SPACE TRIPPING 2
THE CHASER

PATRICK M. EDWARDS

Black Rose Writing | Texas

ISBN: 978-1-68433-851-1
PUBLISHED BY BLACK ROSE WRITING
www.blackrosewriting.com

Printed in the United States of America
Suggested Retail Price (SRP) $22.95

Space Tripping 2 is printed in Sabon

SPACE TRIPPING 2
THE CHASER

WORD SECTION 0001

"They want to eat your head."

Bhanakhana translated the words of the Pyenapor Chieftain, whose community of purple pineapple-shaped aliens crowded the jungle clearing. Well, technically speaking, the Pyenapor weren't the aliens here. This was *their* home world, after all. Bhanakhana, the hulking Dronla; Jopp, the stocky Yoblon; and Chuck, the Earth man... *they* were the visitors from outer space, ergo the *real* aliens here. Again, technically speaking.

"Well, they can't eat my head. I'm using my head."

"That's debatable," said Chuck.

"Shut it, Earth Ape," Jopp snapped back.

Chuck didn't shut it.

"Maybe they like the taste of lemons."

"My head doesn't taste like a lemon!" cried Jopp, his yellow cheeks flushing with veins of purple.

"That's right, it just looks like one."

Jopp unloaded a verbal onslaught of truly vile yet admittedly imaginative expletives. He paused his tirade when he saw the aghast expression on Bhanakhana's face. The muscular, red-skinned Dronla cleared his throat. "I hope you are not expecting me to translate all that."

"No!"

"Do the Pyenapor even have a word for *squibling shit stain*?" asked Chuck.

"As a matter of fact, they do."

"Excuse me," interjected Jopp. "Can we get back to the matter at hand?"

"Don't you mean the matter at head?"

"I'm so glad you're enjoying this, Earth Ape." Jopp then looked back to Bhanakhana. "I don't care what you tell them. Just know that I plan on shooting anyone who gets too close." His thick yellow fingers grazed over the pulse pistol at his hip.

Bhanakhana grimaced. "Why must you persist in carrying that *thing*?"

Jopp glared at Bhanakhana as he pointed to the top of his own head. Yoblons like him typically had a pair of three-inch hearing nodes. Jopp had a three-inch node and a one-inch nub that *used* to be a three-inch node. It had been cut off during a spirited interrogation session with a homicidal marauder.

"I think you look cool with only one node," offered Chuck.

"One and a half!" snapped Jopp.

"Nevertheless, you do not see Chuck toting around a deadly weapon on peaceful missions. We are merely here to study the day-to-day existence of these beautiful peoples."

"Eh, actually, Rohi got me a pistol as a gift last Splendor's Day. I just forgot it in my room."

Bhanakhana frowned. "Why would you feel the need to arm yourself? I have been assisting you with your physical fitness and teaching you limb-to-limb combat."

Chuck shrugged. "Rohi says the best punch in the universe doesn't mean much when you're staring down the barrel of a mecha rifle."

An indiscernible yet stern sounding voice pulled the trio's attention back to the crowd of Pyenapor tribesmen. They reminded Chuck of five-foot-tall purple pineapples with arms and legs. He'd mentioned that to Jopp and Bhanakhana when they'd first arrived. The next five minutes had been spent attempting to explain what a pineapple was.

"What's he saying?" asked Jopp.

"*She* is telling me that outsiders must appease Tufu."

"What's a Tufu?" asked Chuck.

"Tufu is their god. He rules over the jungle."

"And Tufu wants to eat Jopp's head?"

"Apparently."

"Is there any other way to make an offering that doesn't require me dying?" asked Jopp.

Bhanakhana spoke to the tribal chief. She conferred with her fellow elders for a moment, and then gave Bhanakhana a rather long-winded response. Bhanakhana kept glancing back and forth between Jopp and the tribe, his eyes wide with shock.

"So, what'd she say?"

"Well... she has informed me there is indeed another way to make an offering to Tufu."

"Okay, what is it?"

"Well... the offering to Tufu must be a gift of life. Giving yourself as sustenance is one way of providing life. The other way to give life would be..." Bhanakhana stalled.

"Spit it out, already."

"How shall I phrase this...the Chieftain... she thinks you're cute."

"Nope. I am not doing the nebula nasty with her. Fuck that noise."

"Wait," said Chuck with a devilish grin, "so Jopp has to get freaky with an old pineapple lady?"

"*No*," said Bhanakhana, "That is the wrong context of cute. Not cute in a romantic sense. Cute as in..."

"Spit it out already."

"She wants you to be her pet."

The Pyenapor Chieftain held up a length of rope they assumed to be some sort of leash and said, "Eeleeo. Eeleeo."

"That means pet."

"We figured," said Chuck.

"No. Fucking. Way," growled Jopp.

"Dude," said Chuck, "just act like a shnarfling for a little bit. Crawl around, bark, and you'll get probably get treats 'n stuff."

"I only need a few days to complete my research. Two, three at the most."

"Do you realize what you're asking me to do?"

"I will give you my entire share of the publication earnings."

Jopp groaned and huffed in a deep breath.

"If either of you tell anyone about this, I will literally... I mean *literally* murder you."

"Oh shit oh shit oh shit oh shit oh shit...." screamed Chuck and Jopp as they sprinted back to the ship.

"I am most displeased with this turn of events," huffed Bhanakhana as he lumbered alongside them. He glanced back over his massive shoulder, saw the hoard of angry Pyenapor chasing after them, and quickened his pace.

"Dude, you bit the Chieftain's hand!"

"She was scratching behind my hearing nodes too rough! She wanted a pet, she got a pet!"

"Most displeased indeed."

The trio burst out of the jungle and onto a soft, sandy beach. Their ship, a late model Estal Cube, rested at the water's edge with green waves lapping gently at its base. A panel slid open on the side of the ship's chrome finish, allowing them to enter the ship at a dead sprint. Bhanakhana used his data bracelet to power up the engine as they rushed to the bridge. Jopp dove into the pilot's chair, and pulled up the navigational interface.

"Ready to leave whenever you are, Big Red," he called over his shoulder.

Bhanakhana glanced at his data bracelet again. "All systems shall be operational in six seconds."

Jopp's hand hovered over the flight console.

"Three seconds..."

Chuck secured his chair's safety restraints.

"Proceed."

Jopp slapped the propulsion icon.

Outside, four dozen anthropomorphic pineapples ceased hurling stone knives at the ship in order to gawk as the giant silver cube shot up into the clouds. That night there would be much revelry amongst the Pyenapor to celebrate the ousting of the strange intruders. Tufu would certainly be pleased.

WORD SECTION 0002

The Estal Cube exited the planet's atmosphere, entering a wide stretch of open space. Jopp let the navi-matic take over and leaned back in his chair, resting his feet on the console.

"Man!" he said to no one in particular, "That was a real cluster phoob."

Bhanakhana shot Jopp a dirty look, "Please remove your feet from the navigation sensor screen."

Jopp swung his legs back down to the floor, "Sorry, jeez... What's got your krilbits in a whush?"

"I was very much hoping to conduct a comprehensive study of traditional Pyenapor culture. It is a subject on which surprisingly little has been published."

"Maybe that's because the only way to get close to them is to either die or pretend to be a lap cat," offered Chuck.

"Indeed," concurred Bhanakhana, his broad shoulders slumping forward.

Chuck leaned over to Jopp and whispered, *"Ah man, the big guy is sad. You couldn't have taken one for the team?"*

"Excuse me?" retorted Jopp, "If you're so worried about his work, why didn't you volunteer?"

"They weren't interested in me, remember? They told Bhanakhana using an Earth Man would have been an insult to their god... which, by the way, is super racist."

Jopp waved him off, "You'll get over it. And besides, I'll bet they were just saying that to save your feelings."

"How does telling me my species is too inferior to even be *sacrificed* save my feelings?"

"Because then it's not personal. Whereas if they'd told you it was because they find that sorry excuse for a beard revolting, you might have been offended."

Chuck pawed at his fledgling peach fuzz. "Hey, give me a break. I've never grown facial hair before. It just needs time to come together is all."

"Dude, you could wait from now until the universe collapses in on itself. Those bare patches ain't filling in. You need to shave that shit." Jopp turned back to Bhanakhana and added, "But, in all sincerity, I am sorry about your research, Big Red."

Bhanakhana nodded and said, "It is alright. It would have been both unfair and unprofessional of me to ask you to undergo such an intimately intrusive ordeal." His massive chest heaved as he sighed.

"Aw, hey, don't be sad."

Jopp snapped his fingers. "Hey! I know! We could stop by an intergalactic animal shelter. Play with the scritch-kitties for a bit... see if they have any newborn muckdogs to adopt. What do you say? Would you like that, Big Guy? We could get a whole litter of muck puppies for the Chieftain?"

Bhanakhana smiled slightly. "I appreciate the sentiment, however I feel it would be irresponsible of us to put innocent animals in a situation like that."

Chuck felt his data bracelet vibrate, signaling an incoming comm line.

"Better take this in the other room," he said to no one in particular.

Bhanakhana nodded. "Please pass along my warmest regards to Rohi."

Jopp leaned back with a smirk and added, "Yeah, tell Officer Hot Pants I said 'hi,' too." Chuck gave Jopp a wicked grin. "Sure thing, buddy."

Jopp sat up straight, his eyes widening, "I was just joking. Please don't tell her I called her that."

Chuck laughed as he exited the bridge. Jopp hopped to his feet and announced, "Whelp, I'm gonna grab a drink."

Bhanakhana rolled his eyes.

Chuck entered his personal cabin and pressed the 'receive comm' button. The oval-shaped view screen on the far wall blinked on. The humanoid face looking back at Chuck had silver skin, shoulder length black hair, and a purple tattoo shaped like a backwards 7 on her right cheek.

Chuck gave her his best big, dumb smile. "Hey, Beautiful."

Rohi grimaced. "What did you do?"

Chuck was taken aback. "Uh, what do you mean?"

The bouquet of flowers she pulled into view resembled a cluster of bright blue sea urchins.

Chuck beamed. "Oh, I sent those to you to wish you luck on your upcoming promotional review. Did I screw the date up?"

"No, you got that right... but these are Rysor flowers, Chuck."

He gave her an even bigger, dumber smile. "Yep. There's pretty, aren't they?"

She eyed him skeptically. "Wait, did Jopp help you pick these out?"

"Uh, yeah... why?"

Rohi sighed and chuckled, "Thank Bjordax. I thought I was going to have to kill you."

"Rohi, what's going on?"

She gave him a sympathetic smile. "Fuzlumps..." (*Chuck wasn't sure if he was a fan of this new pet name*) "... Rysor flowers are typically sent as an apology when someone commits an act of romantic infidelity."

Chuck let that sink in for a second, then his eyes flared wide and he jumped up. "Wait! So you thought..."

Rohi nodded.

Chuck cracked his knuckles. "Oh, that little yellow shit is going to get it."

She tossed the flowers over her shoulder and chuckled, "It's okay. I appreciate the gesture. I just wish I could *thank you* in person."

Rohi punctuated the statement with a wink.

Chuck's cheeks flushed. "Yeah, me too."

"How long are you going to be on this latest camping trip?"

Chuck dropped back into his seat. "Actually, we're off-world."

Rohi arched an eyebrow. "You guys finished the research that quickly?"

Chuck shrugged. "Well..."

Rohi rolled her eyes. "You and Jopp screwed it up already, didn't you?"

"Hey, I had nothing to do with it... *this* time. Jopp's the one who selfishly messed things up by not being a good-good little puppy boy and whatnot."

"What does that... wait... I don't even want to know. So are you heading back to the Hub[1] now? I feel like I'm going insane here."

"They still have you on desk work and babysitting duty?"

"Pretty much. The closest thing to actual police work I've done is bodyguard a couple of spoiled aristocrats from Raeth Alpha."

"You'd think two standard annuals of desk work and rookie-level assignments would be punishment enough. I mean all you did was-"

"*All I did*," she cut in, "was break the suspected murderer of a ULE agent out of the holding cells."

"Yeah, but I was innocent! It just seems excessive. But what do I know? I'm just a dumb Earth Man."

"But you're *my* dumb Earth Man," she said with a grin.

"Yeah, and I guess that whole Dashii Kento incident a few months back didn't help."

"Hey," said Rohi. "If they didn't want me taking action to foil a major conspiracy, they shouldn't have had me reviewing the legal permits filed by the corporation at the heart of said conspiracy."

"They probably would've preferred for you to have sent your findings up the chain of command? Instead of bursting into their corporate headquarters with pulsers blazing..."

"That is a gross over-simplification of how it went down, and you know it."

---

[1] *The "Hub" is a commonly used term for the Centrelo Solar System. It contains five fully developed and inhabited planets, not to mention the free-floating mega-city, Pa Nui. It is where both the Sentient Coalition and the Universal Law Enforcement agency keep their headquarters. For all intents and purposes, it is the capital of the civilized universe.*

An excerpt from 'Guuno Hrongo's Cheeky Tourism Guide to the Systems of the Sentient Coalition'

Chuck smiled. "I know. I love you. You're the best... but seriously though, why do you think it's taking so long to get back on full duty?"

"Honestly? I'm willing to bet a certain someone high up in the hierarchy is laser-walling me... a certain someone who happens to share my surname."

"No way. Your dad?! You think he's keeping you put? I would've thought he'd be pushing to get you reassigned quicker."

Rohi scoffed, "Oh no, not High Admiral Roklar Kahpanova. He probably sees this as an opportunity to prove his lack of favoritism toward family. I mean, there are dozens of Kahpanova's in the ULE. Coming down hard on his own daughter is the perfect way to showcase his professional impartiality."

"Well, that sucks."

Rohi raised an eyebrow. "I thought when something was bad on Earth, you say that it *blows*?"

"We say both."

"Those two words mean the exact opposite... yet you use them colloquially to mean the same thing?"

Chuck shrugged. "Yeah, we do a lot of stupid shit on Earth. Contradicting slang doesn't even scratch the surface."

Rohi chuckled, "You'll have to educate me further on those matters when you get back."

Chuck stood up. "Speaking of that, I should probably get back to the bridge to see what our plan is."

Rohi tapped two fingers to her lips and put them up against the screen. "See you around, Chuck from Earth."

Chuck mimicked the motion. "Bye, Beautiful."

•   •   •

Chuck returned to the ship's bridge and dropped into his seat with a sigh.

"How is the personal wellbeing of Rohi?" Bhanakhana asked him without looking up from the touch screen desk that wrapped in a semicircle around him.

"She's hanging in there," answered Chuck. "Still getting lame missions as atonement for her part in our little Black Case Adventure."

"More like the Total Fucking Humpadung Adventure," griped Jopp, "We got stuck on a backwater planet, sent to prison, kidnapped, tortured, almost died a thousand times, exposed an attempted intergalactic corporate coup... and they *still* never told us what the fuck was so important about that stupid fucking black case! Whatever *authority figure* made that decision was a real yokhead. Am I right, Big Red?"

"Mmmm," Bhanakhana added noncommittally, eyes still glued to the screen in front of him.

Chuck craned his neck. "What's got you so focused over there?"

"Yeah!" blurted Jopp as he took a swig from his drink. "You cruising the GIG looking for freaky Kapua porn? Because I've checked, there isn't any. I guess it makes sense... I don't see how living clouds could even have sex in the first place..."

Bhanakhana rolled his eyes. "No, Jopp, I am not scouring the Galactic Information Grid in search of niche smut videos. I am on my private Sentologist network. Sometimes my colleagues will post requests for assistance with their studies. I would like to engage in a new project as soon as possible so as to take my mind off our recent string of debacles."

"Hey!" Jopp pointed at him. "That incident on Yoshnau was not my fault. If the Baron didn't want me drinking his *priceless* wine collection, he should have put a better lock on the door. Really it's his own fault for being so careless. And besides, you still collected enough material to publish your thesis."

"Uh," interjected Chuck, "we did get banned from the planet for life, though."

Jopp narrowed his eyes and bared his teeth in faux growl. "Who's side you on?"

"There was also the matter of the monetary recompense," added Bhanakhana.

"Bah, take it out of my wages."

"I am planning on it. You will be receiving just sixty percent of your normal pay for the next standard annual."

"Slave runner," grumbled Jopp.

Bhanakhana waved his hand, sending the highlighted view panel off to the margins. He flicked his wrist, bringing up the next one in the queue.

"Ah," he breathed with relief. "We may have found our next endeavor in working with Professor Yeidat Phyos, a most respected figure in the Sentology community. She is a Department Head at the Zenith Lyceum on Raeth Beta, and is apparently in need of a groundwork team with experience in the extinct civilizations of the Onalithic Era." He looked up with a bright smile. "I wrote my graduate dissertation on the Onalithic Era."

Chuck raised an eyebrow and looked at Jopp. "Did you follow any of that?"

"Nope! But I did hear the words 'Zenith Lyceum' and that's all I need to know."

"Why?" asked Chuck.

Jopp cocked a thumb at him and nodded to Bhanakhana. "You wanna help him out?"

"The Zenith Lyceum is an institute of higher learning."

"More like an institute of righteous chuz-fests," added Jopp.

Bhanakhana sighed. "Yes... an unfortunate side effect of gathering young adults together in large quantities devoid of parental supervision is that there tends to be a proliferation of nightlife debauchery. Now, excuse me while I send communication to Professor Phyos."

Realization dawned on Chuck. "Oh, it's a college." He looked at Jopp. "And you want to go to a party?"

"Yeah, dude, Co-eds!" Jopp extended his hands out laterally and began moving them back and forth as if he were pushing two walls on either side of him.

"What are you doing?" asked Chuck.

"It's that thing you taught me. *Stretch the room...*"

Chuck sighed. "No, man..." he put his hands above his head. "It's *raise the roof*. And besides, I kinda taught you that as a joke. That stopped being cool on Earth like twenty years ago."

Jopp tapped his chin in thought for a moment. Then a wry smile slid across his face. "Yeah, but the ladies won't know that. And I'll have my bona fide Earth wingman there to verify how cool it is."

"Wait, what? You think I'm going to help you pick up college girls? Hell no. Besides... aren't you a bit old for that?"

"First, fuck you. I'm only like six annuals older than the current graduates. And second, you owe me one! I saved your life from a murderous pirate trying to strangle you."

"*First*, all you did was roll over a bottle of booze. I still had to hit him with it myself..."

"I had been shot!" Jopp interjected, "I couldn't over-exert myself or else I might have bled to death! Also, that wasn't just *some bottle of booze*. That was top notch hooch."

"...*and second*," Chuck continued, "that was over two annuals ago! How long are you going to hold it over my head?"

"I don't know... remind me how long your species typically lives. Listen, just roll with me on this and I'll stop making fun of that dead kajiratch on your face you're trying to pass off as a beard."

"What's a kajiratch?"

"It's a raggedy little rodent. If you wanna know what it looks like, just look in a mirror... there's a dead one on your face."

"Oh fuck you."

"*AHEM!*"

Jopp and Chuck whipped their heads around to see Bhanakhana glaring at them with mouth agape. Their eyes then moved past him to see the visage of an older Puzuru woman filling the eighty-inch view screen on the wall. Her motley jigsaw-patterned skin ranged across a variety of green hues. Her white hair was tied up in a bun with green pins sticking through it. She gazed down at them with an expression that was equal parts amusement and curiosity. Her voice came through the screen's speakers in a lilting tone with just a hint of scratch.

"Colorful team you have there, Sage Bhindo."

"Yes," sighed Bhanakhana. "That is a most accurate descriptor, Sage Phyos."

"I wasn't aware you dabbled in quantum chaos experiments."

"Oh no! I am not... it is just that-"

The professor smiled. "Relax, Bhindo. I'm tugging your cable."

"Ah, I see... a jest. I have heard tales of your affinity for unscheduled humor."

Jopp whispered to Chuck, "*Is he being sarcastic? I can't tell if this is going well or not.*"

"*Don't look at me,*" Chuck whispered back, "*I'm still trying to wrap my head around the phrase 'unscheduled humor'.*"

Jopp shrugged and took a long pull from his blue bottle. They turned their attention back to the conversation between intellectuals.

"Bhanakhana, have you ever dipped your yub nubs into the mind-bending shit pit that is the Ak'alei?"

Jopp spit out a mouthful of fizzy blue beverage. Chuck choked back a roar of laughter.

Bhanakhana stared, mouth open, at the screen for an extended moment before answering, "Er... ah... Well, I certainly have studied the Ak'alei. They are a most fascinating aberration in our universe's history. In fact, they were the subject of one of my earliest publications."

"Oh shit sticks, I remember you now," the Professor's eyes lit up, "You gave a student talk at that symposium that completely upended the long-held Parallels Theorem. That was a phoobing beauty. I love watching stodgy old pseudo-intellectuals squirm as the logic blocks they stand so proudly on erode beneath their pretentious feet."

"Yes, well, while my arguments may have been sound, they did little to endear me to the scientific establishment."

"Bah! They can all masticate a big plate of dowfa dung. Which, by the way, sounds considerably more appetizing than the watered-down refuse that passes for scientific study these days. And besides, it doesn't seem to have slowed you down much. I pulled your professional profile. You've done some good work over the years. And speaking of which, we have business to discuss. I'm giving a public lecture in four standard days regarding some recent breakthroughs in our research. Sage Bhindo, I know I'm prone to vague and flowery fucking language, so let me be clear: I may have found a path that will actually lead to the Ak'alei origin world. I need an experienced groundwork team to escort me."

"Chaos and Cosmos... that would the most astonishing historical discovery of that past century! I would- I mean *we* would most certainly like to be considered for that role. I will prepare a consulting proposal complete with a list of our qualifications and our estimated fee for your immediate review."

"Never mind that shit. You're hired. How soon can you get to Raeth Beta?"

Before Bhanakhana could respond, Jopp shouted out, "For a paying client and an old friend of Big Red, such as yourself? I can get us there before the end of this stretch, probably show up the day after your big speech thingy."

The professor arched an eyebrow. "*Big Red*? Ha! That's a damn good sobriquet given Bhindo's stature and hue."

Jopp glanced at Bhanakhana. "Huh?"

Bhanakhana ignored him. "Thank you, Sage Phyos. We will depart immediately."

The view screen went blank as the connection terminated.

Chuck hopped up. "I'm gonna go message Rohi. Her station is orbiting Raeth Alpha. Maybe she can meet up with us for a bit."

"Jeez," Jopp rolled his eyes. "She's really got your yub nubs gravi-docked to the mantle, huh?"

Chuck slugged him in the shoulder. Jopp winced with pain. "Ah! C'mon man, that's my bad arm. Since when can't you take a joke?"

"That was for the flowers, you dick."

"The what? Oh yeah... Ha! I forgot about that."

After Chuck had left, Bhanakhana asked Jopp, "There are only five standard days before the end of this stretch. Can you truly get us there by then?"

"Don't worry about it," replied Jopp with a wink.

"I find it morbidly fascinating how you telling me *not* to worry consistently results in the opposite effect."

WORD SECTION 0003

"...and that brings us to the frosting on the shit-cake that is today's presentation."

Professor Yeidat Phyos's voice boomed through the vocal amplifier as she gestured to the massive display screen behind him.

"There is plenty of evidence suggesting the Ak'alei were running the show for a long time among the now-extinct civilizations of Gjenlu... and if you didn't already know that, you're likely in the wrong room. Remedial Flatulence Studies is down the hall." The professor paused for a laugh that didn't come. She shrugged and continued, "Gjenlu has three things going for it that make it critical to locating *Hirth-Ak'alei*, the Ak'alei home world: First, it holds more evidence of Ak'alei presence than any other planetary dig site. Second, this evidence is all in relatively excellent, unmolested condition, due largely to the fact that Gjenlu remains a mostly undeveloped planet. Chalk that up to the mighty corporatocracy having yet to figure out a way to make money there. And third, it was where the original pioneer of Ak'alei study, Cestoras, first began his work over a century ago. Unfortunately for us, Cestoras was that special kind of asshole who liked to brag incessantly, yet still kept the juicy details to himself. He claimed he knew not only where the Ak'alei originated from, but also how they traveled across galaxies in an era well before the first recorded evidence of space flight. These supposed revelations of his are famously held within his Diary. The problem, as you are all painfully aware, is Cestoras wrote in his Diary with a seemingly impossible cipher. It might as well be the random scribbling of a baby Gorthan for all the sense they make. No academic team has been able to translate it."

The Professor grinned.

"Until now."

An image of Cestoras' Diary appeared on the screen.

"Unfortunately for you data duds, I'm not going to share the full breadth of our translation matrix." She winked and added, "but I can give you all a taste-"

The professor froze mid-sentence.

Alu Glyf leaned his seven foot frame back in a chair far too luxurious to actually occupy a lecture hall.

"Dowfa shit," he cursed as he slammed his palm down on the projection controls.

The frozen projection of Professor Phyos, the stage, and the surrounding auditorium flickered for a moment and then dissolved, revealing Alu's darkened, empty office. His oval-shaped eyes landed on the liquor counter on the far end.

"Damned rancid dowfa shit," he grumbled to himself as he stalked over, passing by the dozens of digital accolade certificates on the office wall. He snatched up a bottle of cloudy orange Tahleese whiskey, taking a long pull without bothering to use a glass. When he set the bottle down, he caught his reflection in the mirror hanging over the bar. His long, narrow features and deep purple skin were typical for a high-born Tahl. Creases and wrinkles had begun to form around the eyes of his otherwise youthful face. It was a toss-up whether work stress or Alu's nightlife were more to blame. He took another swig of the whiskey and spoke into his custom, jewel-laden data bracelet.

"Janeesa."

"Yes, Doctus Glyf?" replied the professionally pleasant voice of Alu's third-shift assistant.

"Send word to my contact at Neb-Tech. I've reconsidered their last offer and decided to accept."

"Are you certain? If I recall, you referred to their last offer as being *not good enough to wipe a humpalope's ass with*..."

"Just do it... immediately. And tell my flight crew I want my personal vessel prepped for interplanetary travel as soon as possible."

Alu pressed his thumb to a button on the underside of his data bracelet, causing a panel in the ceiling, some fifteen feet above him, to slide open. A metal safe was lowered to Alu's eye-level by four hydraulic arms. He pressed the fingertips of his right hand to the safe's door and it lit up as it popped open. Alu retrieved a stack of untraceable currency cards, a pulse pistol, and half a dozen sliver-chips, before the safe slid back up into its ceiling hideaway. All of these items found their way into Alu's designer attaché case. He paused for a moment to admire one of the sliver-chips. It was translucent, thin as paper, shaped like a teardrop, and contained half a petabyte of digital information.

He mused to himself, "In the grand scheme of things... I guess early-*early* retirement isn't the worst fate."

Alu stuffed the sliver-chip in his attaché. He sealed the bio-lock and collapsed into his couch, briefcase in one hand, whiskey bottle in the other. Dusk had fallen, and Alu gazed through his expansive office window as the countless lights of Pa Mahinga, capital city of the planet Raeth Alpha, blinked to life.

Janeesa's voice buzzed through the com, "Your pilot says it will take three hours to prep your ship and get the required clearances."

Alu huffed, "Tell him to do it in half the time and I'll bonus him five thousand Tahlians."

After a moment, Janeesa replied, "He says he's not a *phoobing magical shaman* and that these things take time, but also that he'd see what he can do."

Alu glowered down at his bracelet. "Remind him who approves his pay-wires and that there are plenty of skilled pilots in the galaxy that know how to conduct themselves with proper decorum."

•　　•　　•

"Fucking move it! You scroll-shoving tome-domes!"

Chuck's eyes shot open and he sat up in his chair. As he rubbed the sleep from his eyes, he mumbled, "Wha- What's going on?"

Jopp shot him a sidelong look. "Oh I'm sorry, did I wake little precious from his dreamy naptime? Were you busy in magical fa-fa-land dancing through the technicolored meadows with a candy coated mega-vixen? Why don't you make your hairless primate ass useful and send a commline to these superstitious squib kids? Tell them to get the holy fuck out of our way!"

Chuck stood up with a yawn, strolled over to Jopp, reached out and poked him square in his wide, flat nose while saying, "Boop."

Jopp glared up at him while huffing a few silent breaths. Finally he said, "What was that?"

"I needed you to calm you down."

"By *booping* my nose?"

Chuck shrugged. "First thing that came to mind. What had you so worked up? Also, where's Bhanakhana?"

"He's in his lab pulling up his old research notes on the Aklee- the Akla- the *old-dead-as-shit-ancient-assholes*."

"Ak'alei," corrected Chuck.

"Shut it, Pronunciation Pansy. And I'm *all worked up,* as you put it, because we're sitting outside our last anomaly jump, but can't hit it because these shuttle-thumpers are clogging up the line."

Chuck examined the view screen that was the current target of Jopp's ire. It displayed a colossal black spot, larger than most moons. If they flew into it at the proper speed and trajectory, they'd come out the other end in the Centrelo System, some thirteen light years away. From that point, it'd be less than a day until they reached the Lyceum on Raeth Beta.

Something about the situation: the colossal black nothingness looming before them, Jopp angrily spewing wanton obscenities, made Chuck think back to the first time he'd been in this situation. He'd just been accidentally abducted by an inebriated Jopp and subsequently pressed into service by the universe's largest corporation. Pirates had attacked him and Jopp on their first delivery run, forcing them to escape through a previously undiscovered anomaly. For much of the civilized universe, jumping through these anomalies was as routine as traveling across town on an errand.

The problem currently vexing Jopp was that there were a half dozen interstellar shuttles sitting between their ship and the anomaly. The shuttles reminded Chuck of cruise liners back on Earth. He zoomed in on the insignia emblazoned on each shuttle's side hull. The background of the insignia was a solid black circle. It displayed a pair of gold horizontal lines above two pairs of gold vertical lines spaced apart under the ends of the horizontal lines, reminiscent of the symbol for pi.

"Hey... I've seen that symbol all over the place. Who are they?" Chuck asked.

"They're a bunch of damn 'Nac Whackers, that's who they are!"

"Hey buddy?"

"What?"

"I'm gonna need you to dial back the dramatic ranting a bit and explain."

Jopp huffed a few times and said, "They're the Church of Rhonac. Bunch of humpalope-heads worshipping their collective imaginary friend."

"So, it's a religion."

"That is correct, Charles." They looked back to see Bhanakhana step through the doorway. He smiled at Chuck and added, "Though I am impressed you were able to discern that from the crass explanation offered."

Chuck grinned. "I speak fluent 'Jopp'. And, uh, you can go back to just calling me 'Chuck', okay?"

Bhanakhana cocked his head to the side. "But you told me your formal name was 'Charles.' I wish to show you the proper respect and admiration I feel for you as a friend and colleague."

"Seriously, just Chuck is fine."

Bhanakhana smirked. "Okay, Juschuck."

Chuck burst out laughing. "Oh my god, I forgot about that. From when we first met, right? You know, if we hadn't met back on the Prime Partners corporate frigate, Jopp and I would either be lying dead out in that Gorthan desert or still being force fed booze by Dagwam and his brethren..."

"Death or a life amongst Gorthans; I probably would have opted for death by now," groused Jopp.

"Now you're just being a dick," said Chuck, "Dagwam was a good guy...oh yeah, and he said to say *hi* to both of you. Actually what he literally said was," Chuck's voice adopted a thick twang, "*Tell Yellow Butler and the Big Brain Fella ol' Rocket Beer says Pow-Pow-Kachow!*"

"Excellent vocal impression, Chuck," said Bhanakhana.

"Yeah, he's a real mimic-bot. What the fuck does that even mean?" asked Jopp.

Chuck shrugged. "I don't know."

"Wait, when the hell did you talk to Dagwam?"

"Dude, he calls me like once a week. Nine times out of ten it's a video-comm and he's at a bar trying to impress a Gorthan woman by showing off his *real live Earth buddy*. He keeps asking when we're going to come back for a visit."

"Yeah, try *never*," Jopp waved at the view screen. "I got enough problems right here without intentionally surrounding myself with Gorthans."

Chuck looked back toward the line of shuttles sitting between them and the anomaly. "So, what's the story with these shuttle people?"

"The Church of Rhonac is one of the older religious organizations in the Sentient Coalition. They were something of a fringe group for many centuries, but have seen their numbers swell in recent decades." Bhanakhana nodded to the shuttles. "This is due largely to their offering free anomaly transportation between the major systems."

"*Free* my ass," Jopp added. "Sure, they don't charge any currency, but your entire trip is one big heavy-handed sales pitch on the virtues of *The Divine One*." He punctuated the point by wiggling his fingers in the air.

"And," he continued, "they clog up all the interstellar traffic ways."

Bhanakhana added, "Their custom is to offer prayer before entering an anomaly. I understand the ritual can, at times, take a while."

Jopp spread his arms out wide and shouted to the ceiling, "Oh, great Rhonac! Please carry us safely through the scary space hole. Never mind the ten deka-tons of mechanical innovation that went into the ship we're sitting in, 'fore we know it is by your grace alone that we shall survive this journey."

Chuck rolled his eyes. "Nice performance. So, why do you have such a pocket-rocket over this?" He smirked. "Wait, don't tell me... Jopp, are you a member of a rival religion? Are your people locked in a centuries old faith war? How have we spent so much time together and I never realized what a zealot you were?"

"I must admit: I, too, am curious regarding your hatred of this organization."

"Huh? Oh, no..." Jopp started. "I don't *hate* their religion. They can worship Rhonac, Bjordax, ZuZu the Erinaceous, or even the Hovering Nudell Beast for all I care. It's just that these prayer rituals take so long."

"Well- *wait*, what was that last one?"

Bhanakhana cut in. "Your statement begs the question as to *why* you are in such a hurry?"

Jopp folded his arms and made an attempt to look stern. "We told your professor pal we'd be there in six days. I'm trying to keep us on pace. Pace is important. Punctuality is the mark of a true professional."

Chuck and Bhanakhana traded glances.

"Hey! What's with the funny looks?"

Chuck arched an eyebrow. "In the past two years, you've shown, oh, I don't know... *zero* regard to the concept of professionalism. Spill it, Lemonhead."

Jopp threw his hands up. "Fine! You got me! I want to get there as soon as possible because of... well, because of Nemesis Day."

Bhanakhana sighed. "Of course."

Chuck raised his hand. "Dumb Earth Man need info."

"Nemesis Day! The Zenith Muckdogs are playing their big rivals, the Akonga Warp Hawks. Both teams are undefeated! It's gonna be tops epic... not to mention all the festivities!"

"That sounds more like the Jopp we know."

"Excuse me for wanting to mix a little fun in with our work."

"I would appreciate it if, for once, you were to mix a little *work* in with your work."

Chuck burst out laughing and held his fist out to Bhanakhana. He gently tapped his own massive fist to Chuck's and added, "I believe that is what you refer to as a *burn*."

"A sick burn," Chuck added.

"Bah!" grumbled Jopp, "I don't need to put up with this... and you know what? I don't need to wait around for the pious prayer posse anymore. Strap in!"

Bhanakhana barely made it to his seat before Jopp slammed the ship into maximum acceleration. Meanwhile, aboard the transport shuttles, the Children of Rhonac were about to complete the ritual of the sacred snack when they were suddenly interrupted by a silver Estal Cube that screamed past them and disappeared into the anomaly. Many of the parishioners took it upon themselves to say an additional prayer, asking Rhonac to bless the passengers of the cube ship with some gosh-darn manners.

WORD SECTION 0004

Alu pulled up the time display on his data bracelet. His ship should be ready any minute now. He figured he'd better head down to the hangar. He snatched up the whiskey for one last drink. *"Funny,"* he thought, *"I could have sworn this was brand new bottle, but it's only got a quarter left now..."* He shrugged and took a long pull, setting the bottle back on the table next to his attaché. He admired the exquisite custom design stitched into the outer layer of the case. Hardly anyone used organic fabrics on luggage anymore. It was costly and more fragile than other materials. But Alu could afford little luxuries like that. He smiled to himself. *"Shit, with what's in here I can afford the little luxury of my own custom-built planet."*

"Good evening, Alu."

Alu whipped his head around to see a Venovan woman stepping through his office door. The skin of her humanoid face was a deep navy blue. Her coiffed blonde hair was pulled back, the hair on the sides of her head woven into tight rows that combined into one thick braid hanging just past her shoulders. She wore dark, loose-fitting pants tucked into black boots with gold ribbon wrapped around the calf. Her black shirt had a mandarin collar stitched with gold. The left sleeve clung tight to her arm. Her right sleeve ended at the shoulder, revealing cords of well-toned muscle. A wide bracelet, black with gold script, encircled her right wrist. A pendant hung from a thin rope around her neck. It was a circle painted black. Two gold horizontal lines ran parallel across the top half of the pendant. Underneath were two more gold lines.

They were spaced further apart and ran vertically down the lower half of the circle.

Alu waggled his long, lean fingers in a lazy wave and said, "Hello, Grand Herald Dac'eth."

She smiled warmly. "No need for titles... *Serru* will suffice. Mind if I grab a seat?"

Alu waved lazily at the space next to him. "Last time I checked, we're still a free Coalition."

She nodded graciously and moved toward the couch. Generally, Alu didn't find Venovans and J'Kari to be all that appealing. They were too short, most standing under six feet; and their facial features were too rounded. His own tastes notwithstanding, he recognized her to be a handsome woman by most standards. It was her eyes, really, that intrigued Alu. The irises of Venovan eyes typically ranged from brown to yellow to gold, but Serru's eyes were colored an unnaturally brilliant shade of orange. Alu felt his own eyes grow heavy as she took a seat at the opposite end of his couch. He gestured to the bottle of whiskey on the table.

"Want a pour?"

Serru smiled again. "No, thank you. I don't drink."

Alu arched an eyebrow. "You mind if I..."

Serru nodded. "Don't abstain on my account. Do *you* mind if I smoke?"

Alu shook his head and allowed himself another thirsty helping of liquor. Serru slipped a thin gray cinder-stick in the side of her mouth, produced a personal igniter, and lit it.

"That stuff'll kill you," noted Alu.

Serru exhaled a thin cloud of green vapor. "This isn't your common deepleaf, Alu. It's an herbal blend. Calms the mind without dulling the senses. And all the potential health risks have been engineered out of the plants on a genetic level. It's totally clean."

She took another drag and added, "If only we could say that about people."

Alu set the bottle back down and said, "S'pretty late- doin' some pray'rs- I mean *prayer service* down at the chapel?" Alu discovered both his tongues had become a bit sluggish.

Serru gestured at her attire. "Dressed in my casual wear? No. I'm afraid I'm here on more... *secular* matters. It's been quite impressive to see what you've been able to achieve over these past years, Alu. You should be proud."

Alu lazily shook his head. "Team effort. Couldn't have done it without the church's... *moral* support." He chuckled.

Serru gave a small nod. "You're too kind."

"Lucky for me your god has deep pockets and a fondness for the historical sciences."

Serru's smile remained firmly in place, yet responded with a hard tone, "Rhonac is *everyone's* God..."

She turned to look out the expansive office window at the illuminated skyline below. "...some just haven't realized it yet."

Alu shrugged. "Sure -*urp*- sure thing."

"I take it you've seen Professor Phyos' lecture?"

Alu waved lazily. "S'lucky break... doesn't matter. We're so far ahead... Cesto-*urp* Cestoras' Diary is just one piece of the puzzle."

"A piece you've been working on for quite some time." Serru's gaze moved from the window to the attaché case. "Taking your work home with you, Alu?"

"Oh nah. I mean, *yeah*. Yes. I'm going to my place down the shore for a few days. I figure a change of scenery might, uh, help us on the next breakthrough."

She breathed green vapor through her nose and said, "You will, of course, take every available precaution. Can't have any briefcases full of vital secrets floating around in the universe, now can we?"

WORD SECTION 0005

"MUCK DOGS! MUCK DOGS! MUCK DOGS! MUCK DOGS! MUCK DOGS!"

"Holy shit..."

Chuck gazed out the office window down at the chanting throngs of crimson-clad Zenith Muckdog fans filling the Hex yard. He then scanned the five other buildings that encircled the open space at the center of the Lyceum campus. The buildings were built from white stones marbled with black veins and they towered over the miniscule students below. Columns of multi-colored stone orbs twirled around each other like colossal strands of DNA stretching up toward the pink sky overhead. A gigantic 360-degree display screen hovered above the masses. It finished running a video of team highlights from the season so far, and the head coach was about to give what was sure to be a stirring rally speech to the assembled student body.

A thick yellow hand slapped Chuck square in the back.

"Pretty freaking sweet, ain't it, Earth Man? All of Luga City was pretty much built up around the Lyceum. The entire town basically shuts down to watch the games."

Chuck winced at the stinging in his back for a moment, but then gave Jopp a devilish grin.

"I thought we had an *agreement* when it came to you slapping my back?"

Chuck gave a faux lunge forward and Jopp hopped backwards, bumping into a table that held a decorative bowl. He caught it at the last second, barely preventing a disastrous crash. As soon as the antique was safely returned to its perch, Chuck and Jopp shot a pair of nervous glances across the room.

Their gaze was met by the glare of Bhanakhana. He pointed at the couch next to his chair and silently mouthed, *"Sit. Down. Now."*

They shuffled over to the assigned couch and plopped down. The trio sat in a waiting parlor just outside Professor Phyos' office. The furniture and the decor created a motif that was a bizarre cross section of exotic alien life and Victorian England. The table in front of them was a glass surface supported by a complicated tangle of metal tubing that pulsated with dull amber light. A large stone slab was bolted to the opposite wall. It displayed a crudely painted image of some four-armed humanoid beings throwing oblong objects at a spike-coated beast with an oversized jaw. Chuck figured Bhanakhana would describe the room something like *charmingly antiquated.* Jopp hadn't bothered to examine the room, as he was too busy playing "Galacti-Quest" on his data bracelet. It was one of those games where you tried to build up as big a fleet of spaceships as possible in hopes of conquering the virtual universe. But, of course, it had a feature where you could pay real money in exchange for the game's biggest and best ships. Chuck and Rohi had a secret bet going on how long it'd take before Jopp asked them for loan to help pay off the debt he'd likely incur for the game's new "Annihilation Class Interstellar Galleon".

"This decor is charmingly antiquated," mused Bhanakhana.

Chuck rolled his eyes. Jopp offered a non committal grunt, his fingers busy wiggling across the projected game screen. Bhanakhana nudged Chuck and pointed to an object that reminded Chuck of a grandfather clock. It stood almost seven feet tall. The peach-colored wood had been carved to look like a dozen tentacles stretching down to the floor, where they curled up slightly. At the top, the tentacles morphed into a bulbous head with a wide mouth and three tiny eyes. Set into the carving's gaping maw were five wheels lined up side by side, like on a combination lock. The outer edge of each wheel was covered in unfamiliar runes.

"Chuck, do you know what that is?"

Chuck arched an eyebrow. "Do you really expect me to say anything other than no?"

Bhanakhana frowned. "If you had completed the list of suggested readings I GIG-mailed to you, you would know."

"Dude, there were like twenty books in that list."

"Exactly. I gave you a truncated selection so as to help ease you into the subject matter."

Chuck sighed. "Just tell me what the weird clock thingy is."

"Oh! So, you did do the reading! Yes, that is one of the rare Bu Creso Time Tellers. It is an exquisitely well preserved piece... must be at least fifteen hundred years old."

"Uh..."

Chuck was saved from having to come up with a more eloquent response by a sudden burst of sound resonating from the opposite side of the office door. They heard muffled grumbling, some stomping, more grumbling. The office door slid open and besuited Mahimon with bulging eyes and a fish-like head stumbled clumsily into the parlor. His awkward gait was the result of the gnarled green stick prodding him in the back. Holding the other end of the stick was a short Puzuru woman, whom Chuck recognized as Professor Yeidat Phyos. Her camouflage patterned green skin looked much more vibrant in person... or maybe that was just because she was worked up at the moment. She had roughly eight to ten pins stuck through her hair bun, and wore loose-fitting brown robes with a green floral pattern.

"Now now," sputtered the Mahimon, "There's no need for such barbaric physicality!"

"Physicality seems to be the only way to get the message across to you people."

"But Sage Phyos! The offices of Carpian & Bassinette are prepared to offer whatever accommodations, financial or otherwise, you might require!" He turned around to face her. "How can you refuse such a lucrative offer?"

"Oh, that's easy, Mr. Carpian. I do it like this."

She prodded him firmly in the chest with her stick and bellowed, "Get the fuck out."

Jopp whispered to Chuck, "*I love her.*"

Once Mr. Carpian had huffed and puffed his way out of the parlor, Professor Phyos turned to her other visitors with a big smile.

"Well hello, gents. How was your trip in?"

"Oh," started Bhanakhana, "It was-"

"I'm not really interested. I was just being polite. Follow me."

She spun on her heel and disappeared back inside her office. The three "gents" looked at each other, shrugged, and followed after.

Chuck had expected the cozy theme of the waiting parlor to extend into the Professor's office. He had also expected a desk and a few chairs... you know, an *office*. What he had not expected was to find himself stepping into a laboratory that looked like it'd been ripped straight from the set of an old James Bond movie. White metal tables holding a myriad of rare-looking artifacts lined the right half of the cavernous space. The entire left wall was made from large sandy blocks, as if it were the wall of some long lost temple. A series of spiraling, unfamiliar runes formed a fifteen foot circle at the center of the fake temple wall.

Professor Phyos led them over to a table at the center of the room. The table was covered with a setup that reminded Chuck of his great uncle's model train displays. The texture and color of the table's ground looked like desert. Clusters of spiny orange trees peppered the landscape. A painted river cut through the center of the table, splitting in two and wrapping around the miniature fortress of purple towers at the center of the table. Figurines of pink-skinned humanoids wielding tiny curved spears occupied the fortress's battlements. There was an open space in front of the fortress with more of the humanoid figurines. They were apparently locked in perpetual battle with a few dozen statues of bipedal rock people.

"What do you think?" asked the Professor.

"Rad," said Chuck.

"Sweet," said Jopp.

"Marvelous," said Bhanakhana. He moved in closer, studying the incredibly detailed carvings of the model foliage, the layout of the fortress, the path of the painted river. "Yes, yes," he mused to himself. "Such a place as this must hold a great many ancient secrets." He looked up at the Professor. "This fortress, is it on Gjenlu? Is this our destination?"

"What? No!" scoffed the Professor. "This is a recreation of the Battle of Rubble Keep from the War of Irreconcilable Differences. Do you know how much time this shit takes to build and colorize? Or how expensive these physical materials are? Why would I spend that kind of time and money on *work*? This is my hobby."

"But if this has nothing to do with our job, why did you make it a point to show it to us?"

"Because it's fucking spectacular and I wanted to show it off."

"Uh..." stammered Bhanakhana.

Jopp gave her a thumbs up. "Tops work, Prof."

She gave him a little finger-gun motion and said, "Thanks, Yellow."

"Oh, I'm Jopp."

She repeated the finger-gun motion and said, "If you say so." She turned to Chuck and added, "You, Earth Guy. C'mere and let me get a look at you."

"Uh, okay." Chuck walked up to her. "My name is Chuck, by the way."

"If you say so."

The Professor brought her face to within inches of Chuck's. She studied his eyes and looked up his nose. She gave his left ear a gentle tug. Chuck shot a nervous glance at Bhanakhana who could only shrug in reply. She cupped his chin with her hand and asked, "Can you please open your mouth?"

Chuck was nervous, but complied nevertheless. She tapped his front teeth with her finger. Then she leaned back and nodded with satisfied expression. "You're a lot more hygienic than I expected."

"Uh, thank you?"

She pulled a piece of brightly wrapped candy out of her pocket and handed it to Chuck with one hand while tousling his hair with the other. "Good boy."

Chuck was too busy tearing into the candy to be offended.

"Well," She stepped back and beamed at them, "aren't we the motley bunch? Tell you what, Sage Bhindo, you may take the jubla when it comes to interesting field teams: running around with an Earth Man and a booze-soaked Yoblon with only one antenna."

"One and a half!"

"Er... indeed," concurred Bhanakhana. "Shall we discuss your plans for the field?"

"Bah, we'll get to all that later. We won't depart for at least two days. And besides, I got us all tickets to Nemesis Day. It's gonna be a station-stormer of a game."

"YES!" Jopp pumped his fist.

"So, for today, go get some food, some rest, explore the campus." Her eyes fell on Bhanakhana. "I'm guessing you're the sort who'd rather spend the evening pouring over research files."

Bhanakhana smiled. "That would be splendid."

She nodded. "Thought so." Her hand disappeared into her robes and came out holding a sliver-chip. "There's some real deal secret research type shit here. Stuff I don't trust on even the most secure encrypted GIG-drive. Enjoy."

Bhanakhana accepted the chip with a hungry expression. He looked to Chuck and Jopp and said, "Shall we head to the local, as you put it Jopp, *Hydration Station?*"

Jopp pumped his fist. "Ah yissss!"

"Wait," said Phyos. "I thought you wanted to work on my files?"

"Oh," said Chuck, "See, we so often find ourselves in bars that the big guy thought he might as well re-train his brain to be able to work in them."

Bhanakhana nodded. "This is true. Now I sometimes have trouble focusing on my research unless I am surrounded with sounds of thumping music and inane banter."

"We're really good at that second one," noted Chuck.

Phyos chuckled, "Well, it ain't the *weirdest* thing I've ever heard. You boys have a nice evening. Now if you'll excuse me, I've got a date with that new Imaginary Mathematics professor. At 50 standard annuals, he's a bit younger than I usually like 'em. And he's a dreadfully boring conversationalist. But, damn, the man is good with his hands, if you catch my drift."

Chuck and Bhanakhana exchanged mortified stares.

Jopp held his hand out for a high four, "Get it, girl."

WORD SECTION 0006

"Kahpanova!"

Rohi awoke from a daydream and jumped to her feet at the sound of the Division Leader's voice. She stood at attention and watched the late-middle aged J'Kari man waddle toward her. The width of his shoulders and thickness of his forearms indicated he might have once possessed an imposing build, however, years of commanding a division of "paperwork police" had left him with some extra cushioning around his midsection and a backup chin. You know, in case anything should happen to the first one. Even the customary J'Kari tattoos on his silver face seemed to sag, just like the rest of him.

He was breathing hard by the time he reached Rohi's desk.

"Something I can help you with, sir?"

The Division Leader tapped his data bracelet and a holographic file display appeared in the air between them.

"You got a case," he huffed. "Senticide of some VIB. This file is already in your data drive. You need to be on the next chute headed dirt-side. From there you're headed to Pa Mahinga... *the jewel of Raeth Alpha.*" He added that last bit with a heavy eye roll.

Rohi scanned the floating file display for a moment. She flicked her wrist, pushing the projection to the side, and peered down at the shorter Division Leader

"You're giving me a murder? I thought I was still in High Command's *Deadenders List*. And besides, isn't this a case for the city cogs?"

"Turns out the *dead-o* isn't the only Very Important Being in his family. His mother is a big timer in planetary politics. She requested you specifically."

Rohi looked for the mother's name in the file.

"I don't know this person."

"Yeah, well she knows you." He pressed another button on his bracelet, causing the visage of an older Tahl woman to appear. Rohi stared up at the six-foot-three purple hologram. The woman's outfit was the very epitome of opulence. Her robes were covered in high end brand logos. Her head-scarf alone cost more than a ULE agent made in a quarter span. Rohi didn't even want to guess how many lifetimes it'd take her to earn enough to pay for the woman's electric-diamond necklace. The Division Leader waved his hand and the hologram sprung to life, playing back one half of a recorded conversation.

"Do you honestly expect me to let some common city 'police' handle this? One of my sons has been murdered! I don't think so! I'll tell you what you're going to do... you're going to find me that spunky agent from that corporate-sponsored disaster on Takutai. No, I don't know her name. How many violent incidents with scruffy hooligans occurred at a Takutai resort in recent years... Really?! That many? Well, someone should talk to a manager about security protocols. Nevertheless, you will find that agent or I will rescind my family's annual donation to the Coalition Defense Fund. I don't care if she's on the opposite end of the Mishinyo Rift. Find her!"

The Division Leader paused the video and took a bite from an oozing gobjam pastry. Rohi wondered where the hell it'd come from.

"So, anyway," he continued through a mouth full of flaky dough and green jelly, "Imagine her delight to learn that you were stationed in orbit above the very planet where her son met his untimely demise." He held up the remainder of his pastry. "Now if you'll excuse me, I got a Gorthan's Dozen more of these beauties and a fresh mug of wahu back in my office that require my undivided attention. The next chute leaves in twenty minutes. Be on it."

Rohi shook her head. "There's no way my father—I mean, *High Commander Kahpanova*—signed off on this."

"Already done."

"How?"

"Never underestimate the unholy triumvirate of money, politics, and bureaucracy."

The Division Leader stomped off back to the pastry orgy waiting for him in his office. Rohi gave the floating case file projection another quick scan before waving it out of existence. She clipped a standard issue pulse pistol to her waist and shut down her workstation interface panel. As she turned to leave, the officer in the desk next to hers called out, "Make the rest of us desk-pilots proud out there, Kahpanova!"

Rohi glanced over her shoulder with a smirk. "I'll try, Nep. You just make sure my desk stays clean. I don't want to come back to find it being used as a repository for all your Oogie Bar wrappers."

"Hey, I'm off the sweet treats. Wife's got me on that Dronla Diet."

Rohi rolled her eyes and gave him a casual salute as she left. After a short elevator ride, she stepped onto the orbiting precinct's lowest level. It was an open circular room with two dozen doors spaced around the walls at equal intervals. One of the doors glowed with a soft green light while the rest were awash in red. Through the green door, Rohi found a series of individual pods containing nothing but a cushioned seat. She hopped into an empty one just as the departure countdown began.

A minute later, the pods descended. They crawled along the four hundred kilometer cable that tethered the orbiting precinct to the planet's surface, specifically to a reinforced platform standing just off the shore in the Mahinga Bay.

Rohi stepped out into bright afternoon sunlight and glanced out at the Pa Mahinga skyline crowding against the rocky coast. She breathed in the distinctly unfiltered air of... *the outside*. The blended smells of dirty saltwater, metal, industrial fumes, and general *life* made her nose rankle.

"And people wonder why we like our precincts to stay in orbit."

A row of matte black ULE street cruisers stretched out before her. Rohi thought of the time she used one to drive herself and Chuck to a concert on Tasa Major. He'd almost enjoyed the ride into town more than the show itself, and kept calling the cruiser something like "Lamor-jeeny"... whatever the hell that was.

She slid into the nearest one and pressed her data bracelet against the receiver panel. The cruiser's internal computer scanned her officer credentials and pulled the file on her active case. It charted a route to her destination and displayed a message: *"Vehicle will depart once all passengers are secured."*

Once Rohi fastened her shoulder harness, the cruiser whipped out of the parking deck, merged onto the suspended bridge way, and accelerated toward the city. Whenever traffic threatened to slow her progress, the ULE cruiser's computer would send a signal to the nearby vehicles, causing them to automatically move out of her lane. She zipped along the elevated byway that bordered the city's densely packed downtown while gray waves crashed against the rocky shoreline below.

A quarter hour later, Rohi's cruiser pulled into the parking lot at her destination. The building towering over her looked like one gigantic sheet of blue glass. A half dozen local law enforcement vehicles crowded the pavement near the entrance. She saw a pair of city cogs, dressed in the local grey uniforms, leaning against the open double doorway. One was flipping through GIG sites on his data bracelet. The other looked on the verge of falling into a deep standing sleep. They snapped to attention when they noticed Rohi, dressed in her ULE blacks, approaching.

The uniform on the right, a humanoid Puzuru woman with mottled brown and blue skin saluted and said, "Can we help you, Agent...uh..."

"Division Officer Rohi Kahpanova," she corrected, "I've been assigned jurisdiction on this matter. Can you please point me in the direction of the current officer-in-charge?"

The uniform on the left, a young, a blue-skinned Venovan man answered, "Inspector Kaloce has been running things. He's up on the top floor."

Rohi gave them a nod as she entered the building. She stopped mid-stride when she saw the blubbery, frog-faced Bogtek dressed in a medical examiner's coat hunched over the lobby security desk. He wore a pair of thick glasses and was studying the neon outline that marked where a dead body had recently been.

"I thought the victim was up on the top floor."

The examiner glanced up with an annoyed expression. "*The* victim? We shipped off *five* corpses to the lab this morning."

"Hey, I was just told about the one."

The examiner huffed, causing his rubbery green jowls to quiver. "Of course, I'm sure it was the rich boy. That's all that matters, right?"

Rohi gave him her perfectly-honed '*I don't have time for your shit*' look.

The examiner sighed and nodded his head toward the back of the lobby. "The lifts are over there. The other four victims, including your rich boy, were all on the top floor."

Rohi pointed at the body outline at the examiner's feet. "Who was that?"

The examiner tapped the 'Security' sign etched into the desk's surface. "I can see why they put *you* on the case."

Rohi put on her most terrifying smile. "Okay. I'm going to go up the lift now. I'm sure I'll want to come back later and check this particular scene out in more detail. I would highly advise that by the time I get back down here, you get that pesky bug up your ass removed. If you need any help, I'd be happy to loosen things up back there with my boot."

The Bogtek's heavy-lidded eyes bugged out. Rohi noticed a bright red wrapper sticking out of his coat's breast pocket.

"Is that Terp Root?" she asked. "I haven't had one of those since I was a kid."

"Uh, here," the examiner handed her the candy-bar sized wrapper. "I chew too much as it is. All yours."

Rohi tore it open and gnawed on the bittersweet stick inside. "Hey, look at us, becoming fast friends. See you in a bit."

When the lift doors opened on the top floor, Rohi found herself looking at another neon body-shaped outline next to a receptionist's desk.

She asked the uniformed officer standing near it, "Receptionist?"

"Assistant," the uniform replied.

"Close enough. I'm giving myself credit for that one. I can't start out 0-2 on the investigation scoreboard."

"Huh?"

"Never mind. You Kaloce?"

"No. He's through there." The officer pointed toward a wide, open doorway at the end of the hall.

The hallway's sleek decor didn't so much say *"opulence"* as much as it screamed *"I want you all to think that I am in fact quite opulent!"* Rohi noted two more neon outlines on either side of the office door. She entered the office and saw a pair of officers standing near a couch in the center of the room. Both officers were Venovans: blue-skinned humanoids, which was not uncommon for the major cities in this corner of the system. Civil conflict has been a constant backdrop on their species' home world for the better part of a century. As a result, most Venovan immigrants that make it to the major Coalition cities arrive with barely more than the jumpsuits on their backs. They get funneled into poor neighborhoods where, more often than not, the most two most lucrative career options are either law enforcement or crime.

Or a combination of both.

The two officers in front of Rohi were middle-aged. The one on the left had a thick yellow beard and a shaved blue dome for a head. The one on the right was clean-shaven and his amber hair was neatly parted. The bald, bearded one rolled his eyes and grumbled when he saw Rohi enter. "Oh look, our chaperone is here."

The clean-shaven officer shot a quick glare at his comrade before giving Rohi a polite smile. "You must be Division Officer Kahpanova."

Rohi nodded at him. "Please tell me you're Inspector Kaloce."

"That is correct." He nodded to his bearded partner. "This is Yuhf."

Rohi sighed, "Tops. Let's get star-" she stopped when her eyes fell on the table in front of the couch. More specifically, she was staring at the hole in the table. It was a perfect circle, exactly two feet in diameter, ringed with violet scorch marks.

"That's... interesting."

"Indeed."

"What's the story there?"

"You tell us," grumbled Yuhf, "Isn't that why you're here? 'Cause you're so much smarter than us city cogs?"

Kaloce glared at his partner.

Rohi smirked. "Oh, I don't know, Inspector. I can't imagine my being here has anything to do with my own intelligence."

She crouched down next to the table, bringing her face to within a few inches of the burned hole. She glanced back up at the officer.

"I mean, I got myself assigned to work this case alongside *you*... so I can't be *that* smart."

He took a step forward. "Just what the hell-"

"Alright," Kaloce cut in. "Settle down."

"You're gonna let her talk to me like that?"

"You're acting like an unprofessional dung muffin."

"A what?!"

Rohi chuckled. "I heard you city boys were rough around the edges, but I never expected such harsh words."

"Pardon the language, Division Officer."

Rohi looked up. "I'm fucking with you." She stood and gestured down at the smoldering, glowing hole. "Have you sent a sample of the accelerant down for testing?"

"We did," answered Kaloce.

"But we didn't need to," added Yuhf. "It's Moto Kuvu... most call it Rage Flame."

"We don't know for certain," started Kaloce.

"*I* know for certain." insisted Yuhf.

"Rage Flame?" Rohi asked. "How do you know?"

"Because I was born on Venova Prime, in Old Kanisa. All them psycho, religious rip-heads loved the stuff when it came to killing off the *heretics*. The smell... it ain't something you forget easy."

Kaloce looked mortified.

Rohi nodded. "Fair enough." She gestured at the hole, "But have you ever seen it used in such a controlled method?"

Yuhf shook his head. "Nah, that's a new one on me. That shit is usually raw, scorching chaos."

"So, keeping the destruction to such a tight, specific area would take some next level chemical wizardry?"

"Well," Kaloce chimed in, "our Deceased here did business across a variety of technological industries... maybe it was something he was working on. Or maybe this is an extreme case of corporate sabotage."

"Then that leaves us with the question of what was so important for our Crim to utterly destroy that he'd risk using such a volatile substance..."

"Naked videos of him in a kinky four-way with a trio of Vashnii bug babes? Who cares? Ain't five murders more important than an oversized cinder-stick burn?"

Kaloce gave Yuhf another death glare.

Rohi snickered, "Thanks for putting that image in my head. But you do make a point. Let's examine the bodies. I assume you documented the scene?"

"Indeed," answered Kaloce.

"We ain't savages," added Yuhf.

As if on cue, another medical examiner walked in carrying four opaque visors. She was Puzuru woman with camouflage-patterned lavender and purple skin.

Yuhf sucked in his gut and smiled, "What's hopping, Miss Ghin?"

"Not my patients, that's for sure," she quipped back.

Yuhf chuckled as Ghin handed out the visors and everyone slid them over their eyes. When Rohi tapped the activation button, her vision flashed white for a moment. Everything in the room looked the same, save for the couch. Where the neon outline had just been, the reclining body of a Tahl man now rested. His gangly arms lay limp, palms up. His elongated, purple, slack-jawed faced stared up at the ceiling.

They huddled over him.

"And here is how we originally found the body of Mr. Alu Glyf."

After a moment, Rohi sighed, "Well, I don't see any obvious cause of death..."

"Don't beat yourself up," said Ghin, "I had to do a full xeno-scan to figure this one out... and I *still* have questions."

She pointed to the base of the man's neck. "You see that little bruise?" Ghin waved her hand over the spot and the skin disappeared, revealing the internal physiology of the Tahlese neck. "Not only is the windpipe collapsed, but the primary nerve cord that sits right behind it is pinched, which would make him lose control of his arms and legs."

"What exactly does that mean?" asked Kaloce.

"It means he had to lay here, unable to move, while suffocating. Tahls have two primary and one reserve lung. The reserve can hold about ten to fifteen minutes of air, which probably felt like an eternity to him."

"That's fucked up," noted Rohi.

Kaloce coughed uncomfortably and added, "What- I mean, do you have any ideas as to what murder weapon was?"

"That's the thing," said Ghin as she waved her hand back over the neck, causing the skin to reappear. "Take another look at that bruise. It's barely the size of my thumb."

"So... someone shot him in the neck with a non-lethal bullet?" asked Kaloce.

"Looks pretty lethal to me," noted Rohi.

Yuhf snorted back a laugh.

Ghin pointed to the floor space between the coffee table and windowed wall opposite the couch. "The furthest someone could have stood from him and fired would be up against that glass. That's what? Ten feet at most? You all carry non-lethal rounds, don't you? Tell me, what would happen if you took that shot?"

"The wound would be a shit-load messier than that," noted Rohi.

"Same with our rounds," added Yuhf.

"So perhaps someone hit him with something?" posited Kaloce, "like a combat wand?"

"If they had enough pip on their swing?" answered Ghin, "Yeah, that could crush a Tahl windpipe, but again, the damage radius would be much larger. Remember-"

"Yeah, yeah, tiny bruise." noted Rohi.

"Could it have been a punch? Like someone's knuckle caught him just right?" asked Yuhf.

"The Tahl windpipe has a protective layer of cartilage," noted Ghin, "Whatever hit him was going at least seventy feet per second. That would be one mighty hell of a punch."

"Damn," grumbled Yuhf, "Now what? Canvas all the local fighting gyms for a grapple-tapper with freakish strength and a homicidal demeanor?"

"Half the clientele fits that description," answered Kaloce.

"Actually," mused Ghin, "You might not be too far off. Whoever did this knew how to handle themselves. Sure, Mr. Glyf here is something of a mystery, but it's painfully obvious how the rest got dusted. I'll show you."

She led them back into the hallway. Two holographic bodies lay waiting for them on either side of the office doors. Like the first, both were Tahl men, each at least seven feet in height and dressed in security uniforms. The one on the left's neck had been snapped. Rohi nodded to the one on the right. "What got him?"

Ghin gestured to the angular ornamental stormstone statue behind him. "Got his head cracked open on that overpriced piece of *art*. If get closer you can see there's still blood on the one edge."

Yuhf chuckled, "Could probably sell it for double price to some memorabilia freak now."

Rohi nodded, thinking Bhanakhana probably knew someone who knew someone who'd be interested.

"Pretty straightforward from here," said Ghin, "Alu's personal security detail all carried pulse pistols. The holster was empty on our 'art piece' victim here. The receptionist at the end of the hall and the security guard in the lobby were both shot in the head. Any of you fine detectives want to take a wild guess at what type of gun they were shot with?"

"Does it rhyme with Mulse Mistol?" asked Rohi.

Ghin rolled her eyes.

Yuhf snorted again.

Kaloce was silent.

"That's really all the medical team has for you right now." Ghin removed her visor and the others followed suit, causing the dead bodies to disappear. "We'll let you know if further scans turn up anything."

"Thank you for your help," said Kaloce.

Ghin collected the visors and left.

The data bracelets on all three officers dinged in unison, signaling the arrival of a new message.

"Nice, the company's legal team finally released the security footage," Rohi tapped her own bracelet and smiled at the others, "I, for one, am very interested to get a glimpse of our mysteriously strong warrior-assassin-psychopath-whatever. I don't suppose you have any steam pops we can spot-nuke for the show?"

Yuhf chuckled. Even Kaloce cracked a small smile.

WORD SECTION 0007

"I'm telling you, there is simply no reasoning with that uncouth *woman*!" Gupsley Carpian punctuated the statement by downing the rest of his Saltwater Brandy. He smacked his wet, scaly lips and reached for the decanter to pour another glass. "It's too bad you couldn't join me in person. I do keep some exquisite terrestrial liquors on hand, in order to better suit my clients' tastes. Personally, though, I find them all quite... *dry*," he chuckled at his own quip.

"No great loss for me," the holographic image in the seat across from him replied.

"Ah, yes, you don't drink. I knew that..."

"Were you able to glean anything useful from the meeting?" asked his virtual guest.

"She has a replica of the Gjenluvian spiral script ruins built over an entire wall of her lab."

"And?"

"And... uh... oh! Crates! A carry-drone was leaving her office with a number of hermetic crates just as I was arriving."

"She's leaving soon."

"Oh! Oh!" Gupsley tapped his webbed hand on the desk. "*Very* soon actually. While she was kicking me—I mean, while I was leaving of my own accord, I noticed some people in her waiting parlor. There was a Dronla, a Yoblon, and... actually, I don't know what the third one was. Some unfamiliar humanoid... I don't even know how I'd begin to describe his coloring... odd looking fellow... or woman, for all I could tell. They did *not* look like students."

"A groundwork team."

"Most likely."

"I will have to accelerate things then. Are you absolutely *certain* that no amount of financial recompense or professional resources will motivate the professor toward a partnership with us?"

"I offered her the proverbially blank currency card. She turned me away, in a rather hostile manner too."

Gupsley's virtual guest sighed. "Unfortunate."

A moment of uncomfortable silence passed.

Gupsley cleared his throat. "May I ask you something? Is the 'no drinking thing' a personal choice or is it a... *mandate from on high*, so to speak?"

"Alcohol consumption in moderation is generally accepted. I choose to avoid it like I do many of life's distractions. I can't afford the slightest chance at having my judgment impaired. At least, not until I have fulfilled my purpose."

"Well, you'll have to let me buy you that first drink... to celebrate."

The face of the projected image smiled, yet her eyes looked almost sad. Her eyes. Gupsley found them intriguing yet intimidating. It was the color. He'd never seen eyes with that hue of orange.

Serru Dac'eth took a drag from her cinder-stick. She exhaled and said, "I don't think that's going to be possible."

Some movement pulled Gupsley's eyes up from Serru to see a young Venovan man enter his office. He wore a simple gray shirt, black pants, and black boots with gold trim. He closed and locked the door behind him without saying a word.

"I will pray for your eternal essence, Mr. Carpian."

Serru's holograph disappeared.

WORD SECTION 0008

"You've got to be shitting me!" yelled Yuhf.

"Hmmm," mumbled Kaloce.

"That's a... a new one on me," noted Rohi.

They stared at the grid of two dozen view screens displaying the office building's security footage. Their cameras provided exceptional coverage of every inch of the space in marvelous detail. That is, except for one particular seventeen minute span of time. The camera in Alu's office showed him lounging on his couch, an expensive attaché resting on the coffee table. Then, the footage went black for five and a half minutes. Then it resumed, showing Alu's lifeless body slumped back into the couch, and a smoldering hole where the attaché case had been. Alu's office camera wasn't the only one to experience a temporary blackout. They could actually trace a clear path of short camera blackouts starting with the camera facing the parking lot, through the lobby, up the elevator, down the hallway to Alu's office. The blackouts then rolled back down to the lobby and out to the building's exterior.

"So, if I'm reading this right," started Rohi, "our Crim somehow rigged the cameras to go dark in perfect time with him showing up at the building, walking through the lobby, riding up the elevator, killing Alu and everyone else, and then leaving. Is that what we're looking at here?"

"It appears so," Kaloce concurred.

"Cool... cool, cool, cool," muttered Rohi to herself.

Yuhf let out an exasperated huff. "Worst case scenario: I figured we'd have a crim wearing a high-end holo-skin."

"You still get many of those down here?" Rohi asked. "We've been cracking down hard on them on our end of things."

"To your credit, it's working," offered Kaloce. "We hardly see any holo-skins these days."

"Yeah, well take away their disguises and apparently the crims can decide to just black out the cameras. You got any fancy ULE tech that can fix the picture?" asked Yuhf.

"I mean, yeah, I'm gonna send it to our people, but I'm not optimistic. This isn't like some digital designer pixilated the image... the cameras are just *off*."

"Is there a central monitoring station?" asked Yuhf. "Could someone there have been in cahoots with our Crim?"

"Let me see." Kaloce pulled a file. "No. The camera feeds aren't monitored in real time. They just record everything for reference in case of an incident."

"A lotta good that decision is doing them now... you'd think the rich prick'd be able to afford some extra oversight."

"Eh, that'd be a hell of a lot of footage to watch," countered Rohi.

"I know plenty of jobless folk down on Venno Street that'd take that work. Do it for next to nothing, too. But, of course, that would've required our dead Tahl friends to actually interact with lowly Venovan refugees."

"Yuhf, I think we should give the class politics a rest for once."

"Easy for you to say, 'loce. You're fourth generation on this planet. You never had to worry about catching collateral damage from some extremist in the Old Planet. You never had to line up in them refugee queues, wondering if you'll starve before they ever get you processed."

Kaloce stood. "I've worked for everything I have. No living person ever gave me anything."

"Boys!"

They turned to Rohi, who had her feet propped up on the desk and hands folded behind her head.

"If you two are done measuring your yub nubs, you think you could pack 'em back up in your pants? That way there'd be room on the desk to do some real detective work... and besides, I'd hate to have to whip mine out and make you both look bad."

Kaloce's mouth fell open. Yuhf started laughing.

Rohi suddenly sat up straight. "Oh shit... that just gave me an idea."

"Sorry, Agent," scoffed Yuhf, "But I'm married... not that I ain't flattered or tempted."

"Ew," said Rohi. "No... just listen. If we're going to do this the old fashioned way, step one is building a picture of who this guy was. We know he was relatively young, very rich, and very successful. Given the fact that guy had an old school hand-painted portrait of himself hanging in his own office, I'm gonna go out on a moon and say he was pretty fucking in love with himself. What's the favorite pastime for pretty much every young, rich, self-possessed guy across the universe? Bragging about himself. And where is the best place to brag about yourself if you're looking to maximize your audience?"

"GIG-Life," answered Kaloce.

"Ah," scoffed Yuhf, "That shit my kids is always wasting time on?"

"I'm willing to bet this guy posted damn near everything about," she mockingly crooked her hand into the 'peace and prosperity' symbol that was currently popular with pretentious young folk, "his *tops epic lifestyle* on his GIG-Life profile."

"Great," muttered Yuhf, "Let's pull the account."

• • •

Rohi picked at the remains of the Vashniien takeout, as she continued scouring Alu's seemingly endless online profile.

"I swear to Bjordax this guy posted from his office almost every day that he was *on my righteous grind*. What the phoob does that even mean?"

"I don't know," said Yuhf as he stared at his own screen, "but this guy was no stranger to the night life. How'd he have the time to always be *on his grind* when looks like he was out getting drunk every night?"

"Zip," answered Kaloce. The other two looked at him and he said, "Full autopsy report came in. The guy had plenty of Zip in his system."

"Well that explains his apparent immunity to sleep," noted Rohi.

"It also gives us a lead," added Kaloce, "Maybe he got into trouble with his supplier."

"What's Zip's legal status here?" asked Rohi. "It's getting hard to keep track these days."

"Prescription only," answered Yuhf. "Dosage is tightly controlled. So we still see it being dealt at street level."

"Okay, there's one lead for the big board." Rohi's work terminal let out an audible *Ping!* "And it looks like we've got another one here..."

"What's that?" asked Yuhf.

"I had the computer run a program searching for patterns, as well as deviations from those patterns in Alu's GIG-Life activity. Here's the report."

She swiped her finger across her screen, sending copies to Yuhf and Kaloce's respective terminals.

"Copious references to work and partying," noted Kaloce.

"We already knew that," grumbled Yuhf.

"Check out *Notable Item Number Six*," said Rohi, "For over three years, same day of the week, same two-hour time frame... no posts, *ever*. We have a two-hour blank spot with zero references to his activity or location occurring on the exact same day, at the exact same time... for *years*."

"So, I assume we start interviewing his colleagues and employees?" asked Kaloce. "See if they know anything?"

Rohi sighed, "Yeah, we should, but I'm not hopeful. I'll bet everyone who might have known something about it is currently laying on a slab in the fridge downstairs."

"Oh shit... now *I* have an idea," said Yuhf.

"I'm equally intrigued and terrified," noted Rohi.

"This Alu guy... he's a yok, don't get me wrong, but he's a smart yok. He knows not to reference what he's doing during this 'special' time. But his security guys... maybe one of them is dumb enough to post something. Bunch of rent-a-triggers like that? One of them had to slip up."

"Careful, Yuhf. I'm starting to think you're an actual police officer." Rohi punctuated the comment with a wink.

Yuhf smiled as he replied, "Fuck you, ya Ulee Boot Smoocher."

"Alright, let's each take a guard's GIG-Life account and re-run the pattern program, specifically looking for posts around that time frame."

WORD SECTION 0009

Bhanakhana rubbed his eyes with one hand and reached for his glass with the other. A new song with head-rattling bass began to hammer through the night club's speakers. He could have sworn this was the fourth time they'd played it. All the young folks' music sounded the same to him anyway. He tilted the glass up to his mouth, but sadly found it to be empty. Bhanakhana moved aside the info tablet that covered the table's digital menu. He pressed the *refill* icon, submitting virtual payment via his data bracelet.

While waiting for a service professional to arrive with his new drink, Bhanakhana scanned the crowd for his companions. He usually had no trouble finding them, with Chuck being the only Earth man in this particular star system, possibly even this galaxy. And while there were plenty of stout yellow Yoblons running around the civilized systems, Jopp was... well... he was *Jopp*. He tended to stick out. But this time, Bhanakhana found his search to be fruitless. He sent up a little prayer to the cosmos that whatever hijinks they were getting into wouldn't cause him *too* much of a headache tomorrow.

There is a strange universal sensation that exists amongst all known sentient races. And that is the subconscious feeling of knowing when you are being watched. Bhanakhana felt this tingling at the back of his neck as he surveyed the crowded bar. Before he could pinpoint his watcher, however, a silver-skinned humanoid J'Kari woman approached his table carrying a fresh cocktail on a tray. Her black hair was streaked with neon purple and a crescent moon tattoo sat just under her right eye. Bhanakhana noted her to be a handsome female by almost any standards.

"Here's your drink, Muscles." She set the glass down with a wink.

Bhanakhana handed his empty to her and said, "Thank you most kindly."

The server took note of the digital files and tablet screens splayed out across the table and asked, "Are you the new professor of campus nightlife studies or something?"

Bhanakhana chuckled. "No. I am a consultant to one of the Lyceum's senior educators. We will be setting out on a research expedition soon. I am merely conducting a little preparation."

"I can't imagine you're actually getting any work done in here. Or is that the point?" She leaned forward on the table. "You come here looking for a distraction?"

"I am actually accomplishing quite a bit here. The pleasant ambiance helps me concentrate."

She laughed. "I'm pretty sure that's the first time anyone has described this place as having *pleasant ambiance*."

Bhanakhana raised his drink. "A toast to ambiance then." He took a sip, a smile spreading across his crimson face. "This is exquisite."

"Thanks, I mixed it myself."

"You are a master of your craft. Thank you, Miss…?"

She shot him a sly grin. "My shift ends in two hours. If you want to know my name, meet me for a drink at that place across the street. That is, unless you have too much work left to do."

Bhanakhana canted his head to the side and said. "I can definitely be finished by then."

She left with a wink.

"Well that was interesting," Bhanakhana mused.

He resumed his work. Over the next hour, the already crowded bar managed to squeeze in more bodies. The thumping music managed to get even thumpier. The relentless waves of stimulus formed walls around Bhanakhana's head. He lost himself in reading the ancient Gjenluvian lore, the theories on Ak'alei interstellar travel, the debunking counterpoints to those theories…

Bhanakhana became aware of a figure standing at his table. He had been so focused on his research, he hadn't even noticed them walk up.

"My dear, I am not certain I deserve this level of enthusiasm, however flattering it may be... I believe there is still another hour until our scheduled-" he looked up and saw that the figure standing there was a Venovan man. He stared at Bhanakhana with pale yellow eyes set against an impassive dark blue face. He wore a gray shirt, black pants, and black boots with gold trim.

"How may I help you, sir?" asked Bhanakhana.

"Give me everything. Everything on the table." Neither his face nor his tone betrayed any emotion.

"Pardon?"

"Give me everything on the table," he repeated.

Bhanakhana straightened his back and folded his thick arms across his wide chest. "Let us set aside the inherent *oddness* of your request for a moment, as well as go ahead a skip the part wherein I ask *why* you want my research files, and just cut straight to me denying your truly baffling demands."

"Uh..." the man let his impassive gaze slip. "What?"

Bhanakhana sighed and added, "No, you may not have *everything on the table*."

The man's confused expression turned hard. "We will take it by force if we have to."

"*We?*"

Bhanakhana noticed two more Venovan men move up to the edge of the crowd. The dim light of the bar made it difficult to discern the expressions on their dark blue faces, but he could feel the coldness of their stares. Bhanakhana's eyes came back to the man in front of him, who had raised his shirt just enough to reveal the sonic dagger on his belt.

"I see," said Bhanakhana. "Well, in that case, please allow me to pack everything up in the proper order."

The man glanced over each of his shoulders, then nodded. Bhanakhana saved and minimized each holographic file, and then carefully folded up his array of screens and digital notepads until the entire workstation was nothing but a slim silver rectangle. It looked like a steel cafeteria tray. Bhanakhana offered it up. The man leaned forward, his blue hands grasping.

In one swift motion, Bhanakhana reared back, raised his leg, and drove his heel into the table. It tore it free from the floor and sailed directly into the chest of the Venovan, who toppled backwards. The other two broke out of the crowd and rushed forward. Bhanakhana burst out of the booth, wielding the compacted workstation. Before the second assailant could even pull his knife free, Bhanakhana cracked him across the face with the metal rectangle. A glob of blood and teeth went flying as the man crumpled to the ground. He turned and reacted just as the third assailant lashed out with his own knife. Bhanakhana caught the man's wrist, the knife tip just barely grazing his chest. He hoisted him up by the wrist until their eyes were level.

"Who *are* you?" he asked.

A shriek pulled Bhanakhana's eyes to the left. The first man had gotten out from under the table, and was rushing at him. Bhanakhana reacted by striking the charging man with the body of the one he held. Both would-be assailants hit the floor in an unconscious heap.

"Blast it," Bhanakhana cursed, "I suppose no answers will be forthcoming."

At that very moment, his data bracelet lit up with a new message. It was from Professor Phyos, and read *URGENT: Get to lab now*.

Bhanakhana turned to find the J'Kari server woman standing there, her eyes wide and mouth open in utter shock.

"I apologize," he said, "but our rendezvous will have to be postponed indefinitely. Please add the cost of the table to my tab." He handed her a digital information card. "Should the local authorities wish to contact me, that is how I can be reached." He smiled and added, "You may also contact me, should you desire."

She grabbed Bhanakhana by the collar, pulled him down, and planted a quick kiss on his mouth. "Sorry," she said, "That was just... fucking hot."

Bhanakhana, his head still being head bowed low, his eyes bulging from the surprise, replied, "Ah, yes, it may be a bit warm in here."

WORD SECTION 0010

Bhanakhana and Professor Phyos stood in her lab. More accurately, they stood in front of a three foot by seven foot rectangular hole in the wall at the far end. A slab of wall lay amongst the scattered dust and rubble at their feet.

They looked up to see Chuck dragging a ranting and raving Jopp through the door.

"Physical space is a lie! We are all one entity! We don't need to walk anywhere! We just need to sync our consciousness with the planet's conscious and then the environment will move to meet our needs!"

"What's up with him?" asked Phyos.

"Oh, uh, we were hanging out with a couple students who'd bought us some drinks... then they offered us some Glitch. I declined."

"Jopp accepted," finished Bhanakhana.

"I recognize that behavior alright... he's glitching hard," added Phyos.

Chuck noticed the twisted mess of stone and metal and looked through the hole in the wall. He saw a small room filled with digital work screens and a row of gray metal boxes that Chuck found to be surprisingly reminiscent of desktop computer towers. He noticed a few of the "computer" boxes were missing from the row. The tense silence was too much for Chuck to bear, and he couldn't stop himself.

"So, uh, doing some remodeling?"

Bhanakhana gave Chuck a disapproving look.

Jopp didn't react as he was too busy staring at the ceiling.

To his surprise, Professor Phyos smiled. "Good. We're going to need a lot of smart ass one-liners if we hope to make it through this thing with our sanity intact."

Chuck couldn't tell if she was being sarcastic, and made an educated guess that it was a feeling he'd be experiencing a lot in the days to come.

"Sage Phyos, what happened here?" asked Bhanakhana.

"What happened here is these fiddle-tits that keep been bothering me finally decided to grow some yub nubs."

"Pardon?"

"Remember that slippery bastard I booted from the office? He represents some big important mystery client that's been trying to get their prehensile appendages on my research for ages. I think my symposium lecture might have been the motivator for them to stop playing by the rules. Curse this colossal ego of mine, justified though it may be."

"Do you have any ideas as to whom these individuals are?"

"Any ideas? Yeah, a few... there's this dunghole professor over at Tasa Technical. We've had something of a rivalry over the past decade. Then there's this band of religious fanatics who're convinced the Ak'alei were descended from their god or some other crap like that. And of course, you've got a handful of corporate-sponsored Research Institutes who love taking new scientific discoveries and sucking out every drop of profit-juice they can muster. Finally, there's my second ex-husband. We had a tendency to play pranks on each other, but we were terrible at drawing a line on the escalation of said pranks. He divorced me when I spent half our joint savings on a satellite laser show that culminated with a photo-realistic image of him in the nude being displayed against the night sky. The whole city could see it." She started chuckling to herself. "I had them draw everything perfectly to scale... except for his jibbly bits. Those I had them shrink to one-tenth size. In retrospect, that was probably the rod that broke the humpalope's butt."

Chuck choked back laughter.

"So, yeah," she continued, "Could have been a number of folks."

"We did it."

They all turned to Jopp, who was still staring up at the ceiling, only now his arms were stretched out to the sides, palms facing up.

"Um, no we didn't," said Chuck.

"I keep telling you: every being in the universe is connected. We are not separate entities but one single consciousness. We are all one being. Whoever did it... *we* did it."

"And there's our friend, Glitch, again," the professor rolled her eyes. "What stage is he on?"

"One, I think... but Two should be starting any minute."

"Makes sense. What with all the philosophical mish mosh."

Jopp turned and gawked at them with wide, dilated eyes. "Yes! Okay! Yes! I *am* Glitching! Sorry for having fun! I must have missed the memo that mentioned tonight was the start of our next shitty adventure!"

"Aaaand there's Stage Two taking over," noted Phyos.

Chuck tried to soothe him. "Settle down, bud. You're yelling."

"I can't help it! It's the drugs! There's not another black case again is there?!"

"Nope."

"Pirates?!"

"Nope."

"Gorthans?!?!"

"Nope."

"Great! Why is Big Red bleeding?!"

Phyos rolled her eyes. "Hallucinations are-" she paused when saw that there was indeed a stain of dried blood than stemmed from a short thin slice across his massive chest.

"Oh shit," said Chuck, "How did we not notice that? Bhanakhana, what happened to you?"

Bhanakhana blinked with surprise as he looked down. "My word, I forgot about that. Just prior to Sage Phyos summoning us back here, I was accosted by three rogues."

"Someone attacked you?! What happened?"

"I handled it. Quite efficiently, I might add."

"What does that mean?" asked Phyos.

"Oh, I imagine once they finally regain consciousness they will all be in need of strong pain-alleviator medications. And one gentleman will definitely need to arrange for some major dental work."

"Damn," mused Chuck, "You're always so prim and proper, I sometimes forget what a stone-cold badass you can be."

"The ping-berries that attacked you, what can you tell me about them?" asked Phyos.

"Not much," answered Bhanakhana, "They were all Venovan men. Nothing remarkable about their attire. My *defensive* efforts rendered them all unconscious before I could ascertain their motive. However, I can say with certainty it was related to our Ak'alei research."

"How's that?"

"They did not demand money. They wanted my work station."

"Well, that cuts out Professor dung-bum and my ex-husband. Neither have the spooj-sacks required to employ violent thugs."

"Will someone please tell that three-headed hoggnoff in the corner to shut the fuck up?!" screamed Jopp, "I can't hear anything you guys are saying!"

They all looked toward the corner Jopp was glaring at. No three-headed hoggnoffs in sight.

Jopp smacked his lips and announced, "I need water!"

Professor Phyos pointed to the opposite side of the lab. "Earth Man... Chuck, was it? There's some water in the cold-closet over there. We don't need him collapsing from dehydration. Make sure you get one of the green bottles. GREEN."

Chuck hustled over. Bhanakhana folded his hands together. "Was any crucial material stolen, Sage Phyos?"

"Unfortunately, yes."

"I am so sorry to hear that. What was stored on the servers they took?"

"Two dozen terabytes of erotic novels. Including a manuscript I was writing myself. Over a hundred thousand words detailing the romantic trials and tribulations of an Ochrean merchant prince and his secret lover, the Magistrate Premier of the Soreshi Empire. Theirs was a love doomed from the start," she sighed.

Bhanakhana glanced awkwardly around the room. Jopp was staring at Phyos with wide, tear-soaked eyes.

Phyos took a breath and then smiled up at Bhanakhana. "But don't let a single molecule in that mountainous muscle-bound frame of yours worry, Sage Bhindo. Not even a secret room hidden behind the wall of my supposedly 'ultra-secure' lab is a good enough place for my Ak'alei data. I'm actually more concerned on how they ripped the door out of the wall. The type of machinery for that wouldn't fit through my door, and I don't see any excavator-sized holes around here..."

Chuck returned and handed Jopp a green bottle of water.

"Would it be safe to assume this incident requires some refiguring of our plans?" asked Bhanakhana.

"I knew they gave you the 'Sage' certification for reason. We should leave sooner than planned."

"When were you thinking?"

"Now. Right phoobing now. Which one of these two is the pilot?"

Bhanakhana and Chuck both pointed to Jopp, who was chugging from the green bottle so greedily that trickles of water were running down the sides of his mouth.

"Of course." She looked to Chuck, "I don't suppose you have much experience?"

Chuck shrugged, "A little... but pretty much always low orbit stuff. I've never flown deep space or through an anomaly."

"Well, shit," sighed the Professor. "I hate flying myself. Oh well, let's make Halka Spritzer from Halka nuts."

"I could pilot the vessel," offered Bhanakhana.

"Nope. I need you to keep soaking up my research. I want you to get as much of that info in your brain as possible. Leave the labor to us."

Jopp sputtered his lips, spitting water everywhere.

"Well, there is *one* piece of labor I need from you, Sage Bhindo. You're gonna have to carry him to the ship."

The Professor led them out of the lab, through the parlor, and to the faculty elevators. They piled in and ascended.

"Out of curiosity," Chuck asked, "why was it so important that I grab one of the *green* bottles? They all said 'water' on the labels."

"Oh," Professor Phyos chuckled, "The blue bottles are just plain old water. The green ones have an additive that counteracts the psychoactive properties of Glitch, pulling you down off your high at a much quicker pace. And of course, you're wondering why I would need that on hand, well, that's because the *purple* bottles actually have powdered Glitch dissolved in them. I use it in rare situations when I need an extremely creative solution to a seemingly impossible problem. The last thing he needs," she pointed up at Jopp, who was slung over Bhanakhana's shoulder, "is more Special G in his system."

"Uh, okaaaaay. Wait... blue, green, and purple are relatively close on the color spectrum. Wouldn't it make more sense to use more opposite colors, like blue, yellow, and red? Don't certain species have differences in the range of colors they can see? Nobody in your lab has ever accidentally dosed themselves with the drug?"

The Professor shrugged. "It's never been a problem bef- Ohhhhh-no, wait- that totally explains one of my student's midterm presentation on the *Myth of Thumbs*. One of his projection slides was just the word 'hands' written over and over again in fifty-six different fonts."

The elevator stopped and the doors opened to reveal a short hallway with another set of open elevator doors at the other end.

"Isn't this fun?" crowed the Professor.

They followed her into the new elevator chamber.

"Where are we going?" asked Bhanakhana.

"Out of the shadows of forced ignorance and into the illumination of enlightenment!" shouted Jopp from over his shoulder.

The Professor ignored Jopp and pointed at a column of buttons with names written next to them.

"For the handful of tenured faculty that also own their own interstellar vessels, the Lyceum provides private hangars."

She traced her finger along the list of names. Bhanakhana noticed she zipped right past her own name and pressed the button next to "Kefa Chareet".

"Pardon me, Sage Phyos, but you may have pressed the wrong button. Who is Kefa Chareet?"

"He's an adjunct professor in the Metaphysical Physics department. Also, he doesn't exist. I made him up to get an extra parking space."

"Why would you do that?"

"Good question."

A moment passed. Chuck and Bhanakhana traded perplexed glances.

"Are you, uh, going to answer his question?" said Chuck.

Phyos rolled her eyes. "I guess so. We're avoiding my 'official' hangar, because I'm assuming the yok knockers who broke into my office also scoped out my ship. I guarantee you there's some kind of monitoring or tracking device in there... or hell, maybe even a bomb."

"We should contact local law enforcement," stated Bhanakhana.

"Way ahead of ya. While I was waiting for you lot to show up, I wrote a comprehensive account of the break-in, complete with a list of what was taken and who I suspect and why. I even noted that my ship may have been tampered with. In a few hours, that message will be sent to the Chief Constable of the local police department. I gave them blanket permission to inspect everything and listed out the answers to a bunch of assumed questions they might have, like what my favorite brand of breakfast num nums is. That's a thing police want to know about, right? Of course it is. You're going to ask me why I delayed the message for a few hours. Well, again, I figure the tit ticklers messing with my work might very well be monitoring my communications. I want them thinking I'm still on the planet for as long as possible."

"So, you own a second ship no one knows about?" Chuck asked.

"No."

Another pair of confused glances exchanged between Chuck and Bhanakhana. Then Jopp started squirming.

"Why is Big Red carrying me like a sack of Duber Spuds?"

Bhanakhana set him down on his feet. Jopp shook his head a few times and rubbed his eyes. The Professor nudged Chuck.

"Green water sobering him up."

"Ugh, my head hurts," moaned Jopp.

"Yeah, speeding up the come-down will do that to ya. I had some pain relievers put on the ship."

"You indicated you did not own another ship."

"Yeah, I don't."

The elevator stopped moving with a *ding* and the doors slid open. The Professor pointed.

"But you do."

A very familiar platinum-colored Estal Cube sat in the middle of the space.

"That... that is my vessel."

"Yeah, that's what I just said."

"What is it doing here?"

"I had it moved."

"Why?"

"You know, I knew you were going to ask that. I just love how easy the Estal models are to customize. They make all these modules that you can get installed in just a few hours."

"Did you tamper with my ship?"

"Me? No! I had some Interstellar Mechanics undergrads do it."

Bhanakhana's mouth fell open.

"You can't just like make changes to our ship," said Chuck.

Phyos looked almost offended. "Of course I can... *I'm eccentric!*"

"I have no clue what's happening right now," announced Jopp.

"I know, dear, I know." Phyos patted his head, then to Chuck and Bhanakhana she said, "Honestly, I think you're going to thank me. I installed some seriously primo upgrades. Some of them are even legal."

She strolled toward the ship's entry.

"Wait, what was that last bit she said?" Bhanakhana asked.

Chuck shrugged, grabbed Jopp by the sleeve and started dragging him forward.

"C'mon, boys!" Phyos leaned her head out the entry panel, "Let's blow this friznitzery!"

WORD SECTION 0011

"Got it!"

Yuhf and Kaloce rubbed the creeping sleep from their eyes and looked over at Rohi. She flicked her wrist, sending copies of her screen to their respective terminals.

"This is from the guard who got his head busted on that sculpture. The time marker is from one of Alu's regular calendar blackouts."

The post was a picture of a cylindrical building made from glossy white stones. The only other notable feature was a pair of large obsidian doors. Together they formed a perfect fifteen foot circle. Two gold lines in a tight parallel across the top and one vertical line ran down the outer half of each door.

"That's the Temple of Rhonac in Bluestone Hills," noted Kaloce.

"Where is that?" asked Rohi.

"It's a relatively affluent, predominantly Venovan neighborhood on the north side of the city," he answered.

Rohi held up a hand just as Yuhf opened his mouth. "Please hold the socio-political commentary and look at the caption the guard wrote."

Yuhf grumbled to himself as he peered down at the screen. The caption under the picture read: *"Boss man getting his weekly dose of religion. Time for me to get my weekly dose of naptime."* The sentence was followed by a little cartoon image of a Tahl fast asleep and another of a purple face laughing.

When Yuhf looked up, all the grumpiness had drained from his face.

"You feeling a little spiritual?" asked Rohi.

"Nice!" replied Yuhf. "Let's head over there tomorrow morning and rattle some cages."

"We can't just barge in there."

Yuhf and Rohi both looked over at Kaloce. His dark blue forehead was lined with frustration.

"We can't?" asked Rohi.

"Yeah, why the hell not?" added Yuhf.

"The Religious Protection Ordinance. We need to request clearance before entering their property in an official capacity."

"I can't imagine this being an issue," started Rohi. "We have a murder victim whose whereabouts are pretty much all accounted for, save for one particular reoccurring time slot. Now we have clear indication of where he was spending that time. Pretty linear investigative progression."

"I'll get to work on the request form right now," offered Kaloce.

"Good idea," added Yuhf. He looked at Rohi and nodded toward his partner. "He's way better at the bureaucracy stuff than me. I'd probably submit the form with a typo or something and we'd have to start the process over."

Rohi sighed, "Fine."

"Why don't you two go get some rest? I'll take care of this request submission. Like you said, it shouldn't be too much of an issue. I'll be right behind you."

Yuhf yawned and stretched. "Works for me. Meet back here first thing in the morning?"

Rohi folded her arms. "I guess if that's the way things are done here, sure."

Kaloce nodded. "Definitely."

WORD SECTION 0012

"How was your nap, Buzz Brain? Still seeing pink humpalopes everywhere?"

Jopp shook his head groggily as he entered the Cube ship's bridge.

"Where are we?" he asked.

"We are four hours out from Raeth Beta's atmosphere," answered Bhanakhana, "and will be at our first anomaly jump in another four."

Jopp's eyes took in the ship's bridge. He vaguely remembered some babbling about upgrades and Bhanakhana sounding distressed. That explained why his usual pilot's station in the center of the room was gone. It its place was a large, semicircle-shaped touch panel with two seats. Phyos occupied one, the other was empty. Bhanakhana sat at a workstation terminal to her left. Chuck was at the terminal to the right.

"You ready to fly the new and improved Estal Cube?" asked the Professor.

"I can fly anything," answered Jopp.

"Really?"

"No. Technically, I'm not certified for any vessel above a Class Nine. But that doesn't sound as cool, does it?"

The Professor smiled and said, "Fair enough." She patted the seat next to her.

Jopp hopped in and cocked his head over at Chuck, who'd yet to look up from his screen or even acknowledge Jopp's presence. "What's up with him?"

"Dude!"

Jopp looked over Chuck, who was beaming back at him with a childlike grin.

"She's got every *Mac Battle* issue ever! I'm reading the one where Mac defeats the pan-dimensional giant space squid with his light-speed jetpack and the Sacred Scimitar!"

"Mac what? Oh... those static image stories you love so much?"

"They're called *comics*, man. I told you."

Jopp leaned closer to the Professor and whispered, *"Good idea. Best to keep him occupied so he doesn't get in the way. How'd you know he liked that one so much?"*

Professor Phyos raised an eyebrow. "I didn't. That's *my* collection. I love *Mac Battle*, especially the one where he saves an entire planet from an evil army of aliens that feed on sound waves by playing such an intense rock opera that it causes them all to die of over-excitement."

"Ah c'mon!" shouted Chuck, "No spoilers!"

"Chuck." Bhanakhana tapped the screen in front of himself. "How about you instead start reading up on the Ak'alei. You may be able to provide a unique perspective on everything."

Phyos arched an eyebrow at him. "You really think so?"

Bhanakhana chuckled. "I have been traveling with him for over two standard annuals... and am still nowhere near comprehending the cognitive processes of the Earth human mind. You will not find a 'fresher' pair of eyes in the galaxy."

"Ah heck yeah!" Chuck waved away the holographic comic books. "Long lost historical mysteries... an unknown enemy nipping at our heels... this is so *Raiders*!"

"So what?" asked Phyos.

Jopp rolled his eyes. "Never ask him to explain his references..."

"Raiders!" said Chuck. "Raiders of the Lost Ark... Indiana Jones... possibly the greatest movie series ever... well, not counting that fourth one... we shall not speak of that one. I mean, I see what they were going for, but they could've-"

Phyos turned to Jopp. "I see what you mean... anyway!" she clapped her hands, "Flying School is in session."

"I know how to fly this ship," asserted Jopp.

"Yeah, yeah, but ol' New Cube here has a few... let's call them *non-standard* modifications."

"Did we get a warp drive?!" Chuck asked.

"Dude, we've talked about this. That's not a real thing."

"As a matter of fact, yes," said Phyos, "I had a warp drive installed."

"Seriously?!"

"Yeah," said Jopp, "seriously?"

The Professor chuckled. "Sorry, I'm just yanking your dangle... wait, do Earth males have the dangly bits?"

Chucks cheeks flushed. "I'm, uh, not okay with this turn of the conversation."

"Oh relax," said Jopp. Then to the Professor he added, "He's been bunking up with a scorching little J'Kari woman for the past few annuals, so I can only assume he's got the required equipment."

"Shit, Rohi! I forgot to send her a message letting her know we'd left."

Chuck scampered out of the room to go find a private commline.

"I gave a presentation on Earth human anatomy a while back. I could pull it up for you two," offered Bhanakhana.

"Nope!" replied Jopp and the Professor in unison.

"But," Professor Phyos hopped up and approached Bhanakhana, "I have something for you."

She reached into an unseen pocket within the folds of her clothes and pulled out a leathery, brown rectangular tablet. It was much thicker than most data tablets. Bhanakhana was stunned when she actually pulled the tablet open, revealed it to contain hundreds of flimsy white pages bound on one side.

"What the shit is that?" asked Jopp.

"This..." Professor Phyos waved it through the air with a flourish, "is a notebook."

Bhanakhana gasped.

"I think my great grand-mam had one of those," mused Jopp. "Damn, that's vintage as hell, Prof."

The Professor placed her other hand over the top and presented it to Bhanakhana.

"I needed to ensure my most important findings, my most crucial insights, were stored in a place no one would find. You will not find the data in this notebook in any museum, university library, or in any digital corner of the GIG. More specifically, this is a recreation of Cestoras' Diary, along with my translation matrix. We're in this shitstorm together now, Sage Bhindo. If you're going to help me solve this puzzle, you'll need *all* the clues."

Bhanakhana took the notebook with utmost reverence and gingerly placed it on his terminal's desk. He took a few deep breaths, the thick cords of muscle enveloping his arms seemed to quiver as his delicately opened to the first page and began to read. Professor Phyos grinned at him for a moment before returning to her seat next to Jopp.

"Okay," said Jopp, "Let's talk about these *non-standard modifications*... like this little guy." He reached for the fist-sized, glowing red button in the center of the console.

"Don't touch that!"

Jopp's hand froze.

"Why?"

"Because that button causes a spherical protective shell to materialize around the bridge, while the rest of the ship breaks apart into eight sections, which then fire off in separate directions before exploding with electromagnetic pulses."

Jopp's hand stayed hovering above the button as he slowly turned his head toward the Professor.

"Why do we even *have* that?!"

"In case."

"In case of *what?!*"

"In case we're ever in a situation where we need a spherical protective shell to materialize around the bridge, while the rest of the ship breaks apart into eight sections, which then fire off in separate directions before exploding with electromagnetic pulses... *duh.*"

Jopp stared at her dumbly.

"Now, this area over here controls the ecological makeup of the cargo holds. Like if we need to accommodate the environmental needs of a specimen of Gjeku Fish... oh, that reminds me, these controls control the surveillance masking features. Like in case we needed to hide said Gjeku Fish from the Wildlife Authorities. Got it? Good. And, over here are the defenses: plasma cannons, trailer mines, rapid pulsers..."

Jopp stared at her with his mouth hanging open.

"What?"

"None of this is even close to legal."

"Legal by whose standards?"

"Everyone's."

"Oh, what does *everyone* know."

"I...uh..." Jopp looked toward Bhanakhana, whose hulking frame was hunched low over the workstation. "Big Red? You cool with this?"

"Yes. Yes. Splendid and all that..." Bhanakhana gave a lazy wave without looking up.

"He hasn't listened to a word we've said since I gave him that notebook," answered Professor Phyos. "That muscle-bound brain of his is taking the deepest knowledge dive of its existence. He won't be coming up for air any time soon. Shall we continue our lessons on the controls of this marvelous mobile laboratory?"

"How did you do all this to the ship?! We were only on Raeth for like seven hours."

"Never underestimate the power of unpaid student labor. Now, moving on..."

WORD SECTION 0013

"This is fucking stupid."

Rohi sat with Yuhf in her black cruiser, just around the block from the Temple of Rhonac in Bluestone Hills. She had the windows retracted, letting the slight chill of the morning drift into the vehicle. Two steaming cups of wahu rested between them.

"Still no word from Kaloce?" she asked.

"Nah. He sent me that message first thing this morning about being sick. Claimed the food last night tore up his stomach. Hasn't responded to any of my other messages."

"And nothing from local Command on that special investigative permit thing?"

"Not yet."

"Fucking. Stupid."

"Yep."

Rohi drummed her fingers on the car door. Yuhf took a loud sip of wahu.

"So what's up with you and your people?"

Yuhf gave her a side glance. "Huh?"

"My understanding of the politics on Venova is, well, nonexistent."

"Ever been there?"

"Nope."

"But you've probably got a picture of it in your head?"

"Uh, yeah, I guess."

"What you're thinking of is Sala Ma. It's really the only part of the planet you see in GIG-shows and movies. It's a nice place."

"But?"

"But only one tenth of the world's population lives there. What they don't show you on media is that the ocean and sky surrounding the continent are patrolled constantly by warships. Sala Ma is the only republic on the planet. Every other country is either literally owned by a corporation or controlled by a religious faction. The corporates kill each other over profit. The 'faithful' kill each other over who is more righteous. And of course, they hate each other too. The life worth for an average Venovan basically amounts to either how much profit you can generate or how many souls you can harvest. It's all the same shit, just different lingo."

"Damn."

"Yeah, why do you think so many Venovan immigrants are willing to move into the worst neighborhoods? It's not just here." He pointed a finger toward the ceiling. "Up there in Pa Nui, the Little Venova district isn't exactly swimming in money, is it?"

"Actually, I've heard rumors it's been cleaned up a lot lately, but yeah, it's historically been pretty shitty."

Yuhf sighed, "I guess I shouldn't whine to you...you know, because of..." He trailed off.

"Because I'm a J'Kari?" asked Rohi with a raised eyebrow.

"Yeah, I mean, I guess a *shitty* home world is better than *no* home world."

"I hate when people say things like that. No, a shitty home world is *not* better than none. Venova's problems continue to fuck people up to this day. Ji'a has been a smoldering husk for generations. We had no choice but to forget the old fights and move on." She let out a cynical laugh. "Our whole planet had to fucking *die* before we could unite as a people. It's probably why so many of us are in the U.L.E. Maybe we think we can save the other 'Venovas' of the universe before they annihilate themselves."

"In my experience as a law cog." Yuhf gazed out the window. "...there's no use saving people that don't want to be saved."

Before Rohi could respond, her data bracelet beeped, signaling a new message. She tapped the cruiser's dash-screen, pulling up the message's content. Rohi read it and clapped her hands together.

"Hell yes."

Yuhf looked back from the window. "What's up?"

"So," she started, "I may have went ahead last night and sent a request to *my* commanding officer. I asked about this ordinance Kaloce was so concerned with... and he just sent us official permission to continue the investigation as we see fit. Said if anyone makes an issue of it to send them his way."

"Works for me. Let's do this." Yuhf drained his cup's remaining contents.

They got out of the cruiser and walked around to the front of the Temple. From the street, the door looked like a solid black circle with the golden gate of Rhonac printed on it. As they got closer, they could make out the seam between the doors. Rohi noticed a ringer button built subtly into the white stone frame to the left of the door. She pressed it and they waited. After a few moments, and a voice spoke from an unseen intercom, *"May Rhonac's light illuminate your travels. How may we be of service to you today?"*

Rohi looked up at the top of the door, where she assumed the camera to be. She pointed at the ULE insignia on her uniform with one hand and at the local city law enforcement logo on Yuhf's chest with the other.

"We represent a joint effort between the ULE and Pa Mahinga Safety Enforcement. We are investigating a serious crime and have come across evidence that leads us to believe you may be able to assist us. We would be happy to divulge more information... face to face."

The intercom voice paused for what seemed like an unnecessarily long moment.

"I am sorry. Now is not a good time. We have morning rituals to attend to before the day's first service."

"Citizens are dead. We need to speak with a church representative. Now."

"Do you have an official edict permitting such demands?"

Rohi muttered under her breath to Yuhf, "So, it's gonna be like that, huh?"

"You were expecting a welcome mat?" he replied.

She sighed as she pulled up the writ from her commanding officer and her data bracelet projected a holographic copy of it up toward the assumed camera. Another unnecessarily long moment passed.

"*Welcome.*"

The doors opened inwards, revealing a well lit vestibule. Luxurious carpet ran from the door to a circular pool set against the back wall of the welcoming chamber. The carpet split into two paths running around the pool and ended at tall arched doors on either side. Jet black water flowed down the wall between the doors into the circular pool.

"How do they get the water that color?" asked Rohi.

Yuhf shrugged.

"It's just blended with Eusi mineral."

Rohi and Yuhf whirled toward the unseen voice. A woman dressed in a simple gray robe stepped out from an alcove to the left. She was, expectedly, Venovan, with powder blue skin and platinum hair pulled back in a short braid. She nodded toward the pool.

"It's safe to drink, in case you wondering."

"I wasn't," replied Rohi.

"Really? That was like the first thing I wondered when I got here," said woman.

Rohi glanced at Yuhf who only shrugged again.

"Are you who we were talking with on the comm outside?"

The woman shook her head. "Oh no. I'm just a volunteer here. My name is Lefsa."

"ULE Division Officer Rohi Kahpanova." Rohi cocked a thumb at Yuhf, "Pa Mahinga Safety Enforcement Inspector, Dryan Yuhf. We need to speak with the highest ranking official on the premises."

Lefsa nodded. "I'm here to take you to 'em."

•   •   •

Exalted Herald Sillu Ffoth sat in an opulent gilded chair behind a desk of obsidian, inlaid with auric veins. He wore flowing gold and white robes. Pictures of Alu Glyf and his personal guards were displayed on the tablet screen built into the surface of the desk. He steepled his pudgy blue fingers in thought, showcasing their many gold rings. Rohi and Yuhf sat across from him in noticeably less opulent chairs.

The Exalted Herald sighed and looked up at them, his small yellow eyes peeking over round cheeks. "I am afraid I do not recognize these specific beings."

Rohi tapped her finger on the desk. "They've been coming to this temple once per week for years. I'd think a Tahl would stand out amongst your overwhelmingly Venovan congregation."

The Exalted Herald spread his palms out. "My congregation is open to all beings who seek salvation. And while yes, most who pass through my doors are children of our mother Venova, I have seen Tahls, Puzuru, Yoblons," he leaned toward Rohi with a grin, "and even J'Kari attend our services."

"You seriously don't recognize this guy?" asked Yuhf.

The Exalted Herald gestured in the general direction of the main hall. "Our temple can accommodate upwards of four thousand parishioners per service. It is simply impossible for me to know every one of them... however," he pressed a button and almost instantly a side panel in his office wall opened, and another gray-robed acolyte, carrying a translucent tablet console entered. The Herald spoke to the acolyte, a young Venovan man, "My Child, please show these pictures to our brethren. If anyone recognizes them, please send them here." He swiped his finger across the screen on his desk, sending the images to the acolyte's tablet. The young man bowed and left.

He turned to Rohi and Yuhf and explained, "We do more than simply preach the divine truth here. We like to help support the local neighborhoods. A group of community leaders is currently having a meeting to discuss outreach programs. They would be the best start in your search for someone who knew Mr..."

"Glyf. Alu Glyf. He was quite the local mogul, I'm told."

"I wouldn't know. I am not a businessman. I am a man of faith, a man of the people."

Rohi cast a cynical glance at the sizeable black gemstone on one of the Exalted Herald's rings.

"So, my son..." the Exalted Herald beamed at Yuhf. "Have you accepted the light of Rhonac into your spirit?"

Yuhf folded his arms. "I ain't your son."

"No, no, not mine. Although, we are *all* children of the Divine One."

"That right?"

"It is."

"Even them folks in Old Kanisa? The ones at Shahidi Square?"

Exalted Herald Sillu Ffoth grimaced.

Yuhf continued, "What was the message that guy projected on the GIG before detonating the Rage Flame canisters? *I cleanse these souls in the name of Rhonac.*"

Herald Ffoth's face grew darker for just a moment before he forced a polite smile back to the surface. He spoke to Rohi, "Inspector Yuhf is referring to a truly terrible incident from over ten years ago."

"An incident that killed over five hundred people."

The Herald ground his teeth and continued. "It was a true tragedy. And you might remember, the Church denounced the actions and the individual in question had no formal affiliation with the Faith. He was a mentally ill man, who never got the treatment he should have." He looked back at Rohi and added, "The Church has since become one of the largest private benefactors for mental healthcare across the Coalition."

"Ain't that swell."

The side door of the office opened again, and a new individual stepped in. He was, expectedly, a Venovan, and his straw-colored hair was cropped closed and neatly combed. His face was that of a man well into his late middle-age, however the tailored fit of his black shirt and pants revealed an exceptionally well-maintained physique. The cuffs of his sleeves and the ring of his mandarin-style collar were stitched with lustrous thread. Rohi recognized the symbol on his medallion as the same one from the temple's front doors.

The Exalted Herald swallowed and then said, "Noble Herald Mavros?"

The man smiled warmly. "Herald Ffoth, I believe I can offer some assistance to your guests."

"Are you another member of the local clergy?" Rohi asked.

"Not local," he replied, "I'm visiting from Kovil-Rho, capital city of the Faith. Our Exalted Herald Ffoth here has done an excellent job of cultivating and fostering this particular congregation. I'm here to observe, to see if there are any insights I might glean that could help new temples replicate his success."

"All thanks to the Divine," insisted Ffoth, "The credit is His."

"If you're not from here, how do you think you can help us?" asked Yuhf.

Mavros's smile remained firmly in place. "Seeing as I hail from Venova Prime, the *non*-Venovans that attend service here tend to stand out to me as opposed to someone like Ffoth who is accustomed to such racial diversity. While I never interacted directly with the person in question," he pointed at Alu's picture, "I remember often seeing him speaking with another parishioner whose name I *do* know. I have asked the temple acolytes to retrieve his information from the registry for you."

"Thank you," said Rohi. "Would you be willing to provide a sworn statement that you saw them interacting in the event this person denies knowing Mr. Glyf?"

"Certainly," answered the Herald.

A few minutes later, Rohi and Yuhf exited the temple and headed back toward her cruiser to enter the address of their next stop. Shortly after their vehicle rounded the block, the temple doors opened again. A hooded figure in simple gray robes slipped out and headed in the same direction.

WORD SECTION 0014

"I thought we were going to Gjenlu," asked Jopp.

"Oh, we are," answered Professor Phyos. "We just need to make a little detour first."

"Between the time it'll take to get to this destination and then back to Gjenlu, we're looking at a full week out of the way. You call that a *little* detour?"

The only thing missing from Phyos's patronizing expression was a pair of spectacles for her to peer over. "Young man, our current best guess is that the universe is roughly fifteen billion years old and stretches at least seven trillion light years across from end to end. Thanks to the combined fortune of anomaly jumps and modern technology, we are able to traverse dozens of those aforementioned light years in a matter of days... from that perspective, a week is literally nothing."

"Yeah, but from the perspective of *my lifespan,* an extra week removed from spending our hard-earned fee on nightlife debauchery is literally an eternity."

"You mean figuratively, not literally," corrected Bhanakhana.

"This ain't no grammar class, Big Red."

"Clearly." Bhanakhana rolled his eyes and resumed his studying of the notebooks.

Professor Phyos's index finger tapped the stump where Jopp's left antenna used to be. "Can you still hear with this thing?"

"Hands off the nub!"

Phyos held her hands up apologetically. "Fair 'nuff... now where were we? Oh yeah, seeing as I'm the one paying your *yet-to-be-earned* fee, I'd have to counter your point with: Quit your whining and set the directed flight path, *pilot*."

Jopp scrutinized her for a moment.

"Touché, Prof."

Chuck entered the bridge cradling a mug of steaming liquid. He took a careful sip and let out a contented sigh.

"Hey, did I ever tell you guys we have something similar to Wahu on Earth? We call it coffee."

He was met with three wide-eyed stares.

"What?"

"Wahu *is* coffee, Deary," answered Professor Phyos.

"Every sentient civilization has coffee," added Bhanakhana. "It's the one bit of evolutionary interference the Coalition allows scientists to give to developing planets like Earth. It was deemed centuries ago that denying coffee to any sentient species would be cruel and unusual."

"Wait... what?! Coffee was given to Earth by aliens?"

"Of course."

"How come you never told me this? What else on Earth did aliens do... build the pyramids?"

"No."

"Stonehenge?"

"Is that a band?"

"What about, like, shaping our DNA?"

"Certainly not." Bhanakhana was visibly offended.

"You're telling me, the one and only thing aliens have ever done to affect the Earth... was introduce coffee?"

"You mean the single greatest substance in the universe?" asked Professor Phyos. "Yeah, you're welcome for that."

"Really? No other part of our consciousness, evolution, or civilization has been guided by the Sentient Coalition?"

Phyos snorted back a laugh. "If that were case, someone is definitely asleep at the control panel."

Jopp laughed. "Don't try to pass off your societal failings on us, dude."

Chuck looked disappointed. "Okay, then why does everyone call it wahu?"

Jopp shrugged, "Wahu is just the Prime Partners brand of coffee. It's so popular, people just started using the brand name as a generic term for it."

"Oh, like how in my country on Earth, we call tissues Kleenex."

Chuck was met yet again with a trio of wide-eyed stares.

"What?"

Bhanakhana cleared his throat, "Chuck, I would like to fully understand what you have just said... You are referring to the tiny squares of soft face paper?"

"Um, yeah..."

"And these same bits of face paper are often used to wipe away dirty, germ-riddled olfactory secretions?"

"Does that mean boogers? Then yeah."

Bhanakhana took a deep breath. "Chuck, why do your people use the name of one of the most venerated beings in modern history in such a disdainful manner?"

"*What?!*"

Professor Phyos added, "Klii Naks was the founder of the Benevolence Fund and perhaps the most prolific philanthropist in modern history. He was the heir to one of the largest fortunes in the Coalition and devoted his entire life, along with every bit of currency he owned, on projects ranging from negotiating peace treaties between warring nations to legislation aimed at protecting small federations from corporate oligarchs to feeding entire cities on the brink of famine... and I might add, he was quite a handful in the bedroom."

Bhanakhana coughed in shock, nearly choking on his own spit.

Jopp's eyes lit up. "No fucking way!"

Phyos shrugged, "It was about forty years ago. I was working my way through two simultaneous sage-doctorates at the Lyceum. He came to the campus on speaking tour, fresh off the heels of winning his twenty-second consecutive Cosmic Compassion award. My roommate was working the bar at the reception gala and she snuck me in. We started chatting, *blada blada blada*, and the next morning I'm eating room service griddle-tarts at his hotel, if you catch my inference... see, I was at his hotel the next morning because.."

"Got it," said Jopp.

"Understood," said Bhanakhana.

"Yep," said Chuck.

"...because we had spent the night rubbing our parts together," finished the Professor.

"I have become so very uncomfortable with the direction this conversation has taken," noted Bhanakhana.

"Ditto," added Chuck.

"Wasn't he like over seventy years old at that point?" asked Jopp.

"Seventy-three... and still sprier than guys a third his age. Though, I may have given him a bit of limp that never fully healed."

"You might be the most tops person I have ever met."

"Probably... anyhoo," she clapped her hands together, "all this talk about coffee has given me a thirst." She gave Chuck a wink and a smile, "I don't suppose you could fix me a cup, Deary?"

"Sure thing," answered Chuck. "Any excuse to leave this conversation."

He turned on his heel and scurried out of the room.

Jopp reached for the pilot's controls but froze for a moment.

"All this talk about doing the nebula nasty with intergalactic civil rights icons made me forget... where are going, again?"

"Nautun."

"What's that?"

"A massive 'ocean' of water that exists in space without a planet," answered Bhanakhana. "Truly, the word 'massive' does not do it justice as this body of water is larger than some life-sustaining suns."

"What's there that's so important to us?"

"Currently?" said Phyos. "Nothing."

"Huh?"

"But, by the time we get there, the Golatac Barge will have arrived."

Bhanakhana's eyes lit up. "We are visiting the Golatac? Marvelous!"

Chuck returned to the bridge carrying a new mug of steaming blue coffee. As he set it in front of the Professor, Bhanakhana proclaimed, "Chuck! We are going to see the Golatac."

Chuck's face was blank.

Bhanakhana sighed. "I do not know why I bother forwarding you articles."

Chuck snapped his fingers. "Oh! Wait! I know that one. That's the big traveling museum thingy, right?"

Bhanakhana beamed with pride.

"We're going to a museum?" Jopp whined. "Laaaaaaaame."

Phyos gave him a sly grin. "Not *just* a museum. They have a resort with shops, restaurants, and a bar that boasts the universe's largest drink selection."

"Well, what the shit are we waiting for?!"

Chuck made it to his chair just in time to avoid getting thrown against the back wall by the ship's sudden acceleration.

WORD SECTION 0015

"Where are we, Yuhf?"

"Big Box District... you know, on account of all the buildings just look like big boxes. Way back when, it was a warehousing sector. Then it got converted to housing. For the most part it's been a community of hard working, decent people just trying to get by."

"It's a bit of a ways from the temple, isn't it?"

He shrugged. "People commute into low orbit on a daily basis for work. Driving the occasional hour to get your dose of god-talk ain't too much of a stretch."

The ULE cruiser rolled to a gentle stop.

"We're here."

They climbed out and looked up at the building. It was a five story cube built from weathered tan stone. Everything, from the walls to the windows to the front door, looked old but well-maintained.

"What's the guy's name?"

Yuhf looked down at his data bracelet. "Uh, *Ustep Ptso*. He lives in Suite Thirty."

Rohi looked up and down the street. She saw a few denizens milling about outside the market on the corner. A crisp gust of wind whipped through her hair. She looked back at Yuhf.

"You getting any weird vibes here? Or is it just me?"

"Maybe. It's quiet for midday. Let's go squeeze this guy, see if we can juice any info. Then grab lunch?"

Rohi gave one last look around before answering. "Sure. But let's not eat Vashniien again. I don't blame Kaloce begging off today. I've been burping up that shit all morning."

"I'll take you to Meat Maw's. You gotta try the Triple Greaser."

They approached the outer door of the housing block. Yuhf pressed the comm icon for Suite 30. After a few beeps, a gruff voice answered, "*Whozit?*"

"Pa Mahinga Safety Enforcement, Mr. Ptso. We'd like to come up and ask you some questions about one of your fellow church parishioners."

The door's lock light turned green.

At the far end of the block, a hooded figure watched from the shadows as the law enforcement officers stepped inside the building.

"That was easy," said Yuhf as they entered the building's small foyer. Rohi noticed a building layout map displayed on a view screen. She found Suite 30.

"Third floor."

They passed through the foyer's inner door. The entire first floor appeared to be an open communal space, filled with couches, relaxation chairs, tables, and stationary plug-ins for personal tablets. The building managers had recently made a half-assed attempt to "style up" the place by adding a half dozen cheap ceramic sculptures. A thirty-by-thirty meter space in the room's center had no ceiling immediately above it. Gray sunlight trickled down from the skylight five stories up. The apartments above were supported by thick, square columns that formed a border around the floor's middle.

They took a few steps forward when Rohi noticed two figures sitting in lounge chairs facing the opposite wall. Both had blue-hued heads with close-cropped yellow hair.

"Excuse me, gentlemen," she called out, "Either of you know the guy in Suite Thirty? Ustep Ptso? We just have a few questions for him."

Neither one responded. Neither one so much as flinched. Rohi and Yuhf exchanged wary glances. They each rested their hands on their respective holsters and crept toward the motionless figures. Rather than walk a straight line right toward them, they stayed under the second floor ceiling, keeping the columns between themselves and the open space, and circled around to the right.

When they reached the periphery of the men in the chairs, they stepped to the edge of the open space, between two columns. Yuhf nudged Rohi and nodded at the table in front of the two men. It held a pyramid of orange bricks. Rohi gave him a confused eyebrow raise.

"Unprocessed Zip," Yuhf whispered, *"Probably stolen from a pharmaceutical factory. It's illegal in its purest form. Too strong."*

Rohi leaned ever so slightly forward and glanced up. A concrete balcony wrapped around each floor above them. She leaned closer to Yuhf, *"This is fucking hacked. You check them. I'll keep eyes up top."*

They freed their pistols from their holsters and moved in. Yuhf stayed locked on the two seated men, while Rohi kept her eyes in constant sweep of the balconies above and the shadows beyond the first floor pillars. As they got closer, Yuhf noticed one of the orange bricks had been cut open and there were small piles of zip crystals in front of each person. His eyes then raised to the men in question. He knew instantly that they were dead, partly due to the slack jaws and blank stares... but mostly due to the trio of boltshot wounds each man had in the middle of his chest. He saw the electric blue skulls stitched into their overcoats.

"North Side Reapers," he noted.

"A what?" asked Rohi, her eyes still scanning the balconies.

"It's a local thug club, a street gang."

"I know I'm not from around here, so forgive me if this is a dumb question, but is it normal to find two dead slangers and a stack of stolen drugs sitting in the lobby of a halfway decent housing unit?"

"No. This is hacked up."

Rohi risked a glance at Yuhf, the dead men, and the orange bricks piled on the steel table. She was about to comment, but noticed a flash of movement reflected in the table's gleaming surface. She spun to the left and raised her pistol just as two figures leaned out over the third story balcony. Her eyes snapped to the unmistakably gun-shaped objects they were holding.

She shouted, "Weapon!" and let off a pair of shots. The figures ducked down behind the concrete balcony. "Go!"

Rohi and Yuhf sprinted back to the outer edge of the lobby away from the view of the upper balcony. They dove behind the columns as a spray of automatic gunfire peppered the floor behind them.

"Fucking spitters," cursed Yuhf.

"What?"

"Cheap ass mini shooters. The street yoks love 'em. They won't punch through these columns, but the ammo generator is practically infinite."

He dialed up his comm line. "Control.. Control... Inspector Yuhf requesting emergency assistance... Control?"

He looked up with a grim expression and said, "My comms ain't sending."

As Rohi tried her own communicator, Yuhf peeked around the columns. His eyes fell on the elevators at the opposite wall just as a blue-skinned man and woman stepped into the lobby. They were armed and wearing the same 'Reapers' jackets as the two dead men. Yuhf brought his pistol up but they ducked behind some nearby columns before he could get a shot.

"My comms are down too," huffed Rohi.

"Yeah, well, I got more good news," replied Yuhf. "We got two shooters on the ground with us."

"Same two from up top?"

"I didn't see the two up top."

"We have to assume we've got four hostiles."

"At least."

"Ever the optimist, Yuhf."

"Always assume the worst. Then you're never let down when everything inevitably turns to shit."

Rohi cracked a grin. "*Inevitably* is an awfully big word for a simple city cog like yourself."

"Yeah, yeah." Yuhf shot her a grin back. "You don't need to go file a *'Permission-to-Firefight'* request form with your tight ass ULE bosses before this goes down, do you?"

Their smiles fell.

"They'd probably shred us if we ran for the door, huh?" asked Yuhf.

"Safe bet."

"Fuck. Why couldn't this be a bar fight? I've got way more experience there." He rattled his pistol. "Haven't had to use this thing in a long time."

"Here's a refresher: Point that end at the bad guys and squeeze the trigger... and make sure the safety's off."

"Haha... fucking smart ass." Yuhf glanced at his pistol's safety.

It was on.

He grumbled to himself and switched it off. Rohi unclipped a small black cylinder from her belt.

"I've got one shine bomb. I figure we use it now. They know where we are and we've given them plenty of time to get us pinned. We shine them and sprint around the outer edge, hopefully taking them out before they recover."

Yuhf took a deep breath and nodded. Rohi thumbed the detonator toggle.

"After I toss it, count to 4 Centauri."

"I better get a medal out of this," muttered Yuhf.

Rohi sighed, "Here we go."

She hurled the shine bomb around the column, where it landed in the center of the room with a thud. They shut their eyes and covered their ears. Four "centauri's" later, the lobby erupted with blinding light and deafening sound.

Rohi and Yuhf sprinted along the wall. They hit the first corner and whipped around with pistols raised, finding no one. They ran forward, scanning the center of the room for movement. Yuhf almost crashed into Rohi when she suddenly skidded to a halt. They stood in front of a door that had been built nearly seamlessly into the wall. It had the word "stairwell" printed on it in thick, red lettering. They ducked inside without a word. The stairs wrapped around the walls in a square shape, with landings at each corner. They ascended, taking care not to make too much noise with each footfall.

They were about halfway to the third floor when a voice from below shouted, "Stairs!"

"Shit snacks," grumbled Yuhf.

"Move!" ordered Rohi.

They pounded up the steps, no longer concerned with discretion. As they hit the last landing, the door at the ground level slammed open. Rohi leaned over the railing, her pistol pointed down, waiting for the first sign of their assailants. Yuhf was about to do the same when he noticed movement on the third floor landing. The door opened slowly.

"Fuck nuggets," he growled.

He bounded up the last few stairs, tapping the final reserves of athleticism left over from his younger days. He had no clue what we he was going to do. The door began opening inwards. A blue hand clutching an automatic mini-shooter peaked around the edge. Yuhf did the only thing he could think of in the moment, and hurled himself forward. He slammed into the door, sending the Venovan thug careening backwards. Yuhf spilled out onto the floor of the third story balcony as the thug toppled over the concrete half-wall. The bone-breaking crash of the man landing in the lobby below made Yuhf cringe.

"Well, that's one way to handle 'em."

Rohi came up behind him. He looked up at her from the floor.

"Think he's dead?"

"Don't know. We have more pressing matters."

She punctuated the statement by firing across the expanse. The thug ducked down, avoiding the shot. She pointed back at the stairwell. "If that door moves, shoot it. And stay low."

Yuhf hauled himself up against the balcony wall and aimed his pistol at the door in question. Rohi took off as fast as she dared while staying crouched below the wall. She reached the first corner and turned, pistol at the ready. At that same moment, the thug crept around the opposite corner.

Their eyes met.

Rohi fired.

The thug tried to dodge, but the pistol round punched through his upper arm. He scrambled back around the corner, trailing pale pink blood. Rohi bolted forward in a dead sprint, bridging the distance in seconds. When she was a few feet from the balcony turn, she surged upward, planted her foot on the balcony wall, and exploded forward. Her jump took her at a diagonal trajectory, cutting off the corner, and over the two story drop. She sailed over the wall, saw the thug crouching there, and pumped two shots into him as she fell. He never even got a chance to react. Rohi hit the floor and rolled to her side, firing off another round. The shot went wide, but it didn't matter. The thug was already dead, slumped back against the balcony. Rohi saw a blue light blinking on his data bracelet. She crawled over and lifted his limp arm. The light was a message alert. It'd been sent less than a minute before and read, *"Kin Fevin alive but injured. Status?"*

Rohi gave herself half a moment to think, her eyes falling on the elevator just a few feet away. She grabbed the thug's mini-shooter and fired a quick burst into the wall. She then dragged the body into the elevator. Luckily, this thug was built on the leaner side. Rohi typed a reply message into the bracelet. She pressed the elevator's "lobby" button and hopped off, spraying the interior with another burst of gunfire. Rohi discarded the borrowed weapon and sprinted back around toward Yuhf, careful to hug the wall so as to prevent any lines of sight from the first floor. He jumped when she came around the corner.

"Thank fuck-" he started. Rohi fired her pistol to drown out his words and put a finger to her lips. They heard a woman's voice shout from below, "Elevator!"

Rohi gave Yuhf a nod and risked a peek inside the stairwell, before ducking inside. Yuhf took a deep breath and followed after. Once at ground level, Rohi nudged the door to the lobby open ever so slightly. Through the sliver of the opening, between the gaps in the curving tendrils of one of the decorative statues, she could see one of the Reapers. He hunkered down behind a couch, facing away from them. Given the tears in his clothes, the pink blood stains, and the awkward bend of his right leg, she guessed he'd been the one Yuhf had knocked off the balcony. Unfortunately, she'd have to step out of the stairwell to get a clean shot. She whispered to Yuhf, *"Sweep right. See motion, shoot it."*

"What-"

They heard the ding of the arriving elevator, followed instantly by the roar of three automatic weapons unloading dozens upon dozens of rounds. Rohi burst from the stairwell door. The Reaper behind the couch was too busy firing at the opening elevator doors to notice her.

Rohi pumped three shots into his back as she ran by looking for the others.

Yuhf followed her out from the stairwell, but turned right and ran along the outer wall. He hurried around the thick column in the corner and collided with one of the thugs. They both fell to the ground in a heap, each dropping their weapons.

Rohi weaved through the columns and furniture, looking for her next target. A shot exploded the ceramic sculpture near her head, and she dove for cover behind a column.

"Shit." She had hoped to have taken down two of the three before they spotted her. She looked around, searching for something to help her. There was nothing.

Yuhf and the Reaper thug wrestled on the floor, trading head butts and punches. The Reaper pulled a knife from his boot, but Yuhf caught the thug's wrist. Yuhf spotted his gun and made a grab for it as he felt the bite of the blade cutting into his side. He snatched up his pistol and slammed it into the thug's forehead. Pink blood oozed from a gash in the bright blue skin of the thug's forehead before he slumped backward lifeless. Yuhf felt the pain in his side and pressed his hand over the bleeding wound

He gritted his teeth against the pain and crawled to the nearest couch, daring a peek. He saw a Venovan woman, dressed in Reaper garb, her yellow hair pulled back in a braid. She was making her way toward a column along the far wall, peppering it with gunfire every few seconds. Yuhf raised his pistol. He had a clear shot. He didn't pull the trigger.

Instead he called out, "Drop your phoobing weapon! Drop it now!"

The woman froze in place. She turned her head back toward him with a slight smirk.

"Are you going to shoot me, brother?" she asked.

Yuhf stood, his left hand pressed to his side, his right outstretched with the pistol leveled at her head.

"Not your brother. And yes, I will shoot you. Drop the gun."

The woman looked sad for just a moment, but then she got her smirk back.

"Certainly." She let her gun fall to the floor and turned around to face Yuhf, hands held out to her sides.

Rohi cautiously stepped out from behind the column. She kept her pistol trained on the woman and started walking around toward Yuhf.

"What in the holy hell is going on here?" Rohi growled. She and Yuhf stepped closer to the Reaper.

"Interesting choice of words," mused the woman, amusement gleaming in her brown eyes. "As for your question, well, I believe I have the information you're looking for. All I ask is you spare my life."

Rohi let her pistol lower a bit. "Do you know the name Alu Glyf?"

"Yes, I do. I knew we shouldn't have had dealings with him. I told my friends it would only be trouble. I even recorded a few of our meetings to be cautious. I have the data chip with those recordings here in my pocket."

She reached to her hip. Rohi was about to order her to keep her hands out in the open, but she was preempted...

...by Yuhf firing three rounds into the woman's chest. She hit the floor with a thud. Rohi ran up to her and saw two lifeless brown eyes staring back at her. She wheeled on Yuhf.

"What in the actual *fuck?!*"

Yuhf lowered his gun. As he spoke, his eyes never left the dead woman.

"Ain't no data chip. That's an incendiary detonator on her belt. Rage Flame... the smell... like I said, you don't forget it."

Rohi crouched down and flipped open the woman's jacket. Yuhf was right. She stood up and gave him an appraising look. Yuhf tore his stare away from the dead thug and looked back at Rohi with bloodshot eyes.

"First time you had to put someone down?" she asked.

He nodded. "I think I need to go throw up... then I need a drink... a *lot* of drinks."

"I hear you," she said, "I could probably handle a whole bottle of Soreshi Blaze-Water right now. Let's get Incident Oversight out here, then get you patched up by Medical while I knock out the reports. And then those drinks will be on me."

"Sure... sure... sure..." Yuhf's stare had been drawn back to the corpse at their feet.

"Yuhf."

He looked up at Rohi.

"You did good."

Yuhf would've said 'thanks' but at that moment a gunshot hit him between the eyes, snapping his head back in a cloud of pink mist.

WORD SECTION 0016

Rohi's instincts had her diving over a couch before Yuhf's body even hit the floor. She rolled to her knees and popped up with pistol pointed in the direction of the shot.

She froze with shock when she saw Kaloce standing there with a gun in his outstretched hand.

"What the fuck did you just do?!" Rohi screamed.

Kaloce trembled as he looked at her with wide, shame-filled eyes.

"I- I'm sorry," he answered. "I did not want it like this. I had no choice. I must follow the righteous order."

"Oh yeah?! Command told you to murder your partner?!"

"Not Command, no. A righteous order comes from the Divine... and the laws of God outweigh the laws of mortals." He reached into his collar and pulled out a small medallion. "Again I am sorry, but I must deliver your spirit into the next plane."

"Kaloce, stop. I swear I will shoot you..."

"No, you won't. My hand is guided by God. I will not fail."

There was a sudden burst of gunfire. Rohi and Kaloce stood frozen in place for a moment, eyes locked on each other. Neither of their pistols had discharged. Kaloce's eyes rolled back in his head and he fell face down to the floor. Blood trickled from half a dozen tiny holes in his back.

A figure stepped out from behind the base of a shattered sculpture. The figure clutched one of the mini-shooters and had a gray hood pulled low, hiding their face. They flinched as Rohi fired a shot past their hooded head.

"Drop that gun or the next shot is in your brain."

The figure let the gun clatter to the floor without a word.

"Don't fucking move."

Rohi took a few steps to her right and leaned around the nearby columns. She scanned the area, including the balconies above.

"What are you doing?" asked the figure, her voice noticeably female.

"I'm making sure no one else is here. I swear to Bjordax, if you suddenly get shot mid-sentence by another unseen gunman, I'm going to fucking lose it."

"I think we're good."

Rohi leveled her pistol at the figure. "No, *we* are not good. *We* are so fucking far from good right now. Take that hood off."

The woman slowly pulled back the hood. Rohi recognized her as the young Venovan woman who'd first met them in the vestibule of the temple.

"You're the acolyte... Lefsa, was it?"

"Yeah, about that, my name's not Lefsa. It's Loi. It's so jetty to meet you again, but we gotta warp outta here. Like now."

"You just killed a senior inspector with city Security Enforcement."

"Who was about to kill you... you're welcome, by the way. Can we go now?"

"No! What the fuck is going on, Lefsa... or Loi... or whoever the fuck you are?!"

The blue-skinned woman sighed, "Again, name's Loi. This was a hastily scrapped together setup to get rid of you. These yoks aren't really gang members. You've just bumble-fucked your way into a massive conspiratorial operation organized by a secret sect of the Children of Rhonac. They're exploiting the considerable resources of the Church to further what I'm assuming is some nefarious megalomaniacal objective. Can we please go now?"

Rohi rolled the Loi's words around in her head. After a few seconds, she shrugged.

"Okay."

Rohi holstered her pistol.

"Really?" asked Loi. "Just like that."

"What you just said doesn't even rank in the top five of crazy things I've heard in my life."

"Interesting life."

"You have no idea."

"Mine hasn't been exactly mundane either."

"Oh yeah? You acolyte's get up to some wild nights, huh?"

"Oh this?" Loi started yanking off her robes, "Yeah, I'm not really a church acolyte... I mean I am, but not... I'll explain later. We seriously need to get moving."

Loi dropped the robes in a heap, leaving her dressed in generically casual pants, boots, and a short-sleeved shirt.

"I'll go call this mess in to Control," said Rohi.

"Nope," countered Loi as she walked over to the dead woman in Reaper garb.

"Excuse me?" asked Rohi.

"You step outside in that uniform and they'll know you're still alive."

"Good. I want them to know. They're about to learn what happens when you fuck with the ULE."

"Easy there, Trig Fig."

"What did you just call me?"

"Trig Fig, short for Trigger Finger... it's not a perfect match... we're probably not at the nicknames stage yet, are we? Anyway, yeah, you could go out there and send a signal up top. I'm sure the resulting firestorm would clean out the local cell of this group. But it wouldn't stop their overall plans... oh, and you would definitely not live to see it."

"Let 'em fucking try to come at me again."

Loi stripped off the Reaper jacket, then went to work unbuckling the boots.

"Yeah, yeah, you're a comet-cold badass. But seriously think for a second; they had enough influence to get, to use your words, a *senior inspector with City Security Enforcement* to straight up kill his own partner. Whatever you're investigating, they've decided it needs to get shut down regardless of fallout. You will not leave this city, shit, this *neighborhood*, alive dressed like that."

She'd finished with the Reaper's boots and started shimmying off the woman's pants.

"I need you alive. So please put these thug duds on, and help me get your super sleek, totally not trying-too-hard-to-look-intimidating ULE suit on her."

A minute later, Rohi was dressed in the jacket, pants, and boots of a North Side Reaper. The dead woman was now clad in the armor of a ULE agent, while Loi rummaged through her satchel.

Rohi knelt next to Kaloce, confirming what she'd already suspected; the medallion around his neck bore the Rhonac "Gateway" symbol. She sighed and shook her head, her eyes then catching Yuhf's body laid out on the floor some yards away. She walked over and forced herself to look down at him. She spoke under her breath, *"You were a curmudgeonly klugger, Yuhf... but a good guy nonetheless. I'm gonna get these yoks."*

She noticed Loi had moved next to her and looked up. "So now what?"

Loi held up the thug's incendiary detonator.

"Now we run."

"Oh, you've got to be-" Rohi's eyes went wide as Loi tossed the device back toward the fallen city officers and the corpse currently dressed in ULE armor. They sprinted for the rear exit before the detonator even hit the floor. Their feet hit the pavement of the back alley just as the building's lobby erupted in flame.

"What the fuck have you done?!" cursed Rohi, "What about the other people inside?"

"Nobody's in there... and if there is, they ain't exactly an innocent civilian, you feel me? Now, let's get-"

Loi froze when she saw Rohi had a pistol pointed at her.

"Start spilling."

A nearby window shattered from the expanding heat inside. The rank stench of chemical burn permeated the air.

"Look," started Loi, "I know your brain just got phoobed nine ways from Numsday... I promise you I will tell you everything I know. I swear it. Can we please get somewhere safer? My roller is parked at the end of the alley. I know this discrete bar we can go to…"

Rohi holstered her pistol with a glare. She shouldered past Loi and said, "You're buying the drinks."

Loi rubbed her arm and called after her, "So… I guess I'll get that 'thank you' later, then? You know? For saving your ass? No?"

She caught up with Rohi and they stepped out of the alley to the street side walkway. The vehicle parked in front of them was a long, six wheeled trudger. It had a four-person cab in the front, a rectangular cargo hold in the back, and the Church of Rhonac gateway painted on the side.

"Nice trudge," quipped Rohi.

Loi shrugged, "One of my acolyte duties is- *was* driving delivery for the Domestic Outreach Initiative. You know, bringing the less fortunate food, clothes-"

"Senseless murder."

"That's a *different department*. Like I said-"

"NORTH SIDE!"

Rohi and Loi spun toward the sound of the shout. A young Venovan man stood a few feet away from them at the corner of the intersection. From head to toe, he was decked out in North Side Reaper garb. Rohi glanced down at her own attire and back up at him.

"Uh… yo?"

The man glared at her. "Real North Siders respond with *'til I die*. Don't know what you was thinkin' tryin' to pass as one of us… ain't no silver skin J'Kari bitches like you in the Reapers. We got word some unknowns dressed like 'Siders jumped two of our boys. Tell me where they at and you might not get shredded."

"Easy there," Rohi held her hands out defensively, "threatening a ULE agent is no minor offense."

The man scoffed, "You a Ulee? Prove it."

"Sure, pal. I'm going to reach into my pocket and get my credentials. Nice and slow, okay?" Rohi felt around her right pants pocket, then her left pocket, then her two jacket pockets.

Pistol, check.

Mag-shackles, check.

Telescopic shock baton, check.

One-of-kind-security-certified ULE identification badge... nowhere to be found. Rohi looked up at the man, then to Loi, then back at the smoldering building.

"Well... shit."

"Fuckin' knew it." The man turned around and shouted, "HEY!"

Rohi hadn't waited to see who he was shouting at. The second he turned his head, she had lunged forward with the shock baton. As he crumpled to the ground, Loi stepped up next to Rohi and said, "Nice move... so, uh, what's your plan for them?"

Rohi followed her eyes to the parking lot at the opposite corner of the intersection. A dozen or so Reapers were leaning on thruster bikes. They'd seen the whole thing.

"Well... shit."

WORD SECTION 0017

Loi and Rohi roared through the Pa Mahinga city streets, Loi pushing the engines of the trudger truck well beyond their intended threshold. She whipped across four lanes of traffic, exiting the tightly packed avenues of the city and onto the open expanse of the express byway that circled the city limits.

Rohi screamed into her data bracelet, "Pa Mahinga Security Enforcement! This is ULE division officer Rohi Kahpanova. I am currently traveling inland on the north most byway. Being pursued by hostile elements. Requesting immediate emergency assistance!"

"Here they come!" shouted Loi.

A dozen thruster bikes, each one a glossy blue missile on two wheels, were fast approaching in their rearview. Rohi crawled to the passenger cab's back seat, opened the window on the right side and leaned out, pistol at the ready.

"So," hollered Loi. "How much do you know about the Children of Rhonac?"

"What?" Rohi hollered back.

"The Church. I'm trying to explain."

"Right *now*?!"

"Why not?"

Rohi looked from the gun in her hand, to the dozen violent thugs chasing them, to the speeding traffic Loi was tearing her way through. She snorted. "Why not?"

The trailing thruster bikes weaved around a hydro-tanker to get closer. Rohi could see that all the Reapers wore helmets painted to look like skulls. She grumbled, "Fucking cliché punk ass yoks."

"What do you know about the Church?" Loi asked again.

"Fourth largest religion in the Coalition, counting all the factions. Followers overwhelmingly of Venovan descent. Free anomaly shuttle rides and the usual preachy rhetoric."

"So not a damn thing, huh? Listen, way back when the Venovan system planets first started mingling with intergalactic society, the Church formed a special group."

One of the bikes broke ahead of the others, coming right up to the rear corner of the trudger's cargo hold. Rohi fired. The shot glanced off the trudger's side, missing the Reaper, but causing him to pull back.

"Special group?" Rohi asked

"A sect, an order, whatever! They're called *The Adherent*. Church leaders knew that as Venovan society was going to be integrating with other sentient civilizations, the rules and tenets of the faith would have to adapt to allow for further growth and expansion- *Hang on!*"

Loi swerved to avoid hitting a shuttle bus. The bus's automated driver blared a warning horn.

She continued, "But they also wanted to maintain some semblance of the old ways, so The Adherent were formed to do just that. And for generations, they've been quietly living in peace as monks, keeping the foundations of the faith alive and well."

"Is that it?" asked Rohi as she watched the bikers all maneuver to avoid the same shuttle bus.

"Fuck no," answered Loi, "that's just the load of humpa-shit they teach all the kiddos in Rhonacite schools. The Adherent were created to be 'Defenders of the Faith'. I'll bet in your line of work, you're all too aware of how easily people with an agenda can warp the definition of 'defense' into *seek out and destroy anyone who disagrees with us.*"

Rohi kept her eyes on the trailing assailants and replied, "Yep."

"Yeah, these people are no joke. I don't know *exactly* what they're up to. I just know something big is going down soon and it's bad."

"How do you know that and why do you care?"

"Does that matter? I'm keying you into a bunch of yok-heads doing yok-head things. Your job is to stop them."

Avoiding the shuttle bus had caused the bikers to split into smaller groups. One group of three had caught back up to them. Rohi saw them pull out mini-shooters. She took aim and fired. The middle biker reacted by jerking his steering throttle right, apparently forgetting about his comrade. The two bikes collided, and both Reapers hit the street, rolling away like a pair of tumbleweeds in a wind storm. The remaining biker responded with a wild spray of gunfire.

Rohi ducked back inside the cab and fixed Loi with a stone-cold stare. "*How* and *why* always matter."

Loi sighed and said, "I'm Venovan, but I didn't grow up there." She raised her index finger and tapped it against the cab's moon-roof window. Rohi didn't have to ask to know what she meant. High above them, way out in space, floated the gigantic mega-city Pa Nui.

"I spent a solid chunk of my childhood in Pa Nui too," offered Rohi.

"I'll bet our experiences were pretty different."

"You were in the Little Venova District."

"Good guess. You must be a professional detective or something."

"Little Venova is rough."

"Don't have to tell me, I lived it. My parents died when I was young. I couldn't tell you a thing about them. Wound up in the local Church-sponsored group home amongst three hundred of my fellow orphans."

"Even rougher."

"Building yourself a new 'family' was crucial if you wanted to survive. The older kids were your aunts, uncles, parents... the younger, your brothers and sisters. I learned quick, the best way to get what you wanted was thieving. Thieving got you better food, better clothes... and the respect and protection from the older kids. I took to it easily. That, plus the fact that I never hesitated to smack anyone who looked at me funny meant I was pretty much left alone.- *On your right*!"

Rohi saw the biker. He was three lanes over, but had pulled up even with them. He let off a burst, but the shots passed overhead. Rohi returned fired just as Loi jerked the wheel. Her shot went low, missing the thug, but hitting his bike right in the engine block. The Reaper flew through the air, his body slamming into the front of an expensive sport roller in the next lane.

Rohi looked back at Loi with raised eyebrows. "Why aren't I just aiming for the bikes in the first place?"

Loi shrugged, "Maybe you like near-death experiences to be more of a challenge? Back to my story: There was this other girl, though, just a bit younger than me. She just didn't have that *edge* to her. Her problem was, if you ask me, she still had hope. I felt compelled to look out for her. I think I just needed something to give a shit about. We looked out for each other for years. I made sure the other punks didn't hassle her. She made sure I didn't devolve into a total scrogbag of a person. Then, when I was thirteen, I got caught trying to pinch cards from this shitty little casino in the neighborhood. Nothing major. The local Law Cogs didn't really want to bother with the filings, so they just gave me a lecture and tossed me in a cell overnight to *think about my life choices.*"

"But?" asked Rohi.

"But it just so happened the day I got caught was the same day the group home got a visit from the Church of Rhonac's Second Start Initiative. Two dozen kids got adopted by the Church that day. My sister was one of them."

Loi gave Rohi a pointed look. Rohi responded with, "And the kicker is?"

"The *kicker* is that the Second Start Initiative is run by The Adherent. They recruit kids and indoctrinate them." Loi gripped the throttle tighter and spoke through gritted teeth. "If I had been there I could have, I don't know, stopped it somehow... but I *wasn't.* And now she's been stuck with those fanatical fucks going on fifteen years."

"Why were you working at that Church if you hate them so much?"

"My Rhonacian Guilt won't let me ever say I full on *hate* the Church. Too many hours spent in mandatory religion classes growing up ingrained that shit in me. What I do hate are the people that use the Church as an excuse—"

"Hold that thought!" said Rohi as she scrambled to the opposite backseat window. A cluster of four bikers closed the gap. She leaned out, but a barrage of gunfire forced her to duck back inside. Rohi looked out the front windshield. A large delivery crawler was up ahead of them in the lane to their left. Rohi tapped Loi on the shoulder and pointed at the vehicle.

"Stay in this lane, but keep close to that crawler when we pass it."

"You got it," answered Loi. She hammered the accelerator, and as they came up alongside the vehicle in question, let their trudger drift over to be mere inches away from a sideswipe. Rohi leaned out the window just as they cleared the delivery crawler. As she expected, the four bikers were too busy maneuvering around that vehicle to shoot at her. She raised her pistol, but didn't pull the trigger. The four bikers regrouped into a tight formation. Rohi took aim and fired. Her shot found its mark: the front wheel of the closest bike. It erupted in a burst of sparks. The Reaper and his bike careened into his neighbor. The other two narrowly avoided the collision. Rohi winced as the delivery crawler rolled over one of the prone thugs.

"I'm going to be in so much fucking shit for this..."

"Huh?" asked Loi.

"Oh, uh, this is actually my first case back in the field. I've been chained to a desk for the past two years because I... well, let's just say I breached some *major* ULE protocols on my last case. I doubt this many bodies dropping on my first case back is going to go over well with my division chief."

"Wow, I had you pegged as the tight-pants Rulebook Rider type."

"Shut up and finish your story."

"I'll let the nonsensical nature of that sentence slide for the moment. So, my sister got herself scooped up by The Adherent. I've spent the last fifteen years doing two things: making as much money as I can and scanning every Rhonacian Temple's registry looking for traces of my sister. I've been a lot more successful as a thief than I have a 'sister-finder'. Try not to hold it against me, Law Cog."

Rohi looked at the formation of remaining bikers catching up to them, then to the ammo gauge of her pistol, which hovered barely above zero.

"Yeah, I'm not exactly worried about that at the moment. Do you have any weapons?"

Loi reached under her seat and came up with a compact pistol. It had a wide, short barrel and only carried a dozen rounds. It was commonly known as a "popper". Rohi took it with trepidation.

"Got anything with a longer range than ten fucking feet?"

A flash of movement pulled Rohi's eyes left. She found herself staring directly into the skulled helmet of a Reaper. He reached through the window with his weapon. Rohi grabbed his wrist. He fired, the shot shattering the front passenger window. Loi screamed. Rohi put the popper gun right up against the "eye" of the Reaper's skull helmet.

"Bye Bye."

She squeezed the trigger. The helmet visor imploded. The Reaper fell away.

"Rho-damn-it!" cried Loi as she picked a tiny pebble of glass out of her right temple, causing a bead of pink blood to appear.

Rohi tucked the popper into her waistband. "Well, that'll be my contingency plan if any others get that close." She retrieved her own pistol with its dwindling ammo, from the cab floor.

Loi weaved through the traffic with one hand, while dabbing the blood from her temple with the other. "Or if you could make sure they never get that close again at all, that'd fucking spectacular."

"Hold on," Rohi cut in. "You see that rig loader?" She pointed to the gigantic transporter up ahead of them, two lanes over. It toted a pyramid of massive metal piping. Each length of pipe was at least ten feet in diameter and one hundred feet long.

"Yeah?"

"Get us up alongside it," Rohi ordered. "I have an idea."

Loi pushed them forward and over a lane. Their pursuers followed in kind, gaining more ground. Rohi readied her pistol. She zeroed in on the thick industrial strap holding the pipes in place. She knew she'd have to time it just right.

Loi had them right alongside the rig loader.

The Reapers were in the lane behind them.

They got closer.

And closer.

Rohi pulled the trigger.

Her shot found its mark. The harness strap snapped apart with a spark. And the towering payload of pipes...

...didn't budge on account of there being thirteen other safety harnesses keeping them in place, not to mention a magnetic field emanating from the truck bed to hold them down.

"Fuck."

"*That* was your plan?!"

"I saw it work in a movie once."

"Yeah, I once saw a movie where the 'power of love' thwarted the evil Galactic Alchemist's plans for universal domination... doesn't mean I'm about to start kissing you!"

Rohi noticed the twinkle of another minuscule bit of window glass lodged in the side of Loi's head and pulled it out.

"*Ow-* Fuck!" Loi hollered. "Well now I'm *definitely* not kissing you."

"I'm devastated," said Rohi. "Are you going to tell me how you wound up posing as an acolyte in Pa Mahinga or do I need to find more glass to yank out of your skull?"

"I found my sister," answered Loi, "Well, I didn't *find her* find her. I found her name in a new temple's registry about a year and a half ago. Since then, I've seen her name popping up in registries around the major systems. I've been planet hopping, trying to catch up. But every time I get there, she's moved- *Whoops!*"

The front of their truck clipped the rear corner of a much smaller roller that'd been too slow in getting out of her way. The smaller vehicle's driver lost control and swerved across the lanes. The pursuing Reapers scattered to avoid it. One wasn't quick enough and he careened headfirst into the vehicle's broadside. The rider sailed like a ragdoll over the vehicle's roof and slammed into the pavement with a crunch.

Rohi stood up through the roof window and counted the remaining bikers. Five left. She checked her pistol's ammo gauge. Four left.

"Well ain't that just fucking tops," she grumbled.

She canted her head to the side and watched as three of the Reapers allowed themselves to fall back a bit. The two still out front maneuvered to be right up next to each other. Rohi saw one of them hand the end of a thick black cord to the other. They split apart, the cord stretching between them until it was as wide as the traffic lane. The cord came alive, glowing and crackling with blue electricity.

"What the fu-" Rohi started.

"It's a ripline!" Loi answered the unasked question. "If it touches the trudger, it'll short out our power systems!"

The two Reapers revved their engines and roared forward with such a force that their front wheels lifted off the ground. They kept their front wheels up in perfect balance as they accelerated. Rohi fired at the underside of the right-hand Reaper, her shot glancing off the protective plating with barely a scratch. The tilted angle of the bikes prevented any decent sightline on the riders. She could try to shoot the ripline out of their hands...

Five Reapers.

Three shots left.

One fast-approaching, electrified ripline.

Rohi ducked her head back into the trudger's cab. "What cargo are you hauling?"

Loi answered, "Clothing donations... why?"

"Fuck yes." Rohi saw the panel just behind the rear seats that lead into the storage trailer. She slid it open, reached in, and pulled out a lacey, practically see-through bodysuit.

"Nope." She tossed it aside and reached back in.

"What the shit are you doing?" asked Loi.

Rohi's arm came out again, this time holding a long, shaggy, desperately-in-need-of-a-wash Home Robe.

"Here we go." Rather than stand back up through the moonroof, Rohi opted to leaned the top half of her body out the left side window. The bikers were mere meters away from the back of their trudger.

"Whatever you're planning... fucking do it!" shouted Loi.

"Just keep driving straight for a few more seconds!"

Rohi held the robe out the window, the rush of air almost tearing it from her grasp. She zeroed in, spread the garment out as wide as possible, and let go. The wind took hold and propelled the robe backwards, where it caught on the sizzling ripline, whipping the rider on Rohi's side right off his bike. A moment later, the biker holding the other end of the cord was pulled down to the pavement.

The trailing three Reapers could not avoid the still-crackling ripline splayed out across almost three lanes of traffic. Their bike engines terminated at the very instant they touched the ripline. The sudden stoppage of momentum causing them all to fly forward over the front of their bikes, slamming hard into the street.

"*Wooo-fucking-hooooooo!*" hollered Rohi. She ducked back inside the trudger cab and slapped Loi on the shoulder. "Clean up on Lane Three! Someone spilled a whole bucket of thug-punks!"

"And would you look at that?" Loi nodded toward the rear viewport. "Of course *now* the reinforcements decide to show up!"

Rohi looked and saw the red & violet lights from a pair of City Security Enforcement cruisers merge onto the byway.

"Let's find a spot to pull over. We can have these guys send a comm to get the whole damn station staff over to that temple. I'll have my people take a ride down from orbit too."

Loi shook her head. "Even if you could get your ULE platoon-division-thing here within the hour, they wouldn't find much. The Adherent has already starting cleaning up their local operations. That one Herald you met, Mavros, he's definitely with the Adherent. I've seen his name a couple times at the same temples where my sister had been. The guy whose murder you're investigating? I'd bet a million Tahlians they contracted him for some kind of technical work and *tied off the loose end* once he'd finished the job. I say we go after the fob-gobblers, like *right now*. You send word to your HQ once we're clear of the city and they can follow us with the cavalry. I guarantee you whatever they're planning involves people dying. We can stop it, you and I…" Loi took a deep breath before adding, "And I don't know to what degree my sister is wrapped up in this, but it's definitely against her will. She doesn't have it in her to hurt people."

The City cruisers fell in behind Loi's trudger, lights still flashing.

Rohi told her, "That's fine, but you should still pull over. Otherwise they might assume we're fleeing a crime."

"We *are* fleeing a crime."

Rohi rolled her eyes. "These City Cogs can look me up in the ULE database. Once that's taken care of, we track down these Adheer-whatever-fucks. Where do we need to go next?"

Loi opened her mouth but paused.

"Uh, well," she muttered, "I'm not sure."

Rohi glared at her.

"Okay, look," Loi started, "I've seen some patterns develop wherever Adherent members are active. If they are in a specific city, it's because something or someone is there that can be useful to them. What was your murder victim into?"

"Alu Glyf? He ran some technology research institute or something like that."

"Perfect. We should find out more specifics on what types of research he did."

"Fat fucking chance. The institute's legal team is being... uncooperative."

"Not surprising. I've tried to piece together their plans based on those business-type associations. I got nothing. But the *other* pattern I've noticed, is their presence often makes waves amongst the local criminal element. Usually it renders down to the local thugs either agreeing to play along or getting themselves smoked out. I figure with the two of us being tangentially related to that world, one of us has got to know somebody who knows something."

Rohi smirked. "Of the two of us, only I am *tangentially related* to the criminal world. You are straight-up in the family photo, Ms. Master Thief."

"Very funny."

Rohi added, "But yeah, actually I know someone who could probably help."

"Who?"

Rohi looked up toward the sky. "You ready to take another trip home?"

"FUCK!"

Rohi looked at Loi with a raised eyebrow, "I know you might not be super stacked on going back to Pa Nui..."

"Not that... look!" Loi gestured at the rear viewport.

Rohi looked just in time to see a trudger truck, similar to theirs, barrel into the back of the trailing police cruisers. The force of the collision sent both cruisers spinning out of control. One spun into the path of another rig loader and was practically pulverized.

"Holy shit!" shouted Rohi and Loi in unison.

"I've seen that truck before... usually bringing Herald Mavros to and from the temple," breathed Loi.

"Mavros, as in...?"

"As in part of the psychotic prayer posse a.k.a. The Adherent."

"Damn."

The mystery truck moved into their lane and started closing the gap.

Rohi stood back up through the roof window, the rush of wind blew her hair all around her. She focused on the pursuing vehicle. It was almost identical to theirs, save for the solid black paint job. Rohi saw a flash of movement on the vehicles roof. A ceiling window, albeit twice as large as hers, slid open.

The figure that emerged from the opening was something Rohi would never have even thought to expect. It was humanoid, as evidenced by its head, two arms, and, after climbing completely onto the roof of the vehicle, its two legs. While not quite as large as Bhanakhana, the figure's frame was tall, thick, and muscular. Most remarkably to Rohi, however, was that every inch of the figure was encased in bronze and copper armor plating. The only feature on its perfectly round helmet was a strip of dark glass where the eyes would be.

"What the fuck is that," Rohi mumbled to herself.

"What the fuck is that?!" screamed Loi, still staring in the rearview.

"Could be a battle bot," Rohi mused to herself.

"Is that a battle bot?!" screamed Loi.

The bronze figure took one step on the roof of its own truck and jumped. There was at least fifty feet between them, an impossible distance. But nevertheless, Rohi watched with horrified awe as the figure launched itself across the span between two speeding vehicles. Its fingers caught the edge of the cargo hold and dug in, puncturing the metal with ease.

Rohi leveled her pistol at the space between the two sets of fingers.

A metallic head rose up.

Rohi fired.

The head jerked back with the force of the shot, yet the moving suit of armor continued to climb up onto the cargo hold roof.

"Shit."

Rohi fired again, hitting it in the chest. Again, the bot-man shuddered with the impact of her round, but was otherwise unimpeded.

"Shit."

The bot-man started marching forward at a steady pace. The considerable speed of the vehicle beneath its feet gave little hindrance. Rohi unloaded her pistol's last two shots into approaching figure, yet they did nothing to slow its progress. She holstered the pistol, and retrieved the small popper gun. After unleashing another half dozen rounds at the bronze-plated figure with no effect, Rohi's frustration got the better of her and she hurled the popper at it. The gun bounced off its chest harmlessly.

"SHIT."

Rohi ducked down inside the cab.

"What's going on up there?" asked Loi.

"Oh, you know, just an unstoppable armored man-bot thing casually strolling along our roof. I'm sure he just wants to chat. Please tell me you have another, *bigger* weapon in here."

"Oh shit, yeah! Check under the seat."

Rohi felt around and came up with a pistol similar to her standard issue model.

"Not big enough."

"Keep looking," Loi assured her.

Rohi reached down a second time. She felt the grip of a gun and pulled it loose. The weapon she now held was shaped like a pistol, but that word didn't quite do it justice. Calling this gun a pistol would be like calling a sword a butter knife.

Rohi's gawked at the oversized weapon in her grip with reverence. "This is a Bloodfist Hand Cannon."

"Yep, and as to your next question: No, I don't have a legal permit for it."

"Oh, I know you don't... because there's no such thing as a legal permit for this."

Loi's reply was drowned out by the shriek of rending metal as the roof of the driver cab was torn off. They looked up. The bronze man-bot had peeled the metal roof back as if it were merely a can of salted sandfish. The dark visor retracted, revealing two very humanoid looking eyes. Rohi noted the fiery orange hue as those eyes glared down at them with contempt. The evidently living person encased in armor spoke to them in a booming tone.

"Heretics! I am the righteous hand of Divine retribution. Prepare to be smited!"

"Smited?" asked Loi, "that can't be the right tense..."

"Yeah," said Rohi, "Would it be smoten?"

"Or smitten?"

"Silence!" bellowed the armored man. "In the name of the one true God, I send you servants of evil to the next plane of existence! Pray that our Lord is merciful on your spirits!"

"Yeah," said Rohi, "About that..."

She raised the Bloodfist Hand Cannon and squeezed the trigger. The weapon's barrel erupted with a thunderous howl. The blast struck the forehead of his helmet. His head snapped back, taking the rest of his body with him. Rohi poked her head up in time to see him tumble off the back edge of the cargo roof. She glanced at the weapon in her hand and then to Loi.

"I'm keeping this."

Rohi watched the armored man roll and skid along the paved byway before coming to stop in front of swerving crawler. Then, to her astonishment, he sat up. The Hand Cannon had torn most of the helmet's faceplate off. Rohi saw he was a Venovan, as he glowered back at her with his blue-tinted face, peppered with scratches from his shredded faceplate. He either was unable to, or chose not to get back up and chase after them. Rohi kept her eyes fixed on him until he was nothing but a tiny golden dot in the distance.

Loi merged onto the byway leading northwest, away from the city. Rohi hopped down into the seat next to her. For a few seconds, they drove in silence, enjoying the rush of wind in their newly made convertible, savoring the relative peace of not constantly being shot at for a moment. Rohi felt around the pockets of the Reaper's jacket she was wearing and found a pocket torch and a box of cinder-sticks with just two left. She offered one to Loi.

"I quit a few years back, but hell, if there was ever a moment to relapse..." Loi took one.

Rohi took the other and said, "Yeah, I only smoke after narrowly avoiding a violent death."

"So, you're finishing off what? A box a day then?"

Rohi chuckled as she lit Loi's and then her own. She took a long drag and then said, "We need to get to Pa Nui. If they have a history meddling in shady dealings, my contact will know something. Let's burn their whole fucking show to the ground."

Loi nodded. "I like the sound of that."

"Hey," said Rohi, "You never mentioned your sister's name."

Loi looked over her shoulder.

"Serru... Serru Dac'eth."

WORD SECTION 0018

"Coooooooooooool..."

Chuck stared out at the seemingly endless blob of dark blue water that was the Nautun Space Sea.

"Yeaaaah," mimicked Jopp, "Waaaaaater. What's the big deal?"

"Dude, it's a mass of water bigger than most suns, floating through space without a planet. That's fucking cool."

Bhanakhana concurred, "Indeed. The estimated average temperature of the ocean is five-point-five degrees Xelceus. Most cool indeed."

"That's not... I mean... we've talked about this, B. When I say 'cool' in that context..."

Bhanakhana smirked.

"Oh! Were you making a joke?"

"Indeed," he started chuckling, "In truth the average temperature is *fifteen-point-five* degrees. I deceived you by a margin of ten degrees!"

Chuck and Jopp looked at each other and shrugged.

"At least he's *trying* to be funny," said Jopp. "So there's progress."

Professor Phyos snorted, "Listening to you three have a conversation has become my new favorite hobby. I might have to keep you around for future endeavors."

"Oh, that'd be easy," answered Jopp, "Just keep giving Big Red new intellectual mountains to climb, and give Chuck new shiny wonders to ogle at in that special slack-jawed way of his..."

"And as for you?"

"Vubi, please! All it takes to keep me around is straight currency. Peck Peck!" He tapped his first two fingers to his thumbs, the universal sign for money. Phyos flicked his missing antenna nub.

"Ow!"

"Don't call me 'vubi'. I'm old enough to be your mother... hell, maybe your grandmother. And quit acting like you're just a greedy, drunken lutho. It's lazy and, candidly, *boring*."

Jopp shot her a defiant glare.

"Yeah yeah, you can share whatever colorful retort you're cooking up later. But for now," She grinned and pulled out a disposable currency card, "I'll bet you fifty pecks you can't fly into the ocean without a full engine stop and start."

Jopp raised an eyebrow. "Make it a hundred." He tapped the velocity gauge. "And I'll do it with our speed changing no more than five kips."

Phyos' eyes flashed. "Deal."

Jopp turned to the controls with resolute concentration. The floating body of water grew and grew until it enveloped the view screen. Jopp cut the ion thrusters, letting momentum carry the Cube ship into the cloud of water. He switched on the air propulsion in a seamless transition. The velocity gauge barely even flinched.

Phyos slid the card across the terminal. "I guess I'll have to print out a second one of these."

Jopp left the card sitting on the dash, still focused on his controls, "Yeah, well, no rush. You can owe me."

"That was an exceptional bit of piloting."

"I know."

He shot Phyos a quick grin, which she returned.

As they sailed deeper into the ocean, Chuck marveled at the luminescent tendrils of color peppering the seascape around them. Each one was a spiral stretching hundreds of feet, glowing with shades of green and purple.

"What are those?" he asked.

"Plankton," answered Phyos.

"You mean those itty bitty shrimp bacteria algae things?"

"*Itty bitty?*"

"Little."

"Well, the average individual organism in a cosmic plankton spiral is about, oh I don't know..." Phyos pointed at Chuck, "the size of your head."

"Damn, the ones on Earth are like..." Chuck held up his thumb and index finger close together. "Is that the only life out here?"

"No," answered Bhanakhana, "There is-"

"STOP!" Professor Phyos slammed the emergency brake icon. Their stomachs all leapt into their respective throats as the ship came to a rapid halt.

Jopp massaged his shoulder under the harness strap. "What the fuck, Prof?"

Phyos pointed out ahead of them. "It'd be a real shame if our little outing ended so abruptly, and unpleasantly."

"Ah," concurred Bhanakhana, "Coincidentally, Chuck, this is the creature I was about to expound upon."

Chuck leaned forward with wonder-filled eyes at the behemoth rising up before them. It's pale turquoise body looked like, well, Chuck though it looked like a chubby caterpillar... A chubby caterpillar that was pushing a hundred feet tall with a length at least six times that, ending in a vertical tail fin. Thirteen pairs of stubby 'horns' sprouted along the underbelly of its chubby body segments. Its two lateral fins stretched in a long, curved arc. But really, it was the creature's head that drew Chuck's attention. It was absolutely, completely, totally... adorable. Round cheeks. Big sparkling blue eyes. A short snout. A pair of wide, floppy antenna. It looked like a gigantic alien puppy dog... with a caterpillar body... and fins. Chuck couldn't help but let out a "wow" as it opened its colossally cute maw and swallowed a cloud of glowing plankton.

Bhanakhana announced, "Chuck, you are looking at the Gigansau Cetusau. Commonly known as the taharo, gentle giants of the space sea."

"Yeah, yeah," groaned Jopp, "We all learned about them in Interstellar Zoology class in elementary school. Why did you stop the ship? I could have easily drove around it."

"You should've paid better attention in class," Phyos zoomed in the main view screen on the taharo's long back. What Chuck had assumed were a half dozen small lumpy dorsal fins, were actually six much smaller versions of the massive creature.

"Get too close to the mamas during nursing season and they become less 'gentle giant' and more 'horrific hell beast'."

They waited for the taharo to eat her fill and slowly swim off.

"Well, wasn't that a sickeningly sweet display of the beauty inherent in the natural universe?" crowed Professor Phyos. "And hey, look at that, right on phoobing time."

She pointed toward a cluster of dim lights a few miles deeper into the Nautun ocean. Jopp turned the propulsion back on and piloted them forward. As they got closer, Chuck began to see the outline of the immense vessel. It looked like a chromatic purple-tinted cruise liner, except over a quarter mile long and twenty stories tall.

"My word..." Bhanakhana looked like a child the way he grinned up at the looming ship, "The Golatac Barge. The universe's greatest collection of knowledge and antiquity."

"Why is it on a ship?" asked Chuck, "Wouldn't it be safer in a building, like on an actual planet?"

Phyos turned to him, "And why do you think that would be safer?"

"Uh, well, because... the ground?"

"Wow," said Jopp.

Phyos glanced at Bhanakhana. "Sage Bhindo, remind me of what development level have the Earth people achieved with their interstellar travel?"

"They are still at Infancy Stage, Sage Phyos."

Phyos nodded and gave Chuck a kind smile. "I understand why you might think that. But planets have weather, and wars, and can implode... or explode. That ship you see there will likely be around longer than most inhabited planets. If trouble brews, it can leave. Or depending on the nature of the trouble, it can fight back. The Curators maintain a hefty security force. It can go anywhere in the entire universe, which funnily enough, is part of its mission statement. The Golatac has spent the last century traversing the settled galaxies. Any sight worth seeing, the Golatac will see it... eventually."

Chuck leaned back in his chair. "That is awesome. They should make a movie about it."

"They have," answered Jopp, "Many times over. In fact, so many movies have been set in relation to the Barge that it's gone from a popular setting to a worn out trope and now this new generation of movie makers like using it as an ironic joke setting."

"The Barge itself even has an exhibit cataloging all the times it's been referenced in a piece of major entertainment media."

"Dude, wait," said Jopp, "We saw a movie featuring The Barge like a year ago. It was that one starring those Puzuru twin sister comedians. It had that crazy meta scene *in* the actual exhibit showcasing all the *other* times the Barge has been in movies. How do you not remember this? You literally laughed through the entire thing, even the part when their pet dowfa died."

"Oh yeaaaah," said Chuck, "That was when you made me try deepleaf for the first time. Man, I don't remember a thing from that night."

"Lightweight."

Chuck showed Jopp his middle finger.

Bhanakhana cleared his throat. "I would very much appreciate it if we could let this... *banter* rest for a moment and respond to the Security Hail from the actual Barge."

Phyos sighed, "As entertaining as this conversation has been, I gotta agree with Sage Bhindo. They won't hesitate to scramble a defense drone."

Jopp noticed the flashing red "urgent communication" icon and quickly acknowledged, sending back Professor Phyos' identification code. After receiving their security approval, Jopp guided the Cube ship to docking hangar at the rear end of the Barge.

•   •   •

The group waiting for them at the bottom of the ship's ramp consisted of three lanky Tahls, one male & two female, and a large rocky Craglad. The Tahls stood just a few inches shy of seven feet, their stretched faces ranging in various shades of violet and lavender. The Craglad had to have weighed almost two hundred pounds more than them, despite standing six inches shorter. He carried a bored expression on his dark, slate-like face. He was wearing a tan bow-tie, a tan vest, and no shirt underneath. The two female Tahls wore matching suits: tan with pink pinstripes. The male wore... well, the only word Chuck could use to accurately describe it would be "bathrobe". He was wearing a chocolate brown bathrobe with furry, silver trim, and matching slippers. His long, narrow jaw line was rimmed with dozens of the micro tentacles that acted like hair for Tahls, making him look like an alien Abe Lincoln. He spread his arms out and greeted them with a broad smile, "Yeidat! My friend, welcome back. We are honored to have you returned to us."

She returned the smile and gave him a hug, "Phitz, how are you?"

"Excellent, as always." Phitz's eyes narrowed. "I suppose it would be too ambitious of me to hope you've come here to share your recent Ak'alei breakthroughs? The ones you neglected to share in your lecture?"

Phyos playfully wagged her finger at him. "You old pack maggler. You know I can't do that just yet. My actual contribution should have arrived not too long ago."

"Yes, yes. Your package was with the mail drop we received while passing through the Forssa system. I am excited to get a look at it in person, but before all that..."

He gestured to the Craglad, "Chonsee can assist with any luggage you may need carried." He then gestured to the two women, "Qita and Idu can assist with the travel-induced thirst I am certain you've acquired." The Tahl women approached holding trays of tall glasses containing a sparkling silver liquid.

"Mmmmm," cooed Phyos, "You broke out the good stuff for us, huh?"

They all took glasses.

Jopp eyed his skeptically, "This got hooch in it?"

Phitz laughed, "Indeed. This is some of the finest Miru in the galaxies."

"Miru?" asked Chuck.

"Sparkling wine," clarified Bhanakhana.

"Sweet," Chuck replied.

"Actually this vintage is a bit on the dryer side," noted Phitz.

Phitz raised his glass in silent toast. They all followed suit. Everyone took a polite sip, except for Jopp who took down the entire glass in a single gulp. He let out a belch and declared, "That's some swanky bubble glug."

Phitz raised an eyebrow, "Quite the entourage you've got yourself, Yeidat."

Phyos chuckled, "You have no idea. But pardon me, I didn't properly introduce you." She turned to the guys, "Boys, please meet Phitz Phitz, Third of His Name, Head Curator and Proprietor of the Golatac Barge."

She turned back to Phitz, "Meet the Boys..." she pointed at Bhanakhana, "You might have heard of Sage Bhindo..."

Phitz smiled, "Yes! Sage Bhindo, you may be surprised to know that the Barge has acquired some of your previous archaeological finds from other museums in recent years. Two quarter-span ago, we purchased your collection of fossilized Tuhinga spears for a new exhibit."

Bhanakhana beamed, "I am greatly honored my work could be of use to your esteemed institution."

Phyos interjected, "Yeah yeah yeah, you can squeeze each other's dumpers later." She pointed at Jopp, "The loudmouth Yoblon is my new pilot. His name is Jipp."

"Jopp."

"Sure."

"I've never seen a Yoblon with only one antenna," commented Phitz.

"One and a half!"

Then Phyos pointed at Chuck, "I thought you might really appreciate this, Phitz. This little pile of cuteness is a real live Earth Man."

Chuck waved. "I'm Chuck."

Phitz strode over to him and bent down close. His narrow eyes scanned Chuck's face. He leaned to the side and sniffed Chuck's ear. Chuck wondered how many years of living in this intergalactic society it would take before people stopped looking at him like a show-pony.

"Simply marvelous," breathed Phitz.

Chuck stuck his hand out, "Nice to meet you, Mr. Phitz."

"Oh please," he replied, "No need for using my formal surname. You can call me Phitz."

"Okaaaay..." Chuck looked at Jopp who could only shrug in reply.

"Consider him an extra gift for the collection," said Phyos.

"What?!" Chuck, Jopp, Bhanakhana, and Phitz all exclaimed, albeit with four separate emotions ranging from excitement to distress.

"Well, this is certainly a surprise... We rarely take in living exhibits, insurance issues and all that, however for such a rare find..."

"Hold on!" protested Chuck, "You can't do that!"

"Sure I can," replied Phyos, "It was a clause in the employment contract you all signed."

"Well, who actually reads all that?!" Chuck turned to Jopp, "Did you know?"

"Hell no, I never read anything I sign."

Chuck looked at Bhanakhana, "I know *you* read the whole thing."

Bhanakhana was mortified. "To be perfectly honest, I... skimmed it. But in my defense, I was exceptionally excited about diving into the research files."

"But... it can't... no... seriously..."

Phyos cracked a devilish grin and then burst out laughing, "Nah, I'm just yanking you all around." She wiped a tear from her eye. "Alright, enough funning. Chuck and Jott-"

"Jopp."

"Sure. You two show Phitz's people where our luggage is, then we'll go to Phitz's office so I can open up my package."

As they lead the uniformed Tahls up the ramp, Jopp leaned in to Chuck and whispered, *"I hope that isn't a euphemism."*

●   ●   ●

They huddled around Phitz's desk, which was empty save for a rectangular black metal box, roughly the size of a twelve pack case of bottled beer. Chuck suddenly felt thirsty. Phyos laid her hand on the box's lid.

"Behold, my latest contribution to the Golatac Barge."

She pulled open the lid, waving her hand about in a dramatic flourish. They all leaned in closer. A single item rested within. To Chuck, it looked like a copper figurine shaped like a beetle, with a fist-sized emerald where its "abdomen" should be.

"A Yecdo Royal Broach..." uttered Phitz.

Phyos gave him a wide smile, "I know you already got yourself a couple... but last time I checked, you didn't have a green one!"

"Oh yes, that is true. How thoughtful of you." Phitz was smiling and saying all the right things, but they could all tell he was disappointed with the box's contents.

"I shall get this cataloged and prepared for display along the rest of our Yecdo artifacts." After an awkward pause he added, "Thank you, Yeidat."

"Don't mention it," said Phyos.

"Okay," answered Phitz. He summoned an assistant and handed off the Broach. As he reached for the metal box, Phyos placed her hand over it.

"If it's not too much trouble, *Phitzy*. Could I take the box with me? The Lyceum's gotten a bit stingy as of late, making us pay for our own shipping materials and whatnot."

"Oh, certainly. Yes, very good. Well, please forgive me... but I'm afraid there are a great many things that require my attention at the moment."

Phyos slid the box off the table and stepped back, "Of course! We don't want to get in your way. I know you're a busy man. We'll get out of your follics and I'll give my boys here a little tour."

"Which way is the bar?" asked Jopp.

"Two levels down, Four chambers over. I shall send word that your libations are to be gratis as a 'thank you' for the... the *generous* gift."

"Righteous!"

"Thanks Phitz!" Phyos waved and hustled out of the office. Bhanakhana, Chuck, and Jopp looked at Phitz, then looked at each other; shrugged, and followed Phyos.

• • •

"I think I might cry."

Jopp caressed the gleaming, polished red wood of the Golatac Watering Hole's bar and gazed up at the impressive display behind the counter. The wall was a mirrored surface and had shelves running from end to end and rising twelve feet into the air. There had to be close to one thousand colorful and exotic liquor bottles covering every inch of shelf space.

Bhanakhana folded his thick arms and said, "We stand amidst the greatest assemblage of historical antiquity, with relics from hundreds of civilization spanning across the universe, some exhibits even dating back over ten thousand years old, and the thing with which you are most awe struck is a liquor dispensary... I may just cry myself."

Jopp pointed. "I'm fairly sure that bottle of Vashniien Cognac has been aged for like three hundred years. See, there's *plenty* of history right here!"

Bhanakhana rolled his eyes.

Chuck gave him a playful nudge, "Are you seriously surprised by this?"

"No, I suppose I should not be."

Chuck patted Bhanakhana on the broad sea of muscle that was his back. "How about we have a drink or two to unwind from the trip, then we can go check out some exhibits? I bet this bar has some of that Caramelized Dronlish Whiskey you like so much."

Bhanakhana seemed to brighten at this. "A taste of home would be pleasing."

A uniformed Tahl bartender approached.

"How may I serve you?"

Jopp tapped the illuminated menu screen built into the bar's surface.

"Yeah, I'm gonna need a baby taste of every Puzuran Rum you got."

The bartender arched an eyebrow. "Sir, we have *all* of them."

"I guess I better get started then."

"This is a good plan," stated Phyos, "Yes, a good plan...excuse me while I go check in on something... private messages to reply to... and stuff."

"Bye," Jopp waved without looking up.

Bhanakhana and Chuck settled up at the bar next to him.

"Just a couple drinks, then we do some exhibit exploring."

Jopp asked the bartender, "What's your policy on *to go* cups?"

WORD SECTION 0019

"That view gets me every time."

Loi and Rohi were looking out at the bright, pulsing mass that was Pa Nui, the largest city in the Coalition. A city without a planet, it nestled comfortably in its pocket of black space. Easily mistaken for a moon, or perhaps more appropriately, a tiny sun given the intensity of the constant light. They didn't call it the Neon Gem for nothing. Thousands of glowing spires rose up out of a massive half-spherical foundation.

Loi let the city's transit guidance system direct them into an approved flight lane. Their speed declined to a casual drift as they settled into the heavy city-bound traffic.

Rohi sighed, "You know, if I had my cruiser, I could just flip the lights and we could whip right around all this. Being with the ULE has its perks."

"True," replied Loi, "But that would've meant getting all the way to the other side of Pa Mahinga. A little traffic is an easy price to avoid another run in with that gold-plate whatever-the-fuck-that-was."

"Yeah, that was a new one on me. A shot from the Hand Cannon at that range should have -pardon the gory candidness- turned his head into a bowl of mashed *witi* oats. The gun *should* have killed him. The fall off our truck *should* have killed him. But he just sat right up, like he'd simply been sucker punched in a bar fight..."

Rohi drummed her fingers on her armrest and looked around the small cockpit. Loi's ship was one of the smallest classes, but the quality was top-notch. The interior design was sleek, a tasteful mix of off-whites, grays, and blacks. The armrest her fingers were currently tap-dancing on was covered in fine Ochrean-made leather.

"This is a pretty nice floater you got," Rohi commented.

"Thanks," replied Loi.

A moment passed.

"No, I didn't steal it," she added.

"I didn't say that."

"You thought it."

"Might have crossed my mind."

Another moment passed.

"Fine," huffed Loi, "I got the money to pay for the ship by stealing *other* things."

"I didn't say anything!"

"But you were thinking it."

"Well... it's kind of my job- *Oh hey*, there's our stop."

Rohi pointed toward the glowing neon tower looming just a block ahead. A twenty foot sign of glittery letters read: *Welcome to the Gilded Vixen*. Loi immediately pulled them out of the traffic lane and stopped.

"That's where your contact is? You've got to be shitting me."

"What's the problem?"asked Rohi.

"Last time I set foot in there, I was with that guy... from that big score I told you about. We actually had a nice time, that is until we had something of a 'knuckle-bruising' run-in with some old neighborhood associates."

"So he knew you had a dodgy past? And this joker still let you get close enough to him to rip him off?"

"You don't have to be a *kotch* about it."

"Sorry, meant no judgment in my word choice," Rohi pointed to tower rising up before them, "I'm sure you know this place's reputation. It'd be pretty phoobing hypocritical of me to judge your past at the same time I take you to a meeting with a known gangster."

Loi smirked. "Nah, that'd just make you a typical Law Cog."

"*Now* who's being the kotch?"

Loi gave Rohi a wink and merged back into the traffic. After crawling their way through the last block of traffic, Loi maneuvered her ship into the parking hangar.

A hulking Aviape, with a tropical bird's head on a gorilla's body, waited from them at the bottom of the ramp. He wore a plaid patterned suit of green and gold. He gave Rohi a scrutinizing glance and then let out a squawking laugh, "Finally decide to switch teams, Law Cog?"

Rohi looked down at herself and remembered she was still wearing the clothes of a North Side Reaper. She rolled her eyes, "You wish, Nudd. I just finished some undercover work."

He laughed again, "With the Reapers? I thought you's only chased the Top Nogs. Dem Reapers is weak shit. Dey once tried expanding operations from down there in the dirt to up here in the clouds."

Loi thought about mentioning the distinct lack of clouds in an orbital interstellar city, but the muscles threatening to burst through Nudd's suit sleeves helped her stay quiet. She brought her attention back in time to hear Nudd say, "I *heard* dey tried taking the wrong piece of business away from the wrong crew. I *heard* every one 'a dem Reapers what got sent up here earned demselves a tour of the industrial decompression chambers down in the city's plumbin'. I *heard* dem blue skins turn bright red right before their blood explodes out their pores. A'course... dat's just what I *heard*. Ah well, what ya gonna do? Some peoples is just made dumb."

He turned to Loi, noticing her Venovan blue tint, and added with a shrug, "I'd tell you *No Offense*... but really, I doesn't care."

Loi gave him a wide smile. "I can see why they put *you* on the welcoming committee."

Nudd laughed again, "My Ma says I'm a real charmer."

Rohi rolled her eyes. "Yeah, you're practically shitting yourself with charisma. As much as I enjoy our little chats, Nudd, I'd rather not keep *him* waiting."

"Fair 'nuff."

The feather-headed behemoth turned and led them up hangar's low, wide exit ramp. At the top of the ramp, Rohi froze in place, rubbing her eyes in shock. She'd been expecting the same tacky hallway leading into the main hall that she'd traversed many times over the years. The walls and ceiling were still present, but the floor was... well, it was gone. In its place was a shallow river of green water. Nudd waved them over to a row of golden gondolas, each one manned by a skeletal automaton coated in glittery paint.

"Uh," started Rohi, "What the fuck is this, Nudd?"

Nudd made a noise halfway between a squawk and a scoff... a squawff.

He replied, "Dem yok-knockers over at the *Sparkling Siren* turned der whole freakin' lobby into a jungle and is leading guests into the hotel on the backs of live *packyraffs*. Can you's believe dat shit? Dey got like thirty 'a them beasts."

"You mean their lobby turn into a savanna, not a jungle," corrected Loi. "Packyraffs come from the Chirico savanna. Not a jungle."

Nudd shrugged. "Who gives a shit?"

"Those packyraffs sure do. I would not want to be the janitors cleaning up that mess. Those things eat like six hundred mass-grams of food per day." Loi glanced at Rohi and added, "I love nature documentaries."

"I ain't ask for a freakin' science lesson," Nudd growled. "Anyways, the boss don't let nobody outdo him, so he had this river installed soon as he heard 'bout it."

He clambered into a gondola, the boat giving surprisingly little sway under his added bulk. Rohi and Loi followed suit, and the single eye of the otherwise featureless automaton lit up. He spoke in a synthesized voice with an accent that seemed, to Rohi's ear, to fluctuate between three different faux-exotic dialects.

"*Bon-hello! Upon where might I do ferry thee?*"

"The lifts," answered Nudd. "And no freakin' singing!"

The automaton either had not registered Nudd's anti-song request, or simply didn't have that programmed in as a viable command. As soon as their gondola started sailing forward, the robotic pilot began belting out a bittersweet ballad.

The indoor river took them down a hallway and into the cavernous main hall. Hundreds of blinking, flashing, and humming game-tables filled the space. Projection screens hovered in the air, each one displaying competitive events for the patrons to bet on. The river split into four directions. Their gondola followed the tributary to the right, circling around the seething mass of intergalactic beings who were so eagerly gambling away their hard-earned Tahlians, and came to a stop at a bank of gold-plated double doors.

"May thou soar upon new heights within our luxurious elevation tubes!" crowed the automaton.

"I hate deese bolt-heads," grumbled Nudd as they all climbed back onto the firm stone floor. He led them to the furthest pair of doors, stopping in front of the right one. He cocked his hairy thumb at the left one and said, "He'll be waitin' for ya."

Both doors opened and Nudd stepped into the right-side elevation tube.

"You're not coming with?" asked Rohi.

"Nah, I gotta deal with an unruly VIB up in the suites. Some Craglass princess has been gettin' handsy with the staff."

"Ha!" laughed Loi, *"Handsy!"*

Rohi and Nudd shot her a pair of raised eyebrows.

"You know," she explained, "because Craglasses have four hands... they're *handsy*."

Nudd huffed in annoyance as his door slid closed.

"What's wrong with you?" asked Rohi.

Loi threw her hands up. "Two minutes ago that guy was joking about straight-up murdering people."

"The context was different, you gotta read the room."

Loi looked around incredulously. "What?"

Rohi stepped into the left tube. "Let's go."

Loi sighed and joined her.

Their elevation tube opened at the top floor with a ding. The foyer was just as gaudy as Rohi remembered it. A stone statue of a two-headed humanoid woman held a cup that poured an endless recycling stream of water into the pool at her feet. Two tacky couches flanked the fountain; their spiraling gold frames likely forgoing any measure of comfort in favor of flashy aesthetics. Plants that were obviously synthetic lined the walls. The tall pair of dark wooden doors on the opposite wall stood slightly ajar. A voice called from behind them, "Pwoceed within."

Rohi and Loi passed the threshold, and entered a room that made the antechamber look modestly tasteful by comparison. Green marbled stone covered the walls. Two thin sheets of water fell along the stone into narrow troughs. The troughs formed something of a river that encircled the room, and zigzagged its way across the floor. This series of narrow rivers divided the room into a handful of white marble islands. Tiny bridges connected the 'islands' over the trickling water. Half of the island landings housed large detailed sculptures. The running theme appeared to be barely dressed beings from a variety of alien races. An unnecessarily wide stone desk with a figure seated behind it took up the space on the far side of the room.

Rohi started to lead Loi over the tiny bridges toward the desk. When they were about halfway there, Rohi came to a sudden stop. Loi didn't noticed in time, and bumped into Rohi's back.

"Shit, sorry..." Loi saw the dumbfounded expression on Rohi's face. "What's up?"

Rohi's mouth opened, but she couldn't muster an audible response.

Loi's eyes followed Rohi's gaze to one of the decorative statues. Given its glossy sheen, Loi guessed it was a new addition. The statue was a humanoid male, completely nude. She couldn't quite put her finger on it, but something seemed off...

"I can't tell if it's supposed to be a Venovan, J'Kari, Puzuru, or a-"

Rohi found her voice. "It's a- *he's* an Earth man."

"Huh, random."

"No, not random. This isn't some generic Earth man... this is an exact likeness of a very specific Earth man... *my* Earth man. This is... this is a statue of Chuck."

"Whoa-wait... the head of an interplanetary crime syndicate has a naked statue of the dude you're bunking up with in his office?" Loi's eyes drifted below the statue's waist. "Oh! Hey, good for you."

"What?! Oh, no... that's not what it actually... it doesn't have three-*never mind.*" Rohi stomped the rest of the way over to the desk at the far end of the room.

As Loi hurried to catch up, she saw that their host was waiting for them with a wide smile. Being a Pa Nui native as well as a career thief, Loi was all too familiar with the name, the face, and the reputation of the person sitting in front of them, but she'd never been in his physical presence. Honestly? She had expected... more.

Their host had narrow shoulders, and boney arms poking out from under his silver and red, pin-striped bathrobe. Loi noted an oily shine over his mahogany skin. Jowls hung below his bulbous nose. A thick brown mustache curved over his upper lip. Two tufts of brown hair protruded from the sides of his large, round, otherwise bald head. Beneath his bushy eyebrows, his eyes were hidden behind a pair of octagonal, red-tinted glasses.

"Hello, Mr. Brondo," said Rohi.

Mr. Brondo nodded. "Division Officer Kahpanova... Oh! Pawdon me for asking, but you still wetain the wank of Division Officer?"

Rohi sucked in air and replied, "Yes."

"Spwendid. A wittle Fwitterby told me you had been demoted. I must vet my sources better."

"Oh yeah? And who is this little flitterby giving you information about me? I'd love to meet them."

Mr. Brondo giggled. "I am sure you would... though I assume they would not enjoy meeting you, would they? You know I am not one to weveal sources. Pwease, won't you and your fwend have a seat?" He tilted his head to the side slightly, as if looking behind Rohi and Loi. "Shall I send for another chair? You don't have anyone *else* with you? Perhaps a certain little swice of Earth cake?"

Rohi folded her arms across her chest. "No. Chuck is not with me."

The corners of Mr. Brondo's mouth drooped, as Rohi and Loi took their seats.

"But since you brought him up," Rohi continued, "I have a question for you... about that newly forged statue back there..."

Mr. Brondo's face lit up. "Yes! Indeed! Ma-ve-wous, is it not? Evewy curve and detail sculpted to pewfection. I did have to take some artistic wiberties with certain... anatomical features."

Loi choked back a laugh.

"Yeah, I *noticed*." Rohi sighed and rubbed her forehead. "Mr. Brondo, why do you have a naked statue of Chuck?"

"He is one of the most unique and fascinating cweatures I have ever come acwoss. How could I not incwude him in my cowection? Honestwy, I am surpwised at your surpwise. I assumed he told you."

"Who told me?"

"Chuck. He knows about the statue. I asked him for permission before having it made."

Loi was eternally grateful she didn't have a drink, because it would have been spit out all over the floor at this point.

"What?!" asked Rohi, "When did you talk to Chuck?"

"He and I talk all the time... I wike to think we are fwends. He's given me a whole new perspective on things. These days, I don't automaticawy wesort to violence to solve my pwoblems. I haven't had half as many people killed as I normawy do by this time of year. It feels nice."

Rohi could only stare back at him in shock. Mr. Brondo turned his head toward Loi. "And who might you be?"

"Oh, uh," she replied, "I'm Loi. Pleasure to meet you..."

"Pweasure to meet you too, Woi. How do you know our mutual fwend, Agent Kahpanova?"

"Oh, you know..."

"No, I don't. That's why I asked." Mr. Brondo's face was stone cold.

"Ha, yeah, we're working together on a case."

"Are you a Universal Waw Enforcement Agent, as well?"

"Nooooooo..."

"Well, what are you then?"

Loi looked to Rohi who shrugged. *Fuck it*, she thought and replied, "I'm a thief."

Mr. Brondo leaned forward. "You ever steal from any of my business intewests?"

"Well... not that I'm aware of."

Mr. Brondo beamed. "Excewent! So, why has this case bwought you back to my doorstep?"

"We were hoping you might have some information."

"My dear, I have more information than I know what to do with."

Rohi rediscovered her voice. "Which is exactly why we came to you."

Mr. Brondo turned his head back toward Rohi. "Intewesting... I bewieve you still owe me one fwom our wast meeting, yes?"

Rohi sighed. "Yes, that's true."

"And you wish to double up your debt?"

"Why can't she owe you one?" asked Rohi, nodding toward Loi.

"What good would that do me? A favor from an Agent is worth more than a common thief."

"*Common* my as-" Loi cut off her protest when she saw the glare from Rohi. Loi noted Mr. Brondo's raised eyebrows and frown and took a second to compose herself. She remembered she was dealing with someone who, as the rumors say, is never wrong... and if he *is* wrong, it's only because he meant to be wrong in order to prove some other, much more important point the likes of which an insignificant peon like you could never fathom. And even if, given enough time, you could fathom such a grandiose idea it wouldn't matter, as you would likely be killed for having proven Mr. Brondo wrong in the first place.

Loi smiled. "The Sparkling Siren... it's controlled by the Unacilo Clan, right? And they're your number one competition- uh, excuse me- they're the closest thing you have to competition, right?"

Mr. Brondo's expression shifted from displeased to curious. "That is a fair statement."

Rohi gave Loi a look that said *I have no idea where the hell you're going with this, but it'd better be good.*

"Obviously you don't need any help beating them in... business. But have you wondered how they can afford to offer such supposedly high end food and drink for the same prices as a chow-chow stand vendor?"

Mr. Brondo's left eyebrow raised, then lowered. Then his right one rose up. "Perhaps."

"Yeah, it's because none of it is authentic. Every liquor is same cheap tummy chum, just treated with coloring and flavor, then poured into top tier labeled bottles. Same with the food... literally everything from the humpalope steaks to the roasted spudzies is just a mush made from bili worm larvae. They color it, flavor it, and texture it to mimic any food they want. Exposing that secret would be a real embarrassment for them, wouldn't it?"

Mr. Brondo stroked his chin with one finger in a circular motion. "Indeed it would. But how is it you know this to be twue?"

"I grew up in this city: Little Venova District. The only way out of there is to find yourself a hustle. As we already covered, my hustle was stealing shit. And I make some good money selling stolen shipments of industrial grade alcohol in off-book deals to a local consumables factory... that happens to be owned by the Unacilo's."

Mr. Brondo reached into a green marble bowl on his desk. "Would either of you wike a candied spindle-fly wing?"

He pulled out a glittery, brightly dyed insect wing and popped it in his mouth.

"No thank you," answered Rohi.

"Yeah, I'm good."

No one spoke for the next eighteen seconds while Mr. Brondo chewed his confection. Finally he swallowed and said, "Vewy well. I accept this tidbit of intewigence and will answer your question." He beamed. "How may I help?"

Loi cleared her throat. "Um, well. We're trying to track the movements of this secret organization."

"Cult," clarified Rohi, "They're a cult."

"Intewesting," noted Mr. Brondo.

"Fair enough," said Loi, "Anyway, they're pretty widespread and often get involved in, how should I say this... businesses that are unencumbered by the regulations of the Sentient Coalition."

"Illegal shit," clarified Rohi, "They often get involved in illegal shit."

"Vewy Intewesting," noted Mr. Brondo.

"Yeah," said Loi, "We want to stop whatever scheme they're up to... but our trail has gone cold. We wanted to know if you've caught wind of any of their recent activities..."

"Happy to help," said Mr. Brondo with a polite grin, "What can you tell me of this gwoup?"

"Oh, lots" said Loi, "They're an offshoot from the Church of Rhonac... they call themselves The Adherent-"

"Get out."

Mr. Brondo's grin evaporated.

"What?" asked Rohi.

"Out," he commanded, "get out."

"But..." stammered Loi.

"Mr. Brondo..." Rohi started.

"Get out now, or I will have you thwown out."

"Please don't," said Loi, "I'm trying to find my sister. Her name is Serru-"

Mr. Brondo hopped to his feet and pointed back toward the door. To Rohi he said,

"Get out wight now and I will consider this your favor weturned. Never mention those names to me again."

Rohi saw a bead of sweat trickled down Mr. Brondo's bulbous forehead. She grabbed Loi's sleeve. "Let's go."

Loi started to protest, "But you said he'd know something..."

"Let's *go*." Rohi dug her fingers into Loi's arm.

Loi looked from her, to Mr. Brondo, and back to Rohi.

"Okay."

•   •   •

"What the fuck was that?"

Loi and Rohi stepped off the elevation tube back in the lobby.

"I honestly don't know," answered Rohi. "I once saw Mr. Bronco react to the news that a Soreshi hit squad was on their way to assassinate him by giggling himself to tears... I have *never* seen him get scared of *anything*."

"So, what do we do now?"

Rohi's eyes drifted across the gaming floor to the ring of golden columns that encircled the main lobby bar. "We get a drink."

WORD SECTION 0020

The man reclined on a pile of car tires. His perfectly spherical potbelly peaked out from under his sweater vest, which was the only shirt he wore. Instead of pants, he wore a loose-fitting, ankle length skirt. His right foot was stuffed into a red gym shoe, while a flimsy flip-flop dangled off his left. A large soft drink cup was wedged between his thighs. He only had four fingers on each hand. One of those fingers was lodged deeply in his nose. He wore a monocle over his left eye and a chef's hat on his head. His other hand stretched out in front of him, holding a revolver. However he was holding it at the wrong end so that the handle of the gun was pointed outward as if it were the barrel.

Chuck stared at the statue and the digital plaque next to it that read: EARTH MAN.

"What the *fuck*, guys?"

"You inquired as to whether the Golatac Barge possessed any exhibits on your kind," answered Bhanakhana.

"And *this* is what they've got?"

"It's like I'm seeing double," said Jopp, "I bet if you stopped moving, people wouldn't be able to tell which of you was the statue."

"I do not look like this!"

Jopp answered with a loud slurp from his Yum Dum Rum Punch. It was also a long slurp, and his beverage had to travel the twelve inches of plastic tubing that formed the curly straw for his to-go cup.

Chuck turned to Bhanakhana. "Do you really think this *thing* and I look alike?"

"Hmmm... well... hmmm..." Bhanakhana scratched a non-existent itch on the back of his hand, while avoiding eye contact.

"I knew I'd find you three here!"

Bhanakhana breathed a sigh of relief at the sound of Professor Phyos's voice.

She sauntered up to them and said, "We got some work to do, fellas-" she paused when she saw Chuck standing next to the EARTH MAN statue. "Oh wow, it's like I'm seeing double."

"That's what I said!"

Phyos shook her head. "Okay, enough play time. Let's go."

She took off down the expansive exhibit hall at a brisk pace. The others looked at each other, shrugged, and followed after.

After they caught up, Chuck asked, "Where are we going?"

"To get the next piece of the puzzle," she answered.

"Oh."

They moved past the exhibit on Kapua mating rituals. Chuck and Jopp couldn't help but stare at the holographic simulation loop.

"How 'bout that? Sentient clouds *can* have sex," noted Jopp, "Anyway, Prof, which puzzle were you referring to? We've got like three of them."

Phyos replied to the question with another question, "You boys familiar with the Ta'ke Ta'ke Accords?"

"I think I saw them in concert once."

Phyos rolled her eyes at Jopp, and then glanced at Bhanakhana. He nodded, "I am somewhat familiar."

Phyos looked at Chuck expectantly.

"Oh," he said, "yeah, I have no idea what that is... did you honestly expect me to?"

She chuckled, "Fair point. Quick back-story: the Curators have been collecting rare artifacts for centuries, long before this Barge was built. And they weren't always the most scrupulous when it came to procuring new additions for the collection. The Ta'ke Ta'ke are a race of sentient beings that got royally phoobed over by the Vashnii Armada's early colonization campaigns. And the Curators of the time, having no qualms purchasing relics from conquered civilizations, accrued quite the Ta'ke Ta'ke collection. This was before the formation of the Sentient Coalition put the Vashnii in check. The Ta'ke Ta'ke Accords were drafted, and the next couple decades were spent making amends for the sins of past empires. The Curators supposedly returned any and all ill-gotten relics to their peoples of origin."

"The key word there being *supposedly*, right?" asked Chuck.

"Correct," answered Phyos with a slight grin, "For the most part, the last few generations of Curators have conducted themselves with ethical and moral professionalism However there are still artifacts in their possession from ages ago that were gained through... why mince words, unethical tactics. Now, do you want to know why the Ta'ke Ta'ke homeland was such a hotbed of interest?"

Chuck shrugged. "Sure."

Bhanakhana prided himself on his attentive listening skills, however they were currently walking past the two-hundred-yards-long exhibit on the Jaggodashi people of Renay 6. One of his early research papers in Sentology 100001 had been on the Jaggodashi. The exhibit detailed their civilization's industrial evolution and subsequent self-annihilation. He found it positively riveting. Coincidentally, he was just examining the display of the Jaggodashi Construction Clan discovering the technology for rivets, when he heard Jopp blurt out, "Ta'kenite. That's why the Vashnii wanted the land."

Phyos arched an eyebrow. "Well douse me in sauce and feed me to a Pfraza, how did you know that?"

Jopp answered between slurps of his drink, "Yoblon Defense Academy <slurp> You learn about the major militaries in the Coalition. Strengths, weaknesses. The Vashnii wanted Ta'kenite because it's virtually undetectable. Even with today's technology. <slurp> A ship made of Ta'kenite could be inches away from your own and you'd never know unless you were looking through glass right at it. Something about its molecular structure drives electronic machines nuts. Even cameras can't pick it up. <slurp> Ta'kenite on film just looks like empty blackness. The rumor is the Vashnii still have a few fighters made from the stuff <sluuuuuuurp>"

"Well damn," said the Professor, "that's actually correct."

Bhanakhana rested his broad hand on Jopp's shoulder and beamed down at him with pride. They turned down a dimly lit hallway. There were no exhibits and no signs of life.

It was then that Chuck noticed the Professor was still holding the delivery container from before.

"Oh shit, that box you shipped here is made of that same metal, isn't it?" he asked.

She wheeled around on him with a bright smile. "Absolutely correct! I don't think I've ever been prouder of a student."

Chuck considered pointing out he wasn't actually her student, but then figured he should just shut up and take the win.

Phyos waved her finger around in a circle. "Back in the Arrivals Hangar, they've got every security measure in existence. I couldn't just walk off our ship holding a box made of a material famous for concealing things. You see how that might raise a red beacon or two? But a personal package from me to Ol' Phitzy? Why would they ever think to check if the delivery container was contraband?"

"This is... uncomfortable for me to admit," said Bhanakhana, "but I am less than certain I understand what is happening."

"You don't get it, Big Red?" laughed Jopp, "We're in the middle of a heist..."

Bhanakhana scoffed, "That certainly cannot be the case. Sage Phyos, please set my friend straight."

Phyos sucked air through her teeth and said, "Well..."

"You are intending to engage in illicit thievery?!"

"Man," noted Chuck, "even *stealing* sound fancy when *you* say it."

"No no no," Phyos protested, "We're just borrowing something... probably permanently... and without permission."

"Yeah, there's a word for that," said Jopp, "it's *stealing*."

"Pssshaw! Besides, they aren't even using it. It's been in their storage vaults for the better part of a decade... and here we are!"

She stopped them in front of a circular vault door. The glowing yellow letters above it read, SECTOR CLOSED FOR MAINTENANCE.

"Professor, I am afraid I must protest this course of action-" Bhanakhana started.

"*Listen...*" she placed a reassuring hand on his thick forearm, "Phitz is a decent fellow, but his first priority is the prestige and renown of the Barge. If he found out he was holding such an important Ak'alei artifact... well, not only would our little excursion be stalled indefinitely, but our nefarious competitors, whoever they may be, would certainly come a calling. And on top of all that, the item we're going to take is originally from Gjenlu. We're just returning it to its rightful home. Really, we're rectifying a centuries old transgression against a disenfranchised indigenous people. We're like Righteous History Heroes... or something."

Bhanakhana opened his mouth, but nothing came out. He couldn't decide whether the Professor's argument was flawless logic or an utter crock of humpalope shit. Before he could finish pondering the ethical arithmetic, Professor Phyos flipped up the box's lid and popped open a false bottom. She pulled out a tray with five glass cylinders and a keyjack fob. Chuck remembered Jopp using something like that to break into the cargo hold after their first ship crash landed. Phyos took out the keyjack and handed the tray of cylinders to Chuck.

"Hold on to these, Deary. Try not to drop them."

With that, she used the keyjack to unlock the sector door and slipped inside. Chuck and Jopp wasted no time in following after her. Bhanakhana looked around for a moment, breathed a heavy sigh, and disappeared into the darkened sector beyond.

WORD SECTION 0021

"Shut up... are you serious?" Loi folded her arms across her chest, "You broke a suspected murderer out of a ULE frigate? On a hunch?"

Rohi downed the last of her Liquid Bliss. "A hunch that turned out to *right*."

Loi rolled her eyes. "And not only is this same suspected murder..."

"*Formerly* suspected murderer. He was innocent, remember?"

"Yeah yeah... that's the *same* guy you've been bunking up with? And on top of all that, he's from motherphoobing *Earth*?! I need to stop underestimating you, Law Cog."

"You and everyone else." Rohi tried to flag down the bartender, but she was preoccupied chatting up a pair of well dressed Tahls. "But that's enough prying into my personal affairs. What about you, Ms. Intergalactic Thief... I imagine you've had more than your fair share of risqué liaisons... what's your bedroom poison of choice? Dronla men? Puzuru women? Bogteks?" Rohi chuckled, "You like 'em slimey?"

"Honestly, haven't done much in the way of dating. And when I do it's usually a guy who seems incredibly charming... for about a day. Then I realize he's a total scrogbag. There was one guy a few years back though..." she laughed, "He was so far from my usual type. I don't have much tolerance for loudmouths. But there was something weirdly endearing about his otherwise annoying antics."

Rohi felt a vibration on her wrist. She looked down and saw a new message. Her eyes lit up when she saw the subject matter.

"What's up?" Asked Loi.

"While you were flying us up to the city, I posted a flier in the U.L.E. active case database."

"A flier?"

"Agents can put tags on key phrases, and if a report is ever filed that references those phrases, the listing agent gets an alert. I posted a flier that tagged both the Church of Rhonac and the word Adherent."

"And you just got one?"

"Yeah. I'm pulling the report now. Holy shit this is a big file."

"What's it about?"

"The topline summary says it's from some lawyer, a Mahimen named Gupsley Carpian. He was found dead in his office a few hours ago. A data file was sent from his GIGmail address to the U.L.E. orbital precinct above Raeth Beta." Rohi continued to read aloud, "So apparently this message was preset to be sent out every day unless a password was entered. Evidently no password was entered today."

"It's a 'Fuck-You File'."

"Huh?"

"Let's say I was running a heist for a handler, and I suspected there was a chance that handler might screw me over or even kill me. I might set up something similar to what this lawyer dude did. So, if this hypothetical handler did betray and kill me, I'd at least get one final Fuck You in by exposing whatever dirt I had on them."

"Oh shit, you are so right. Damn, there's a lot to unpack here... Order us another round. I'll finish downloading this and send you a copy."

"Are you allowed to show me this?"

"Not really worried about that right now. We need to sift through this as quick as possible."

While Loi flagged down the bartender, Rohi broke out two collapsible tablet screens and sent a copy of the file to each one.

Two more drink rounds and one picked over platter of spicy crunch-chunks later, and Rohi and Loi were just barely scratching the surface of the information contained within Gupsley Carpian's posthumous confession.

"Holy Mud Humping Gorthans..." breathed Rohi, "these yoks are into everything."

"Told you," said Loi. "You'd think we were looking over the portfolio of a Tahlese billionaire entrepreneur rather than a freaking church."

"Here's a reference to Alu Glyf's company. It's marked as a Closed Account. Damn, there's a lot of Closed Accounts here. You were right, they're cleaning house."

"WAD GOBBLING MOTHER PHOOBER!"

Loi's sudden outburst made Rohi almost fall off her stool. Loi looked up from the tablet to Rohi with fire burning in her eyes. After a few deep breaths to calm herself, Loi said, "I know one of these names: Butahn Bazzinthi. Or as those of us who grew up in Pa Nui's Little Venova district knew him, Big Bazz. He's been receiving payments for a few years now. Him, Rinch, and Gam Gam are the bosses of the three major crime crews in Little V."

"Wait, say those other two names again."

"Rinch and Gam Gam."

"Oh shit," said Rohi, "I knew they sounded familiar. They're right here... under Closed Accounts."

Loi gulped the remainder of her drink and said, "I think it's time we hop over to my old neighborhood and pay someone a visit."

WORD SECTION 0022

"Oh, wow, that is gnarly."

Chuck stared up at the dust covered hunk of stone leaning against the wall. Its nearly twenty foot diameter had been carved to resemble the howling face of some demon beast monster. Its mouth formed a shallow basin with four fangs protruding from the corners.

"Ah, yes," mused Professor Phyos, "the Gegethu Sacrificial Altar."

"This thing is an *altar*?" said Chuck.

Phyos explained, "They laid it flat, with the face looking toward the sky. The chosen one had their arms and legs tied to the fangs, which suspended them, face down, above the mouth basin..."

"Yeah yeah," Chuck interrupted, "then they'd cut the guy's throat and let his blood fill the basin... and then they'd probably all drink it, right?"

Chuck noticed three horrified stares looking back at him.

"Excuse me?" said Phyos.

"Chuck, that is not... well..." stammered Bhanakhana.

"Holy Bjordax, dude, what kind of sick shit you got up in that brain ball of yours?" asked Jopp.

"But you said... I mean..."

Phyos shook her head, "No... no they don't commit senseless murder... but thank you for asking."

Phyos continued to lead them through the closed off wing, navigating through a seemingly endless hoard of dusty artifacts collected from hundreds of civilizations scattered across dozens of star systems.

At one point they passed by what appeared to Chuck to be a literal pile of Stargates.

"Hey!" Called Jopp, "Anybody want breakfast?"

They all turned to see him holding up a half-meter long fossilized egg. It looked like it was made from black granite. Chuck saw about fifteen similar eggs arranged in a basin that resembled a wading pool made of a charcoal grey wood.

Professor Phyos and Bhanakhana had barely gotten their mouths open when Chuck blurted out, "Oh hell no! Put that thing down right now, dude! If I know anything about anything about *anything*, it's you do not mess with strange alien eggs! Put it down... NOW."

Chuck noticed he was wagging his finger like a disapproving parent. Jopp laughed and set the egg back in the basin. "Man, you look like my dad right now... except taller, skinnier, and less yellow and- ah, man! I think my drink is leaking. Anyone got a wash wipe?"

"Please do not touch anything else," said Bhanakhana, "I honestly did not think you would actually need to be told that."

"My fault," added Phyos, "I assumed everyone just knew that there should be *no touchies* when sneaking into an off-limits sector filled with priceless antiquities."

The two intellectuals and Chuck resumed walking. Jopp called after them, "Hey! For real, anyone got a wash wipe?"

He hurried to catch up, leaving the leaky remains of his Yum Dum Rum Punch on the edge of the basin, right above the plaque fixed to the front of it that read:

Under no circumstances should the Igg'rreh Eggs be exposed to moisture of any kind.
Seriously.
We mean it.

WORD SECTION 0023

"C'mon, Loi, I don't want trouble, okay?"

The tall athletic Venovan man looked down at Loi and Rohi.

"And I don't want to give you any trouble, Heggie," Loi replied, "So step aside. We just need a quick chat with your boss."

The big man continued to block the doorway. They all stood in an alley behind the gray box of a building. Around in the front, the glowing sign read *"B.B.'s Gas Bar: Authentic Venovan Smokes."*

A hundred feet above them, digital lights twinkled like stars in the simulated bio-dome sky. Loi let her gaze drift over their surroundings in a faux casual manner.

"Lot of changes to the neighborhood since I've been gone, huh Heg? I couldn't help but notice that big fucking Rhonacian temple taking up the entire block where Rinch's place used to be. Not to mention the new apartments in the same spot that used to house Gam Gam's bakery. But look at your crew... still sitting pretty in the same spot as always."

"Loi, I don't know nothing 'bout it. I just tend the door."

"What if I told you I'm with the U.L.E.?" said Rohi.

"I'd say show me credentials and a writ of justified entry," Heggie answered.

"Damn," Rohi cursed to herself, "I seriously gotta get a new badge."

Loi tried a softer tone. "How's your Grandma? I liked her. She didn't treat the group home kids any different than the ones with families."

"She's hanging in there... I just work for Bazz to help pay her rent. You know this. C'mon, Loi..."

Loi sighed, "We're walking in there, Heggie. The only thing that's up for debate is what happens to you in between now and me standing in front of that fat phoobing boss of yours."

The otherwise imposing man whined, "But he's in a meeting..."

"I'm gonna make the decision for you in about two seconds."

Heggie let out a defeated sigh and stepped aside. Loi headed through the doorway. Rohi started to follow, but stopped and looked up at Heggie.

"Sorry," she said as she punched him in the face.

"Ah! What the hell?!" He groaned and massaged the welt that had sprouted from his cheek.

Rohi shrugged, "Now it looks like you at least *tried* to stop us. You're welcome."

Loi lead Rohi down the dimly lit hallway, stopping at a door whose sign read, *Boiler Room*.

Rohi gave Loi a quizzical look. Loi rolled her eyes, "His lazy attempt at subterfuge." She tapped the hilt of her holstered pistol. "Hey, uh, this might get a little dodgy... legally speaking."

Rohi held up her own weapon. "Yeah, pretty much every minute we've spent together has been dodgy. Let me ask you," she nodded at the door, "He really that much of a scrogbag?"

"With the heinous shit this guy's done? If he's still breathing when we leave, we'll be letting him off easy."

"Works for me. Want me to kick the door down?"

Loi arched an eyebrow. "Easy there, Battle Babe. I'm a thief, remember?"

In a rapid sequence of movements, she pried the faceplate off the locking mechanism, produced a small tool that resembled a pair of pliers crossed with a calculator, and jammed it in the tangle of wires. The door beeped three times and slid open. Rohi and Loi burst into the room with weapons raised.

They found themselves in a spacious lounge decorated in what could only be described as "Sleazy Chic". Purple velour and faux gold plating were the primary themes. Shelves lined the wall to the left, displaying dozens upon dozens of pipes, bongs, hookahs, and other ornamental smoking implements. A panoramic window stretched along the back wall. To the right was a small wet bar, replete with a healthy selection of local spirits. Next to that was a couch, purple with gold stripes. The body of a young Venovan woman lay across it, her eyes staring lifelessly at the floor. But what drew Rohi and Loi's attention was the gaudy desk in front of them, or more specifically, what was next to the desk. A Venovan man dressed in black stood over another Venovan man who cowered on the floor. The one on the floor was middle aged, and severely obese. Years of poor health choices had faded his once blue skin. The standing man was fit and young, barely 20 annuals of age. His head and face were clean shaven, and he stared at them with eyes that burned with an unnatural orange glow.

"Help me!" cried the man on the floor.

The standing man appraised the two women with a cold stare. In what appeared to be the greatest of self indulgences, he cracked a slight grin and said, "Rhonac has blessed his child this day."

Rohi and Loi raised their pistols.

"I am a Division Officer of the Universal Law Enforcement agency. Don't make any aggressive moves."

"Yeah," added Loi, "and step away from that yok blob. We got dibs on smacking him around."

The unnatural color of his irises expanded until his eyes were just two glowing orange ovals.

"Do not be afraid. The Lord Rhonac will carry your souls to the next dimension."

"Do we look afraid, chaak face?" Loi waved her pistol.

The man's grin grew. "Your heart rates are quite elevated. And the air is dense with the pheromones of panic."

"Okay, you weird mother-phoober, get on your knees and put your hands behind your head."

The man made a move to reach behind his back. Rohi squeezed her trigger, aiming for his arm. With a seemingly impossible reaction speed, the man turned his shoulders and leaned just out of the way of the shot. He produced a black baton. Rohi didn't plan on giving him the chance to use to it, whatever it might be.

"Put him down," she said to Loi.

They each fired a pair of shots.

In a physics defying display of agility, the man avoided the first shot, and then the second. The third barely grazed his arm. The fourth found its mark in the side of his abdomen. He let out a pained grunt and dropped to his knees. Rohi holstered her pistol and retrieved her mag-shackles.

"Keep him covered," she said as she approached the kneeling, wheezing man. "That was one thriller trick, buddy. I hope you don't die before we get you some medical. I'd like to hear how you-" Rohi noticed the man was breathing normally, no more wheezing. Before the synapses in Rohi's mind had a chance to comprehend what this might mean, he burst up from his knees, picked her up as if she were a child, and hurled her across the room. Loi barely dove out of the way in time to avoid the airborne J'Kari woman. Rohi slammed into the wall, crumpling to the floor.

Loi rolled and tried to bring her pistol up for another shot, but the man was already on her, ripping the gun from her with unnatural strength. She looked up with terrified shock as he took the weapon in both hands and, with just the barest hint of strain, snapped it in half. He then hoisted Loi off the floor by her collar, bringing her eyes to his.

"You turned your back on our people's savior. But do not despair. The Lord will forgive you..."

Loi's eyes flirted over his shoulder, and saw Rohi pulling herself together. The man noticed her gaze and turned his head just as Rohi raised her pistol. The man tossed Loi and leapt out of the way as Rohi fired. Loi landed on the bar top, smashing a pair of spirit glasses, cutting up her forearm, before rolling off the other side.

Rohi continued to fire and the man continued to dodge the shots in a flurry of rapid acrobatics. Rohi's errant shots pierced the panoramic balcony window behind him, causing a spiderweb of cracks. Then a liquor bottle sailed past the man's head. It was shortly followed by second, which collided with the window, shattering the glass. Shards of jagged glass jutted up from the bottom window pane, like a row of transparent stalagmites. Rohi glanced toward the bar and saw Loi throw a third booze missile.

The man saw it too. To their astonishment, he made no attempt to avoid the bottle, but rather squared up and head butted it. It shattered in a spray of pungent alcohol. Trickles of blood and liquor rolled down his face. He wiped it away with a smug grin, just as Rohi pumped four rounds into his stomach.

The man staggered.

Rather than cry out or moan, he began to chuckle. He reached up with both hands, gripped his collar, and tore open his shirt, revealing the four gunshot wounds.

"You heretics are vermin to me. You cannot harm a true child of Rhonac," he crowed, while inadvertently stepping on the loose bottle at his feet. Perhaps it was the series of lacerations to his forehead. Perhaps it was the four nano-carbon bullets in his torso. But his athletic prowess failed him at that moment and he fell backwards...

Right onto an upright, dagger-like shard of window pane glass. It pierced clear through the back of his neck and protruded out the front, just under his chin. The man gurgled, his body shuddered, and he went limp.

Despite the painful protest from her ribs, Rohi pulled herself up. She hoped it was just some bruising, and no breaks. Loi wrapped a bar towel around her bleeding arm, and clutched it to her chest. They cautiously limped over to the motionless body with the glass shard sticking up through its neck.

"So that's officially the most messed up way I've ever seen someone die," said Loi.

"Meh," said Rohi, "I once busted an illegal weapons dealer named Rinz 'Juice' Jenzin. He liked to get rid of his competition by dropping them into an industrial juicing machine. Hence the name."

"You know that's not normal, right? To be so casual about stuff like this. It's really unsettling."

"Don't you start trying to psychoanalyze- *holy shit,* are you seeing that?!"

They stared down in complete disbelief as the four gunshots in the dead man's torso closed up, leaving a perfectly unmarred patch of blue skin. Rohi braces herself for a sudden movement, but the man remained dead; the shard of glass still jutting up from his neck, his vacant eyes, now devoid of any unnatural orange glow, still staring blankly upward.

"He's a shepherd," croaked a voice from behind them.

They whirled around to see the obese Venovan man still laying on the floor.

"A what?" said Rohi.

"The shepherds are a myth, Bazz," said Loi as she reached down with her good arm to snatch up the bottle the man had tripped on. She appraised the label, a limited batch Venovan cognac. She nodded, yanked off the magnicork with her teeth, and took a swig.

"Yeah," said Bazz, "Well that *myth* is laying right there at your feet."

"What's he talking about?" asked Rohi.

"It's a fancy tale Venovan kids tell each other," said Loi.

"Again, that *fancy tale* is laying right there in front of you!" barked Bazz, "Now will you please help me up?"

"Nobody does a fucking thing until someone explains what the fuck you two are talking about," demanded Rohi.

Loi took another healthy swig from her bottle and offered it to Rohi.

"In Rhonacian lore, the shepherds are the chosen defenders of the faith. Blessed with divine powers…"

Rohi pulled the bottle from her mouth, "Like dodging gunshots? Or insane strength? Or an inexplicable healing ability?"

"Yeah, but c'mon, there's got to be another expla-" Loi's eyes fell on the dead woman at the couch. She grimaced, snatched back the bottle from Rohi and stomped toward Bazz. She pulled over the desk chair to lean against and glared down at the prone mound of a man.

"This is some good shit, Bazz," she sipped at the bottle. "Probably costs more than most people around this neighborhood earn in a month." She took one more swig and then started drizzling the cognac over Bazz's gut, chest, and then his face.

He sputtered and coughed, "What the phoob are you doing?!"

"Getting justice."

"For what?!"

"Take your pick. For setting me up to take the fall for that last job we did together. Or for selling out the neighborhood. From what I gather, you're the only Hustle Buddy left breathing. You helped check off the other crews so you could save your own ass. You flipsiding kajiratch." Loi's eyes again found the young woman, too young to be in a place like this, and painfully too young to be dead. "Or maybe it's justice for whoever she was, you skeevy fuck."

"I didn't kill her! That psycho did!"

"Yeah, but she was here because of you. You and your worthless promises." To Rohi, she said, "You still got that Reaper's pocket torch?"

Rohi tossed it over without a word.

Loi lit it up. "That good hooch you're wearing is high proof. I bet if I dropped this you'd light up like a Yoblonese fricassee."

"You want to blame someone for that tart's death? Check the mirror!" blubbered Bazz, "The Adherent knew you were in town, snooping around. They're dusting anyone who might be able to help you."

This caught Loi off guard. She paused for a moment. Rohi picked up the slack.

"I guess you'd better tell us what they don't want us to know."

"Huh?" said Bazz.

"Yeah, *huh*?" said Loi.

"You said he came here to kill you to prevent you from helping us. Which means you know something that can help us. So tell us what it is."

"Fuck if I know!" cried Bazz. "It's not like I actually work for them... I just do a favor here and there so they leave me alone!"

"There's something," said Rohi, "Something you know."

She crossed the room, crouched down close to Bazz's face, and spoke in a low raspy tone, "Honestly, I don't know if my friend here has the kotch-knots to actually set you on fire."

She gently pressed the barrel of her pistol to his head.

"But I sure as shit know that *I* will turn your brains to scrambled fujo if you don't tell me something useful in about four... three... two..."

"Gjenlu!" shrieked Bazz.

"What the phoob does that podunk planet have to do with anything?" asked Loi.

"The Church... the Adherent... they've got some project going on. They needed cheap labor... I asked where the job was, they looked like they wanted to kill me for that, but I reminded them the workers would need the right cocktail of immunization drugs and gravitational adjustment. Whatever they're doing, it revolves around Gjenlu."

Rohi stood up and gave Loi a hard look.

"We need to go, *now*."

She started heading for the door.

"What about him?" Loi asked, gesturing at Bazz.

"Do whatever you want. We just need to go."

Loi gave the splayed out, soaking wet obese Venovan man an appraising glance and sighed with disgust. "Killing you isn't worth the stain on my soul, although..." She yanked open the bottom drawer from his desk and pulled out a stack of slim metal rectangles. "I will take your stash of untraced currency cards."

"You're robbing me?" he whined.

Loi shrugged, "It's kind of my thing, remember? All things considered, I'd say you're getting off light."

"What do you think you're going to accomplish, huh? You're nothing but a three-peck thief. They have real motherphoobing *super soldiers*. Do you hear what I'm saying? You're just a bug on the view screen of their star cruiser."

Loi tilted her head toward the dead man with the glass through his neck.

"They ain't so tough."

"Ha! Pure luck. And besides, I remember that one. He was the weakest of them. You should run, Loi. That's also *your thing*, isn't it? Run far away."

"Loi!" called Rohi, "Let's GO."

Loi headed for the door. She was almost out of the room when Bazz called after her, "You don't actually think you're going to save *her*, do you? I promise you, that ship has launched! The person that was your sister is long dead, Loi. Who do you think approached me with the deal? Who do you think orchestrated the recent renovations of the neighborhood? The person who killed Rinch, Gam Gam, and their crews? The person who scorched the children's home? She's a monster, who just happens to wear Serru's skin."

Loi looked back at him with fire in her eyes.

"You fucking lie!"

"Ha... sure, yeah, I'm lying. You know what? I wish you all the luck in the universe, Loi. I hope you find her. Really, I do. Then you'll see what she is for yourself. I'll bet the look on your face will be priceless."

Loi huffed and glanced around the room.

"You should really clean this place up, Bazz. All that booze soaking into the carpet... you're gonna get mold."

"*All that booze*? It was only like two bott-"

Loi picked up a barstool, spun around, and hurled it into the liquor-laden shelves behind the bar. Dozens of glass bottles shattered, spilling their pricey contents onto the floor.

"Good catching up with you, Bazz. See you on the other side of never."

•   •   •

Loi and Rohi were back aboard their ship. Each of them had had their aches and pains checked out in the med bay. Loi was sporting a new bandage over almost the entirety of her left forearm. Rohi's ribs, thankfully, were not broken. Just badly bruised. She manned the controls, sifting through comm messages. She found the one she was looking for and sent it to the big screen.

"Why am I looking at this?" Loi asked.

She had asked this because the message Rohi had pulled up was from Chuck. After a hefty handful of minutes spent on inane small talk and cutesy platitudes, the recorded Chuck said, "*So, then the hostess at the waystation restaurant slapped Jopp. Anyway, it sounds like after we make a quick stop at that Barge museum thing, we're going to a planet called Gjenlu...*"

Rohi stopped the recording.

"We need to get there, like yesterday. However, I'm about to beat your ship's computer to death with my bare hands because it's telling me it's going to take over a week to get there."

"One sec." Loi's fingers danced across her screen. "Actually, I can get us there in two days."

Rohi arched an inquisitive eyebrow.

"Can you keep a secret?" asked Loi, as she started punching commands into her console. Rohi watched as a new route was traced from Pa Nui to Gjenlu, a new route that dropped their estimated travel time from eight standard days to just two. Not only that, but a host of informational bullet points about the route appeared on the screen. The content of these bullet points ranged from laying out the patrol routes of nearby U.L.E. regiments to highlighting way stations with the best food.

"Um, please explain."

"You know how when a new anomaly gets discovered, and then the Sentient Coalition goes through its whole mapping process, shooting drones through it to see where they come out... then, if it leads anywhere useful, the anomaly gets added to the official Interstellar Mapping System?"

"Yeah..."

"So, what do you think happens if an anomaly is discovered by a person who, let's say, has no interest in being noticed by the Coalition?"

"Like a smuggler? Or a thief?"

"We're going to have to work on your tone with those words if we're going to be friends. But yes, if a smuggler discovers a new anomaly, they likely won't share that information with the same authorities trying to pinch them. And in the service of mutual self-interest, a loose network of smugglers and smuggler-adjacent professionals was formed to share information on unreported anomalies. That information was compiled into an unofficial Mapping Program that you can acquire if you know the right people." Loi waved at the display. "And thus was born the Hooligan's Atlas, the *real* map of the known universe."

"Seriously? That's what you call it? The *Hooligan's Atlas*?"

Loi grinned. "Us thieves, smugglers, and general miscreants are a cheeky bunch, aren't we?"

WORD SECTION 0024

"It's a building…" said Chuck.

"Technically, it is a *yurt*," said Bhanakhana.

"More like a shack, if you ask me," said Jopp.

"You know you three have something of a repetitive conversational pattern?" said Phyos. "Anyway, yes, this structure is the actual dwelling that Cestoras lived in on Gjenlu while finalizing the research on the Ak'alei.".

Bhanakhana held up the notebook. "And where he created his infamous diary."

"Ah, yes," said Phyos, "something like that."

"It's just funny to me is all," said Chuck, "Like an entire building inside a room, inside a spaceship."

"It must be nice… being so easily amused," quipped Jopp.

Chuck slugged him in the arm.

"Ow!"

"Does that actually get him to hush up?" asked Phyos.

"No, I don't think that's possible," said Chuck, "When the last star burns out, and the weight of the universe has grown so much that all reality collapses in on itself, the last snippet of sound to ever move through space will be a smart-ass quip from Jopp."

Jopp rolled his eyes. "Har Har, you're so- holy shit, Big Red, are you crying?"

They all looked at Bhanakhana, who wiped away a tear and smiled at Chuck. "You read the book I gave you… *We Are All Going to Die: Twenty Probable Methods of Universal Destruction.*"

"Oh, I actually read that one too," said Phyos, "My favorite apocalypse was the one where all life spontaneously transforms into cake and we eat ourselves to death."

"Huh, maybe I should give books another chance," said Jopp.

Phyos rolled her eyes and headed toward the yurt. As they approached, Chuck noticed the structure was a made from a weird mix of primitive and semi-modern technologies. Thousands randomly shaped stones acted as the building blocks. They were held together with a green tinted, industrial polypoxy. A tubular light ran along the top of door frame. The walls formed a near-perfect cylinder, rising up about as high as a single story house. The conical ceiling was made from a gray, plastic-like material. A fine layer of dirt coated the whole of the building.

Phyos placed her hand against the door, "Cestoras' house here was uprooted from its original location on Gjenlu a few decades back. The planet is gorgeous, however, much of it is… *unwelcoming* to outsiders. Cestoras decided to squat himself down in a particularly inhospitable sector of the planet. At first, they tried conducting studies on site, but they lost too many research assistants to the jungle."

Jopp and Chuck traded nervous glances. Bhanakhana was too busy being enamored with the building's stonework to react. Phyos continued, "So, they opted to extract the whole thing. They had planned to make it an exhibit here on the Barge, open for all to study at their leisure. That is, until they saw the writing on the wall."

"I assume you mean the obvious observation that allowing such unfettered access could result in a contamination of any substantial archaeological discovery?"

"No," said Phyos, "I mean the literal writing on the wall."

She pushed the yurt's door open and ducked inside. The others followed and found themselves in a walled off section of the yurt. The interior had been divided into four quadrants, with a small, circular room at the center. Phyos took one of the glass cylinders from the tray Chuck had been holding and set it in the middle of the floor. They repeated the process on each of the main quadrants and then placed the fifth in the small round room at the yurt's center. The stone walls were devoid of any markings, images, or text.

"Sage Bhindo," said Phyos, "How's your study of that diary coming?"

Bhanakhana held up the book and sighed, "Honestly, Sage Yeidat, I am somewhat flummoxed. I attempted to use your cipher, however my results are confusing..."

"Yeah, so... contrary to what everyone believes, *that*," she pointed at the book, "is not the diary of Cestoras."

Bhanakhana's eyes widened. "But the opening pages are not in code, and they make clear references to the crucial information contained within, and I quote..." he opened the book, "*my diary holds all my knowledge pertaining to the Ak'alei...*"

Phyos nodded, "Don't trail off. Finish the quote."

Bhanakhana grimaced and said, "*...Good luck figuring it out, Turd Gurglers.*"

Chuck and Jopp choked back laughter.

"It's not a huge surprise Ol' Cestoras shacked himself up out in the proverbial middle of nowhere to do his work. He and the established scientific community of the time weren't exactly the best of friends. They found him too weird for their tastes... can you imagine that? The governing body of academia being lead by old stuffy Stumps who can't be bothered to pry their blubbery asses out of their desk chairs? Some things never change. But here's the thing, at his core, Cestoras a purist. The *Knowledge* was more important than any personal differences he might have with peers. He could never hide his findings, nor would he outright lie. Mislead a bit? Sure. So yes, he left the original copy of that book for the community to find. And yes, it references a diary. Everyone just assumed that was it and went about the century long task of decoding his cipher."

"So, what *is* that little book Bhanakhana's been tinkering with this whole trip?" asked Chuck.

"For the most part? A bunch of dirty limericks Cestoras wrote to amuse himself."

Bhanakhana exhaled a sigh of relief. "That explains so very much. There are quite a few entries about this *Man from Xan'Wuckit* and for the life of me, I could not work out how it fit into the bigger picture."

Jopp threw his hands up in the air. "Okay, we get it, you're both giga-smart... so where's the actual diary?"

Phyos winked. "We're standing in it, Jirp"

"Jopp."

"Sure."

She pressed a button on her data bracelet, and the five glass cylinders burst to life with pale blue light. The previously bare stone walls were suddenly coated in bright blue text, complex diagrams, and crude drawings.

"Oh my," said Bhanakhana.

"Wow," said Chuck

"What the fuuuuuuuuuck?" said Jopp.

"I told you the writing was on the wall," said Phyos.

Chuck found his eyes pulled toward a particularly graphic sketch what he assumed was two beings having sex. Phyos saw his stare and said, "Yeah, in addition to the limericks, ol' Cesty liked to draw different species zoinking each other. That's why they pulled his hut off the exhibit floor. Felt it wasn't appropriate for the masses. Okay!" she clapped her hands, "Enough gawking. Everyone open your data bracelet cameras and start taking pictures of every inch of blue scribble. We'll piece it all together once we're back on the ship. Hop to it."

Chuck, Jopp, and Bhanakhana fanned out and started doing as she'd asked. After a few minutes, Chuck noticed that Professor Phyos was not taking any pictures. Instead, she was intently studying the ceiling above the small central room. He finished cataloging the walls of the room he was in and went over to join her. He couldn't help but laugh when he saw what was on the ceiling. The image was rough sketch of a long, thin man, presumably a Tahl, naked and in a squatting position. There were words arranged in a pyramid shaped underneath his posterior, as if the writing was meant to symbolize feces. Put together in a sentence, the words read: *The key to everything is shit.*

"Creative," mused Chuck, "Is that supposed to be a self-portrait?"

"Yep," said Phyos, "Cestoras was a little nutty, but he was also one of the smartest motherphoobers to every bounce his way around the galaxy. This isn't random. There's a reason this particular image is right in the center. There's only a few dozen academics who know about these scribblings. And that's all from memory-based notes people took after visiting the site... before the Barge Lords pulled it off public viewing status. Most of the information we capture here will be brand new to me, but this..." she cocked her thumb upwards, "This phrase has been kicking around the inner circles of Ak'alei enthusiasts for some time. People have their theories, but no one seems to have the definitive meaning."

Chuck looked at Phyos, then up at the picture, then back at Phyos, then back at the picture.

"Honestly?" he said, "I think you're all over thinking it."

"Come again?"

"It's like these literature classes I had as a kid in school on Earth. The teachers and other students loved to find or inject secret meaning into every little thing in every book we read. But maybe, most good books are just good stories. Like, maybe *Lord of the Flies* isn't some big allegory for conflict between varying socio-political ideologies or an exploration on the inherent good vs. evil nature of man... maybe it's just a story about a bunch of shitty kids on a shitty island."

Phyos raised her eyebrows. "I was with you until that last bit."

"Okay, take the first part: *The key to everything...* are we looking for a key?"

"There's always a key with stuff like this, isn't there?," said Phyos, "In his writings, Cestoras often referenced *unlocking the path to Hirth-Ak'alei.*"

"Great," said Chuck, "now the rest of it... *is shit.*"

He tapped his chin a few times and then his eyes lit up and he started laughing. Phyos stared at him like he had matofish wriggling out of his ears.

"Hey Jopp," Chuck called, "Come look at this."

Jopp sauntered over and followed Chuck's pointed finger upward.

"They want to know what he could possibly have meant," Chuck explained.

It took Jopp all of fifteen seconds before he too started laughing.

"Feel free to clue me in anytime," said Phyos.

"Yes, myself as well," said Bhanakhana as he joined them.

Chuck and Jopp looked at each other and nodded.

"Whatever you're looking for, it's in the toilet," said Jopp nonchalantly.

"Pardon?" said Bhanakhana.

"How do you know?" asked Phyos.

"It's what I would've done," answered Jopp.

"Yeah, c'mon," said Chuck, "the bathroom was back in this quadrant that I just photographed."

Chuck led them to the quadrant in question, where a curtain of plastic-like material cordoned off a small space in the back corner. Chuck pulled the curtain aside, revealing a stone bathtub and a stone toilet. Neither appeared to be very comfortable.

Jopp shook his head. "This plubb of a dude had to have a short circuit in his brain. Why live in a dump like this when he had a ship to go back to. I mean, I know spaceship living quarters weren't quite as cushy a century ago, but it had to be better than this."

"He would not have been able to keep his ship grounded close to his research sites," said Bhanakhana.

"The valley jungles of Gjenlu are... not friendly to, let's say *non-natural* things, like large gravity-defying machines. I'll explain more when it becomes relevant, but I believe you two have a theory about the toilet?"

Jopp gestured at it. "Go wild, Prof."

She snorted, "I don't know exactly what we're looking for, and this is your theory, fellas."

Jopp held his hands up. "I'm not sticking my nose in a hundred year old toilet."

Chuck rolled his eyes. "Fine."

He walked over to examine the toilet. The bottom was a large spherical stone, with the top half removed and the inside hollowed out. The back rest was rectangular construct of stones held together by the same polypoxy as the yurt's walls. It didn't appear as if the top of the back rest was removable. Chuck got down on his knees to scan the underside and rear of the toilet. He found nothing of interest. He stood up and stepped back.

"Short of breaking it apart with a pickax, I'm out of ideas."

"Why does it have a disbursement handle?" mused Bhanakhana, pointing at the oblong length of rock protruding from the back rest.

"Huh?" said Jopp.

"There is no plumbing system here. It is merely a hollow rock. Yet there is a handle for dispersing the waste."

"Oh, you mean flushing," said Chuck.

"Valid point, Sage Bhindo."

Bhanakhana crouched down close to inspect the handle. After a few seconds, he shrugged to himself, gripped the handle and with minimal effort, snapped it clean off.

"Nice use of the scientific method there, B"

Bhanakhana ignored him and as he turned the dull rock over in his hands, he noticed flecks of gray pigment chipping off. He started scratching at the rock, causing larger bits of paint to flake off. Then, actual pieces of the rock began crumbling to dust, as if they were made from old plaster. Phyos handed him a sterilizing cloth and Bhanakhana wiped away that last of the gray. He was left holding a curiously shaped object. It reminded Chuck of a feather quill sculpted out of pink steel.

"Well, okay then," said Phyos.

"What is it, Prof?" asked Jopp.

"A key, I guess."

"Key to what?"

"How the phoob should I know?"

"Isn't it literally your job to know?"

Phyos pulled out the concealer box and examined the quill-shaped key. "Yeah, that should fit. Drop it in."

Bhanakhana placed the metal object neatly in the box.

"If you didn't know about the key, what were you originally going to smuggle out?" asked Chuck.

"All the pictures we took."

"But they're, like, digital…"

"Ah yes," realization dawned on Bhanakhana. "The scans."

Phyos explained, "Most of the Barge exhibits are open viewing. Meaning you're free to take pictures, video, whatever and keep it for yourself or even post it to the GIG. But some exhibits are Sight Only. Before leaving, we'll have to submit our data bracelets to a scan to make sure no unapproved images or information is leaving with us. I was going to store all the photos we took on a sliver-chip, wipe them from the bracelets. The box is for the sliver-chip."

"Oh... okay."

"Speaking of, let's take care of that and blow this Friznitz stand."

It was in that moment that emergency alarms began to wail throughout the Barge.

WORD SECTION 0025

Phyos, Bhanakhana, Chuck, and Jopp rushed back the way they'd come. Emergency lights flashed and the sirens continued to scream their disconcerting song.

"We're phoobed... we're so phoobed," grumbled Jopp.

"How will I ever explain this to the scientific ethics review board," moaned Bhanakhana.

"Hey, if we go back to jail, this time can we *not* get in a fight with Soreshi thugs?" said Chuck.

"You making jokes right now, Earth Ape?!"

"Who's making jokes? You ever been almost-eaten by a huge snake-man? It's not fun."

"Hush up, all of you," ordered Phyos, "These alarms aren't for us. If they knew we were back here, they'd have just surprised us with a security detail. Something else is going down."

They heard a muffled, distant bang and felt the walls shudder as if from impact.

"Yep, something is going down."

They rounded the corner and Phyos skidded to a stop. The others barely avoided toppling into her.

"That is... not good."

They followed her eyes and saw the old basin with the granite eggs. Jopp's drink cup lay on the floor in a small puddle. But what really drew their attention was the eggs, specifically the seven of them that had been shattered open. Or perhaps, a better term would have been *hatched*.

"So not good."

"What's the big deal?" asked Jopp.

"Your littering just unleashed one of history's deadliest beasts."

"They should really put up a sign or something."

Bhanakhana, Phyos, and Chuck all glared at him as they pointed in unison to the sign, the one that read:

Under no circumstances should the Igg'rreh Eggs be exposed to moisture of any kind.

Seriously.

We mean it.

"Oh, that sign. I mean, if these things are so dangerous they should be locked away."

"Like in a secure, off-limits sector of the Barge? Like the one we broke into?"

"Fine! But seriously, what's the big deal? They just hatched. They're babies."

"The Igg'rreh attains full maturity within nineteen minutes of birth," stated Bhanakhana.

"Uh, damn... I'm sorry, guys. Guess we need to keep our eyes peeled. What do these things look like anyway?"

"Like that," said Phyos.

They all turned in time to see a dark form drop from the ceiling a short way down the hall. It let out a low, gurgling growl and stalked forward. Bhanakhana and Phyos knew what to expect, yet they gasped right along with Chuck and Jopp as the creature emerged from the shadows. It moved like a gorilla: walking on two hind legs while leaning forward on two thick, leathery arms. A second pair of long bent arms, resembling those of a praying mantis, hung from the sides of its torso. A large curved horn sprouted from each of its muscular shoulders. Its head looked like that of a great white shark's, complete with the dorsal fin, beady eyes, and massive mouth full of sharp teeth. The creature's skin was pure white with a marbling of jet black veins. It let out another, more eager sounding growl.

"Well, it's been *not terrible* knowing you all," said Jopp, "I'm not going to say it's been *great*, you know, because of the whole dying a painful death in the belly of a monster thing."

"Prepare to run." Bhanakhana pulled an ancient ornamental axe off a nearby display. After a couple test swings, the muscle-bound Dronla cracked his neck and took a deep breath.

"B," said Chuck, "This isn't a pair of loud-mouthed drunks making trouble at the bar, or even some pirate thug... that's a fucking *monster*."

"I am keenly aware of what it is, Chuck. Someone needs to draw it away, so the others can escape. I am best suited for this. Rest assured, I too will run when given the chance. I am not looking for a fight to the death with some feral beast." Bhanakhana glanced at Phyos. "Do you take issue with this, Sage Phyos?"

She shook her head while reaching out to place a hand on his arm. "Thank you."

"Oh, knock off the melodrama," said Jopp, "You're not throwing yourself at that thing. And I'm not letting you get away from me that easily, Big Red. We'll think of something else."

The Igg'rreh reared up on its legs, stretched its two arms outward, flexing knotted cords of muscle. They could now see that each mantis arm ended with a wicked looking claw. The creature roared, revealing three rows of razor teeth, and charged forward.

"Just run!" bellowed Bhanakhana as he rushed the monster. Just before they could collide, Bhanakhana pivoted to the side slashing at the beast, scoring a cut across its left arm. Black blood oozed from the wound. The Igg'rreh roared in anger and wheeled toward Bhanakhana who was backing toward a side corridor. The beast crouched low, growled, and charged. Bhanakhana turned on his heel and sprinted down the corridor with the Igg'rreh in hot pursuit.

"Go!" ordered Phyos.

The three of them rushed down the hall, around a few bends, and exited the closed-off section. It took all of two seconds for them to realize that something was very wrong. Emergency lights flashed, sirens wailed, distressed voices echoed off the walls, a thin trickle of smoke was leaking from a ceiling vent.

"Could this all be from the Igg'rrehs?" asked Chuck.

"Don't know," said Phyos, "Let's focus on getting to the ship."

"No," said Chuck, "We need to find weapons or security or something... and go back for Bhanakhana."

Jopp huffed, "Damnit... yeah. We can't leave him. I can't fucking believe I'm volunteering to go *toward* the Igg'rreh."

"Well, of course we are," said Phyos, "I know a shortcut to the hangar and our ship has a minor personal defense arsenal."

"Because that's totally normal for a *Mobile Laboratory*," quipped Jopp.

"Okay, wise-ass, no gun for you. You get to hunt the terrifying deadly monster with a spoon."

Phyos lead them down another corridor, through a side hatch and out onto a catwalk that extended across a room so cavernous they couldn't see its bottom. Chuck looked down and a rush of air swept across his face, bringing tears to his eyes. He felt a hand grab his arm and saw it was Jopp.

"Don't look down, dude. You know better."

Across the open expanse, the wall running parallel to the catwalk was lined with large windows, showcasing different exhibit halls. A blur of motion drew Chuck's eyes. He poked Jopp and said, "Look!"

They saw a squad of Barge security personnel engaged in battle with an Igg'rreh. The Igg'rreh had impaled one guard against the wall with its left mantis claw, and a second guard pinned to the floor with its powerful left arm. Using its right claw and right arm, the beast hoisted a third guard up in the air and toward its open jaws. Chuck looked away feeling nauseous as the Igg'rreh bit down. Jopp tugged him along. Three windows later, Chuck stopped again and shouted, "Holy shit! What is that?"

"Dude," Jopp said, "I know! It's messed up, but I don't really need to watch another monster feeding frenzy."

"I actually agree with Jeep," said Phyos.

"Seriously! Look!"

Phyos and Jopp turned to see what the big deal was. They saw another cadre of Barge security engaged in combat, however they weren't fighting another Igg'rreh. Their opponents were humanoid, Venovans to be specific, as evidenced by the blue faces. They wore gold helmets that reminded Chuck of ancient Roman legionnaires, along with gold and white armor. The Venovans wielded weapons that looked like medieval poleaxes. Both the armor and the weapons seemed more ceremonial than functional. All three of their mouths fell open when one of the Venovans struck the floor with his poleaxe and a burst of orange lightning exploded outward from the axe head, striking down two security guards.

"Oh... shit," gasped Chuck.

"What the fucking fuck is going on?!" shouted Jopp, "Prof! Tell me what we just saw is fake and they're just filming another movie here or something."

The myriad of green shades had drained from Phyos' jigsaw patterned face.

"I..." she started, "I thought they were a myth. It was just too hokey to believe..."

"*Who* was a myth?" said Chuck.

"I'll, I'll explain later. We need to rescue Sage Bhindo and get off this vessel, now more than ever."

Phyos began to run forward at a speed neither Chuck nor Jopp would've guessed her capable of. They reached the opposite end of the catwalk and hopped through the hatch into a dimly lit corridor.

"The hangar isn't far," said Phyos.

Lights flickered and many winked out completely. It looked as if the corridors ahead had gone almost completely dark. They rounded a bend in the hall, stopping short as they found themselves suddenly looking down the business ends of two ornamental poleaxes. The pair of Venovans holding these weapons glared at them with cheerful malice.

"Don't move," commanded one of the soldiers.

They didn't move.

"Gents, I'm just an educator taking two of my prize students on a field trip. We'd be happy to get out of yo-"

"Silence," snapped the other one.

The first one moved his hand up to his face and spoke, "Blessings, Shepherd Dac'eth. This is Faithful Unit Twelve. We've acquired Quarries One, Three, and Four." He gave a quick glance left and right, "Quarry Two is unaccounted for. I am pinging our location now."

"*What'd he call us?*" whispered Chuck

"*Kwaree. It means best-friend-who-I'm-definitely-not-going-to-murder,*" replied Jopp

"Really?"

"No!"

"Be quiet, Heretic," barked the second soldier, "Or I shall remove whatever organ your wretched physiology manipulates into the slur of noises you call speech."

Chuck and Jopp looked at each other and said in unison, "Huh?"

"Hush up or he'll cut out your tongue," said Phyos.

Chuck drew his fingers across his mouth like closing a zipper and gave the angry, armored Venovan man a thumbs up.

"What manner of lewd, sacrilegious gesture is that?"

"Oh, c'mon!" said Chuck, "You guys don't know *thumbs up*?"

"Enough of this! Our divine mandate only requires Quarries One and Two be kept alive."

He raised his poleaxe to strike.

Chuck winced.

Phyos shouted.

Two large, red hands emerged from the shadows behind the soldiers, gripped the sides of their helmets, and slammed their heads together. The Venovans collapsed to the ground unconscious. The hulking crimson frame of Bhanakhana stood over the comatose pair. His shirt was torn, and he had a number cuts and scratches on his arms, his torso, and one above his right eye.

"B!" Chuck couldn't help himself from lunging forward and wrapping, or at least *attempting* to wrap his arms around the muscular Dronla. Bhanakhana smiled as he returned the hug.

"What happened to your new friend with all the pointy bits?" asked Phyos.

"Unfortunately, I had no choice but to engage in the proverbial fight to the death."

"You killed an Igg'rreh on your own?! Dude, that is legendary!" crowed Jopp.

"Don't ever do anything like that again," said a parental sounding Chuck.

"Do not worry," said Bhanakhana, "I believe I am sold out on my supply of heroic acts for the foreseeable future. I do not know the story with these intriguingly adorned gentlemen," he gestured at the two

Venovans, "however my instincts are telling me we should flee with all due haste."

"Good phoobing instincts," said Phyos.

They continued along the curving hallway for another minute, passing into the next sector, where the lights had apparently not been damaged. The corridor expanded into a wide long, hall. The wall at the opposite end had a seam running diagonally across its length.

"There's the back door to the hangar," said Phyos.

They were just thirty or so meters away when a mechanical hissing sound made them freeze. The seam in the wall began to open, as the two halves slid apart. Heavy clouds of coolant mist rolled through the opening. And standing there in the center of the ever-widening doorway, was a Venovan woman. She wore no armor, just black pants, black boots, and a black shirt. The one feature of note being her shirt only had a sleeve over the left arm. Her right arm was bare, revealing lean, wiry muscle under navy blue skin. Her blonde hair was woven into tight rows along the sides of her head, and all of it was pulled back into a thick braid. She stared at them with curious, yet calculating eyes. Eyes that glowed with an unnatural orange hue.

"*Damn, she's jetty, I'm going in,*" Jopp whispered under his breath before calling out to her, "Hey, Girl, there's some dangerous shit going down. You should hang with us. Being with us is the safest place on the Barge right now. Just ask him," he nodded toward Bhanakhana, "I saved him from a ravenous Igg'rreh earlier."

If eye rolling was audible, the sound from Bhanakhana, Phyos, and Chuck's facial expression would've been deafening.

The Venovan woman ignored him and said, "Professor Phyos, I've been a fan of your work for quite some time and am glad to finally be meeting you. My name is Serru Dac'eth. Now please come with me and none of you will be harmed."

Her tone sounded less like a threat and more like a simple observation.

"Appreciate the offer, Dear. But I think we'll stick to ourselves. Have a nice war, or whatever it is you've going on here."

Serru gave a slight shake of her head. "I'm afraid you don't have much a choice. Come with me willingly, or I will force you... which, as I mentioned, will hurt."

Again, no malice in her speech.

Phyos glanced at Bhanakhana, "Sage Bhindo, I hate to impose on you further..."

Jopp patted him on the back. "Looks like you're up again, Big Red."

Bhanakhana sighed and approached Serru. She watched him come closer with curious amusement. She looked up at the muscle bound Dronla, standing a foot taller and weighing at least a hundred pounds more, and asked, "Are you sure this is the path you want to take?"

"Madam," said Bhanakhana, "Please step aside. I do not wish to-"

Serru punched Bhanakhana in the stomach. To the surprise of Chuck, Jopp, Phyos, and most of all Bhanakhana, he staggered backward and doubled over with a grunt.

"I feel like if I did that, my hand would've broken against B's abs," said Chuck.

"Damn," said Jopp.

When Bhanakhana straightened back up with a resolute grimace.

"Very well. Fisticuffs it shall be."

Bhanakhana moved in with a jab-hook combo. Serru leaned to avoid the first punch, ducked to avoid the second, stepped to the right and delivered a quick blow to Bhanakhana's side. He grunted. The others could see the pain etched across his face. He turned left, bringing his thick right arm around in a haymaker. As Serru hopped back to avoid it, Bhanakhana lunged forward with his other hand. He'd been expecting her to dodge his feinted punch, and had planned accordingly. His outstretched left hand caught the woman around her neck.

"Enough!" He bellowed, "*Please* do not make me kill you!"

Serru's expression was serene. The orange of her irises intensified and grew until the light filled her eyes. She reached up and gripped the large red hand currently holding her neck. Bhanakhana could not believe what he was seeing as, despite all his considerable strength, she began to pry open his fingers. He strained against her, beads of sweat forming on his brow, but his hand continued to move away from her neck.

"Not... possible," he breathed.

"All things are possible," she replied before striking the side of his head with her palm. Bhanakhana's mind went fuzzy.

"*Shepherd...*" breathed Phyos under her breath.

Serru grabbed Bhanakhana by the arm and, as if he weighed no more than a small child, hurled him through the hangar door. He hit the floor, skidded for a few feet, and went limp.

Serru turned to the others and asked, "Now will you surrender? Oh... where did the odd one go?"

Jopp and Phyos glanced around and saw that Chuck was gone.

"Chuck?"

"RUN!" screamed a familiar voice from behind them. They glanced back to see Chuck come hauling around the bend, carrying one of the ornamental long-axes from the Venovan soldiers.

"What are you doing?"

"WENT BACK FOR A WEAPON TO HELP BHANAKHANA BUT THAT DOESN'T MATTER WE NEED TO RUN!"

Chuck whipped past Jopp and Phyos, sprinting for the hangar door. They heard a roar echo off the walls, and saw an Igg'rreh round the corner at a full gallop.

"Shit," said Jopp and Phyos in unison and they took off after Chuck.

As Chuck neared Serru, he lashed out with a wild strike. She caught the weapon mid-swing, wrenching it from Chuck's grip. This caused him to stumble, trip, and then fall to the floor. Serru turned back just as Jopp, Phyos, and the hot-on-their-heels Igg'rreh approached. The monster roared again and leapt into the air. Jopp grabbed Phyos by the sleeve and hollered, "Get low!"

The two of them dove for the hangar doorway. Serru had no choice but to focus on the mass of sharp, pointy, white death falling toward her. She raised the pole-axe to a defensive position just in time to block the worst of it.

Jopp scrambled to his feet and lunged for the door controls. The two metal panels slid closed, sealing off the hangar interior from the flailing claws and bursts of orange electricity wreaking havoc in the hallway.

Chuck and Phyos crouched next to Bhanakhana who was sitting up, massaging his throbbing head.

"You good to move, Big Red?" Jopp asked.

"I should be able to, yes."

"Then let's make like my last three debt payments and bounce."

It took all three of them to help pull Bhanakhana to his feet. They staggered through the hangar in search of Phyos' ship, noticing it had gotten a tad more crowded than when they'd first arrived. There was a line of bone-white tactical fighters with gold trim, presumably belonging to the armored Venovans. Across from that sat a pair of those shuttle ships the Church of Rhonac used to ferry people through anomalies. They could see the gleam of the Cube ship parked just beyond.

"There he is," said Jopp, "Let's fly."

"Halt!" shouted an authoritarian voice.

They all froze. Chuck dared a glance. A cadre of six Venovan soldiers marched toward them.

"Why is everyone after us?" moaned Jopp.

"Actually, Old Boy, I believe they came here in pursuit of me."

The tall purple frame of Phitz Phitz stepped out from behind a nearby ship, wearing a bathrobe, slippers, and wielding a triple-barreled pumpshot. He leveled it at the Venovans, who all stopped marching in unison. They readied their golden pole axes. One of them called out, "Proprietor, stand down."

Phitz flipped off his weapon's safety, causing it to whir with electric life. "Afraid I can't do that, Chaps."

"You alone cannot hope to defeat us."

"Fair point," conceded Phitz. He then called out, "Chonsee!"

Chonsee the lumbering rock man appeared from his hiding spot behind the Venovans, carrying a contraption that resembled a Gatling gun. Without a word, as per usual, he pulled the trigger, and a burst of light exploded from the muzzle. The next thing any of them knew, a large net made of pulsing green energy enveloped the soldiers, paralyzing them in place. Qira and Idu, the two Tahl women, hopped out from behind another ship and rushed toward the immobilized cadre, each wielding a pair of pistols.

"What'd he just do?" asked Chuck.

Phitz smiled. "We call it the Time-Out Cannon. Until we deactivate the signal to the energy net, they won't so much as be able to wiggle their fingers. Comes in quite handy when dealing with unruly rabbles of schoolchildren that visit for field trips."

"Nice work, Phitzy," said Phyos, "I hate to leave you in this mess, but I really think we should be going."

"I've encountered worse than this uncouth lot. You should be on your way. I'll send you a communiqué once the matter is resolved."

They'd taken just a few steps toward their ship when Phitz called out, "And Professor Phyos?"

They turned back to see a wry smile on his face.

"I do hope whatever you've borrowed from my collection is exceedingly helpful in your endeavors. And I expect the Barge to have exclusive display rights on whatever amazing discoveries you will inevitably turn up." He nodded toward their ship. "Off you go then."

WORD SECTION 0026

Jopp rocketed the Cube ship through the electro-stasis field separating the hangar from the extraplanetary ocean of water outside. He got them clear of the Barge and hollered, "What the fucking fuck just happened back there?"

"Uh, yeah," added Chuck, "I'm really confused, kind of terrified... and a little bit hungry. I'm going to go check on Bhanakhana in the med bay and then get a snack."

Once he'd left, Jopp shot Phyos a scrutinizing stare. "Time to fill in the details, Prof. Don't even try to dungmouth me. You might have Big Red all enamored with this crap. And Chuck gets enamored with pretty much everything. But me? I'm currently in favor of heading right back home and being done with all this. Whatever you got us into isn't worth me or my friends dying."

Phyos canted her head with a slight grin. "So you do care about something other than money and yourself. I'm afraid I don't know as much as you might think... you know the Church of Rhonac?"

"The shuttle thumpers."

"Heh, right. There's a fanatical faction called the Adjacent, or something like that. Anyway they believe Venovans are descended from the Ak'akei and that on Hirth-Ak'alei is a gateway that will allow their god to come to our dimension and wipe away the non-believers."

"How do you know that?"

"Because early on, when I was making a name for myself as a expert in Ak'alei studies, the Advocates approached me. Offered to bankroll my research. Course it would've meant they got full control over what happened to any significant findings, so of course, I told them to kick biscuits."

Chuck returned holding three bottles of their emergency ale. He passed them out and dropped into his seat.

"Bhanakhana's resting. What're we talking about?"

"Prof was explaining just how deep she's dunked us in the shit."

"Good one," she said, "I'm stealing it."

"Take it. I got a million of 'em."

"That, I don't doubt."

Jopp glanced at Chuck, "Apparently those Venovans playing dress up are part of some whack job cult."

"What about that lady? With the orange eyes..."

"Really?" said Jopp, "That's your go-to descriptor for her? Not the lady who tossed 120 kilos of muscle, a.k.a. Bhanakhana, around like a toy? Because *that's* what caught my attention."

"I'm not exactly sure," Phyos started.

"Dowfa dung," spat Jopp, "Quit dancing around it. I saw recognition on your face back there."

Phyos sighed, "After the Adhesives tried to buy me, I did a little research into them. I didn't find much in the way of reputable information. And what I did find seemed like mythical nonsense, only..."

"Only we just witnessed that mythical nonsense, didn't we?" said Chuck.

"They called them Shepherds," said Phyos, "Chosen warriors in god's army. Blessed with abilities. They were tasked with cleansing the enemies of the faith."

"And by cleansing, you mean killing."

"Fucking sweet," snarked Jopp, "I've always dreamed of having my name on the hit list of a magical murder monk."

"They're not magic. Magic's not real."

"I think magic is just science we haven't figured out yet," said Chuck.

Phyos and Jopp looked at him with blank stares.

"As endearing as I find your moments of childlike whimsy, this isn't really the time."

"Yeah, dude, quit being such a- *ah shit*!"

He quickly decelerated the ship, the seat straps holding himself and Phyos in place. Chuck toppled forward with a shout, spilling his drink over himself. He hopped back up, started wiping beer off, realized the futility of it, and then stared up at the panoramic view screen with wide eyes.

"Uh, guys? Why's there a building floating in the middle of a space ocean?"

The thing looming out in front of them resembled a massive gothic cathedral built on top of a baseball field sized flying saucer.

"Fuck me til Finsday, a *Sanctuary*."

"A what now?" said Jopp.

"Part time mobile temple, part time warship. I'd suggest evasive maneuvers, Juep."

"I save our asses here, and you better start getting my name right."

Jopp wheeled them around and punched the accelerator. After a few seconds, he checked the rear view and saw that the Sanctuary had failed to shrink in the distance. In fact, it seemed to be getting closer.

"Aaaaand they're chasing us. Awesome."

The console started whining.

"And they're shooting at us too. Even more awesome."

Jopp pulled them left, narrowly avoiding the torpedo as it whirred by.

"Open to ideas, folks," he called out.

Chuck pointed. "There! Fly that way!"

Phyos and Jopp peered at the area of dark water where Chuck had indicated. They saw a pale turquoise line slithering through the water.

"You want us to fly toward the taharo? Deary, remember what I said about not getting too close?"

"Exactly," said Chuck.

"What- oh! Oh, I see," Phyos poked Jopp, "Do what he says."

"Have you two fried your circuits? I still remember the video from class on what happens when you piss of a taharo. You *want* that?"

"Yes," said Phyos, "Fly as close as you can without getting us killed. Shouldn't be too hard for such a skilled pilot."

Jopp gritted his teeth, shot her a sidelong glance, and altered their course toward the taharo. In the rear view, he saw the Sanctuary continuing to follow. The warning alarms sounded again. Jopp barrel rolled to avoid another torpedo. It streaked by, continued on, and missed the taharo by a considerable distance. However the ripples in the water from the sun-sonic projectile caught the creature's attention. It lazily curled around to the right, turning it's gigantic adorable face back toward them. It's expression perked up with curiosity and it tilted its head to the side.

As they got closer, the taharo's expression began to morph from curiosity to trepidation. When they got even closer still, the look of trepidation became mild aggression. Its eyes darkened and its lip curled up in a snarl. The Sanctuary kept coming, continuing to close the gap.

They pulled to within a few hundred meters of the creature and the mild aggression turned into full blown hostility. The taharo reared up stretching its full length into a vertical line.

"Here we go!" hollered Jopp.

The thirteen pairs of horns along the taharo's underbelly grew outward, extending until they became thirteen pairs of elongated pincers. A seam appeared, running the length of the taharo's long stomach.

"Um, what is-" Chuck started to say.

The taharo's stomach seam split open revealing rows of teeth, and a gaping, six hundred foot long maw. Three barbed tongues emerged from different points along the mouth.

"Ah! Fuck! What the fucking fuck?!" screamed Chuck.

"Father-phoobing kotch rot! That is intense!" exclaimed Phyos.

"Yep, just like the video from Zoology class. One of those images that burns into your brain," said Jopp.

"Time to earn your pay," Phyos said to Jopp.

He tightened his grip on the controls and continued to cut a path straight toward the behemoth. The alarms sprang to life once again.

"Now!" Jopp shouted to himself.

He yanked the controls, sending them careening in a left-downward spiral, narrowly avoiding the thrashing mandibles at the creature's tail-end. However, right as Jopp made his maneuver, the torpedo exploded with an electrical burst. The ship shuddered and the lights blinked out for half a second. Chuck noticed some minor scorching along the taharo's hide. The creature made no attempt to go after them. It had found a new, more threatening adversary to focus on.

As they continued to flee, the rear view allowed them to watch the battle unfold. The Sanctuary lobbed projectiles and activated defensive fields, but it did little to stop the taharo from draping itself over the floating citadel. The pincers held the Sanctuary in place while the rows of teeth chewed through the exterior plating.

Chuck's mouth hung open with stunned awe as the giant space caterpillar puppy dog monstrosity ate the church-shaped spaceship.

"It's going to be hard to top that one in the Weirdest Fucking Things I've Ever Seen category."

"I never thought I'd long for the days of being stranded in a Gorthan desert," grumbled Jopp, "Now let's see the quickest way out of here… here we go…"

He attempted to steer. The Cube ship failed to change course. There didn't appear to be any major damage, yet nothing Jopp tried seemed to have any effect. He banged on the controls, cursed at the computer, banged the controls again, threatened to pour his beer over the navigation system's intelligence hard drives. Shockingly, none of that helped.

"What the dung-nuggets?! It's like the entire system shorted out. I need to reboot the central core."

"Then why does it feel like we're going faster than a minute ago?" asked Chuck.

"Shit… there's like a current or something."

"It's the Maelstrom," said Phyos.

"Like a swirly water vortex thing?" said Chuck.

"There's an anomaly at the heart of the Nautun ocean. An anomaly doesn't technically have a gravitational pull, yet it's still empty space.

Water by its nature, wants to fill empty space. But it doesn't have the speed to actually pass through the anomaly. So it kind of just whirls and whirls around it until the momentum creates something of a," she shot Chuck a pleasant grin, "*swirly water vortex thing.*"

"Oh, that's kind of cool."

"Cool? If I can't get full power restored, we might not be able to break free of the current."

"We don't want to break free of the current," said Phyos.

Jopp wheeled toward her, "Say what now?"

"The anomaly at the center of the vortex. I want you to fly through it."

"What the fuck are you talking about? You expect," Jopp's console started flashing, "Hey! The shorted systems are coming back on."

"How's the sub-light drive?"

"Looks okay."

"Great. Here's the trajectory."

Phyos swiped her finger across her screen toward Jopp, causing a digital note to appear in his own screen.

"You... are insane."

"Am I? What happens if you manage to break free of the current, hmmm? We'll be in the middle of a massive open ocean in a less than fully functioning ship in the vicinity of a furious taharo and a gaggle of well armed cultists looking to offer your round yellow ass up to their god."

Chuck saw the Maelstrom come into view ahead of them. The ship's speed began to increase as they entered the outer rim of the twisting vortex. At this point, he'd flown through so many routine anomaly jumps the experience had lost most of its luster. But this one, this empty black hole of universe surrounded by a sphere of raging swirling water; Chuck felt a twinge of that old anxious wonder surge through him.

"Uh, guys?" He pointed toward the screen.

Phyos grabbed Jopp's shoulder. "Hit the jump at that trajectory. I promise you it'll take us somewhere a tuku-load safer than here."

"You know how hard it's going to be hitting the right angle while fighting the current at sub-light speed?!"

"Good thing I hired myself such a great pilot."

"You know I'm full of dowfa goosh, right? I'm an Academy dropout turned delivery hauler turned glorified chauffeur. I'm... I'm..."

"...the only person I'd want in that seat. You can do this, *Jopp*."

Jopp stared at her for a moment, then closed his eyes and took a deep breath. He then gripped the flight controls and glared ahead with iron resolve.

The massive black spot drew closer. Their speed quickened. They no longer moved directly toward the anomaly, but rather at a curved angle as the vortex pulled them into a corkscrew trajectory. Jopp killed the engines.

"What are you doing?" asked Chuck.

"No point right now. We'd just be putting unnecessary strain on the thrusters. I need them at full strength."

A sly grin tugged at the edges of Phyos' mouth. They sat in awkward silence as the ship drifted along, the Maelstrom pulling them ever closer in tighter and tighter circles. Jopp punched Phyos' trajectory coordinates into the Navi-system. The anomaly's darkness expanded, filling more and more of the view screen. The Navi-system dinged with an analysis of the proposed flight path.

Jopp chuckled.

Phyos' sly grin slipped away.

"What's so funny?" she asked.

Jopp winked at her. "Just pilot stuff, Prof. You two should buckle up."

The engines roared to life, increasing the speed of their spiraling path around the anomaly. Jopp's hands rested lightly on the dual throttles in a manner that somehow evoked both a focused intensity and serene calm simultaneously. He let out a low breath and said, "Y'all going to owe me some tops drinks for this one."

He punched the accelerator and yanked hard on the throttles. The Cube ship exploded forward. Chuck and Phyos let out shrieks of terrified surprise. Phyos' scream was an unintelligible "Waaaaaaaaaaaaaaaaa!" While Chuck's was something of an elongated version of "Fuuuuuuuuuuuuuuuuuuuuuuuuck!"

It wasn't so much the sudden acceleration. Both of them had flown enough to get used to typical sensations like that. It was the fact that this sudden acceleration came while the ship entered into a dizzying corkscrew, spiraling the opposite direction of the watery vortex surrounding them. As they reached sub-light speed, Jopp's voice joined the shrieking chorus with a joyous, "Woooooooooooooooooooooooo!"

The Cube ship disappeared into the black emptiness.

WORD SECTION 0027

The Cube ship reappeared from within a different black emptiness situated approximately 3,616 light years away from the Maelstrom. It streaked across the star-pocked interstellar landscape for a few dozen miles as Jopp pulled them out of the corkscrew and applied the brakes, all the while his passengers continuing to scream and hurl curses.

"Alright! Alright!" he shouted as the ship slowed to a lazy drift. "Would you two shut the phoob up already?"

Chuck and Phyos replaced their loud screams with heavy breathing and furious glares at the pilot. Jopp gave Chuck a sympathetic smile.

"Sorry for freaking you out, Buddy." He turned to Phyos with a smug grin and said, "To *you*, I'm not sorry. And you can wipe that frown right of your lovely, distinguished, green face. As the person who roped us into this extended cross-galactic near-death experience, you don't get to be mad. You should be smiling like a kid eating an entire slab of frosted jubla because," he forcefully tapped the navi-screen, "I fucking *nailed* that jump."

Phyos opened her mouth to retort, but her eyes caught the readout from the control panel. She blinked, leaned in closer, and said, "Well fling my feces, you actually did it."

"Jopp," said Chuck, "that was fucking righteous. I didn't know you could fly like that."

"Okay, okay. Don't act *too* shocked. It's insulting."

Phyos swiped her fingers across the control panel, tapped a few icons, and pulled up the image of a planet that was mostly green, but with sizable patches of crimson and gold. The caption beneath it read: *Gjenlu, fifth planet of the Alizlos Solar System.*

"Kind of looks like a Christmas ornament," mused Chuck.

"A what, dear?" asked Phyos.

"Is that the Earth holiday you told me about? The one where the creepy old guy breaks into your houses to eat your snacks?"

"I mean, sort of... there's also like a religious aspect to it... and gifts, lots of gifts..."

"Fascinating," said Phyos, "Well, don't fret. When we're on Gjenlu, no creepy fellow is gonna steal your treats."

"Who the fuck said we're going there?" scoffed Jopp, "Look, Prof, I went for the anomaly jump 'cause as you stated, it was our best chance of avoiding an unpleasant death. I never said we'd continue on with this insanity. I'm out. And I think I can safely say the Earth Ape and Big Red are also out."

"As a matter of fact, I am still very much *in*."

Three heads spun around toward the source of the voice. Bhanakhana stood tall in the control room doorway. A large open robe was draped over his shoulders. He wore no shirt underneath, and his torso was wrapped in sani-seal healing bandages.

"Heeeeey," said Chuck, "How you doing?"

"This may shock you, but I have felt better." Bhanakhana let out the tiniest of chuckles. He walked toward his chair, a slight wince of pain with every other step.

"You can't be serious, Red," said Jopp, "C'mon, this is not our problem. We need to bail."

"I seem to remember another time when another dangerous set of circumstances fell into my proverbial lap. I believe that was also *not my problem*." Bhanakhana eased himself into his chair with a grimace. "Perhaps I should have left you and Chuck to your fates back when we all first became acquainted?"

"That was totally different! We were running from psychos trying to kill us and we didn't even know *why* they were trying to kill us!" Jopp pointed at Phyos, "She wants to intentionally go down the path right *toward* the psychos trying to kill us."

Chuck raised his hand. "To be fair to Professor Phyos, the psychos are technically, like, way behind us on this imaginary path..."

Jopp wagged his finger at Chuck. "You know what the fuck I meant."

"Jopp," sighed Bhanakhana, "Finding *Hirth-Ak'alei,* the home world of the earliest interplanetary civilization, would be the most significant discovery of the past century. Additionally, we now know there is a malevolent force also searching for the same planet. And we can most likely assume their intentions lean toward the nefarious. As you are aware, I am not the sort to stand aside in such scenarios. For those reasons, I am going to see this through. You and Chuck are welcome to depart once we reach Gjenlu."

"I'm still in, too," said Chuck.

"What is wrong with you?" barked Jopp, "You know Rohi would kick the shit out of you if she knew you were volunteering for this."

"I'm paying him, so he's not really a volunteer," offered Phyos. She felt a heavy hand on her shoulder and glanced back at Bhanakhana who whispered, "*Not helping.*"

"You've got a good point," Chuck replied to Jopp, "And it actually gives me an idea! I should comm her. Tell her what's going on. Why not loop the U.L.E. in here? They could get those cult people off our asses! Maybe we could even get some kind of escort or something."

* *four minutes later* *

Chuck returned to the bridge with a pale expression.

"So, how'd that call go, bud?" asked Jopp.

"When I told her about it she said, *I already know. Myself and some reinforcements are coming your way. Don't get yourself killed or I will spend the rest of my life searching for some way of resurrecting you just so I can kick the ever-loving shit out of you. Also, I love you. Bye.*"

"I like her," said Phyos.

"Indeed," added Bhanakhana, "Rohi is an exceptional person and a good friend."

"Not to mention way out of orbit for the Earth Ape," laughed Jopp.

"I don't know," counter Phyos. She gave Chuck an appraising once over. "Once you get over the oddness of him being an actual Earth man... if I had been a few decades younger when we met, I might've tossed him around the bedroom a time or two." She gave Chuck a playful wink.

Chuck's pale expression flushed red as he dropped into his seat.

"Now!" Phyos clapped her hands, "We've got about a standard day and a half until we reach Gjenlu. I know we're all tired, but we've got work to do. We need to assemble all the pictures we took into a new notebook and start deciphering it. Now, Jopp, the public transport options on Gjenlu are a bit spotty, but if you could just fly us there, you should be able to find a ride off-world without too much trouble. Worst case scenario, you spend a few days killing time in a couple of shady dive bars. That is... if you're still *out?*"

Jopp looked from her, to Bhanakhana, to Chuck, then back to her. He let out an exasperated sigh and said, "Fuck. I'm in. Someone's gotta be the voice of reason. Besides, if you all die, how am I supposed to get paid."

"A touching sentiment," quipped Bhanakhana with his obligatory eye roll.

"Aw, we love you too, buddy," said Chuck.

"Shut it," Jopp grumbled as he entered their new trajectory into the navi-screen.

"Forward, friends! Let us discover the undiscovered!" Phyos pointed out at the nothing in particular. She glanced around at the others, who all stared at her with raised eyebrows. "I was just trying it out... did it not work for ya? Okay, I'll think of a different one later."

•　　•　　•

Gjenlu had recently shown up as a tiny dot on their view screen. Bhanakhana, Phyos, and Chuck were flipping through notebooks comprised of the images they'd captured back in Cestoras' yurt.

The bridge doorway slid open, and Jopp shuffled in holding a steaming mug of wahu. He shambled over to his seat a dropped into it with a big yawn.

"Oh man, that sleep was the tops." He noticed three sets of annoyed, bloodshot eyes glaring back at him. "Hey, it's not my fault the route took us through twelve hours worth of wide open space. That's what the auto-fly is for."

He sipped at his wahu, and noticed the newly printed notebooks. "What's up with the old school books? Why not just load the info to your data bracelets or a tablet?"

"Couple of reasons," answered Phyos. "The book that everyone believes to be Cestoras' diary is not entirely useless. There are hints peppered throughout, however it's greatest value is it's a primer for decoding the images he left in his hovel. I already cracked that cipher. So, we just apply that same code to the yurt scribbling, and *swish-swish-thank-you-miss*, we get a crystal clear path right to Hirth-Ak'alei."

Bhanakhana cleared his throat accusingly.

Phyos let her shoulders sink. "Okay okay, admittedly, it's not *crystal* clear. It's more like *dirty bath water* clear. You can see through to the end, but might run into some floating nasty bits along the way... I can see I'm losing you."

Jopp sipped at his wahu and nodded.

Chuck tried to explain, "Here's the basics of what we know, dude. We need to find this previously undiscovered Ak'alei temple."

"We do not know for certain the structure in question held religious value," Bhanakhana interjected.

"It's an ancient building built by a mysterious alien civilization! I'm calling it a temple!" Chuck settled down when he saw the alarmed stares. "Sorry... I'm really tired. So yeah, in this *temple* there's a map that points to a place that Cestoras keeps referring to as the *Doorstep*. And that's where it seems to end."

"Great, tops... you all know none of that answered my question, right?"

"What was it again?" asked Phyos. "We're all a bit loopy from the exhaustion."

"Paper," said Jopp, "Why use paper? From what little I've understood here, it sounds like we've got our hands on some rare and valuable information."

"Technically, it is not paper. It is a synthetic material that embodies the flexibility of cloth while retaining the durability of a plastic-"

"That is so far down on the list of things I need to know, Big Red."

"It's safer this way," said Phyos, "Anything digital can be hacked or decrypted. This way, no one sees these books but us. And even if I wasn't worried about that, our data bracelets aren't going to be too useful."

"Why?"

"It'll be easier to explain once you're on the planet's surface."

"Professor, I think I found it," announced Bhanakhana.

"Found what?" asked Chuck with a pleading stare.

Bhanakhana rolled his eyes. "The *temple*."

"Show me where, Sage Bhindo."

Bhanakhana sent a digital overlay map of Gjenlu's surface to the big screen in front of them all. He zoomed in on a collection of small islands near a large continent in the southern hemisphere.

"There is a line that Cestoras wrote: The path home resides beneath the spicy farts in the bosom of life."

Jopp spit out a small sip of wahu, "What the phoob did you just say?"

"Brilliant as he might have been," said Phyos, "Cestoras had a serious affinity for Wash Closet Humor. But can you blame him?"

"I hear that, sister," added Chuck.

Bhanakhana cleared his throat, drawing their attention back his way. "Yes, well, I believe Cestoras was employing juvenile and crass phrasing as a final layer of coding. Please draw your attention to this particular sector of the planet. As you may or may not know, permanent electrical storms occupy much of the planet's sky. There is a particularly potent cloud system teaming with electricity just north from this collection of islands."

"You think that's the spicy fart!" said Chuck.

"Indeed. His reference to flatulence meaning the clouds and 'spicy' referring to the potent electrical bursts originating from said clouds."

"There isn't much on file regarding the geological history of Gjenlu," Phyos jumped in, "However from what I've been able to dig up, these islands used to be attached to be part of a much bigger continent that has long since sunk below the ocean's surface. Only one bio-botanist ever visited these islands."

She looked at the others.

"And he died. But the notes he was able to upload to his remote server have lead others to speculate this lost continent is where the planet's life originated."

She took control of the display and zoomed in further on one of the islands. Specifically, she zoomed in on a pair of circular mountains sitting right next to each other. They were located in a heavily forested valley. The left-side mountain had a river encircling its base that branched out, cutting a barely curved path to the nearby western coast.

"And those would be the titties, wouldn't they?"

This time, Jopp spit out an entire mouthful of wahu, soaking his lap. "Oh, c'mon! Warn a fella before you say something like that! Now I gotta change my pants."

Phyos pointed at the display. "Right in the middle of one of the planet's thickest, richest jungles. The bosom of life."

Bhanakhana chimed back in, "There is a small town on the Northeast coast of the continent. It appears to be the only location where we can safely land an interstellar vessel."

"So, we land there, journey into the jungle to find the Temple." Chuck finished with a yawn.

"Sweet shiz," said Phyos, mimicking Chuck's yawn. "Alright, the three of us need a nap. Jabb, wake us when we reach the planet's atmosphere. In the meantime, try not to crash."

Phyos, Bhanakhana, and Chuck all stood and headed for the door. As they exited the bridge, Jopp called out, "Wait! Could one of you go grab me some dry pants first?! Seriously, my crotch is wetter than a Noridian swamp! Guys?! I know you can hear me! C'mon... guys?!"

WORD SECTION 0028

Rohi rolled over in bed and looked into Chuck's eyes.

"Hey, Beautiful," he said.

Her mouth started moving in response, but no words came out.

"I can't hear- is everything okay?" said Chuck.

From his parrot's perch in the corner of the room, Jopp took a sip of beer and burped.

Rohi's expression became frustrated. Her mouth kept moving, but Chuck still couldn't hear any words.

"I can't hear you!" he tried to yell.

Jopp let out a squawking laugh. Rohi reached out with one hand and grabbed Chuck's shoulder. With unnatural strength, she hurled him into the air.

Chuck woke up just as he hit the floor.

"Ow! Fuck!"

He sat up and looked around his quarters. No Rohi in his bed. No Jopp sitting on a parrot's perch in the corner.

"What the fuck was that all about, Brain?" Chuck asked his own cranium. He almost toppled over again when the shipped lurched to the left. He realized he'd forgotten to set the bed's immobility field before he dozed off; it was an absolute must for galactic travelers who didn't want to get tossed out of bed mid-sleep. Rookie mistake.

As Chuck stood, the ship lurched one more time and then came to a sudden stop. It was Chuck could do to keep from falling face first back to the floor.

"The hell is he doing up there?"

Chuck sprinted to the bridge and burst in.

"What the hell are you doing up here?!"

Jopp didn't look back but rather pointed up at the view screen. Chuck could make out the flare of spaceship engines far off in the distance. The entire left-hand side of the screen was filled with the greenish glow from Gjenlu.

"Those are Church of Rhonac shuttles out there," explained Jopp. They popped up on the recon meter as soon as we got within Gjenlu's orbit. Didn't want to risk them seeing us, so I whipped out some classic evasion tactics."

Chuck noticed the familiar hum of the Cube ship's engines was absent.

"Where are we, Jopp?"

"Latched on to one of Gjenlu's moons. Luckily for us, the Crazies seem to be heading for the opposite side of the planet. We just need to wait until they're totally out of range before we head down to the surface."

"Good thinking, Jinn," said Phyos as she entered the bridge.

"I feel like you're doing it on purpose now."

"Professor," said Chuck, "Why would the Church be sending their people over that way?"

"Best guess?" Phyos pulled the holographic image of Gjenlu back up to the display. "That continent there is where Cestoras' yurt was originally found. Conventional wisdom stands to reason he'd have planted his home near the more significant Ak'alei sites. But now I'm thinking he left his yurt there to fuck with us all."

"How so?"

"It's funny. I never really thought about it before. There's a random factoid about the discovery of his yurt. The building had some dirt caked around the base of it... the dirt was of a soil not found anywhere on that continent."

She looked up at Chuck with a smile. "How much you want to wager the soil on the continent where we're headed is a perfect match?"

"Sage Phyos, are you suggesting that Cestoras somehow moved his dwelling structure from within a jungle on one continent across an ocean, to the opposite side of the planet?" Bhanakhana appeared in the doorway.

"That's exactly what the hell I'm suggesting, Sage Bhindo."

"Seems improbable."

"That could be the title of our group biography."

•   •   •

The Cube ship came in low over the southeast ocean. It wasn't the most direct route to their destination but the Gjenlu electrical storms had severely limited their options.

"What would happen if we just flew straight through them?" Chuck had asked.

"Our entire ship would short out and plummet from the sky," Jopp had answered.

"And that's bad, right?" Phyos had added.

"Sometimes, I can't tell if you're fucking with me or not."

Jopp piloted the ship up the coastline. The green waves ebbed and flowed beneath them. The lush colors of the jungle whipped by on their left. Ahead of them, they could see a thin, tan spire, wrapped in a leafy copper-colored vine, rising above the tree line.

The density of the vegetation thinned until they found themselves flying over an open swath of beachhead. Phyos pointed to a sand-colored concrete slab near the spire that currently held a short range speedster, an interstellar long hauler, and a rusted, dent-covered Goesch hover yacht. "There's the town landing pad."

Besides the spire and the concrete slab, the only objects of note were twenty large trees, each as wide as a house. These trees were arranged to form parallel semi-circles around the inner half of the slab.

"Did I miss something?" asked Chuck.

"Yeah, I don't see any town, Prof." Jopp added.

"Ah, fizzle tits, I didn't explain that part... well, you'll get it once we land. Just set her down."

Bhanakhana looked confused for a half second, then something dawned on him and he said, "Ah, yes. I recall now..." he glanced at

Jopp and Chuck, "I concur with Sage Phyos. You will *get it* once we land."

The Cube ship settled into an easy landing on the sandy concrete slab. Right as they were about to exit the ship, Phyos stopped and looked back at them. "Oh! Snap Shats! I almost forgot. The gravity is here is weaker than Coalition standards. It'll take some getting used to."

As the crew disembarked, Jopp noticed the beat up Goesch hover yacht and whistled, "Man, I'll bet that rig was tops slick in its prime. Can't believe someone would let it get all shitty like that."

Jopp was too busy leering at the ship to notice the discarded buzz wrench on the ground. He tripped and fell... slowly. Chuck reacted by lunging forward to catch him... and soared five feet past into a tumble across the dusty landing pad.

Jopp and Chuck both sat up and looked at each other, saying in unison, "Holy shit."

Phyos clapped. "Well done, boys. Excellent demonstration of the lighter gravity."

Bhanakhana gingerly and easily pulled Chuck up with one hand. When it became clear Phyos wouldn't be offering Jopp any similar help up, he grumbled his way back to his feet.

They made it across the rest of the landing pad without any additional gravity related incidents. Phyos lead them to the largest of the trees that formed the inner semi-circle. It reminded Chuck of an oak except it was as wide as a house and capped with dense crimson foliage. He noticed a double door carved into the base of the trunk.

"Oh, that's all?" Chuck said, "You could have told us they use hollowed out trees as their bui"

The tree's eyes open and its mouth smiled. Chuck's brain shorted out for half a second while it processed the fact that the tree had eye and a mouth.

"Bah what the fuck?!"

Chuck and Jopp instinctively hopped backwards into defensive stances. Jopp with his fists raised. Chuck with his foot in the air, crane kick at the ready.

The tree's wide mouth opened and an off-puttingly cheery voice emerged, "Hellooooooo! How are you?!"

Phyos waved. "We're great! Thanks! We need to make accommodations for our visit to your lovely home."

"Of course!" The double doors below the tree mouth opened. "Please, come inside me!"

Phyos, Bhanakhana, and after a moment's hesitation, Jopp all walked forward.

Chuck threw his hands up. "So, we're just going to let that sentence hang there without comment, huh? And what about the giant talking trees that are also buildings? Totally normal? Cool. Cool cool cool."

The others were passing through the doors. Chuck looked up to see the tree beaming down at him silently. He gave an awkward smile and hurried after his friends. After Chuck had disappeared inside, the tree glanced at its neighbors and said, "What a curious little Meat Thing!"

Then it went back to sleep.

Just as Chuck passed through the doors, they closed behind him. He took one step forward and immediately froze. The tree's interior was strikingly similar to an old western saloon, with a shiny wooden bar, a bunch of wooden tables, and an object that very much resembled a piano. Although the music emanating from it sounded much more like a series of flutes than any piano Chuck had ever heard. However it was neither the music, nor the furniture that made Chuck freeze. Standing behind the bar, sitting at the tables, and playing the 'piano' were...

"Squirrels?" Chuck uttered.

The beings stood between six and seven feet tall, wore clothes, and had fur ranging across various shades of orange, yellow, and red. But despite all that, they were still squirrels. The closest table to Chuck had four of them sitting around it. One of the squirrels gulped down the foamy brown contents from her glass mug, stood up, and stepped in front of him. She wore a strapless top, baggy pants with no shoes, four gemstone earrings in her left ear and two in her right. Her wrists jangled with simple bracelets made from unpolished gemstones. Chuck had to look up as she had a good five to six inches on him. With a series of short, twitchy motions, the squirrel person seemed to be sizing Chuck up.

"Ya ya," she said, "You a nut?"

"Huh?"

"Are you a nut?"

"Um, no...I'm a human."

"You sure, ya ya? You don't look sure."

"He's not a nut!" Phyos' familiar voice called out. Chuck and the squirrel lady turned to see her and Bhanakhana seated at a table in the corner. "He's with us, okay?"

The lady gave Chuck a last once over, her nose rankling. "Ya ya. Bye bye Hoomon."

She returned to her seat and Chuck darted over to the table in the corner. He dropped into one of the empty chairs.

"You seriously couldn't have given me a heads up that the buildings were living, talking trees... or that the inhabitants of this planet were giant, orange squirrels?"

"What is a squirrel?" asked Phyos.

She glanced at Bhanakhana who shrugged and said, "Do the Kisqui resemble creatures from Earth? Fascinating..."

"Never mind," said Chuck, "Where's Jopp?"

"He is at the bar, procuring refreshments."

As Chuck scanned the room, he noticed a few other non-squirrel, or rather, non-Kisqui patrons. At one table, he noticed a lanky Herbling man, his body seemingly comprised of green vines woven together. His thick leafy hair was clumped together, reminding Chuck of dreadlocks. He had it all pulled back in a ponytail. The person sitting across from him was one of those beings that looked like four foot cotton balls with arms and legs sticking out and small facial features scrunched together. This one had salt and pepper colored hair that looked bristly and unkempt. Chuck couldn't hear their conversation, but the cotton ball- *Swabdob! That was what they were called.* The Swabdob's arms flailed about as it spoke.

He saw Jopp at the bar, seated next to the last of the non-Kisqui patrons. She was a Soreshi woman, and wore a thin blue jacket and a blue cap. Chuck stifled a chuckle. He knew it was impolite, but there would always be something about seeing some of the alien species he'd encountered wearing clothes that would tickle him. Seeing a humanoid creature with the head of a snake, wearing a trucker's cap would never not be amusing.

"Be a dear, won't you? Go help Jiff with the trays."

Every eye was on Chuck as he threaded through the tables toward the bar. He swore he heard the word *nut* uttered at least ten times. As he neared Jopp, he could hear the last bits of whatever diatribe he'd been subjecting the Soreshi woman to, "...and that's why, if you're trying to get to Tasa Major, you'd be crazy to take the Wishwa-7 anomaly. You're way better off taking Erso-13 to Crustallos, which dumps you just half a day from the Centrelo System. Trust me, it's faster and saves you from having to skirt the Forsaken Rift."

The Soreshi woman rolled her reptilian eyes and downed the remainders of ale from her mug. Jopp noticed Chuck and waved.

"Hey, come meet my new pal. She's a long haul transporter, just like I was for years and you were for like a minute. We're just swapping shortcuts and routing hacks."

She let out a guttural chortle and said in a raspy voice, "Swap? That implies I've actually gotten a word in..." She stood and dropped a disposable currency card on the bar. "Thanks again, Bris. See y'all again in a couple span."

One of the two bartenders, a pumpkin colored Kisqui wearing a burlap vest with no shirt, snatched up the card and said, "Ya ya, fly safe."

Jopp added, "Nice talking with you! And you're welcome for the advice!"

She either hadn't heard him (unlikely) or chose to ignore him (very likely), but the Soreshi transport pilot ducked out the double doors without another word. Jopp and Chuck turned back to see the bartender staring at them.

"Chuck, this is Bristlecheek. He and his husband over there, Petalberry, own this establishment."

Chuck turned his head toward Jopp. "You've been in here for less than two minutes. How do you know that?"

Jopp gave him a light pat on the back. "You should know better than most. I make friends fast. Ain't that right, Bris?"

The Kisqui had been busying himself wiping out a glass. He set it down and said, "Ya ya, you ready to order yet?"

"What's good here?"

A few minutes later, Chuck and Jopp each set a tray down on the table in front of Bhanakhana and Phyos. Chuck took it upon himself to explain the offerings. He pointed at the first plate.

"Those are kind of like burgers… or humpa stacks, if you prefer. Except the 'meat' patty is made from ground nuts. And the bun is a bread made from nuts."

He pointed at the next plate.

"Those are tiny cakes… made from nuts."

And the next one.

"That's just a bowl of assorted nuts."

And finally he gestured to the four mugs filled with foamy brown liquid.

"Anyone want to guess what this ale is made from?"

"Hydro-grain!"

Phyos was the only one to laugh at her own joke.

WORD SECTION 0029

Serru stood alone in the great hall at the heart of her Sanctuary. The floor directly below her feet was painted black. Blacker than black. The blackness formed a circle, nine feet in diameter. Outside of that, the floor was painted in concentric circles, alternating between blue and gold. Four titanic columns rose from the outskirts of the painted circles, disappearing into darkness overhead. Were an individual to suddenly awaken here, they would have no reason to suspect it was anything more than an ancient temple fixed firmly to a planet's surface. But in reality, this cavernous room lay at the center of a large interstellar vessel.

She kept her posture rigid with hands clasped behind her back, as the holographic images of two people materialized before her. Their visages were so crisp and clear, a passerby could've mistaken them for actually being in the room... not that any underlings would dare to 'pass by' one of these meetings. Both figures were Venovan men. One stood considerably taller than both Serru and the other holograph. His skin was a darker shade of blue. The left side of his clean-shaven head had a series of short golden lines cross stitched into small patches. He wore black pants and black shirt with the right sleeve missing, revealing an arm so muscular it would put much of the hulking Dronla species to shame. His unnaturally orange eyes burned with intensity.

The other holograph was a middle-aged man with paler blue skin. His straw-colored hair was cropped close and neatly combed. He also wore a black shirt and pants, but his shirt had both sleeves and the cuffs bore intricate gold stitching.

In unison, the three of them nodded their heads and said, "We thank the Divine for guiding our path."

The middle-aged man addressed Serru, "What is your status, Shepherd Dac'eth?"

Serru gave him a slight bow, "Noble Herald Mavros, my Sanctuary is en route to Gjenlu. We will arrive in less than two sacred rotations." She then looked up at the taller one. "That must have been quite the fall, Teza... to require the exterior med-patching to your skull."

"The pain was nothing compared to the retribution I shall mete out upon the heretics," he growled in reply.

"I am certain that is true. Too bad your prototype Inquisitor Armor was so badly damaged. I hear it will take weeks to create a new prototype."

"Bah, that was a coward's shell. My faith shall protect me."

"I'm sure it shall... the armor *would* have been helpful to my plan, though."

Mavros cleared his throat, "*Your* plan? It is the Divine who hath laid the path bare for us to follow. Do not forget whose mandate you serve."

Serru bowed her head.

"All praises be to Rhonac." Serru lifted her eyes to meet Mavros's and added, "I have never lost sight of whose mandate I follow, Noble Herald."

"Good. Did I hear correctly that it is going to take you almost two full rotations before you will join us?"

"You did. My Sanctuary sustained a not insignificant amount of damage that must be addressed before we can successfully jump through an anomaly."

"You have been spending too much time amongst the secular dregs and the *scientists*," scoffed Teza. "*Anomaly* is their word for the Blessed Canals."

Serru fought back a smirk. "You are most likely correct. In order to earn their trust over the years, I was forced to adopt some less desirable mannerisms and vocabulary."

"Then rejoice!" cried Mavros, "The time for compromise is over. The age of glory draws nigh! The filth of the non-believers shall be burned away and from those ashes the perfect civilization will rise..."

He eyed Serru. "...that is, assuming you accomplished your mission."

She gave a slight shrug. "Things became complicated on the Barge. I cannot say for certain what the status of the professor and her cohorts is. They could be dead. They could be lost in some unknown corner of the universe. They could still be stuck at the center of the Maelstrom. Or, however unlikely, they could be there on Gjenlu right alongside you. Amidst the chaos, my Sanctuary became embattled with a taharo breed mother, hence the damage I mentioned."

"You seem complacent for someone who failed her objective."

"I never said I failed. A litter of monstrosities was loosed upon the Barge, wreaking havoc amongst both sides of the conflict. I, myself, was forced to battle one of the beasts while the interlopers escaped. I sent word for the Sanctuary to acquire them. From the bodily scents they left behind, I was able to trace their path back through the Barge. I know what they came for."

She tapped the side of her face, right next to her brilliantly orange eye. "A Shepherd's eyes reveal all secrets, even the hidden scribbling on the walls of a madman's hovel. The one they call Cestoras left behind copious notes we've yet to see before now. My historians are working on making sense of them as we speak. With Rhonac's blessing, we'll have deciphered it by the time we arrive."

"The Divine shall illuminate your path through the eyes of your acolytes," bellowed Teza. "I have no doubt we shall find the blessed door to the birth world of Rhonac's First Children."

Mavros added, "And once the path has been opened, Rhonac's might will flow out into creation. All the heretics, the sinners, and the Secular blasphemers will soon receive their final judgment."

"Amen," finished Serru.

WORD SECTION 0030

"Ya ya, 'nother round a Nut Suds."

Chuck and the others watched as Bristlecheek set a tray of brimming mugs on their table.

"Thank you," said Bhanakhana, "But I do not believe we ordered more libations."

Phyos noticed there were actually six mugs. "And your math's a bit off. You brought two too many."

"Why would you ever say that?" said Jopp.

Bristlecheek cocked a furry thumb over his shoulder. "Ya ya, round from them."

They craned their necks around Bris and saw he was indicating the table with the leafy, dreadlocked Herbling and the fuzzy, salt and pepper shaded Swabdob.

Phyos waved. "Thanks, fellas."

The Herbling canted his head toward the Swabdob and said, "Them sip sips come courtesy of my goncho here. Wee KiKi is ubes vibin' to trade hellos with such a flavorful people stew as all ya."

Chuck turned to Jopp. "I think my TellAll translator is busted."

Jopp arched an eyebrow. "Mine too."

Bhanakhana allowed himself a chuckle. "Actually they are functioning quite normally. He said the drinks were purchased by his friend, who is quite interested in meeting us."

"You speak Herb-slang?"

"Chlorophonics is the official term."

"Meanwhile they're still staring our way," noted Chuck.

"Do you want to join us?" Phyos asked them.

"Sunny!" said the Herbling. He stood lazily while the diminutive ball of fur shimmied off his chair. The Herbling dragged over two seats. While the Swabdob scrambled back up into one of them, the Herbling snatched up one of the remaining mugs and drained half of it in a single gulp.

The Swabdob finally got himself settled and slapped his palm on the table. "Me Kipu!"

"A.k.a. Wee KiKi," added the Herbling.

"Kipu!"

"Okay okay. Anyway, around here I'm called Mola Mola Tai."

"What about elsewhere?" asked Phyos, "what are you called there?"

He smiled. "Mola Mola Tai!"

"Well, hello there. I'm Professor Yeidat Phyos."

"And I am Bhanakhana Bhen Bhindo."

"You can just call me Jopp."

"You! You!" Kipu was waving his hands at Chuck. "What you?!"

"Uh, my name's Chuck."

"Yeah, like... and I mean no ill vibes sent her, but what genus are you, goncho?"

"What you?!"

"They want to know your species," clarified Bhanakhana.

"Oh! I'm an Earth human."

"Woooooooooooow," they said in unison.

"You guys know Earth?"

"Nah, sorry," said Mola Mola Tai.

"Um, it's okay."

"You people funny!" declares Kipu as he tossed a small handful of currency cards on the table.

"What's that for?" asked Phyos.

"Again, why would you say that?" wheezed Jopp, his hand already reaching for the cards.

"So like, Lil Kipu-nana here is ubes rich, right? Been on vacation for like a decade. Bopping 'cross the Uni grazing all the fun he can chew. When something amuses him, he lobs spendy squares at it."

"Fascinating. How have you two become acquainted?"

"Zip zap zoom!" declared Kipu.

"Ha, yeah. He hired me to take him storm surfing. Ever ripped the rain, my gonchos?"

Chuck and Jopp traded confused glances.

"I've heard of that!" said Phyos, "You literally glide along the waves of electricity in the storms above the oceans."

"Sunny! Phy Phy coming through with the knowledge blast."

Bristlecheek returned with another Kisqui who wore a plain brown robe with the hood pulled up.

"Ya ya. Tour time for fuzzy nut."

"Oooooooooo!" Kipu shimmied off his chair again. "Bye bye funny peoples!"

"Where's he off to?" asked Phyos.

"Kipper scored himself a tour of the Sacred Nut Orchard. The 'Squee are tops clandestine when it comes to letting outsiders see it, but Ol' Kip found the right price. I hear the nuts all glow with beautiful light when they're ripe for pickin'. Lucky lil' fella."

"Do you live here, Mr. Mola Mola Tai?" asked Bhanakhana.

"Can't say I do, Bhana-rama! I hail from over yonder across the waves. The Big Land. I just cruise over this way for the storms. Best surfin' in all Gjen Gjen. But enough about the Tai-man. What brings your colorful menagerie to our humble pocket of the 'verse?"

They all glanced nervously at each other. After what their little band had just been through, none of them were feeling too eager to share the intimate details of their purpose for coming here.

"We're searching for a hidden route to the undiscovered home world of the long extinct Ak'alei civilization. If we found it, it would be the most renowned discovery in all the Coalition in recent history, probably yielding untold riches and fame to those involved. We think there's an ancient temple near the center of this island that will direct us to the next part of the journey. There's also a powerful cult trying to simultaneously kill us and find Hirth-Ak'alei for their own nefarious purposes. Honestly, it could be dangerous for anyone in our immediate vicinity."

Well, *almost* none of them felt like sharing. Chuck, Jopp, and Bhanakhana all stared at Phyos with mouths agape.

"What?" she said to them.

"That's radtastic," said Mola Mola Tai.

"See, he gets it. Oh, close your mouths. You three look ridiculous."

"Oh dip! You gonna venture into the heart of Unogo island? Just you, yourselves, and y'all?" He shook his leafy head. "Tops dangero, bud buds. That valley is ubes full of opportunities for a painful death."

"Sounds like my first mother-in-law's house," Phyos said with a much-too-pleased-with-herself grin.

"Nice." Jopp clinked his mug to hers.

"Real spit, though. Squiggle too deep and the Topiarians get ubes pugnacious with meaties."

"Ah, I see," said Bhanakhana. "The sentient trees, much like this one we currently recline within, are amiable with Animalian or *Non-Plant* Beings. However the sentient trees near the center of the island may be more hostile toward us."

"Sunny!"

"What if you came with us?" said Chuck. "Like an ambassador or a guide." He noticed Phyos and Bhanakhana staring at him with raised eyebrows. "Sorry, don't mean to overstep or anything, but that's where this conversation was going anyway, right? Might as well get to it."

"Yeah," said Jopp. "What d'you say, dude? Want to help us out with this thing that will probably get us all killed?"

"I might have something to say on that matter," said a commanding voice from behind them.

They all turned. For Chuck, Jopp, and Bhanakhana both the voice and the person it originated from were quite familiar. Phyos and Mola Mola Tai did not know this person. She was a silver-skinned humanoid J'Kari. Her dark hair was pulled back and she had tattoo under her lavender right eye that resembled a backwards "7".

Chuck coughed, "Hey, Babe..."

She cut him off, "You. Come here."

Chuck rushed toward her. Rohi grabbed his collar, pulled him in close, and planted a firm kiss on his mouth.

Bhanakhana's cheeks flushed with embarrassment.

Jopp rolled his eyes.

Phyos and Mola Mola Tai grinned shamelessly.

Rohi pulled away and smiled, "Bhanakhana, Jopp... how's it going, boys?"

Bhanakhana returned her smile. "It is good to see you, Rohi."

Jopp raised his mug. "What's up, Ro!"

Rohi stroked the work-in-progress beard on Chuck's face. "I know I call you fuzzlumps, but I'm not so sure how I feel about this particular bit of fuzz."

"Told you, dude!" hollered Jopp, "Shave that shit."

"It just needs time to come together!" barked Chuck.

Rohi let a warm smile linger on her face for few seconds, before she turned back to the group and said, "Now let's talk about this colossal swimming pool of humpa dung you've all taken a face-first dive into."

"Oh, I definitely like her," said Phyos.

Rohi dragged a chair over to their table and dropped herself down. In one deft motion, she snatched Jopp's mug out of his hand and drained its contents.

"Fucking seriously?!" he whined.

"Oh hush, I'm sure there's plenty enough booze already coursing through your veins." She pointed at Phyos. "I'm guessing you're the Professor."

Phyos smiled, "Guilty."

Rohi turned to Mola Mola Tai. "And you are?"

"Mola Mola Tai, gonchorina. Electric Storm Surfer Extraordinaire. You got a strong vibe. Who're you?"

"Universal Law Enforcement, Division Officer Rohi Kahpanova."

His eyebrows raised. "Oh dip..."

"Exactly. Once my, uh, *partner* gets in here, we'll explain exactly how fucked this situation is."

"Oh, my dear, I think we're very well versed in how *fucked* the situation is," said Phyos.

"Indeed." Bhanakhana's hand instinctively went to his still-healing mid-section.

"You have a new U.L.E. partner?" asked Chuck, as he returned to his seat.

"Not exactly... it's a story. She's outside talking to the tree building."

"Neat, isn't it?" said Phyos, "Anyway, were just discussing having our new friend here," she gestured toward Mola Mola Tai, "guide us to the center of the island."

"Yeah..." said Mola Mola Tai, "So, I'm a have to say no to the guide gig, gonchos. Much sorries."

He stood up from the table.

"There's an epic storm headin' toward the far coast. I got catch me a bit of them electro-waves. I wish you gonchos tops luck, though."

He turned to leave, but paused to add, "Lil' bit of advice... them tree-peeps do not vibe with weapons like guns and stuff. Anything with an explosive nature to it, you sync? No *fire makers*, as they call 'em."

With that, he headed for the doors.

"That did not go the way I'd expected," said Chuck.

"That seems to have become something of a theme with us," noted Bhanakhana.

"No shit," added Jopp.

Behind them at the doors, Mola Mola Tai stepped aside to let a Venovan woman enter before he disappeared into the bright light of the outside. The woman squinted while her eyes adjusted and announced, "Dang, this place is wild-"

Loi's words caught in her throat. Her eyes widened and her mouth hung open. The others followed her stare right to Jopp, who was staring right back at her, though his expression had more of a primal rage flavor to it. After a few tense moments, Jopp broke the silence, his eyes never leaving Loi.

"Hey Rohi, I assumed you're armed?"

"Uh, yeah."

Jopp pointed at Loi.

"Could you do me a huge favor and shoot her?"

WORD SECTION 0031

No one moved. No one spoke. The air was thick with tension, eyes darting back and forth from various parties. Then a burst of frantic shouting cut through the deafening silence.

"Ya ya! No shooting! No shooting!"

Bristlecheek raced over to them waving a bone-white machete that hummed quietly. All the people at the table hopped up and staggered backwards out of the way. Well, all except for Chuck who was too entranced by the image of a giant orange squirrel wielding a sword to react.

Rohi held her hand up and said, "Sir! I am an agent with the U.L.E. Please put down the sonic blade." She gave Jopp a hard stare. "And I assure you no one is shooting anyone."

Bristlecheek lowered his machete.

"Ya ya. I get you 'nother round. For the trouble."

He scurried away.

"Well, that is pleasant of him, providing us drinks on the house," said Chuck.

"Wouldn't it be on the tree?" mused Chuck.

Phyos chuckled, "I'm pretty sure he means we're *buying* another round from him for *his* trouble."

"Intriguing business model." Bhanakhana tapped his chin.

"Remind me later to look up if permits are required for blades that large," said Rohi.

They all suddenly remembered Jopp and Loi, who were still standing stock still, staring at each other with fiery intensity.

"So, uh, you two know each other?" Rohi ventured.

"Are you going to shoot her, Rohi?" Jopp asked.

"No, Jopp, I'm not going to shoot her."

"Okay... hey! On a totally unrelated note, can I just check something on your pistol? It'll just take a sec."

"I think if you give it to him, he's going to shoot her," said Phyos.

"That's what I was thinking too," said Chuck.

"Indeed," added Bhanakhana.

Rohi turned her a hard gaze their way and spoke through gritted teeth. "Thank you. Please stop talking now." She looked back to Jopp. "Jopp, I'm not giving you my weapon. Can you try to calm down a bit?"

Loi swallowed and said, "Jopp, hey... uh, funny meeting you he-"

"Fuck you!" he shouted. "Fuck you, you fucking fuck!"

Jopp huffed and puffed and tried to catch his breath. A purple vein bulged from his bright yellow forehead. Chuck had never seen him so worked up before. Bhanakhana leaned over and whispered, *"You should boop his nose."*

"I think he'd bite my friggin finger off if I tried," Chuck replied. Then to Jopp he said, "Hey, bud, hey... maybe take it down a notch, huh?"

Jopp's head swiveled toward Chuck. "Take it down a notch? Do you know who the fuck this is?!" He pointed at Loi.

Chuck threw his hands up. "No, dude! None of us do!"

"She's Loi," said Rohi. "We linked up in Pa Mahinga."

"Holy shit!" barked Jopp, "So not everything was a total fucking lie, huh?! At least you had the decency to give me your real name!"

"I got no idea what's happening here," said Phyos.

All the ranting and raving and confused side chatter was put on hold as Bristlecheek returned with a tray full of nut ales. Everyone waited patiently while he passed them around. He asked if anyone needed anything else, no one responded. When he finally left, Chuck looked at Jopp and said, "Dude! You seriously need to explain what the hell is wrong with you."

"It's her!" answered Jopp, pointing at Loi. "She's the girl!"

"The girl?"

"Yes! The one who- *remember?!* The reason why I crashed on Earth in the first place!"

"Oh… *Oh!*" Chuck's eyes lit up with recognition. "The one who stole your cargo and left you stranded in space."

"Hey," said Loi, "*Stranded* is a harsh term. He had the escape pod. That thing was more than capable of getting him to a nearby waystation."

"But it didn't!" Jopp protested.

"To be fair to the argument," Bhanakhana chimed in, "I believe Chuck had mentioned to me you crashing on Earth while considerable intoxicated. We may have to mark this up to user error rather than equipment inefficiencies."

"What he said," Chuck added.

"Fuck both of you. Whose side are you on?"

"Yours, buddy, yours." Chuck tried to reach a reassuring hand out, but Jopp swatted him away.

"Okay, yes," said Rohi, "I'm aware Loi is something of a thief…"

"*Something of a thief?*" scoffed Loi, "I'm a Hall of Renown level thief, thank you very much."

Rohi threw her hands up as if to say *what the hell, dude?* and then said, "So apparently, she stole something big from you. We will deal with that later…"

"It was more than just that," Jopp growled through gritted teeth.

"Oh yeah!" said Chuck, "The only reason she got close enough to steal your cargo in the first place was because she seduced you."

"Hey, *me* again," Loi held a finger up, "Sorry to be so nitpicky, but I'm gonna have to take issue with the term *seduced*. You see…"

"Loi! Seriously?!" snapped Rohi. She took a deep breath and said, "Okay, you two have a fucked up history but, and I'm *sorry* Jopp, we're going to have to set it aside for now. We've got bigger issues to address."

"You mean The Adjudicators," said Phyos.

"They're called The *Adherent*," corrected Loi.

Rohi pointed at Loi and nodded, "Yes. The *Adherent* are powerful, malicious, and as she and I have personally experienced, quite dangerous. So, we might want to try to at least get their name right. What do you know about them?"

Phyos shrugged, "They're powerful, malicious, and as *we've* personally experienced, quite dangerous."

Rohi looked at Chuck, "Is she fucking with me? Does she know I shoot people who fuck with me?"

Chuck glanced at Phyos, "*She really does.*" Then to Rohi he said, "But no, I honestly don't think she's fucking with you."

"I'm eccentric!" Phyos announced.

Rohi pinched the bridge of her nose. "Guys... why are you here? Why haven't you hauled ass back to civilization?"

Bhanakhana leaned his considerable bulk forward. "Rohi, this may seem foolish to you, but we are determined to continue forward. We believe these fanatics are searching for *Hirth-Ak'alei*, as are we. We intend to find it first so as to prevent them from completing whatever, as you put it, *malicious* machinations they have planned."

"These three are determined to continue," grumbled Jopp. "I'm just tagging along for who knows why... loyalty?" He shot a glare toward Loi. "I guess I don't like abandoning people I claim to give a shit about."

"Oh, cry me a puddle, Short Stack," growled Loi, "Maybe I should take a cue from you and have one of my ears cut off. Then I wouldn't have to hear as much of your whining."

Jopp instinctively reached a hand up his antenna nub. His cheeks flushed and he said, "Fu-"

Rohi slammed her fist down on the table, creating a spider web of cracks in the wooden surface. Everyone stiffened up. Rohi fixed her stare on Phyos, "I believe you, that there is something very big and important at the end of this... Not because of your word, but because behind Loi and myself, is a literal trail of bodies. These people have built an intricate and powerful network of resources across the Coalition... and now they are burning it to the ground in pursuit of... what was it again?"

"Hirth-Ak'alei, undiscovered home world of the Ak'alei," answered Bhanahkahana.

"Thank you," Rohi's eyes fixed back on Phyos, "Please, in as plain of language as possible, tell me what could possibly be worth all this."

Phyos took a deep breath.

"The Ak'alei reigned over dozens of peoples spread across dozens of planets during an era when there is no recorded evidence of interplanetary travel. I believe the *Adherent* believe they will find the means to subjugate all civilization."

"And do you believe that's what they'll find?"

"I believe it is a possibility."

Rohi nodded.

"Okay. Let's take a walk through the woods."

WORD SECTION 0032

Serru's Sanctuary came to a steady orbital position above Gjenlu's large eastern continent. She entered the Sanctuary hangar and boarded the Emissary, an oblong mid-size vessel that was a hybrid between a personnel transport shuttle and a gunship. Waiting for her aboard the Emissary were two anointed historians, thirty armed acolytes, and a pilot. Serru ordered the pilot to head down to Gjenlu's surface and turned back to see thirty-two sets of eyes staring at her expectantly. She realized they were probably waiting for her to bless this mission with a prayer or something. Frankly, she didn't have the patience for the grand emotional inflections the traditional prayers required and instead opted for a more direct speech.

"My Kin," she started, "My companions in salvation. We are so very close to achieving what millions upon millions of souls have attempted and failed. We are so very close to bringing the Lord back into our universe."

"Praise Rhonac!" they exclaimed in unison.

"Yes. We are going to open the door to the Divine Worlds. Rhonac will return and with his power, save the lost souls of this universe. But now is not the time to celebrate. The closer we get to the end, the more difficult it will become. The Great Deceivers are unleashing every last bit of their power to try and stop us. We must be prepared to do whatever we must to succeed. I will not lie to you, there is a possibility even our fellow Kin in Faith have been corrupted."

Thirty-two sets of eyes nervously glanced between each other.

"No. No one aboard this vessel has been tainted. My blessed eyes show me that." Serru made her orange irises brighten for a moment to sell the point. "There are a lot of our brethren down there on the surface working toward the same goal. But I've been gifted with a vision. I know it is this collection of pure souls I see before me that will finish the task. You've all been chosen... not by me, but by Divine Mandate."

"Praise Rhonac! Praise Rhonac! Praise..."

The chant died down when the first bit of turbulence hit them. One of Gjenlu's infamous electrical storms was wreaking havoc in the lower atmosphere above their destination. After a twenty-minute detour around the storm, they touched down on a wide disc of flat rock that had been designated the landing pad for the Adherent's base of operations. This base was a small village of transport shuttles that had been converted into temporary buildings. Rows of temporary light posts were arranged in a grid of roads. Dusk was taking over the sky. As Serru and company exited their ship, the first thing she noticed was the smell. She could tell it wasn't originating from the village, but rather from a further distance out. Nevertheless, it was rancid, pungent, and wholly unpleasant. However one thing it was not to Serru was surprising. She and her historians had deciphered many of the scribblings from inside Cestoras' yurt during their journey to Gjenlu, and because of those discoveries, she'd expected an unbearable stench to be a possibility. She saw the people in the village, mostly Venovans but also some reptilian Soreshi and some thick, tawny-skinned Ochrean laborers, all wore masks protecting their noses and mouths. Serru glanced back at one of the acolytes, "Go get the masks."

Three minutes later, Serru and her retinue were all wearing air filtration masks. Just as she was about to march into the village, a pair of boxy multi-terrain trucks hummed their way around the corner of the nearest ship building. They rolled to a stop in front of her, and a young Venovan woman clad in a gray shirt and pants and wearing a filtration mask hopped out. She bowed to Serru and said, "Shepherd Dac'eth, welcome to this most sacred of spaces. Noble Herald Mavros and Shepherd Lo are at the dig site. I am to bring you there. There air can be quite- Oh! I see you have already procured cleansing masks. Excellent."

"Would I be correct in assuming the smell is coming from the excavation site?"

"Indeed it does! Herald Mavros says it is a ward placed there by the Great Deceivers to scare away those lacking in faith."

"That sounds like something he would say."

"Pardon me?"

"Nothing. Shall we go?"

"Yes, of course!" The woman's eyes drifted past Serru to her entourage. "Though I am afraid my vehicles can only accommodate nine additional passengers. I can-"

"It's fine. Don't worry about it, my kin." Serru turned to the historians. "You two are with me." She then looked to the acolytes. "Faithful Unit One will also come with me. The rest of you wait here. Be ready for anything. Remember what I told you..." her nose rankled a bit. "... and feel free to wait back on the Emissary ship if you prefer."

Serru, the historians, and six acolytes loaded up into the trucks. They sped off, circumventing the edge of the makeshift town, and headed toward a rocky ridge on the horizon. Serru sat next to the driver of the first truck, the same woman who'd greeted them.

"What's your name?" Serru asked her.

"I am Takoi, Shepherd Dac'eth. And may I just say how honored I am to be driving for such a renowned defender of the faith as yoursel-" she cut herself off by swerving to avoid a scattered pile of logs. "Cursed scale-skins! Can hardly follow the simplest of instructions. I don't know why we bother with these shifty Soreshi workers... or the brutish Ochreans for that matter."

Serru opted not to acknowledge the ignorant interspecies commentary and instead said, "I've used trucks like these before on other missionary endeavors... I don't ever recall them being so nimble."

"It's the lower gravity," Takoi explained, "That's been the one blessed thing about this mission. We've been able to excavate great swaths of the target site in a much shorter span that previously estimated. Despite the... less than ideal labor force, Herald Mavros' leadership has yielded exceptional results."

"Hmmm," said Serru, only half listening as she surveyed the passing encampment. "I'm curious... where are all the acolytes? Besides yourself and the other truck's driver, I've only noticed a half dozen guards."

Takoi exhaled, "Most of the Faithful Units in Mavros' care were lost to the indigenous dangers when the excavation first began. This once holy land has become infested with servants of the Deceivers. It's unfortunate for us, as we miss our kin. Yet fortunate for them, for their essences must surely be in the embrace of our Lord."

"Intriguing," Serru whispered to herself.

As their truck crested the ridge, the stench cut through Serru's mask like a surgeon's mechanized plasma scalpel.

"Rho-dammit," Serru coughed, ignoring Takoi's judgmental glance aimed at the blasphemous curse, "That is putrid."

"Yes, it is a true test of faith."

Serru looked out over the scene laid before her. The ridge rolled away from them in a gentle downward slope. Three converted ship buildings and a raised observation platform occupied the base the of the slope. The area that stretched out from there had once been forested but all the trees in a kilometer radius had long been cleared. At the center of this barren space, sat a curious structure. A thin stone tower, roughly ten meters in height rose up out of the ground. From its midsection, six stone arches sprouted out like spokes, each one connecting with identical stone towers set some twenty meters away from the center. This structure appeared to be relatively untouched, which is more than Serru could say for the rest of the area. All of the ground that wasn't holding up the stone structure had been dug up. Serru looked down into deep, cavernous pits and as the odor made her eyes water she cursed this planet's electrical storms. If not for them, she could have delivered her message via secure commline and saved herself the displeasure of this trip. Her watery eyes drifted back to the raised observation platform, where the unmistakably thick frame of Teza Lo stood next to the quite normal sized frame of Noble Herald Mavros.

Serru pointed toward them and the trucks descended the slope at a cautious pace. She couldn't help but begin to resent Takoi for this, whether warranted or not, her slowed speed was extending the amount of time Serru had to endure the smell. The trucks finally came to stop at the base of the observation platform and Serru practically leapt from the passenger seat. She signaled for the two historians to follow her as she bounded up the zigzagging ramp. As she reached the top deck, Teza and Mavros turned back to face her. Serru was stunned to see that while Mavros wore a filtration mask, Teza's mouth and nose were bare.

Serru gave the cursory bow, "Greetings, Herald Mavros."

He paused for an annoyingly dramatic moment before returning the bow and saying, "Greetings, Shepherd Dac'eth."

Serru's eyes immediately darted toward Teza, "How can you stand the smell without a mask?"

The large, blue skinned man raised his arms and bellowed, "Tis the smell of righteous victory, My Kin! For any moment we shall uncover the path to the home of Rhonac's First Children!"

"About that," Serru said, her gaze moving back to Mavros. "We've uncovered new revelations." She waved the historians over.

"I am afraid, O Noble Herald, that I may have some frustrating news regarding this excavation site."

WORD SECTION 0033

"Did you just say *dung mine*?"

Chuck was staring at Phyos in disbelief. She laughed, "Technically not a literal dung mine...but if anyone were to follow the big blinking, obvious clues in Cestoras' writings they'd find themselves digging up a whole heap of crystallized carbium sulfane."

"Which is a mineral that emits an exorbitantly unpleasant odor, not unlike rancid animal feces," explained Bhanakhana.

Phyos giggled again, "How much you want to bet that's where the predatory prayer posse is right now? That shuttle we saw was headed toward the Eastern continents, after all, heh heh heh."

"So, you think Cestoras did that on purpose? Went to all that trouble of leaving clues, on the off chance someone would dig up a geological stink bomb? Just for like... a prank?"

"A good one, isn't it?"

"That seems to be a considerable amount of effort to achieve what is essentially juvenile washroom humor," noted Bhanakhana.

Phyos turned to him with the sternest of expressions. "No amount of effort is too much for a good poop joke, Sage Bhindo."

Chuck patted Bhanakhana's massive arm, "I gotta side with her on this one, buddy."

"Hold up, guys!" called Rohi.

The party all stopped. They'd been walking for just over an hour. Chuck readjusted the strap that held the sonic machete on his back. All of them currently carried a similar blade. Rohi and Loi still carried pistols, but had them concealed in satchels. A quick conversation with Bristlecheek had confirmed Mola Mola Tai's advice that while the vege-life at the island's interior wasn't a big fan of Meaties, they'd likely be left alone as long as they kept to themselves and didn't disturb the foliage communities too much. However were the trees to see guns or anything that could be misconstrued as a *fire maker,* they would immediately see the visitors as mortal enemies and do whatever they could to kill the threat. Bristlecheek then assured them the interior trees were indeed very capable of *killing the threat.* So they make sure to keep their electronic supplies to a minimum and purchased five sonic machetes from their large squirrel shaped friend. Chuck had wondered aloud why the trees wouldn't object to them wielding large blades specifically made for cutting foliage. Bristelcheek's husband, Petalberry, had explained that often the trees like their excess limbs removed. It gives them a chance to stretch a bit, or for some it might feel like getting a fresh haircut. You just need to be sure to ask permission first.

Chuck, Phyos, and Bhanakhana had been leading the way through the jungle, which so far had offered a relatively clear path inward. Jopp sulked by himself off to the side. Loi hung back with Rohi, who was busy abusing her data bracelet, "C'mon, you stupid thing! *Send Message!*"

"Who're you trying to reach?" asked Chuck.

"Backup," answered Rohi, "I sent a request for support before we got here... however this phoobing planet is so far off the GIG there's only one U.L.E. frigate in the general vicinity and it's responsible for patrolling four entire star systems! I stressed the importance of the issue and they said they'd start making their way over. Been trying to send an update..."

"It's not going to work, dear," said Phyos, "All the electrical storms make commlines almost useless here."

"Shit," Rohi growled.

"Set it to auto-ping your position every, I don't know, like fifteen minutes or so," said Loi. "The galactic positioning function uses a different wavelength and it can sometimes get through the storms."

They all looked at her.

"How do you know that?" asked Bhanakhana.

Loi shrugged. "It's like she said, there's only one U.L.E. frigate trying to cover four whole star systems out here. Makes planets like Gjenlu popular meet up spots for *business* partners trying to avoid too much oversight. Since comms don't work, we- I mean *they* had to think of alternative ways to touch base with each other."

"Nice," said Rohi and she tapped the command into her bracelet.

Chuck noticed the tree next to him had woken up and was looking at him. When it noticed Chuck make eye contact it said, "Hi! Want to chew my fruit?!"

Chuck sighed, "No... I don't."

"Okay!" the tree closed its eyes and went back to sleep.

This was the umpteenth time a tree had asked Chuck that so far. He was starting to look forward to the less friendly trees at the island's center. Rohi quit fiddling with her data bracelet and they started walking again.

Jopp spoke up for the first time in the past hour, "Remind me again why we can't just fly there?"

Bhanakhana answered, "There is no guarantee we would find a suitable place to land, and if we did find one, the inner island vege-life would be extremely hostile toward such a piece of machinery. Not to mention there is always a chance one of the storms could roll in."

"I've flown us through tough chop before."

"I know a fun fact about that," said Loi, who ignored Jopp's eye roll at the sound of her voice. "Gjenlu was actually discovered by Venovans, two of them... shit, I forgot their names. Anyway, they were a pair of intergalactic explorers who're famous for two things: One, discovering Gjenlu. And Two, discovering that the storms short-out ships, making them drop out of the sky like rocks... they uh, they died."

"Why does every story about a person exploring this planet end with the planet having killed them?"

"Not *every*one..." countered Chuck, "Our main dude, Cestoras, lived here for like, what, over twenty years?"

"Yeah? And how did he die?"

"Oh, uh, I haven't actually finished his biography."

Jopp looked at Bhanakhana and Phyos with an accusingly raised eyebrow.

Phyos sighed, "You tell them."

Bhanakhana answered, "Cestoras had developed a friendship with one of the trees near his yurt. It let him consume its fruit freely whenever he pleased. However the tree right next to the friendly one hated Cestoras... well, they absolutely hated each other. One night, Cestoras became exceedingly intoxicated on homemade wine and he plucked a fruit from the tree that hated him. Whether it was an accident or an intentional slight, no one knows. What we do know is the tree had secreted copious amounts of a toxic enzyme into its fruit on the off chance Cestoras ever ate one. We know all this because the tree told the search party the whole story when they found the encampment."

"I knew it," grumbled Jopp.

As they ventured deeper into the island, the trees appeared to get taller, with more dense vegetation. Less light found its way through the lush tangle of branches, vines, and leaves above them. Chuck noticed the frequency of trees asking him to cheerily sample their harvest start to diminish. Once in a while, he'd see a tree look at them, twist its face into a disapproving stare that screamed *if this jungle had a manager, you can bet I'd be calling them to complain*, before then falling back asleep.

Then, to Chuck's surprise, he heard birds chirping. He peered toward an upcoming clearing and saw small winged things fluttering from tree to tree.

"I didn't think we'd find animals toward the inner island," he mused.

Phyos grinned at him. "Just wait and see."

They stepped into the clearing and subsequently had their collective minds blown. The creatures were shaped just like parakeets... parakeets that had been sculpted out of beautiful purple and pink flowers.

"My word," breathed Bhanakhana.

"They're Gerbudgies," explained Phyos, "I understand they're quite friendly." She stepped further into the clearing, raised her arms out, and kept still. In a manner of seconds she had two of the little creatures land on her, and start hopping up her arm. The others followed her lead, and before long they had dozens of the things fluttering around them, landing on their arms, hopping around their feet.

Chuck and Rohi locked eyes and smiled.

Bhanakhana had a Gerbudgie perched on his thick finger, which he slowly brought up to his face.

"Hello, little friend."

Even Jopp's grumpy shell couldn't help but crack a bit as two of them play-fought with each other along his arm and up to his shoulder.

Then, as if on cue, all the Gerbudgies simultaneously hopped into the air and took off, disappearing through the leafy canopy high above with a chorus of chirps.

"That was rad," said Loi, her eyes falling on Jopp, and then on the amber dollop of goo on his shoulder. "Oh dang, they got you."

"Yeah," said Phyos, "Check your clothes for sap droppings. You'll want to scrape it off right away. Once that shit hardens, it's there forever."

Loi reached toward Jopp, who instinctively flinched.

"Oh chill out and let me help you," she chided.

Jopp settled down and let Loi pinch the sticky goop off his shoulder. She flicked it away, and gave him a once over.

"I think you're good."

Jopp rolled his shoulder and cracked his neck.

"Yeah, thanks," he said.

"Okay," announced Phyos, "That's enough horticulture humping. Let's keep moving."

She double checked the map in her notebook against the compass function of her data bracelet, which thankfully, still seemed to be fully operational. She pointed and said, "That-a-way!"

From that point on, the route became much narrower and more winding. The group was forced to squeeze closer together, and Loi found herself inadvertently sidled up next to Jopp at the back of the line. And dang it all to heck, she just couldn't help but attempt a little small talk.

"So, uh," she started, "Must be some kind of story how you wound up out here paling around with a Dronla scientist, a U.L.E. agent, and an Earth Man, huh?"

"You have no fucking idea," Jopp replied in a neutral tone.

Loi kept finding herself glancing at Jopp's antenna nub.

"In all sincerity though, what happened to your head?"

Jopp sighed, "Big Red and I had been captured by some marauders. They wanted to know something we didn't want to tell 'em. They thought giving ol' lefty the snip snip would loosen my lips."

"And did it?"

"Did it what?"

"Did it work? Did you cave in?"

"That's a weird fucking thing to ask someone who just shared their most traumatic experience with you...but no, I didn't tell em anything. Except maybe how I liked that one thing their mothers did in bed."

A loud guffaw burst from Loi's mouth.

Jopp couldn't help but smile a bit.

"Sounds like you've been taken on quite the ride since we first met."

"Pffft, something like that."

"I mean, it hasn't been all bad, right?" Loi waved at the gang in front of them. "Seems like you've got yourself a solid crew of friends here... and shit, personal injury aside, don't tell me these last few years haven't at least been interesting. You're palling around the universe with an Earth man-thing or whatever. I've never even seen one of them before. I didn't know they'd joined the Sentient Coalition."

"Earth is still officially unaware of the Sentient Coalition's existence," Bhanakhana called back over his massive shoulder. "Through some joint advocacy between ourselves and key personnel from both the Universal Law Enforcement agency and Prime Partners Intergalactic Consortium, Chuck was granted a Unique Citizens Acceptance."

"I'm special!" Chuck announced.

Rohi glanced back with a playful eye roll. They all had a nice chuckle. After a moment of quiet, Loi looked down at Jopp again and said, "For what it's worth, I think the one antenna look is kinda badass."

Jopp sighed, "One and a *half*."

WORD SECTION 0034

"Are we there yet?" Jopp whined as he swatted another buzzing blossquito, preventing the tiny flower with wings from stabbing him with a minuscule thorn proboscis

"Did you really just ask that?" Chuck glanced back at him.

"We've been walking for hours," Jopp complained, "And I'm pretty sure Loi pick pocketed my Rzackio snack bars."

"You got no proof of that," countered Loi.

"Then open your pack and show me."

"I shouldn't have to acknowledge these baseless accusations."

Rohi wheeled around, "Fucking seriously, you two? Knock it off."

"Can't really blame them for getting a bit antsy," Chuck whispered to her.

Rohi sighed and called ahead, "Hey Professor, what's our current ETA? Should we be looking for a place to bed down for the night?"

Bhanakhana and Phyos looked up from their notebooks.

"Gjenlu has thirty-eight standard hours per planetary rotation," answered Bhanakhana. "We have ten to eleven additional hours until dusk settles."

"Yeah and besides," said Phyos looking back down at her notebook, "We *should* be getting close."

Rohi nudged Chuck. *"What's in those books?"*

He shrugged and held up his own copy. "Mostly the ranting of a mad man.... basically what this entire endeavor is based on."

She nodded. "Tops... tops tops tops." Then to herself, "*What the hell was I thinking?*"

Chuck heard her and slipped his arm around her waist. "I think you were thinking it'd be fun to embark on another adventure halfway across the universe with the one and only Chuck from Earth."

Rohi gave Chuck a quick kiss on the cheek... then rolled her eyes and flicked him in the forehead. "I think you need to quit drinking your own Hua Juice, Earth Man."

Ahead of them, Professor Phyos kept flipping through her book while continuing to move forward.

"I swear we should've hit the Whaiti Gorge by now..." she declared right as her foot burst through the dense foliage and found no ground to land on. She tipped forward and started to fall. Bhanakhana burst forward, the planet's lighter gravity giving him some extra oomph. In one deft motion he grabbed an overhanging branch with one hand while barely catching Phyos' shirt with the other. For a moment they both admired the sheer four hundred meter drop waiting below them. A lazy creek, bordered by rainbows of bright flowers, meandered its way along the bottom of the gorge.

"Whelp, there's the gorge...hmmm, pretty," mused Phyos as she hung at a near flat angle over the precipitous drop.

"It is quite picturesque," Bhanakhana conceded before hoisting Phyos back up over the ledge. He released the branch he'd be using to anchor them and the tree it was attached to groaned, "You're a heavy meat thing!"

"Apologies, my botanical friend. You have my utmost gratitude for the use of your limb."

The tree grumbled and said, "S'okay. Just be wary of them stump-heads across the gap. They ain't so kindly like. Must be something in the soil."

Bhanakhana wanted to say thank you again but the tree had already fallen back asleep.

"Are you two okay?" Rohi and the others had caught up to them and they all peered down the drop.

"Better than okay! That was splooshing exhilarating! And what's more," Phyos pointed to their right, "There's the Boletus Bridge we've been looking for!"

They saw what could have once been considered a bridge. Directly across from each other sat two rocky outcroppings that each stretched a ways out over the gorge.

Chuck noticed the sizeable gap between the outcroppings and said, "Doesn't something have to like, actually connect two points to be called a bridge?"

"Oh hush! You'll see when we get there."

"Last time you said that I almost had a heart attack when the giant tree started talking to me. Is the bridge going to talk too?"

Phyos didn't answer, but rather started carefully picking her way along the edge of the drop toward the so called bridge. Bhanakhana and Rohi followed. Chuck looked to Jopp and Loi and said, "The bridge is totally going to talk."

They just shrugged and headed after the others.

"I love how nonchalant you all are about this," Chuck called after them, "I get it with the trees and whatnot. Plants are living things, so it only stands to reason a level of sentience would be attainable. But a bridge? C'mon! Architecture shouldn't talk!"

He noticed a scrutinizing glare from the tree next to him. Chuck pointed at the others and said, "Meat things, am I right?"

"Hmmmph," groaned the tree before closing its eyes.

Phyos was waiting for them all in a small flat clearing at the base of the outcropping, which did turn out to be a purposefully carved stone bridge. There were low walls on either side of a smooth, inclined pathway. It looked like an exceptionally sturdy and functional bridge. Or it would have if not for the fact that the middle third of it was completely absent. As he approached, Chuck noticed beige vines, dotted with mushrooms draped across much of the stone.

"Okay," said Phyos, rifling through her satchel, "We just need to... phoob it, where is my note- Oh!" She cast a longing glance back toward the bottom of the gorge. "Fizzle tits! One book down. Oh well, at least we have two spares." She waved Chuck over. "Let me see your copy, dear."

Chuck handed her his copy of the Cestoras diary and said, "So what's the story here? Some kind of leap of faith or-Aaaagh! Fuck!"

Chuck hopped backwards as a large mushroom with a face had suddenly extended upward from one of the end pillars of the bridge.

"Greetings," drolled the mushroom, "I am the Boletus Bridge."

"A ha!" exclaimed Chuck, "I fucking knew it!"

Rohi patted his arm. "Good job, sweetie."

"In order to cross, you must answer a question," the mushroom continued.

"Don't ask him to clarify whether it's an African or European swallow," quipped a noticeably-pleased-with-himself Chuck.

Nobody reacted.

Phyos glanced at Bhanakhana, "That's one of them *references* he likes so much isn't it?"

"Indeed."

"How many rootcubes of dirt are in a hole that is twenty twigtips long, thirty twigtips wide, and forty twigtips deep?"

Bhanakhana and Phyos started tallying off imaginary numbers with their fingers in the air.

"Zero!" blurted Chuck. "It's a hole, so there's no dirt in it!"

"Correct."

Dozens upon dozens of beige roots suddenly emerged from the porous stone. They coiled around each other into thick braids that intertwined until they formed a root bridge spanning the gorge.

Bhanakhana beamed down at Chuck with pride. "Well done!"

"Yes yes," added Phyos, "Let's hurry up."

She took a step forward and the root bridge immediately started to disassemble.

"Only the meat-thing what answered the question may tread the span," Boletus the mushroom announced.

"What he say?" asked Jopp.

Phyos sighed. "It means only our Earth fellow here can cross over. Then, I assume, we get another question and whoever answers that one can cross too... and so on."

Rohi grabbed Chuck's arm. "Be careful."

"Always," he replied with a wink.

They all watched with bated breath as Chuck cautiously stepped out on to the bridge made of sentient fungus. He found it to have give and sway, much like a rope bridge, but otherwise it felt strong. He glanced back at the others, gave them a thumbs up, and then crossed over. The moment his foot touched the opposite side, the roots pulled themselves apart.

Phyos clapped her hands together. "Alrighty, Mr. Boletus. Next question, please!"

A low growl and a stir of movement pulled Chuck's eyes toward the nearby tree line. He gawked as what appeared to be a bush bearing bright purple berries began to move. It deftly detached itself from the surrounding foliage and stepped into the clearing. Chuck's voice caught in his throat as he realized he was staring down what was essentially a large tiger made out of thorny bushes.

"Uh, guys?!" he called back to the others.

"Oh, fizzle tits," breathed Phyos, "Bramble Cat..."

WORD SECTION 0035

Bhanakhana called across the way to Chuck, "Do not turn your back on the bramble cat! Ask the Boletus on that side for a question to cross back over!"

Chuck noticed an identical face-having mushroom out of the corner of his eye.

"I want to cross over," he rasped at the Boletus.

The mushroom took a breath and said, "I go on four legs in the morning, two in the afternoon, and three in the evening. What am I?"

"I know this one too! It's a man! Or a person?"

"No. Guess again."

"I've heard this one before! I'm telling you that's the answer!"

"No. Guess again."

"Fuck."

The bramble cat let out a more aggressive growl.

"Double fuck."

"Chuck! Use your machete!" Rohi hollered.

Chuck unslung the sonic blade from his back.

"And don't stop hackin' until it stops moving!" added Phyos. "It ain't like an animal beast! Cutting off its head will only make it mad!"

"How fun," grumbled Chuck.

Phyos snapped her fingers at the Boletus head on her side. "Next question! Let's go, let's go."

"What has roots nobody sees, is taller than trees, up, up it goes, and yet never grows?"

The bramble cat lunged.

Chuck reacted with a wild swing. The white blade hummed through the air, slicing off the creature's front left paw. It let out a high-pitched shriek as it limped backwards.

Chuck started to feel pleased with himself. The sentiment quickly faded however when a low chorus of growls rolled out from the tree line.

"How's that next answer coming?!" Chuck called over his shoulder.

"Working on it, sweetie!" Rohi yelled back. Then to the group she said, "Okay, so the answer has roots…"

Four more bramble cats prowled into the clearing. Chuck exhaled, "Shiiiiiiiiiit."

"And the answer is something exceptionally tall," Bhanakhana noted to the others.

"But it doesn't grow," noted Jopp.

One of the thorn-covered predator plants broke away from the others and rushed at Chuck. He lashed out, cleaving a leafy chunk off the creature's head. However, its other paw managed to get a swipe at Chuck's left arm, leaving three parallel gashes below his shoulder. Chuck cried out in pain but kept his resolve and struck again. This time, he severed an entire leg. The bramble cat, now missing its head and one leg, opted to retreat to be near the first one that Chuck had cut. Their three unmarred brethren did not seem deterred as they slowly approached in unison.

Loi had been trying to split her attention between watching Chuck's battle and listening to the others. She found her eyes drawn upwards, past the tree line to the pair of gigantic spires of rock stretching toward the sky.

"Mountain," she said quietly, then louder to the others, "Mountain! The answer is mountain!"

"Correct," said Boletus.

The roots rebraided themselves forming the bridge once again.

"Move your ass, dude!" Jopp called, "Get back over here!"

"No!" said Phyos, "it won't let him cross. Only the person who answered!" She looked to Loi, "You better get your tight blue behind over there."

Loi pulled out her own sonic machete and shot Rohi a wink, "I won't let anything happen to your fella."

"Better not," Rohi replied.

The three bramble cats were closing in. Chuck realized in another few seconds, he'd be hopelessly cornered. He took a deep breath, said "Fuck it," and charged the cat on his right. The creatures flinched with surprise and Chuck took advantage as he lunged into his target, hacking and slashing with reckless abandon. The bramble cat got one good slash in on Chuck's right thigh before it found itself reduced to a pile of kindling. The pain of the new wound took hold, and Chuck dropped to one knee. He looked up just as the next plant beast pounced. Right as the two tangled wads of thorns acting as paws were about to rake across Chuck's face, a white blade flashed across his vision with a high-pitched whine. Both paws were severed off, and the cat stumbled to the ground. Chuck grabbed the outstretched blue hand and pulled himself up to eye level with Loi.

"Thanks," he said.

"Yup," she replied, "Now look alive!"

Across the bridge, Phyos barked at the Boletus, "Next question! C'mon!"

"Many have heard me, but nobody has seen me, and I will not speak back until spoken to..."

The one unhurt bramble cat lunged and Loi gave it a ferocious chop, eliciting a high-pitched shriek that reverberated off the rocky walls of the gorge below.

"I believe I know the answer," announced Bhanakhana.

"Wait, don't say it!" said Jopp.

"What are you doing?" hissed Rohi. "We can see Chuck is bleeding over there. They need help!"

"No shit. So wouldn't it be better if we could all cross over right now?"

"Again, that's *not* how this system works," noted Phyos.

Jopp smiled, "So let's game the system."

He waved everyone in close and they started whispering.

"What the fuck are they doing?" Loi peered back across the gorge.

"Oh, they're hugging... that's nice. I'm want a hug too."

Loi glanced down at Chuck with a raised eyebrow, "We should really stop your bleeding, huh?"

Some odd motion pulled Loi's eyes back to their assailants. To her shock, the four damaged bramble cats separated into two pairs. Then all four seemed to come apart, unwinding their thorny, berry-laden vines until they resembled normal bushes. They only stayed that way for a second before each pair started wrapping themselves together, melding and reforming until all that was left were two, fully formed bramble cats.... much larger than normal bramble cats. Their snarls sounded almost like amused laughter.

"Ok, I know you're hurting," Loi said in a coaching manner, "But I need you to get up. You've gotta have a solid pair of yub nubs on you if you were able to lock down Agent Badass over there. So let's *go*!"

Chuck gritted his teeth and pushed up off his knee with a determined growl.

"Hell yeah, Earth man!"

Back across the way, the others had lined up shoulder to shoulder.

"Okay, ready?" said Jopp, "On three...one, two, *three*!"

In unison, Bhanakhana, Phyos, Rohi, and Jopp shouted at the Boletus.

"Echo!"

For a moment, nothing happened. Then the beige roots appeared and reformed the bridge.

"Go ahead... cheaters," grumbled the Boletus.

The four of them sprinted across the bridge with sonic machetes drawn. Rohi broke away from the back and hurled herself at the large bramble cats with a howl. Intergalactic bio-botanists have long debated the level of consciousness in Gjenlu's plant animals, or plantimals. Had any of them been present, they would've been thrilled to observe the bramble cats acknowledging the added threat of four additional blade-wielding adversaries, presumably calculating this to be an unacceptable reversal of momentum and opting to make a hasty retreat. Out of sheer spite, Rohi managed to clip the tip off one of their tails as they disappeared into the dense foliage.

"Hey guys," waved Chuck, right before he stumbled, and dropped straight down on to his backside.

Everyone except Phyos rushed to him. Bhanakhana started pulling items from his satchel and giving orders.

"Jopp, Loi, clean his wounds with these sterilizer pads. Then use that Wound Sealant spray foam stuff to close them up. Rohi, talk to him, try to keep him calm, and get him to drink this electrolyte tonic."

Phyos sauntered up to the nearest tree and cleared her throat. It woke up, looked at her, and scoffed, "I'm in no mood to deal with meat things this season."

Phyos held up a small sack. "I see you fine folk are sprouting karakaro fruit. I need some. In trade I can offer this bag is a pure blend of nitro-phosphate. No fillers."

"Peddle your filth elsewhere, stinking meat thing."

The tree closed its eyes.

"Pssssst!" hissed a voice to her left. Phyos glanced over at the tree, two stumps down.

"Interested?" she asked.

"Does that nitro-phosphate have potash in it?"

"Of course it does. I'm not a savage."

"I'll drop three karakaro fruits for it."

"Deal," Phyos said with a smile.

The tree's thick, bushy top wriggled a bit and three lime green orbs dropped to the ground. Phyos hopped over and held up the sack. "Want me to go ahead and sprinkle it all around your base?"

"Yes, please!" answered the tree.

Phyos upended the sack, and the crimson dirt crystals spilled out. She spread it all around evenly, patted the tree's trunk and said, "Thanks."

"Ooooooo, that's good," moaned the tree.

Phyos scooped up the fruit and hurried over to the others. She tossed one of the karakaro fruits to Rohi.

"Crack that open and make him eat all the 'fruit meat' inside. Bramble cat thorns release a slow-acting venom when they strike something. This fruit has enzymes that'll counteract the venom."

Rohi pried open the green orb and handed it to Chuck who attacked the fruit with eager greed.

"Mmm, tastes like a lime crossed with a mango," he said.

"If you say so."

"You okay, bud?" Jopp asked.

Chuck swallowed the mouthful of fruit and nodded. "Yeah. I think so. You know, it's the weirdest thing... I tried to get back across to you guys by answering another question... and the thing asked me this riddle that's virtually identical to this one we have back on Earth... I answered but it said I was wrong."

"What was the riddle?" asked Rohi.

"I go on four legs in the morning, two in the afternoon, and three in the evening. What am I?"

"Oh, that's easy," said Phyos.

"Yeah, even I know that," said Jopp.

"The answer is a Wae Wae," explained Bhanakhana, "It is a scaly amphibious animal that awakens early in the morning with four legs. At midday, when its native sun is highest in the sky, it sheds two legs. A third then regrows at dusk, and then the fourth grows back while it sleeps. The cycle begins anew at dawn."

"Oh," said Chuck. Then he fell asleep.

WORD SECTION 0036

Chuck opened his eyes to see Rohi standing over him.

"Sorry, I must have really needed to rest. How long was I out?" he asked with a yawn.

She arched an eyebrow. "Fifteen minutes."

"Oh... well I feel a lot better."

She held her hand out. He took it and pulled himself off the ground with a pained wince.

"You good?"

"Yeah," he answered, "us Earth men aren't quite as squishy as you all might think."

"Yeah, you are," said Jopp through a mouthful of freeze-dried snack rations.

Chuck saw Bhanakhana, Phyos, and Loi with their faces buried in notebooks.

"What's going on over there?" he asked.

"Loi's getting a quick download on what those two already know, sharing any insights that might be helpful."

"Yeah, you know that old cliché on how slimy thieves are always so well versed in ancient history," scoffed Jopp.

Rohi shot him an annoyed look. "She's been sniffing after the Adherent since long before we knew they existed, not to mention she grew up in an group home run by the Church of Rhonac. And look, I know she fucked you over about as bad as one person can do to another, short of causing them serious physical harm... but if that hadn't happened, all of us would've never met. Your current best friends wouldn't be in your life at all. So, think about that next time you feel like making a snide comment about that incident…" She gave Chuck a quick glance, letting him see the mischievous glint in her eye, "because every time you do, you might as well be telling Chuck and Bhanakhana you wish you'd never met them."

"Wait," said Jopp, "What? That's not… I mean, that seems a little…"

Chuck put on a show of looking disappointed, shaking his head and muttering, "Not cool, dude."

He and Rohi headed over to others.

Jopp scratched the side of his head. "What just- you're fucking with me, right? Chuck? You're just being a dick, right?"

Chuck and Rohi fought back a giggle as they approached, arriving just in time to hear Phyos say, "So, that's what we need to do if we want to fuck this cake properly."

"Well, that was either the best or the worst time to join a conversation," quipped Chuck.

"Hey!" said a smiling Phyos, "Look who's not writhing in venom-induced agony while dying a slow death!"

"Chuck, how are you?" asked Bhanakhana.

"I'm hanging in there, big guy."

"We got a plan?" asked Rohi.

"Kinda," answered Loi, "The Ak'alei site should be in or around those twin mountains we've been heading toward. If you remember the planetary map display, the western one has a river around it, so we should start with the eastern one. It's a pretty straight shot down that path through the trees over there."

She pointed toward a narrow, but open lane between a cluster of the thick trees.

"Should we be fortunate enough to avoid any further impediments," added Bhanakhana, "It will only take less than an hour to arrive at the base of the eastern mountain."

"Great," said Rohi, "What are the odds of us actually avoiding any impediments?"

"It's not exactly zero, but mathematically close enough that I feel comfortable rounding down. There's virtually zero chance we avoid all impediments."

"Impediment is a fun word," said Chuck.

"It is, isn't it?" concurred Phyos.

"Super great," said Rohi.

"Um, hey…" said Loi, "where'd the path go?"

They all looked over and saw the previously open path had been completely filled with vines, branches, and leaves.

"Impediment!" announced Chuck.

"Honestly, is it too much to ask for you uncouth meat things to cease sullying our home and just go back where you came from?" whined a crusty voice.

They noticed a nearby tree peering down at them with open disdain.

"Oh would you give that nonsense a rest?" Phyos shot back. She waved at the tree with whom she'd traded plant food for fruit. "That one didn't have any problem with us."

The tree rolled its eyes. "Of course not. Jon loves being a contrarian just to aggravate the rest of us."

"Shove it up your stump, Nancy!" Jon the tree snapped back.

Chuck scanned the faces of his friends, looking for any kind of reaction to the trees' names.

Nancy the tree rolled its eyes again and said, "Please leave. None of us normal trees want you in our grove."

"Being on the receiving end of unabashed racism from a tree is not something I ever expected to experience," mused Rohi. "This is a weird day."

"Almost as weird as two days ago when we saw a giant space caterpillar puppy fish eat a spaceship," noted Chuck.

Rohi gave him an inquisitive look. Chuck nodded, "Yeah, it's been one of *those* types of adventures."

Bhanakhana attempted to placate the tree. "Greetings, my photosynthetic friend. My name is Bhanakhana and I have dedicated my life to studying fascinating and under-appreciated sentient civilizations across the universe. I find you and your brethren to be truly spectacular. I would be greatly honored if you might allow me to learn about your kind. I could write a dissertation that would earn your society the intergalactic respect it so rightly deserves."

Nancy closed her eyes. The sound of leaves rustling ripples through the trees like a wave. She reopened her eyes and said, "We'll pass."

Bhanakhana started to protest, but Jopp interjected, "We're the meat thing decontamination squad!"

"The what?" said Nancy.

"Yeah, the *what*?" echoed Phyos.

Jopp pointed ahead, "See, just on the other side of your, uh, lovely grove here is a bunch of meat thing junk..."

"*Junk*? What is junk?"

"Refuse," answered Bhanakhana, picking up on where Jopp was heading.

"Yes! Refuse! There's some refuse... uh, like..."

"Flesh waste," said Bhanakhana, causing nauseated expressions to appear across the faces of the others.

"*Flesh waste*," reacted Jopp, "What the shit is- I mean yeah, totally! Flesh waste! There's some big piles of flesh waste back there. It was left by some real uncivilized meat things..."

"That's a redundant phrase."

"Okay, well, we're here to remove it from your grove. It's by that big mountain."

"I haven't heard any rumblings from the interior. I can't imagine that is something our community would be quiet about." Nancy eyed them with cautious suspicion.

"Because it's still up in the mountain," Chuck jumped in. "But, like, if left unattended... meat thing flesh waste can... self-multiply?"

"Why did you voice go up like you were asking a question?"

"It's not a question, it's a certainty," Phyos picked things up. "Meat thing flesh waste will self-multiply if left unattended. If we don't get back in there to remove it, it will slowly grow, spreading out from the mountain, and eventually reach your grove, consuming everything in its path like a meaty, fleshy fungus."

"Pardon me, I take serious offense to that. All the fungus I know are exceptional beings, and all much more sophisticated than any meat things I've encountered."

"We apologize," said Rohi, "But that doesn't change the fact that this is a real threat to you fine tree folk."

"Yeah," added Loi, "We just need to get in and out. We'll get back in there, decontaminate the..." she fought back a grimace, "the flesh waste, and then leave this place forever."

Nancy closed its eyes again, and once more the sound of rustling leaves rippled back and forth among the trees. Nancy re-opened its eyes and said, "Please hurry. And try to touch as little of the foliage as possible."

The tangle of vines and branches rustled and parted, revealing a very clear, very straight path straight back toward the eastern mountain.

"Thank you," said Bhanakhana.

"Just go," was all Nancy said before returning to sleep.

WORD SECTION 0037

The crew moved quickly down the provided path, finding the ground to be remarkably smooth and level. And while they encountered no more real hindrances to their progress, the near constant glares and barely muffled mutterings of things like "Well, I never…", "What a disgrace…" and "Tsk tsk, the grove's really gone to peat…" had started to wear a bit thin.

Finally, they emerged from the tree-enclosed path into an open, sunny clearing. The gigantic mesa of tan rock rose up hundreds of meters into the air above them. The trees had kept their distance from the rocky tower, leaving a wide strip of bare ground between the edge of the grove and the base of the mountain. To their left, they could see the western mesa looming high above the trees.

Bhanakhana kept looking from his notebook up to the mountain and back again. He started meandering around the clearing, gradually getting closer to the rock.

"So…." said Jopp, "what now?"

Rohi noticed a light start blinking on her data bracelet.

"Hey, I'm finally getting a bit of a signal out here. Oh shit, there's like twenty-two new messages. Let's see…

U.L.E. detachment unit arrived in orbit… Waiting for further instructions… obviously I couldn't send any. Hopefully, they've been reading the latest Standard Operating Procedure newsletters and followed Protocol 19-15-19… heh heh, the last newsletter had this funny cartoon about an agent who accidentally enacted Protocol 34-10-6 when he *meant* to follow Protocol 6-10-34. Ha!"

Rohi noticed everyone staring at her with raised eyebrows.

Jopp coughed and said, "Nerd!"

Chuck slugged him in the arm.

"I'm not judging you," said Loi, "but I am reevaluating our friendship."

"Oh hush! The long and short of it is they should be scanning for my bracelet's location ping."

"They aren't going to try to fly a ship out here, are they?" said Phyos.

"Everyone!" Bhanakhana's voice rang out, "I have found something most intriguing!"

They looked around and saw he'd apparently wandered off.

"Where'd you go, B?" Chuck called.

"Circle around to the east side!"

They followed the sound of his voice to the right and around the mountain, finding him gently tracing his fingers over something in the rock face. When they got closer, they saw he was brushing off dust, revealing a series of glyphs carved into the stone. The patch he was brushing began to form a vertical strip, about a half meter in width.

"It looks like writing," noted Rohi.

"Why aren't my ReadAll contacts translating it?" Chuck asked.

"It's the language of the Ak'alei," said Phyos. "Not much motivation for the ReadAll manufacturers to expend resources coding in the language of a ten thousand year old dead civilization..."

"Unless they found a way to make money off it," quipped Jopp.

"Ha, yeah," said Chuck, "you know Prime Partners would be all over that shit."

"Hey, you got some more over here," Loi stepped over and joined Bhanakhana in dusting off the rock.

They revealed two parallel columns of script, about two meters apart. They both stretched up higher than anyone could reach from the ground level. They even tried having Bhanakhana hold Jopp up to dust off more of the script.

"This is the most embarrassing thing that's ever been done to me," he grumbled.

"Even worse than the Pandilyx Incident?" asked Chuck.

Bhanakhana couldn't help but let a small snicker out.

"What's the..." Rohi started.

"Nothing!" snapped Jopp.

"I feel like you have to tell us now," said Phyos.

"As long as I'm alive, that story will never be repeated! And you can put me down, Big Red. I can't reach any higher."

With the combination of Bhanakhana lifting Jopp, they'd been able to uncover three meters worth of Ak'alei runes. Bhanakhana set Jopp down and stepped back to take it all in.

"So what's the part we can see say?" asked Rohi.

Bhanakhana and Phyos started looking back and forth from the ciphers in their notes to the runes and making notes.

"Door," said Loi, "It basically just says door."

They all looked back at her.

"That's a lot of fucking scribbling just to say door," noted Rohi.

"The Ak'alei were a long winded bunch," countered Loi. "They loved using as many words as possible to say as little as possible."

"Oh," said Chuck with a wry grin, "I didn't know Jopp was part Ak'alei."

That earned him a robust middle finger from his stout yellow friend.

"May we move the conversation backward for a moment?" asked Bhanakhana, "You can read the Ak'alei language?"

"Read, write, speak... yep," answered Loi.

"I think we need move the convo backward a little bit more," said Phyos.

"What's the most artifact rich, extensive Ak'alei archeological site ever found?" Loi asked.

"Besides this one we were about to uncover before you went all cryptic on us?" said Phyos.

"Jattuir-3," answered Bhanakhana.

"According to the Sentient Coalition, yes. But there's a site much larger and better preserved than Jattuir. It's under Old Kanisa on Venova Prime. You just don't know about it because it's the property of the Church of Rhonac. They've never let the outside universe know. One of the more closely guarded beliefs the church holds is that Venovans are descendants of the Ak'alei. The language is taught as a sacred gift in Rhonacian children's homes."

"Technology," said Phyos.

"What?"

"They found working Ak'alei technology there, didn't they?"

Loi nodded.

Phyos pinched the bridge of her nose and breathed, "Fuck, that explains a lot."

"Cool story," said Jopp, "So what do we do now?"

"We open the door," said Phyos matter of factly.

"That's not a door. That's a wall of rock with cave-alien graffiti on it."

"It says it's a door," insisted Loi.

"So what do we do?" asked Rohi.

"We use a key," said Bhanakhana. He held his hand out to Phyos. "May I have the Ta'kenite box, Professor?"

"Oh yeeeeeaaaaaah," she snapped her fingers, and retrieved the box from her satchel. She tossed it to Bhanakhana, "Feel free to do the honors."

Bhanakhana opened it and held up the pinkish metal quill.

"Well that's interesting," said Phyos.

The others saw she was staring back at the rock face. They looked too and were surprised to see something new. A small section of one of the rune columns was now glowing with a soft yellow light.

"It started when you took that little doodad out of the box. The Ta'kenite must have been blocking whatever signal it emits."

Bhanakhana took a few cautious steps closer to the light. When he was less than a meter away, a small hole appeared within it. He stopped and looked back at the others with eyebrows raised.

"Dude," said Jopp, "what are you waiting for? Stick it in already."

His comment hung in the air for a brief moment before all six of them, even Bhanakhana, allowed themselves a giggle.

"But seriously," said Chuck, "Let's go. It's ancient alien temple time! This is the kind of stuff I've been waiting for ever since Jopp's drunken ass got me accidentally abducted by aliens in the first place!"

"Best day of your life. You're welcome by the way."

Bhanakhana reached forward, sliding the narrow end key into the hole.

Nothing happened.

"Well, that was anti-climactic," noted Rohi.

"You guys smell something?" said Loi. "I smell something... weird. It's vaguely familiar..."

"It wasn't me," said Phyos.

"So do we like go home now?" asked Jopp.

"Wait," said Chuck, "It's a key. Try turning it."

Bhanakhana tried to turn it. The key rotated smoothly for ninety degrees and then seemed to stick in place with an audible click. The carved text closest to the key lit up with a pleasant yellow glow. Then the light extended upward, illuminating the vertical band of runes. It traveled almost four meters high, revealing the text they'd been unable to reach before, then the light curved, forming an arch of glowing script. It traveled straight down, connecting with the other vertical strip of text. They were all now staring at a glowing, arched doorway of runes etched into the flat rock face.

There was a creaking and a cracking and the stone inside and around the doorway began to crumble away. They all stepped back and stared up in stunned awe as large swaths of the outer rock layer on the mesa towering over them dissolved and fell to the ground as dust. They stepped back even further to avoid the falling debris. Wherever the tanned rock dissolved, a protuberance of stonework, colored pale gray with orange marbling, remained. There were decorative arches, buttresses, balconies... The rock within the original doorway has melted away to reveal a staircase that wrapped around the outside of the mountain for a short stretch, before turning to lead inward.

When the literal dust finally settled, they found themselves looking up at an ancient temple that appeared to have been genetically spliced with the mountain. Some areas had remained unchanged, looking like a perfectly natural patch of tan rock. Then, right next to that, an balcony of glossy gray and orange stone hung defiantly out over the forest below.

"Wow," said Rohi.

"Holy shit," said Jopp.

"Damn," said Loi.

"Marvelous," said Bhanakhana.

"Not too shabby," said Phyos.

"That. Was. Awesome!" said Chuck.

"Yes," said an unfamiliar voice, "It is indeed awe inspiring."

They turned to see almost two dozen Venovan men and women wearing Rhonacian garb come from around the corner of the temple-mountain hybrid. Their eyes were drawn to the two men out front. One stood head and shoulders above all the others, and while he was plenty imposing in his own right, he was obviously putting considerable extra effort into the murderous scowl he wore. The other man out front was more average in build. His facial expression was curiously serene, unsettlingly sinister, and to Rohi and Loi, dishearteningly familiar.

Chuck raised his eyebrows. "Impediment?"

WORD SECTION 0038

Rohi and Loi glared at the lead Venovan and snarled in unison, "Mavros."

The middle aged man smiled wide and said, "Hello again, Agent." Then to Loi he said, "And our wayward acolyte... what was your name again?"

"Fuck yourself," Loi growled.

"How dare you spit such filth in front of the Noble Herald!" the tall Venovan bellowed while raising a fist clad in a gold plated gauntlet. "Your smiting is long overdue, heretics!"

Rohi noted the golden gauntlet, the size of the fellow, the use of the word heretic...

"I think this is our friend from the Pa Mahinga byway."

"Did you bring the Bloodfist Hand Cannon?" Loi asked.

"Yeah, but it's buried in my satchel. Doubt they'll give me the time to root around for it."

"Damn," said Loi, "guess we'll have to improvise."

The big Venovan cracked his neck. "Shall I break these heretics, Noble Herald Mavros?"

"Not just yet, Teza. They may yet prove useful to our Lord." Mavros looked over his shoulder to an acolyte, "Send up the flare. Signal the ship to come in."

"That's a bad idea," whispered Phyos.

The acolyte raised a small metal cylinder, and a narrow beam of red light shot straight up into the sky.

Loi rankled her nose as the vaguely familiar odor wafted through the air again. She noticed Phyos sniffing at the air as well. The professor addressed Herald Mavros.

"I suppose you're the fella in charge? Tell me, how did a... *menagerie* such as yours get through the tree line? I've only known you for a few seconds, but honestly you don't strike me as the sort that'd groove well with the locals."

She focused on him, straining to avoid a direct glance at the dozens of vines delicately snaking their way out of the trees behind the Venovans.

He gave her a smug grin. "You're referring to the soulless abominations that infest this planet?"

Mavros held his hand out to the side and an acolyte place a metal thermos in his palm. He then casually tossed it forward. It landed with an empty thunk and rolled to a lazy stop just a few feet away from Phyos and the others.

Loi gasped, "Rage Flame."

"Why waste my valuable time trying to reason with *plants* when I can just burn a path straight through them?"

Phyos' mottled green face flushed purple, "That was an even worse idea."

The big one, Teza, let out a deep guffaw, "Heathen, do we appear frightened? We are the Faithful, protected by the divine blessing of the one true God. We have been chosen, and nothing, especially not a patch of overgrown weeds, will stand in our-"

The moment he said 'weeds' the vines behind them snapped forward, wrapping around necks, arms, legs, torsos... The acolytes screamed as half of them were immediately yanked back into the dense foliage. It was a tossup whether the cracking sounds that punctuated the shrieking came from tree branches or Venovan bones.

"Kill the trees!" cried Mavros, "Burn them!"

The remaining acolytes looked around at each other and realized none of them had any Rage Flame canisters. Everyone who'd been carrying them had been taken.

The vines lashed out again. Some acolytes fought back with their poleaxes, either chopping at the vines with the blade or blasting orange electricity in the hopes of scorching the assaulting vegetation. Some did nothing, their wide eyes starting at Mavros, waiting for orders.

Mavros watched two more of his disciples get dragged away before shouting, "Pull back!"

His followers were more than happy to oblige and they all sprinted toward the base of the mountain, putting as much distance between themselves and the murderous plant life as possible. They skidded to a halt, breathing heavy while leaning up against the tan stone. The vines recoiled, slithering back to disappear within the tree line.

Mavros panted, "Once we've returned Rhonac's glory to this dimension... I'm making it my personal mission to come back here and turn this entire island into one large pyre."

Teza glanced around and said, "Noble Herald... where have the heretics gone?"

WORD SECTION 0039

Rohi lead the way as they raced up the stairs into the Ak'alei temple. Loi stayed at a close second, clutching the temple key in her hand. Bhanakhana held third place, while Chuck and Jopp brought up the rear. Phyos, due to her hip being 'so brittle a vigorous fart could turn it to dust' had opted to hop a ride on Bhanakhana's broad back. Chuck couldn't help but smile at that.

"What the *huff* hell are you so *puff* happy about?!" grunted Jopp.

"Total *wheeze* Yoda moment right there."

"What?!"

"Reference."

"We're literally *pant* running for our lives... knock that shit off."

They wound around a corner and skidded to a halt on a landing overlooking the interior of the temple. Twisting, curving pathways and stairs branched out in every possible direction. A veritable stew of gears and clockwork machinery churned below them.

"It's like an Escher painting," gasped Chuck.

Jopp slugged him in the arm. "No more references."

"Ow, that one doesn't count. It's fine art, not pop culture."

"What is this place?" asked Rohi.

"The Stairgate," said Bhanakhana.

Chuck coughed, "Did you just say Stairgate? Sounds like a terrible parody flick."

Jopp punched him again.

Bhanakhana flipped through his copy of the notebook. When he found the page he was looking for, he held it up so Phyos could read it over his shoulder. The page held a crude drawing of criss-crossed staircases with a few words scribbled below it.

Phyos read aloud, "The Stairgate guards the bridge to the map. Take the wrong stair and be lost until you die of thirst. The wrong answer is never right."

A loud clicking sound echoed off the walls and the staircase directly in front of them broke away from the landing and reconnected with another platform across the way.

"Damn!" said Chuck, hopping back from now precipitous landing edge.

Rohi looked back down the way they'd come. "We need to move."

"Okay, Science People," Loi looked from Phyos and Bhanakhana to Chuck, "and quirky dude who apparently knows lots of weird but sometimes useful nonsense, which way do we go?"

"I'm really sick of all the cryptic shit," groaned Jopp, "For once can't we just have some clear directions?"

Bhanakhana grinned, "We do. The wrong answer is never right. The right is never wrong. We take the stairs to the right."

"Hot plops," said Phyos, "I think he might be onto something."

Above them came the clicking of another staircase shifting positions. Behind them came the stomps of their pursuers.

"Works for me," said Rohi, "Let's go!"

They rushed up the stairs to the right, reached another landing with three options, and took the stairs to the right. This lead them downward in a gentle curve to another landing. From there they went up and to the left, down and to the right, up and to the right, down, down, and down again where the rightmost path took them on a flat, winding journey through the bowels of the temple. Finally they came to a landing with stairs to the right that spiraled directly upward.

They took a moment to catch their collective breathes.

"I kind of hate the Ak'alei right now," huffed Jopp.

"Yeah," said Loi, "This just seems like some totally unnecessary dickery."

"This reminds me of the first quarter of my typical exercise warm-up regiment," said Bhanakhana, "Another twenty minutes of this and I might actually begin to perspire."

"Quit showing off, B," said Chuck.

Rohi tried to peer up to the top of the spiraling stairs. "I think this might be a straight shot to the top of the temple."

Phyos lightly tapped her heels into Bhanakhana. "Mush, mush."

The hulking Dronla smiled and began to climb. The others all took deep breaths and followed. After a tiring trek up the stairs that, as it turned out, did reach all the way to the top, the group stepped out onto the flat, dusty surface of the mesa. Phyos slid down off Bhanakhana's back and looked north to the roiling jumble of clouds.

"Storm's a coming."

Two stone pylons protruded from the edge of the mountain, perfectly framing the nearby western mountain. None of them had a chance to admire the view, however, as they all focused on the lone Venovan woman sitting atop one of the pylons. A thin smoke-stick hung from the corner of her mouth, and she was casually twirling an orange-bladed dagger with one hand. They all stood still, save for Loi who slowly stepped forward, her mouth hanging open.

The woman tossed aside the smoke-stick, sheathed her dagger, slipped down off the pylon, and smiled at Loi as she said, "It's been a long time, Sister."

WORD SECTION 0040

The uncomfortable silence hung in air for a painful handful of seconds before Loi finally found her voice.

"Se- Serru?"

Serru Dac'eth nodded.

Loi caught herself instinctively moving to embrace her, eyes falling on Serru's black clothes and the Rhonacian symbol around her neck.

"How..."

Serru smirked. "...did I get up here? I have a spaceship, Loi. It's picking up my associates down on the ground. They'll be joining us in a moment."

"What are you doing here, Serru?"

"The same thing you are: searching for *Hirth-Ak'alei.*"

"*They're* looking for that shit," Loi flung her hand toward the others, "I was just looking for *you*! That's *all* I've done! For fifteen fucking years!"

Serru canted her head. "*All* you've done?" She then gave Phyos, Bhanakhana, Chuck, and Jopp a glance. "Hello, again. I see you all made it through the other side of the Maelstrom alive and well."

"Hello again to *you*, Psychotic Murder Monk," replied Phyos.

Bhanakhana and Jopp coughed in surprise. Serru let another grin tug at the corner of her mouth.

Rohi whispered to Chuck, "*You know her?*"

Chuck gave a slight nod, "*From the Barge... She handed us our asses on a platter.*"

Before Rohi could respond she saw the pair of brilliant orange eyes fix on her.

"You're the agent who's been nipping after my heels since Pa Mahinga."

Rohi's eyebrows raised. "You killed Alu Glyf?"

Serru nodded, "Sadly, yes. One of the many sacrifices my path has forced me to make."

"Your *path*?" Loi spat, "Serru, knock the shit off and help us get out of here."

Serru held her hand up. "Loi, I know you're confused and I'm sure you have many *many* questions. But we simply don't have the time. In a few seconds, my..." she glanced at Phyos, "*esteemed colleagues* will be joining us. Give me the key, agree to comply with us for the remainder of this journey, and I can promise none of you will be harmed."

"Cause you've got such a great track record of *not* harming people, right?" snipped Rohi.

Loi looked back at her, "Please, *please* let me handle this."

"There is nothing to handle, Loi. It's over. Your choice is either comply with us or die."

The whirring of a ship's engine drowned out whatever retort might otherwise have been offered. Everyone, save for Serru, took a staggering step backwards as her Emissary cruiser rose up from behind her into the air above the mountain top. The side portal slid open as a ramp extended down to them. A squad of ten acolytes descended first. Their crisp and clean uniforms indicated they had not been part of the kerfufflc with the trees. After them came Mavros, Teza Lo, and three acolytes who all definitely looked like they'd gotten the shit kicked out of them by vengeful plant life.

Mavros fixed a murderous glare toward Phyos and the others.

"You will all pay for what you've done."

"Hey, fuck you, dude!" Jopp couldn't help himself, "Not our fault you picked a fight with an entire forest!"

"The lad has a point" added Phyos. "This is obviously a misunderstanding... like I've said before, we're just on a school field trip."

Mavros' cheeks flushed with violet rage. He opened his mouth to undoubtedly shriek for someone's head to roll, but another voice cut him off.

"And besides," Serru strode across flat dusty mesa, stopping between Mavros and Phyos, her eyes locked on the latter, "They've seen the error of their ways, and have agreed to comply with our objectives. At least, that was my understanding. But if I was *mistaken*, by all means, Noble Herald, I agree they should be cleansed... starting with the mouthy yellow one."

Serru held her hand out, palm up. Phyos let out a defeated sigh, and rolled her eyes as she dropped the key in Serru's hand. The Venovan woman smiled, her orange eyes brilliant against her dark blue skin, as turned around and held the pink, quill shaped key up.

"Would you like to do the honors, Noble Herald?"

Mavros' smile resembled a gluttonous child sizing up a frosted slice of jubla. He practically hopped over to Serru to snatch the key. After a moment of ogling, he composed himself, cleared his throat, and declared, "Our faith has been rewarded! We are so very close now, my kin!"

The acolytes pounded their pole-axes against the stone ground in a wordless chant. As Mavros approached the twin stone pylons, a yellow light appeared on the right one. He reached forward and inserted the key into the hole at the light's center.

"Behold the majesty of our divine ancestors!"

He held his hands out in triumph

Nothing happened.

The stomping of the pole-axes awkwardly petered out. Mavros glanced nervously over his shoulder and then leaned forward to pull the key out and put it back in. Still, nothing happened.

"Sir?"

Chuck flinched as every set of eyes wheeled around to stare at him.

"You, uh, you gotta turn it a little."

He mimed the key-turning motion.

Bhanakhana raised his hand, "I had that issue, as well."

Mavros huffed as he gave the key an unnecessarily hard turn, and then stepped back with his arms crossed.

The creaking of ancient gear works echoed through the valley. A tan stone slab sprouted from between the pylons and extended outward. An identical length of tan stone emerged from the opposite mountain and stretched toward the other. Support beams hewn from metal and stone grew out below the lengthening planks above. They met in the middle with a heavy thud. Everyone gawked at the newly formed stone bridge that now spanned the half kilometer distance between the twin mountains.

The show wasn't over. The west mountain began to shift and change, much like the one they all stood on. Balconies jutted out in all directions. Curved walkways swirled around the exterior. Long spires stabbed toward the sky. Much more of the seemingly plain rock face dissolved away to revealed the complex structure within. Finally the transformation ended. Chuck thought the final product looked like a roller coaster had been wrapped around a Roman coliseum. As if to put a pin in the whole spectacle, the looming storm unleashed a thunderous clap.

Mavros held his hands out again and proclaimed, "Behold the"

A sudden discordant siren wail cut him off. Everyone looked up to see three small short-range scout ships, charcoal gray with neon purple trim. They fanned out to get proper targeting coverage of the Emissary vessel as well as the people on the mountain top. An amplified voice sounded from the middle ship.

"This is the Universal Law Enforcement Agency, Pacifier Squadron 2319. We order you to stand down."

WORD SECTION 0041

Rohi saw it in Mavros' eyes, maybe even before he knew it himself. She saw the look of desperate determination that often preceded some foolish crim going down in a 'Blaze of Glory'.

"Herald Mavros, please don't do anything foolish…"

Not a word of it registered with the Venovan man as his expression morphed into grim resolve.

"Defend the faith!" was all he needed to say to unleash pure chaos. The acolytes scattered. The U.L.E. ships opened fire. The Emissary fired a volley from its port-side cannon. The U.L.E. Pacifier dipped to avoid the shot. Teza burst upward, leaping impossibly high toward the lowest U.L.E. ship.

They watched in terrified awe as the bestial Venovan soared through the air, landing right on the Pacifier's cockpit windshield. He reared back with a closed fist.

"No way," said Rohi, "That glass is strong enough to handle flights in low orbit. No way."

Teza's knuckles connected with the windshield. A single crack appeared. He struck again. The crack blossomed into a spiderweb. Finally, the U.L.E. agents inside snapped out of their shock. They banked to the side in an effort to dump him off, but it was too late. Teza's grip was too strong, and his third strike was already in motion. The windshield shattered.

"No fucking way," Rohi's felt a primal need to help her fellow agents rise up from within. She pried her eyes away from the airborne spectacle, tore open her satchel, and started rooting around for her weapon. A hand gripped her arm, and she immediately swung a defensive punch toward the unknown assailant.

Chuck has fully expected Rohi to react with a mean left hook and he ducked to avoid the blow.

"It's me! It's me!"

"Oh shit. Sorry."

"No worries, but c'mon. We're making a break for it."

A scream pulled their gaze skyward. They watched Teza single handedly yank an agent out of the cockpit and toss him toward the ground. The agent hit the rock just a few meters in front of them with a sickening crunch. Rohi sprinted to him. She knelt down to check the agent's pulse. He was gone. Rohi steeled herself as her training instincts took over and she checked his gear for anything useful. His sidearm had been smashed in the fall, but the pair of incendiary shinebombs on his belt appeared unmarred. She quickly transferred them to her own belt and stared up at Teza with fiery hatred. She felt her fingers wrap around the handle of the Bloodfist Hand Cannon within her satchel.

"Rohi, we gotta go," Chuck pleaded.

"One. Second. Sweetie."

She raised the over-sized pistol, lined up a shot, and fired. She'd been aiming for Teza's midsection but hitting a humanoid-sized target on a flailing scout ship, forty meters in the air would've been a tall order for even the universe's best marksmen. Nevertheless, her shot managed to take a chunk out of Teza's right thigh. He rolled off the front of the cockpit, barely managing to hang on to the ship with one hand.

"Okay," said Rohi, "Let's go."

•　　　•　　　•

"Almost there," Phyos thought to herself as she crept toward the bridge. She reached out and plucked the quill key from the pylon. Before she could even enjoy this small victory, a strong hand grabbed her shoulder and spun her around. Serru looked down at her with an expression that was more disappointed than mad.

"Professor, give me the key or I will kill you. Apologies being so curt, but as you can see…"

She nodded her head upwards where one of the U.L.E. Pacifiers took a glancing hit from the Emissary. It returned fire, knocking out one of the Emissary's few turrets.

"…I don't have time to mince words."

Phyos took a deep breath and tightened her grip on the key. "I'm sorry, dear. But I think I've yielded to you and yours for the last time today."

Serru's eyes glowed with orange light. Just as she started to raise her hands, Loi dove between them. Serru hesitated. The two of them locked eyes.

"Serru, please."

"Move."

"I can't let you hurt her."

This seemed to almost amuse Serru, the glow subsided from her eyes. "Loi, do you really think you could stop me?"

Loi shook her head. "No. But he might."

Serru turned just in time to watch Bhanakhana's open palm connect with her own sternum. The air exploded from her lungs as she was sent hurtling backward, right over the mesa's edge.

"I didn't mean for you to kill her!" Loi hollered at Bhanakhana.

"I would be stunned if that were the case," Bhanakhana replied, "We have traded blows before. Trust me when I say I could not afford to give her the slightest chance to counter my attack."

"Yeah, she's not dead." Jopp was leaning out over where she'd fallen. "She caught herself on one of them outside staircases. She looks more pissed than hurt. Oh fuck yeah, she's pissed. We should run."

Chuck and Rohi caught up.

"What's happening?" asked Chuck, "We running for it?"

"Yep, good ol' *Plan A*," said Jopp.

Bhanakhana took off, scooping Phyos up with one arm as he bounded out on to the bridge. Jopp followed closely behind. He saw Phyos looking down at him from over Bhanakhana's shoulder.

"Be-been in th-this sit-situation be-fore?" She asked as the bouncing of Bhanakhana's gate jostled her about.

"Ki-*huff*-kind of," answered Jopp, "Swap out the culty psychopaths for more pirate-y and corporate-y psychopaths."

Chuck unsheathed his machete and looked to Rohi.

"Go," she said, "I'll cover us."

He nodded, and then sprinted after the others.

Teza let go of the Pacifier he'd been clinging to, just as the small ship slammed into the mountain top. The large Adherent enforcer bounced across the dirt. The lone U.L.E. agent inside stood up in the cockpit and started firing shots at the acolytes, who in turn unleashed waves of orange lightning from their pole-axes.

Loi stood with her hands on her head, scanning the chaos with a thousand yard stare.

"Loi!"

Rohi put her face right in front of her friend's.

"Loi!"

"I- I have to find my... Serru."

"Loi! We will figure things out with your sister later. But for now, RUN!"

Loi flinched as a tremendous thunder clap, so loud the sounds of battle might as well have been firecrackers, rattled the sky. Her eyes blinked back into focus. They nodded to each other, before running out onto the bridge.

Rohi hung slightly behind Loi, looking over her shoulder every few seconds to guard against any pursuing threats. She saw one of the two U.L.E. fighters take a bad hit. Saw the Adherent Emissary lose another cannon. She saw the pilot of the downed Pacifier fall to a strike from an Adherent pole-axe, and swallowed the nauseous rage that tried to rise up from within.

They reached the landing on the western side of the bridge, where the others waited. Bhanakhana cocked a thumb toward the spiraling staircase that descended into the labyrinthine mountain temple. "This way. Let us go."

Phyos looked out toward the west, where the river that encircled this mountain could be seen cutting a meandering path through the dense forestation for dozens of kilometers before finally spilling into the dark blue of the ocean on the horizon. She held her hands up. "Hold on. I want to get a really good mental image of this view. We all get so wrapped up in our own little worlds, we rarely appreciate moments like this."

"You're... you're fucking with us, right?" stammered Jopp.

Phyos smirked, shrugged, and said, "Maybe."

Chuck had been looking at a different view, back the way they'd come. The sky had grown significantly darker as the edge of the storm crept out over the battle. Within the clouds, he noticed a flash of green light. The thunder that followed made them all jump.

"Holy hell," said Chuck.

The others turned around just in time to see a bolt of emerald lightning burst from the clouds and cut a jagged arc through all three airborne vessels. Both U.L.E. Pacifier ships immediately fell from the sky.

"No!" cried Rohi.

The Adherent Emissary ship stayed aloft for a full two seconds longer, before it too lost all power and fell. Unlike the two U.L.E. fighters, the Emissary had been partially hovering above the eastern mesa. It crashed into the mountain top, most of its oblong hull hanging out over the jungle floor below. Immediately, the ship began to tip over the edge.

A booming roar that sounded like "Faith and Glory!" echoed across the bridge span as Teza, his leg newly healed, leapt into action. He grabbed one of the bridge pylons with one hand, and, against all laws of universal feasibility, grabbed one of the Emissary's tail fins with the other just as it was starting to fall.

Teza Lo, Shepherd of the Adherent, Servant of Rhonac, was holding an entire transport spaceship with one hand.

"Impossible," breathed Bhanakhana.

Teza cried out, "My hands can hold anything! My body can bear any burden! I am the favored child of our Lord! With his blessing there is noth-"

Then his torso ripped in half from left shoulder to right hip.

"Ohhhhhhhhhhhhhhhh!" Chuck and the others groaned in disgusted shock as the pulpy remains of Teza rained down after the falling ship.

Jopp started retching.

"Okay," said Rohi, "That's definitely worse than Juice Jenzin."

Chuck noticed the surviving acolytes across the bridge starting to regroup.

"Guys... seriously, we should go."

"Chuck is correct," Bhanakhana added.

"Yeah," said Phyos, "This view isn't quite so pleasant anymore."

WORD SECTION 0042

Serru ground her teeth in pain as she methodically climbed up the side of the eastern temple-mountain. While the Shepherd enhancements would soon have her broken ribs all healed up, the process still hurt as if all six weeks of the normal healing process had been jammed into just three minutes. She saw a flash of green in the dark clouds overhead, immediately followed by a crack of thunder. Seconds later, the din of ballistic weapons fire ceased and was, replaced by the sounds of multiple ships crashing. She felt a reverberation through the temple as one of the ships struck the mountain.

She paused when she heard Teza's voice cut through the cacophony. He was screaming something about 'his hands' and his 'body' and the 'blessings of Rhonac' but then he suddenly went quiet. The next thing she heard was the Emissary vessel crashing into the trees below. Pain be damned, she doubled her climbing speed.

Half a minute later, Serru pulled herself up over the edge and stood up to survey the scene. She saw the remains of one U.L.E. scout fighter, two dead U.L.E. agents, multiple dead acolytes, eleven living ones standing aimlessly, and the top of Mavros' head peeking up from the stairwell leading back into the heart of the temple. She saw no sign of Loi or her companions.

Serru rushed over to the bridge pylons.

The key was gone.

She looked across the bridge, toward the western temple where they have undoubtedly gone. The first drops of rain began to fall.

"Form up, Adherent!" she bellowed at the surviving acolytes, "We still live, which means we still have work to do!"

"Just what do you think you're doing?" snarled Mavros as he stepped up from the stairwell. "I am in charge here, Dac'eth. Something you seem to keep forgetting."

Serru didn't so much look *at* him as she did look *through* him.

"Herald Mavros, will all due *respect*, if we are to succeed this day, I feel I must take the lead from here on out."

"What?" Mavros' voice rose to a shrill pitch, "You insolent child! You blaspheming wretch! How dare you attempt to usurp my authority?!"

He stomped toward her.

"*I* have been chosen by Divine Mandate! *I* am the favored son of our Lord!"

He stepped to within arm's reach.

"*You* are nothing but a tool of my Holy Will. Consider this your last warning, Shepherd Dac'eth. The next time you step over the line, you will find yourself being judged by our Lord in the next life."

Serru just stared at him. A streak of green shot across the sky, thunder roared, and the rain fell in buckets.

"Now!" Mavros barked through the downpour, "Given our extensive losses here, we must return to the encampment. I have faith our lord will hinder the heretics long enough for us to easily catch back up to them once we've procured reinforcements."

"Coward."

"What did you just say?!"

Serru's hand shot out, grabbing Mavros' throat. His eyes bugged in terror.

"I called you a coward because that is what you are. You are a small, weak, ineffectual little man... and I am tired of putting up with you."

She squeezed.

Seconds later, the limp body of Exalted Herald Mavros crumpled to the ground.

Serru addressed the stunned acolytes.

"I'm going to give you something Mavros would never have offered: a choice. You can leave and tell whatever superior you find that I ordered you to go. Or you can come with me, and I will show you what every faithful child of Rhonac has dreamed of seeing... Now, choose."

The acolytes traded uncertain glances. Then one stepped forward and saluted. Then another. Then another. Then the remaining eight did as well.

Serru peered through the rain to the western mountain, her eyes blazing with determination.

WORD SECTION 0043

Chuck and the others descended into the western mountain temple. Despite the complex honeycomb of stone causeways and staircases, it was a considerably airy, open space. The clockwork gears that hogged so much of the eastern mountain's interior were nowhere to be found. The rush of water echoed up from far below them. Grey light drifted in from the many wide openings that lead to balconies hanging out over the jungle below. The stone railings were polished smooth and their supporting spindles held patterned carvings. At about a third of the way down toward the bottom, they started seeing sculptures of local creatures decorating the various landings between pathways. They saw a Kisqui, a tree with a smiling face, a bramble cat...

"What's this dude about?" Jopp asked, pointing up at a statue standing half a meter taller than all the others. From the shoulders down, it resembled a broad, athletic humanoid. A perfect featureless sphere, painted bright orange, sat where the head should be.

"Seriously?" said Chuck, "Jopp, that's an Ak'alei. There are doodles of these guys literally all over the notes we've been compiling."

"Hey, reading that shit was not in my job description. I just make the ships go fly-fly."

"And you've done an exceptional job of it, dear," said Phyos, patting his head.

"Thank you- hey, knock it off."

The natural light dimmed noticeably. The temple shivered under a sudden crack of thunder. Rain began to pelt the stone of the outer balconies.

They continued threading a path downward, eventually walking out onto a central landing with three separate causeways branching out in separate directions. A large table occupied the middle of the landing. As they approached, they could see the table held what appeared to be an expertly crafted diorama. It quickly became evident that they were looking at a three-dimensional map of the area. The table was not a perfect circle, but rather shaped like a teardrop, with the island continent taking up the wider end. Models of the two mountain temples rose up amidst hundreds of little painted trees.

"So freaking cool," Chuck murmured to himself.

"This must be the map that Cestoras referenced," said Bhanakhana, "The map that leads to the *Doorstep*."

"I'm guessing this would be said Doorstep." Phyos stood down at the narrow end of the table.

The gently curving trail of green paint, signifying the river, fed out into the swath of green paint the made up most of the table's narrow end. There was one single feature of note near the tip of the table: multiple rings of rocks positioned around a perfect circle of bright orange.

"Neat," said Jopp. "So, what is it? And how the hell do we get there?"

"I think I can answer the second question," said Chuck, his face mere inches away from the island models. "Look at these little black things in the river. I thought they might be rocks or like sea creatures... but I think they're boats or something."

Bhanakhana rubbed his chin. "That would make sense. The Ak'alei would arrive on the planet there," he pointed at the orange circle out in the map's ocean, "And these mountain structures would serve as their base of operations."

"Oh, that makes sense?" said Jopp.

"Yeah, seems needlessly complicated," noted Rohi.

"Not if they wanted to keep the means of their interplanetary travel a secret."

"And what would those means be?" asked Rohi.

"That, my dear," said Phyos, "Is the quintillion Tahlian question."

"Realistically, what could that orange circle be?" mused Chuck. "Everything else on here is crazy detailed... but that's just... orange."

"Good observation," noted Phyos.

"Could be a launch pad, for like old timey rockets," offered Jopp.

"That it could be," noted Phyos, "However if this is to scale, that's a pretty small launch pad."

"Maybe fifty meters or so in diameter," surmised Bhanakhana.

"Holy shit."

They all looked at Loi who had her hand held up to her mouth.

"It makes sense," she said, "All their talk of opening doors to new worlds and dimensions and shit... I know what that is..."

"Well, don't leave us hanging with a case of the blue bits, dear. What is it?" asked Phyos.

"It's a portal... like, a small anomaly."

"Impossible," said Bhanakhana.

"*Improbable*," Phyos wagged a finger at him.

"That would explain how the Ak'alei showed up on all these different worlds," noted Chuck.

"Well," said a grinning Phyos, "Let's go find out."

WORD SECTION 0044

As if in response to Phyos, the air outside flashed green, thunder cracked, and the entire temple vibrated. They heard voices float down from high above.

"Here we go," Rohi readied the Hand Cannon.

"You'd be better off throwing it at them then trying to shoot," said Phyos.

"What?"

"She is correct," assented Bhanakhana, "Those vibrations we just felt were likely a result of the lightning striking this structure. This air is filled with unstable ions. We cannot use any electronics."

"What could really-" Loi started to ask.

"HERETICS!" cried a voice from overhead. They looked up to see an Adherent acolyte looking down over a railing, some thirty meters above.

He raised his pole axe.

From a different landing, Serru leapt into view, calling out to her minion, "No! Don't!"

The acolyte swung his weapon, attempting to unleash a blast.

Instead of firing a jagged web of energy, the pole axe simply exploded. The acolyte's body was hurled backwards. A large chunk of the stone causeway broke off and careened downward. Chuck and the others scattered to the staircases, escaping the central landing just before the falling chunk of stone smashed clean through it. Bits and pieces of the marbled rock and shattered bits of the map tumbled to the depths below.

"In the name of all that's holy!" Serru's voice could be heard bouncing off the walls, "I said no charged blasts! Only use the blade!"

The all looked back to see a wide-open gap where the landing had just been. Rohi and Chuck were together on the left pathway. Bhanakhana, Loi, and Jopp had dived to the right stairway. And Phyos was by herself on the forward path.

"I think with enough speed, I could manage a leap across the span," said Bhanakhana.

"Don't be stupid, B," said Jopp.

"Bjordax help me, Jopp's right," said Rohi, "Look, everyone just try to keep heading downward as fast as you can. Don't fight them if you can run. Go!"

They all turned and took off down their respective paths.

·　　·　　·

It took Chuck and Rohi all of two minutes before they had their first run in. They were hurrying across a wide span that looked as if it led to a downward, spiral staircase. Out of nowhere, two acolytes dropped down right in front of them from a landing above. They brandished their weapons. While Chuck had initially considered their weapon design to be mostly ceremonial, he now could see the blades were very real and very sharp.

Chuck raised his machete, shooting a sideward glance at Rohi. Her eyes never wavered from their adversaries.

"Remember," she said, "Speed over power. No wild swings."

"Protect myself, let the opportunities come to me. Got it."

"And don't get killed."

The acolytes charged.

·　　·　　·

As Bhanakhana lead Jopp and Loi up a short curved staircase, he caught some movement below them and saw Phyos slinking along the opposite wall, trying to keep herself bathed in shadow. Their eyes met, and without a word, both immediately began tracing paths along the stairway network, searching for an opportunity to meet up.

And there it was, one of the larger outdoor balconies. Phyos had an easy, almost straight shot right to it. Bhanakhana, Jopp, and Loi had a bit more zigzagging to do to make it there, but it was doable.

They traded a silent nod. Bhanakhana pointed to the balcony and said to Jopp and Loi, "We need to get there to rendezvous with Sage Phyos. Keep your foliage pruning tools at the ready."

Loi looked at the sleek white machete blade in her hand, "He's really good at making cool things sound lame."

"I'm very aware," noted Jopp.

·   ·   ·

Chuck hopped back, avoiding the acolyte's downward strike. The poleaxe sunk into the marbled stone with a thunk. Chuck drove his heel into the back of the axe head, launching himself up and forward. The acolyte released the poleaxe in time to catch Chuck's machete-wielding wrist. With his other hand, the acolyte attempted to wrench the blade from Chuck's grasp. With his free hand, Chuck punched the acolyte in the face. The acolyte returned the gesture, splitting Chuck's lip open. The machete fell from his hand, clattering to the floor. The acolyte, still holding Chuck's wrist with one hand, grabbed Chuck by the throat with his other hand. The acolyte braced his arm, expecting Chuck to try breaking the chokehold. But Chuck didn't try to break it, rather opting to drive his foot upward, kicking the acolyte right in the crotch. The acolyte grunted in pain, both his hands letting go. Chuck, wasting no time, grabbed the acolyte's chest plate and pulled, while driving his own head forward. Chuck's forehead connected with the bridge of the acolyte's nose. There was a sickly crunching sound, and they both collapsed.

Chuck, his lip and head throbbing, quickly sat up to defend himself. But the acolyte wasn't moving. He then looked to see if Rohi needed help, and saw her leaning against the railing, just a few meters away. The other acolyte lay unconscious at her feet.

"How long have you been just standing there?" Chuck asked.

"Like a minute."

Chuck gestured at his acolyte with one hand, and his own bleeding lip with the other. "What the fuck, Ro?"

She grinned. "I wouldn't have let anything happen to you, Fuzzlumps. Just wanted to see how you'd do."

•　　•　　•

Phyos stood on the wide balcony. A hundred or so meters below, the river branched out from the temple, cutting a gently curving path through the thickly forested valley. The rain had slowed to a light drizzle, which she found a bit refreshing. Behind her, she could hear shouts, screams, bangs, and clangs. She looked down at the Ak'alei key resting in her palm.

"Please give that to me," said a voice.

Phyos turned around to see Serru standing in the broad archway. Two bridges branched off behind her, each connecting to a landing on opposite sides of the interior space. Three acolytes stood at each landing, facing away from the balcony.

"Give me the key. I will order my people to stand down. You and the others can keep your lives. I just want the key."

Phyos canted her head to the side. "Do you even know what's waiting for you at the other end, dear?"

"Do *you*?" Serru shot back, "No. No, you don't. *Hirth-Ak'alei* is like a buried treasure. You 'scholars' and all the Church's Grand Heralds have been reclining in gilded lounge chairs... content to twirl your fingers in the dirt, while *I*," she pounded her chest, "have been relentlessly digging."

"Doesn't sound like you hold your superiors in much esteem... you sure your god will like that when you find him?"

Phyos found herself in the rare circumstance of being caught completely off guard when Serru reacted with a hearty chuckle. "Oh, Professor, I thought you were more perceptive than this... Rhonac is a story for children and fools. I am neither."

There was a commotion behind them. Bhanakhana, Jopp, and Loi stepped down on to the left landing and the three acolytes there attacked.

"Then why?" Phyos had kept her focus on Serru. "You're neither historian nor zealot... *Why* do you want this so bad?" She asked this with total earnestly, her trademark smarm completely absent.

"I'm going to save the people of this universe. Corrupt leaders of every faith, race, political faction... their time is over. The planets under Vashnii subjugation, the Ochrean slave-servants of Gralt, the Venovans who suffer under religious extremism... Once I control *Hirth-Ak'alei*, I will be able to dismantle any regime that threatens innocent lives. Even the U.L.E. and the Sentient Coalition will yield."

Jopp and Loi quickly found themselves getting pushed back. Just as it seemed as if Bhanakhana would best his own opponent, two more acolytes dropped down on top of his hulking frame from the staircase above.

"So, that's it?" Phyos said in a disappointed tone. "That's what this is about? Universal Domination? How unoriginal..."

"Domination? No. *Liberation*. I don't want to rule anyone. I'm setting them free."

"Because no tyrant has ever said that before."

Chuck and Rohi emerged on the right-side landing. The three waiting acolytes rushed them.

"I don't care whether you believe or not. The point is moot. Give me the key."

Phyos stood sideways, her left shoulder facing outward from the balcony, her right facing toward Serru. She looked down at her right palm, at the small piece of metal it held.

"I'm starting to think maybe this isn't really worth all the wub-wub. Maybe it's best for everybody if no one finds the planet."

"Don't," said Serru.

Jopp blocked one strike, ducked another, and totally missed the sweep of the pole-axe's reverse end as it took his feet out from under him. He slammed backwards into the floor, the back of his head bouncing off the hard stone. His vision went hazy, and he held his hands up in submission.

"You know," said Phyos, "I wonder how far down the river I could throw this thing. With the lighter gravity, I bet it'll really sail."

"Please. Don't."

The three acolytes had Bhanakhana down on one knee. In desperation, he roared, grabbed one from his back, and hurled the man over the railing.

"Over-under," said Phyos, "How many times you think I can skip this along the river's surface?"

Loi held one hand up in surrender, while slowly reaching to set her blade on the floor.

"Don't!" bellowed Serru.

Rohi disarmed one acolyte, but then caught a blow in her gut from the blunt end of another's weapon. She dropped to her knees. Concern distracted Chuck just enough for his own Adherent foe to bat away Chuck's machete.

Still dazed and on his back, Jopp's head lazily turned toward the balcony. He saw Serru unsheathe a long, orange dagger. Phyos faced away, toward the graying sky.

"Yeah," Phyos said, "It's not worth it."

She raised her hand, and then gasped in pain. The key fell from her hand, clanking against the stone floor. She then crumbled forward, the hilt of an orange knife sticking out of her back.

Bhanakhana let out a pained, guttural moan.

Loi elbowed her distracted acolyte in the gut and broke away from the others, racing toward Serru, machete still in hand.

She lunged.

Serru spun on her heels and caught Loi's wrist with one hand and her neck with the other.

Loi stared into Serru's eyes. Eyes that, shockingly, appeared strained with sorrow and anguish.

Serru's voice was pained and gravely. "Thank you for coming to save me. But don't worry, Loi. This time, *I'm* going to take care of us. I'm going to take care of *all* of us."

With surgical precision, Serru tightened her grip on Loi's neck just enough to make her pass out. She gently laid Loi's unconscious frame on the floor, stepped over to Phyos' body, and whispered, *"I'm sorry,"* as she retrieved the key.

"Adherent!" Serru shouted before sprinting toward the inside of the balcony and hopping right over the railing. In a flurry of motion, the acolytes quickly followed suit. The thudding chorus of the Adherent descending into the temple's depths quickly faded away. Soon the only sound was the slow drip of waning rain.

WORD SECTION 0045

Nobody spoke or moved for what felt like an eternity. The sight of Loi's unconscious body starting to twitch snapped Rohi out her daze. She rushed forward, crouched by Loi's side and cradled her head. Loi's eyes fluttered open.

"Hey, hey," said Rohi, "You okay?"

Loi sat up, not saying anything, her eyes locked on Phyos.

Chuck, Jopp, and Bhanakhana slowly approached.

Rohi stood up straight and held down a hand for Loi, who ignored it.

Jopp, his eyes bloodshot, moved forward kneel next Phyos.

"Why couldn't you have just given her the fucking thing?" he croaked. "Why'd you have to be such a smart-ass?" His voice became a sob, "*What was the fucking point?!*"

He rose and stomped to the outer balcony railing and screamed, "*FUCK!*"

Chuck glanced up at Bhanakhana, and saw tears streaming down the Dronla's crimson cheeks. Chuck swallowed and said, "Wha- what do we do?"

"I have to keep going," said Rohi, "I can't... I can't let her get away with... whatever she's trying to do."

"I'm coming with you," Chuck asserted.

"Chuck..."

"Don't, Rohi," He cut her off, "Just don't. *I* am coming with *you*."

Rohi sighed.

"I shall also continue," said a hoarse Bhanakhana.

On instinct, Rohi started to protest but caught herself and nodded.

"Bunch of gumble-phoobing yoks."

They turned to Jopp, who glared back at them.

"Uh, what?" said Chuck.

"Did those psychopaths shoot you all with a Make-Me-Stupid Gun? What is this *continue on* shit? It's over! We fucking lost!" he pointed at Phyos, "They killed her! She's fucking dead! And you're ready to just keep on cruisin', huh? Who cares about Yeidat Phyos, right?!"

"Jopp... bud... we care. We just need-"

"Just need what, Chuck? Just need to keep the adventure rolling? That's all this is to you, right? And *you*," he pointed at Rohi, "What's one more bit of collateral damage to enforce the U.L.E.'s authority? Just an extra paragraph in your report." His eyes moved to Bhanakhana, "And you already learned everything you needed from her, right? All the data's been collected, so her life isn't vital..." he looked out toward the valley, "She was more than all that, you know. She was a person. She was smart, she was funny...." when he turned back toward them, they could his eyes were filled with tears, "She treated us all- she treated *me* like... like I was worth something... like I was more than just a fuck up."

"Jopp, you're not-"

"Just go, Chuck. Go have your adventure. I honestly hope you survive, I do. But I'm done, man. I'm *done*."

Chuck opened his mouth, but Rohi placed a hand on his shoulder and shook her head. She looked down at Loi, who still sat on the floor. "Loi, c'mon. Let's go."

Loi looked up at Rohi as if she'd forgotten anybody else was here. "I came to save my sister... she doesn't need- doesn't *want* to be saved. There's no reason for me to be here anymore."

"You could still-"

"Help you save the day?" Loi pulled herself to her feet, "No thanks."

"You don't want to help do some good?"

"Us thieves aren't exactly known for our altruism. You should know, Law Cog."

Rohi sighed.

Bhanakhana gestured to Phyos' body. "I can assist you in moving her."

"Don't trouble yourself, Big Guy," said Jopp, "She can't weight that much, plus with the lighter gravity, I'm sure I can manage. Besides, you've got bad guys to stop."

"Jopp," said Chuck.

"Goodbye, Chuck."

Rohi started moving toward the nearest staircase, followed by a dour-looking Bhanakhana. Chuck spared one last glance at their friend, before heading down the stairs.

•   •   •

Jopp and Loi sat against the base of the eastern mountain and rested, slurping down the nutrient packets they'd fished out of their satchels. The body of Phyos had been lain delicately against the mountain, about a half dozen meters away. Jopp had managed carrying her over his shoulders back up through the western temple and across the bridge. Rather than carry her all the way down, through the maze of stairs in the eastern temple, they'd been fortunate to discover that the downed husk of the U.L.E. scout ship had a long tow cable. This had allowed them to carefully lower Phyos' body down to the ground, using the cable and the bridge pylons like a crude pulley system.

"You know," Jopp said as he polished off his second packet, "If she could see all the trouble we're going to, she'd probably laugh at us and tell us to quit being so foolish. *That's not me anymore, it's just a hunk of dead meat*, she'd say, *reminds me of my second husband in bed...*" he started chuckling, stopping himself just before it turned into a sob.

"I'm sorry, Jopp," Loi said, "I obviously didn't really know her... she seemed pretty great..."

"Yeah," Jopp flicked away the single tear that had dared to show its face, "Well, technically, I didn't know her that well either. We only met like barely a week ago... but damn, she was something else. She *saw* people, you know? Like saw who they really were. She -as lame as this sounds- she believed in me."

Loi put her hand on his shoulder. "You're a good pilot, Jopp. A really good pilot... why do you think I picked you to rip off? Prime Partners only give the best pilots the really valuable swag."

Jopp spit out a guttural laugh, "Ha! Fuck you.... oh man, ha ha... thanks, thanks for that."

Loi stood and then held a hand down for Jopp. He took it and pulled himself up.

"There's something I've been meaning to ask you," Jopp started, "You must be like shu-shu rich now."

"That's not a question."

"How many mansions do you have?"

"Ha, zero."

"I see, invested in one giant estate? Like your own island on Chylaang-4?"

"I'm not rich, Jopp."

"How is that possible? That cargo you jacked from me was worth like twelve million Tahlians!"

"Not in the dark market, it wasn't. Right out the gate, cut your value in half. Then cut it in half again to pay the Fence their cut."

"Still... three million."

Loi bobbed her head, "Yeah... then you pay off some debts to get the kill contracts on your head cancelled, treat yourself to a shiny new ship, have a really weird night at a gambling outpost near the Ko Raha system, and then pour everything into tracking down your, as it turns out, homicidal maniac sister..."

"Please don't tell me you blew three million Tahlians."

"Nooooo. I've managed to hold on to a little nest egg."

"Wow. I thought I was the fuck up."

"Shut it."

•   •   •

Jopp had Phyos slung over his shoulders again, while her slight frame and the planet's light gravity had indeed helped, an achy exhaustion crept through his neck, back, and shoulders. They walked around the mountain, stopping when they found the charred black, muddy path that Mavros' Rage Flame had cut through the trees. They'd noticed his corpse among the others on the eastern mountain top.

"That colossal asshole," Loi muttered.

"At least he got his."

They carefully walked down the ugly path, emerging at a familiar spot near the Boletus Bridge.

"I'm really not in the mood for riddles," Jopp groaned.

"I know, it's-"

"Hello, meat things," said a low voice.

Jopp and Loi turned and saw the closest, unharmed tree was looking at them. It had recognition in its sad eyes.

"Jon?" asked Loi, "Is that you?"

"Yes..."

"Oh, hey man- er, hey," said Jopp.

"They killed Nancy," Jon the tree lamented, "Nancy was a pain in the stump, but she was my friend. They were all our friends. We'd been neighbors for... I lost count after the nine hundredth season. Why did those other meat things do this?"

"I am so so sorry," said Loi, "They were bad meat things. They, uh, they won't hurt anymore trees though."

"You felled them?" Jon asked hopefully.

"Yeah, kinda," Jopp answered.

Jon's eyes noticed Phyos' body draped over his shoulders. "Oh no! Your friend is wilted!"

Loi nodded, "The bad meat things... they killed her."

"Where are you taking her?"

"We don't know," Jopp answered, "I don't know what to do... I just," he felt tears try to rise up, "I just couldn't leave her back there."

"I remember, many many seasons ago, when I was a sapling, there were some strange meat things wandering around. They had tiny little suns for faces! Some of them died, and the others planted them. They planted them in the dirt! I remember thinking, *how strange, meat things don't have seeds...*"

"It's called burial," said Loi, "Some meat thing cultures bury their dead in the ground as a sign of reverence."

"Oh... well, I liked that one. She had good dirt spice. Would you like to plant her next to me? My roots will protect her."

The patch of ground between Jon and them rumbled, roots sprouted up, curled back down, and parted the dirt, creating a person-sized hole.

"I would be honored to watch over her."

A tear managed to break free from Jopp's eye. He sniffed. "Thank you, Jon."

Loi helped Jopp slide Phyos off his shoulders and carry her toward the hole.

"Wait," said Jon, "You don't want her to have that thorn stay in her, do you?"

They looked and saw Serru's knife still in Phyos' back.

"We are dumb shits," said Loi.

"She'd really be giving us hell for this one," noted Jopp.

Jopp looked away as Loi removed the knife and slide it into her belt. They carefully laid Phyos' body in the hole. Jon's roots then covered her up with dirt before sliding back under the ground.

"What did you call her?" Jon asked.

"Yeidat Phyos," Jopp answered. "She was the best."

Jon did the closest thing to a nod a giant tree could manage.

"I'll tell any other meat things that pass by the rest of my seasons. Here rests Yeidat Phyos, best of the meat things."

Jopp smiled.

They turned back to see the talking bridge mushroom had woken up.

"Greetings, I am the Boletus Bridge. In order to cross you must-"

"Oh, for soil's sake, Bol!" Jon shouted, "Let them cross, you *stomatal pore*."

The Boletus sighed and the root bridge formed for them to cross. They looked back at Jon.

"Thanks again," said Loi.

"Yeah," added, "See you around, Jon."

"Honestly, I hope not. I like you two well enough, but meat things always bring trouble."

Jopp chuckled, "Fair enough."

WORD SECTION 0046

While the rain outside had fully subsided, the sound of lapping water grew louder as Chuck, Rohi, and Bhanakhana descended into the temple depths. The reason for this became apparent when they reached a landing that overlooked the bottom floor, which wasn't actually a floor, but rather a wide pool of dark green water. One last staircase led down to a catwalk encircling the pool. Two small vessels, resembling boxy submarines with glass canopies, were held in place by pairs of mechanical arms. Two additional sets of arms hung empty, where two more of the vessels supposedly should have been docked.

Bhanakhana spoke the first words any of them had said since they parted from Jopp and Loi, "It appears as if your assessment was correct, Chuck. The Ak'alei must have used these vehicles to navigate between here and the *Doorstep*."

"Let's hop in," said Rohi.

"I have been meaning to ask," Bhanakhana started, "how do we plan to subdue our adversaries once we catch back up to them?"

"Well," said Rohi, brandishing the oversized pistol. "Hopefully, this Doorstep takes us somewhere that doesn't have weapon-neutering electrical storms."

"A gun is not a plan."

"Maybe for you, it's not."

"We'll do what we always do," Chuck slapped the side of the sub, "Figure something out on the fly- er, I mean, on the... *sail*?"

Bhanakhana and Rohi shared an eye roll.

Chuck found the entry hatch and added, "I just hope we can figure out how to work this thing."

For three average sized humanoids, the sub would have been just barely on the side of comfortable. However, Bhanakhana's considerable girth meant they found themselves getting quite cozy with each other. They quickly learned complicated controls would not be an issue. A single lever was all the interior had in the way of controls. The leaver was pulled all the way to the right. Chuck did the closest thing to a shrug the confined space would allow and pulled the lever back to the left.

The sub sprang to life with a symphony of hums and clicks. They felt a jolt as the mechanical arms released them. The sub began to vibrate and move forward through the water, skidding along the circular edge of the pool, until it straightened out in line with the only exit. The vibrations intensified and the sub propelled through water, out of the temple, and into the gray evening light.

"Avast, mateys," Chuck playfully growled.

"Chuck..." Rohi started.

"Perhaps a respite from your humorisms is in order," Bhanakhana cut in.

Chuck sighed, "I'm sorry. On the inside, I'm utterly devastated about what happened. I'm pretty sure the only reason I'm not crying is because I'm so dehydrated... but look, Jopp had a point; there's a really good chance we're going to die. And I get why you two chose to carry on. I respect you both so much, and I know I could never forgive myself if I didn't come too... but my coping mechanism for dealing with shitty life stuff is corny jokes, and on top of that, if I *am* going to die out here, I'd like to at least have a fraction of fun while I do it. Fair?"

Bhanakhana raised his eyebrows, "As I believe you would put it... damn. I rescind my comment."

Rohi nodded, "Okay, fair enough... but me and him," she cocked a thumb at Bhanakhana, "get to veto any jokes or references we're really not in the mood for."

"Deal," said Chuck.

Rohi said "Here, take this," and handed him a hydration pouch from her satchel.

Chuck said, "Thanks," tore it open, and sucked down the gel inside. It sent a pleasant chill down his spine, prompting him to add, "Shiver me timbers."

"Veto!" Rohi and Bhanakhana barked in unison.

• • •

The sun had barely begun to set when Jopp and Loi reached the village edge. Everything was bathed in an amber gold light. Their legs ached as they trudged up the main lane, heading for the landing pad.

"I am so phoobing tired," groaned Jopp. "Shit, what's our plan now? I can't just take Bhanakhana's Estal Cube..."

"Rohi and I came in my ship," Loi answered, "We can take that."

"Tops. I'll need to grab some things out of my room on the cube."

"Take your time. We should probably catch a nap before trying to fly anyway."

Jopp's eyes fell on the big tree near the landing pad.

"There is only thing I might be more interested in right now than sleep..."

Loi nodded. "Fuck yes. Drink first. Then nap. Then get the hell off this planet."

Jopp sniffed himself. "Oof, maybe squeeze in a hygenizer-bath too."

• • •

"I spy something that is... *red*!" said Chuck.

"Me, again," answered Bhanakhana.

"Chuck, this game is-" Rohi started.

"No, look!" Chuck pointed toward the watery horizon in front of them, where a narrow beam of red light stretched up into the darkening sky. Beyond that, they could see a mass of looming storm clouds.

"Laser flare," Rohi noted.

"Summoning reinforcements," Bhanakhana added.

"So, we're fucked?" asked Chuck.

"Probably," said Rohi, "But we've been operating from that position for a while now."

"We have to hope we can reach the storm before whatever vessel she summoned arrives."

"Sweet. Just hope things happen to work out for us. Solid plan, team. That sounded like I was being a dick, I'm not. I'm just really anxious, and you know, I tend to lose my inner monologue when- *oh my god*, look at that fish! It looks like a rhino boned a squid!"

WORD SECTION 0047

Petalberry dropped the second round of ales in front of them with a thud, sloshing a bit of the nutty beverage over the mug lips.

"Uh, thanks," said Jopp, glancing around the virtually empty tavern. "Hey, where's your husband? Bristlecheek?"

Petalberry sniffed. "Ya ya... bad blue nuts," he shot a glare at Loi, "they hurt my Bris. Asking questions about you nuts. Bris don't spill seeds on customers. So they hurt him. Bris in bed, resting. Rotten blue nuts." He spit on the floor, conspicuously close to Loi's foot.

Jopp opened his mouth, but Loi hopped up. She looked Petalberry directly in the eyes and held her hands out in surrender.

"I am so so sorry that happened. We... we tried to stop them."

"Ya ya. Did you?"

"Some of them, yes. Unfortunately, not all of them..."

"Boss nut?"

Loi thought back to Mavros' body lying on top of the eastern mountain.

"Boss nut won't be hurting anyone ever again. I promise you."

Petalberry sniffed. "Ya ya. I get you some food. Only charge fifty percent extra... for the trouble."

"Fair enough," said Loi as she sat down with a heavy sigh.

"Man, those guys are dicks. Can't wait to put some real distance between us and them."

"Yeah..." said Loi absently as she stared at her beer.

"Dark days, huh, gonchos?"

Mola Mola Tai dropped down in the chair across from them. He had a black bruise encircling his left eye, which was swollen shut. Another bruise covered his right cheek, and his lip had been split.

"Did they do that to you?" Loi asked.

He nodded. "Retributes for trying to dial the emotional temperature to an even chill."

"You tried to pacify things when those other Venovans were here and they hit you."

"S'what I uttered."

Petalberry reappeared with a tray of food and dropped a drink in front of Mola Mola Tai.

"Thank you," said Loi. "You can put his drink on our bill."

"Ya ya. Already did."

"Sorry about that," Jopp gestures to the black eye, "They were looking for us... hey, where's your little buddy?"

"Kipu? Kipu-chini dusted stars the second he peeped their sky boats. He knew them Blues were bad news. If only them gidgies," he pointed at their data bracelets, "worked around here. Wouldn't have to lax around, waiting for mail."

Mola Mola Tai dropped a rolled up sheet of thin, flexible plastic on the table. He unrolled it, and it automatically hardened into a rigid, flat surface. Small, lettered writing filled one side.

"This note-roll came from my cousin over on Big Land. They destroyed his village. Tore up half the valley. Torched hundreds of tree-folk. He was tryin' to warn ol' Mola."

Loi buried her head in her hands.

"I'm sorry. I'm sorry for what they did to your planet and your people. I tried to stop them..."

"Did ya?"

Loi stared at the floor.

"We tried, man," Jopp jumped in, "We fucking tried... and got one of our own killed."

"Ol' Mola counts four missing."

"Yeah, well, the others decided to keep trying... to, uh, do something about."

"Huh, good on them gonchos."

Mola took his drink back over to the bar.

Jopp huffed, "Yeah... good on them gonchos."

.   .   .

Serru climbed up out of the old sub and stepped onto the dark rock. She turned around in a slow circle, taking in the scene. She stood on a near solid ring of black rock. A light, misty rain drizzled down from above. The ring of rock was surrounded for a kilometer in every direction by hundreds of black stone pillars jutting up from the emerald water. Their sub, guided by some unseen force, had perfectly weaved around the stone to reach this point. Her remaining acolytes stood patiently near the boats. She looked back the way they'd come and saw a dot in the sky above the horizon.

Good, she thought, *they saw the flare.*

Her eyes drifted up to the darkening clouds overhead.

It will be a close call to beat the storm. Nevertheless...

A light, misty rain had begun to pepper the ocean's surface. She turned back toward the center of the rock ring, which held a pool of water that stretched some fifty meters across. Serru massaged the key in her hand, and took a few steps along the rocks, her eyes scanning for some feature of note. At last, there it was: a length of black rock sticking straight up, the pointed tip giving off a faint pink glow. As Serru approached, a small opening appeared. She held her breath and inserted the key. Within seconds, the water in the pool began to bubble and churn.

WORD SECTION 0048

Chuck, Rohi, and Bhanakhana peered up through the glass canopy as their boat passed underneath the edge of the roiling storm clouds. The 'forest' of rocky sea stacks loomed ahead of them. They had a brief moment of panic when it looked as if they might crash into the first black, rocky spire, but their boat adjusted its trajectory just enough to sail around it. The ancient machine chugged along a gently twisting path through the black stones until came to a halt alongside two identical vessels against a swath of black rock. Rohi popped out of the boat, ready to take on any would-be assailants.

No attacks came. No one was there. Besides the soft patter of light rain, the only sound was a low, constant hum. Rohi turned back to help Chuck and Bhanakhana climb out from the sub. They surveyed the area and realized that, while the rocks surrounding this place may have been naturally formed, this inner ring was an Ak'alei structure that had been 'activated' with the key. A bit to their left, there appeared to be something of a stone gazebo, completed with table and benches. To their right, they saw a short stone stairway that led down along the inside of the rock ring to a flat stone platform. They stepped to the inner edge of the rock ring and looked down.

"Oh, wow," said Chuck.

"Fuuuuuuuuuuuuuuck," said Rohi.

Bhanakhana dropped to his knees, his hands clasped over his mouth.

The substance filling the interior of the ring almost looked like water, however it appeared thicker, more viscous. Not to mention that fact that they could see right through it. And what they saw was most definitely not an ocean floor.

They saw a circular patch of dark purple stone with a symbol had been carved into its center. It was a large circle, with eight lines branching outward, each ending in a smaller circle. Inside the large, middle circle, there were two parallel horizontal lines over two, wider-set vertical lines.

"That's..." Chuck started, "I mean, we're... we're looking at another planet, right?"

Bhanakhana's lip trembled. "A-against all probability... yes. Yes, I believe we are looking at a location on *Hirth-Ak'alei*. Dear mother of stars, Loi was correct. It is a portal."

"Rad."

"*Rad?* Chuck, this changes *everything* we know about the laws of reality."

"I mean, it's wild, yeah. But don't we have something similar with the anomalies? They kind of work like portals."

"They are called *anomalies* for a reason. They are always massive, and located in empty corners of space. To this day, we don't truly know how they work. Sensory probes have never been able to get a single reading. Nothing. Exploratory probes sent into them either disappear or show up in a new location. That is all we know. This is something completely different. The ability to presumably manufacture a gateway at will has titanic universal ramifications."

"Let's go, you two."

Rohi had already descended the stairs to the stone platform.

Chuck placed a hand on Bhanakhana's shoulder.

"All the more reason to make sure we stop Serru, right? C'mon, big guy."

Bhanakhana gave Chuck a paternal smile, stood back up, and they joined Rohi down on the platform.

"So we just... jump in?" Chuck asked.

"Looks that way," said Rohi.

Chuck looked up at Bhanakhana. "Honor's all yours, big guy."

Bhanakhana had his eyes closed and his brow furrowed.

"Are you okay?" Rohi asked.

Bhanakhana opened his eyes and smiled at them, "Yes, I was attempting to think of a profound statement to punctuate the moment."

"And?" Rohi asked.

"I have nothing."

With that, he stepped off the platform. Chuck and Rohi looked at each other, shrugged, and did the same.

•   •   •

Jopp burst out of the tavern with Loi hot on his heels. They raced past the landing pad, to the southern edge of the town. Jopp stood on the edge of the cliff, the ocean splashing against the rocks below, and looked west.

"You have an Amp-Lens, right?" he asked.

Loi handed it to him and Jopp placed the device over his eyes. He notched up the range, saw the dark storm clouds in the distance. He caught a speck of movement, and notched up the range again. The Adherent Sanctuary was moving toward the storm.

"What you got?" Loi asked.

"You know those big church ships?"

"The Sanctuary."

"Yep."

"We can't fight a Sanctuary, Jopp. My ship has zero weapons."

"Mine does."

"Enough to take on something like that?" Loi asked.

"Probably not," Jopp answered.

"So, we'll be improvising."

"Yep."

"My specialty."

"Decided to try and *do something*, huh gonchos?" said a third voice.

Jopp and Loi turned back to see Mola Mola Tai. He was wearing a silver, skin tight bodysuit and holding a long silver board.

"Yeah," said Loi, "yeah, we are."

"Sunny."

"You want to come help?" Jopp asked.

Mola shook his head. "Nope. But would I be astute in conjecturing that your intention is to zip by that top-top storm out there?"

"Uh, yes?"

"Sunny! Can I scoop a lift?"

"We're about to take that little cube ship over there and attack that gigantic battle-cruiser out that way, likely resulting in our grisly deaths..." Jopp started.

"...and you want to hitch a ride so you can go storm surfing?" Loi finished.

"Sunny!"

Jopp and Loi looked at each other and shrugged.

"Yeah, sure," said Loi.

"Why the fuck not," said Jopp.

WORD SECTION 0049

Chuck, Rohi, and Bhanakhana tumbled awkwardly onto the dusty purple landing pad. They helped each to their feet, all feeling a little wobbly. The transition through the portal had been a bit mind-bendy and disorienting. From the Gjenlu side, it appeared as if they would be approaching the purple landing at a direct downward angle. However the second they passed through the membrane, gravity shifted and they found themselves hitting the ground at a forty-five degree angle, hence the awkward tumbling.

"Oh... *WOW*," said Chuck as he took his first at their surroundings.

"Fucking *fuck*," said Rohi.

"Chaos and Cosmos," breathed Bhanakhana, "... it is breathtaking."

They stood on an outcropping that branched off a tall spire of uncertain material. Upon closer inspection, the 'stone' appeared porous and reminded Chuck of sea coral. Behind them, a ramp leads upwards at a forty-five degree angle to the Gjenlu portal, which was wreathed in a circular construct that had been affixed to the peak of the purple spire. The portal frame, as it were, appeared to be made from copper-colored metal and an orange crystalline substance.

Six smaller versions of this 'frame' encircled the landing. Three were simply hollow rings they could look right through. The other three were 'active,' displaying a familiar translucent membrane.

They got a good idea of what their own spire looked like, because off in the distance, they saw many more rising up from the planet's surface. They almost resembled tree trunks, with wide 'roots' that merged into a thinner spire stretching hundreds of meters into the air. They could see clumps of the orange crystalline material clinging to the purple tree-mountains like moss.

Far below, the planet's surface appeared to be little more than a desolate, rocky landscape. From their vantage point, they noticed clusters of black, dome-shaped buildings. Standing alone, not too far away from the base of their vantage point, was a single dome large enough to house an entire sports arena within its walls. They saw no obvious signs of life.

Bhanakhana stroked his chin as he stepped to the edge of the landing. He looked down at the long drop, giving Chuck a minor case of vertigo by proxy. Bhanakhana then examined the portal rings that appeared to be 'active'. One was completely opaque and black. Another looked as if it lead to similar landing like the one they currently stood on. The third appeared to lead to a spot on the planet's surface, next to one of the dome structures.

"At the moment, my most adequate conjecture would be that all the portals leading to different planets are located atop these curious tree-spires. As to *why*, I could not hazard a guess..."

He sounded as if he was more verbalizing an inner monologue than actually engaging in dialogue. Chuck jumped in anyway. "You think these smaller portals lead to other parts of this planet?

Bhanakhana gave him a smile and nod. " And those domes must be the cities or towns of the Ak'alei..."

"Man, this is so bonkers..."

"... truly, this is perhaps the most fascinating discovery of the past millennia..."

"Boys," said Rohi, "Have you looked *up* yet?"

Chuck and Bhanakhana simultaneously tilted their heads toward the sky.

"My word..." Bhanakhana breathed.

"Okay, my brain is now officially broken," said Chuck.

The sky wasn't blue with clouds, nor was it dark and spotted with stars. The sky was streaked with pale colors, as if some gigantic demigod had lazily swept a paint brush across the heavens. The colors were all pale and faded, however there were too many shades to count. It reminded Chuck of that Starry Night painting by that one artist who cut his own ear off. The streaks of color completely blanketed the sky, save for one small dot of pure blackness. The color streaks closest to this dot seemed to bend and curve around it.

"What're we looking at, Bhanakhana?" Rohi asked.

"I... I do not know, Rohi."

"Okay, well, we haven't asphyxiated or been crushed by the gravity. So, we should assume our Adherent friends are out there somewhere trying to do whatever fucked shit they're here to do. The mystery of the freaky sky and the purple tree-mountains will have to wait until we do something about that."

"Agreed."

Chuck gestured at the smaller, activated portals. "So we taking Door Number One, Two, or Three?"

As he said "three' he smacked the frame of the all-black portal, much in the way a used star cruiser salesman smacks the hood of a thrust-engine. The portal shuddered, a crack formed in the ground near the portal's base. Chuck hopped backwards as the portal and the chunk of stone supporting it broke free from the larger structure. It tumbled end over end, it's fall lasting uncomfortably long, before shattering against the rocky ground.

Bhanakhana let out a long, pained sigh.

"Chuck, sweetie," said Rohi, "Maybe we try being more gentle with the two thousand year old artifacts."

•   •   •

The cube ship zipped across the water toward the darkened horizon. Jopp manned the helm. Loi sat to his right, familiarizing herself with the special 'upgrades' Phyos had installed. She scanned the digital control menus.

"Plasma cannons, trailer mines, rapid bolters... phoobing hell, Jopp, what were you guys planning?"

Loi noticed the glowing, fist-sized red button.

"What's that?"

"Don't touch it!"

"Why?"

"Just don't."

"What's up, goncherinos?! It's your main Cloud Kid, Mola Mola Tai, comin' atcha from the ship of my new bud-buds, Joppopo and Loi-Joy. Say hi to everyone!"

Jopp and Loi turned their heads toward Mola, who was staring at them with a huge smile. A small orb with a tiny red light hovered near his head.

"Are you Surging this on your GIG-Life page?" asked Loi.

"No insta-surging. The cranky clouds out this way won't let the signal out. I'll post the recorded vid-vid later on."

"Dude, this isn't... how many followers you got?"

"A small but tops dedicated batch of a hundo-twenty thou!"

"You have one hundred and twenty thousand people that watch your videos?" Loi asked.

"Sunny."

Loi pointed at the floating orb. "Am I on camera now?"

"Say halla-halla, Loi Joy!"

She stared at the orb. "My name is Loi Dac'eth. There is a dangerous subset of the Church of Rhonac called the Adherent. They are responsible for many atrocities across the settled systems. Here on Gjenlu, we have personally witnessed them murder Universal Law Enforcement agents as well as Professor Yeidat Phyos of the Zenith Lyceum. You are about to watch us engage with an Adherent Sanctuary, a vessel they claim to be a mobile church of peace but as you are all about to witness, is actually a dangerous battle frigate in disguise. Whoever is seeing this, contact the U.L.E. Contact the Sentient Coalition. Recycle this video on your own Profiles. The Adherent have to be stopped."

"Whoa, that's some heavy contenterino."

"Just make sure it gets posted as soon as you can."

"I give you my verb, Lady Loi. If ol' Mola don't get himself kersplattered, ol' Mola will surge your message."

"That's a big *if* on the kersplattering," said Jopp, "But let me see if I can't get you a better view. Watch this."

Jopp pressed an icon labeled 360° View, causing a full sphere of view screens to appear around them. There was an entire ship between the control room and the outside world, however the sphere of screens made it look, from the inside, like they were flying through the air in a glass orb.

"Whoooooooa!" said Mola Mola Tai.

"Fuck! You gotta give a better heads up next time! That is fucking disorienting!"

"It's rad as heck is what it is. Now everyone get ready. We'll be on them in a few minutes."

WORD SECTION 0050

Chuck, Rohi, and Bhanakhana had chosen the portal that led to a crossroads in what they presumed to be a town. They saw one tree-mountain with an active portal about a kilometer away. Bhanakhana stepped back through to test it. Chuck and Rohi saw a red dot appear atop the tree-mountain. The red dot disappeared as Bhanakhana returned.

They began to walk down a dusty path that divided two rows of dome-shaped buildings. Some were as small as a single-story house and some were the size of five-story apartment complex but all were completely dark and showed no signs of life.

"This must be taking a lot of self-restraint, B," noted Chuck. "I'm sure you're dying to explore every inch of these buildings."

Bhanakhana kept his eyes forward with grim resolve, "We must first complete the task at hand." His expression softened and he shot Chuck a quick grin. "But should we both succeed *and* survive this ordeal, then yes, there shall be much scientific research to be done."

Rohi chuckled, "You're the only person I know that talks about scientific research in the same tone a kid talking about eating frosted jubla."

"I would argue mine is much sweeter... of course, I intend that sentiment in a wholly metaphorical sense."

Rohi stopped short, her body noticeably tensing.

"What's-" Chuck saw what she was staring at.

A small, rocky hill stood a short ways past the edge of town. They could see a zigzagging path had been carved into the hillside. What caught their attention, however, was the tower sitting at the hilltop. Tower might have been a generous term. The structure was cylindrical, but not nearly as tall as one might expect an ominous tower on a mysterious, ancient alien planet to be. Chuck thought it looked like a three story can of beer.

The tower itself was not the reason they stared, rather it was the dull light drifting out from the top floor windows. Besides the portal tree-mountain they'd arrived through, it was the only other light they'd seen.

Rohi glanced back at the other two, "Just so we're all clear, I plan to shoot first."

"And ask questions later?" ventured Chuck.

Rohi deactivated the Bloodfist Hand Cannon's safety setting. The weapon hummed with deadly life.

"I don't have any questions."

She took off at a quick but careful pace. Chuck and Bhanakhana followed close behind. The trio swept down the remainder of the street, halted briefly at the town's edge to scan the surroundings, and then sprinted across the open ground to the hill. They darted back and forth up the zigzagging path.

At the tower's base, they found a door. It was a rectangular slab of material that looked and felt like stone, but easily slid open with a light push. The interior of the tower was mostly one big circular room. Six stone-like chairs sat around a hexagonal table. The table had a grid pattern carved into it and was covered with a few dozen small carved figures. A lower counter ran along the back wall between two spherical objects, each the size of a refrigerator. A shallow basin had been carved into the center of the counter. To their right, a staircase had been built into the wall. A heavy layer of dust coated every surface.

"This may be some manner of living quarters," Bhanakhana whispered.

Rohi waved them over to the stairs and they began to climb. About halfway up, Chuck noticed they were leaving footprints in the dust. He looked at the stairs ahead of them, seeing that the dust appeared to be undisturbed. He tapped Rohi on the arm, pointed behind them and whispered, "*Footprints.*" He then pointed up ahead of them. "*No footprints.*"

"*Curious,*" added Bhanakhana.

"*The only other light we've seen is up there,*" countered Rohi, "*Maybe the psychos climbed up the outside of the tower like a pack of frizzle-apes. Who knows. Not taking any chances. Now hush.*"

They climbed the rest of the stairs in silence, finding themselves on small landing with one door in front of them. They could hear an electronic hum whirring from within. Rohi held her weapon up with one hand, while carefully gripping the door with the other. Chuck unslung his sonic machete. Bhanakhana resisted the urge to crack his knuckles. Rohi glanced back at them and nodded. She slid the door open with a thud, and burst into the room with Chuck and Bhanakhana right behind her.

They quickly assumed this space was some sort of lofted bedroom. An orb of yellowish-orange light, the source of the light they'd seen from outside, hung on a cable above an oval shaped pod. It looked almost like a cryosleep stasis chamber hewn from stone and laid flat. This had helped contribute to the theory that this was a bedroom. What further contributed to that theory was the pod opening to reveal a figure lying within. At the sound of their entry, the figure sat up and looked at them. Chuck, Rohi, and Bhanakhana's respective mouths fell open in shock.

The being had a fairly normal, if not a tad wide, humanoid torso. Two somewhat gangly humanoid arms, and two somewhat short humanoid legs. Its only clothing was a pair of loose pants, and its skin tone was a pallid pink. Its head was... it didn't have a head... or a neck. It's large eyes, wide mouth, and flat nose were all set into its chest.

The being blinked a few times and then screamed, "AAAAAAAAAAAAAAH!"

Chuck, Rohi, and Bhanakhana screamed in reply, "AAAAAAAAAAAAAAH!"

WORD SECTION 0051

The Sanctuary loomed in front of them. It was heading for the jagged black rocks on the horizon. The large construct hovered low over the water, cutting a wide, angry wake.

"Shit, it's bigger than I remember," noted Jopp.

"We might as well be a spit-fly compared to that thing," added Loi.

"Except my plan doesn't involve us splatting against their windshield."

"You actually have a plan?"

"Kinda... Step One: piss them off. That's where you come in."

"Fuck," said Loi.

"Mega thrills, bud-buds! Ol' Mola is feelin' the adrenalitini kicking in."

They closed the gap further, getting to within a kilometer of their adversary.

"Shoot them, Loi."

"Shoot them with what?"

"Anything. It doesn't matter."

Loi traced her finger over the control panel.

"I don't know what these things do!"

The Sanctuary was only a half-kilometer away. They saw lights blinking and turrets starting to rotate.

"Loi! Just pick something and fire!"

"Uh, okay, how about this one." She opened the targeting screen and lined up the shot. A hole opened in the side of the cube ship; a plasma cannon extended. She pressed *fire*, unleashing a burst of blue energy. It screamed through the air, connecting with one of the Sanctuary's tall spires. The explosion tore through the spire, sending its top half toppling into the ocean.

The cube ship zipped right past the Sanctuary on a bee line for the storm's edge.

"Oh shit! Think that got their attention?" asked Loi.

Jopp pulled up the rear view on his console just in time to see four sleek, angular fighters emerge from underneath the larger vessel.

"Yup. They noticed. Hang on!"

Jopp cranked up the thrust, sending them hurtling toward the 'forest' of rocky protrusions. The fighters gained on them with little effort and unleashed a volley of rapid pulses. Jopp cut to the right just in time to avoid the attack. The shots shredded through a tower of black rock.

"Loi! You need to do something!"

"I'm not a fucking ship's gunner, Jopp!"

"Right now you are! And you can either die as the universe's worst gunner, or figure it out, get us through this, and go back to being a three-peck thief!"

Loi stopped herself from retorting, but rather focused on the defensive resources at her fingertips.

Jopp zigzagged through the rocks, barely avoiding more shots from their pursuers.

"Fly us straight up in five seconds!" said Loi.

"What?!"

"Just do it.... now!"

Jopp yanked hard on the controls, arcing the cube ship upward at a dangerously sharp angle. The fighters followed suit.

"This is top-top righteous!" squealed Mola Mola Tai.

Loi pressed the *fire* button.

Another hole opened at the cube ship's rear, and a payload of trailer mines tumbled out. The fighters all attempted evasive maneuvers. Two of them were successful. The others had their wings torn off by the mine explosions. The ships fell back toward the frothing sea below.

Jopp quickly adjusted course to get them back down to the cover of the rocks. The remaining fighters began to circle back on them. High overhead, a wave of green light rolled through the clouds. One of the fighters got low enough in time. The other wasn't so quick. Green lightning crackled across the sky with a deafening thunderclap. The lightning branched out in dozens of directions, one arc striking home against the lagging fighter. The power immediately went out, and the small jet tumbled into the ocean.

Jopp whipped through the rocks, staying as close to the water's surface as possible. Proximity alerts started flaring.

"I know! I know about the water! Stupid thing..."

Another arc of green lightning danced across the sky. Jopp checked the rear view, and saw nothing chasing after them.

"Where you at, you little squib kid..." Jopp grumbled to himself.

"Gonchos..." Mola Mola Tai was pointing at the front-right angled view screen. They could see the fighter weaving through the rocks in an attempt to cut them off.

"Loi!"

"I see him!"

Loi pressed a button, causing an analog joystick to extend up from the panel. The flanking fighter curved back toward them, lining the cube ship up in its gun sites.

She fired.

A barrage of rapid fire peppered the rocks near and around the approaching fighter, but the ship remained unscathed. It returned fire, and Jopp just barely corkscrewed out of the way.

The fighter pulled around hard, and Jopp did the same, putting them into another head on trajectory.

"What are you doing?"

"We have to get out from under the storm!"

"You're flying us right at him!"

"So, get him out of our way!"

She fired again. The fighter engaged a rocket-bomb targeting lock on the cube ship.

"Loi... Loi... Loi!"

"Shut up! I'm concentrating..." Loi tightened her grip on the joystick. "And for the record... I'm at least a four if not a five-peck thief, thank you very much."

She squeezed the trigger.

A bolter shot hit the fighter's wing. Then another hit the cockpit windshield. Then another hit. Then another. And another. A dozen shots tore through the Adherent jet. It wobbled, it's wing dipping into the water. The pilot tried to stabilize and over-corrected, causing him to careen off a rock. The fighter toppled end of end, crunched off another rock, and crashed into the sea.

"Holy phoobing Gorthan tits," said Loi.

"Yessssss," Jopp pumped his fist.

"Supe-supe intense, gonchitos! Got the whole thing recorded!"

They whipped by a sea stack just as a crack of lightning connected with the black rock. The cube ship lights winked out for a millisecond.

"Don't you fucking take a nap right now," Jopp hollered at the ship.

"Get out of the storm, Jopp."

"Thanks, Boss."

They could see the Sanctuary just outside the storm's edge. It had lowered itself onto the water's surface and appeared to be mostly powered down.

"That's how they're getting to the center..." Loi said, "sailing in, all analog style."

"Well, let's see if we can't be just a little bit more of a nuisance."

Jopp banked to the right, trying to make it look as if he was running away from both the Sanctuary and the storm. When he'd gotten a good way out, he swung them around again to face the titanic vessel.

"What's the plan, goncho?"

"Yeah, what are we doing?" Loi asked.

Jopp kept his eyes focused straight ahead. "How sure are you that it's a small anomaly... a portal, at the center?"

"Uh, pretty sure... I guess."

Jopp exhaled deeply, "Okay, Mola, you should go get ready to jump ship."

"Righteous!"

He was sealing up the various seems on his bodysuit as he rushed out of the control room.

"Loi, what's our weapon situation?"

"Looks like three more plasma cannon bursts... one more payload of mines... a half barrel of rapid bolter rounds."

"Great. Shoot it at them."

"Which one?"

Jopp gripped the throttles. "All of 'em."

The cube ship shot forward, heading straight for the Sanctuary. As they got closer, four of the defense turrets began powering up.

"Ah, look at that, they're turning the lights on for us."

"It's that good old Venovan hospitality," Loi added as she pressed the fire button.

A blue plasma beam tore a hole through one of the turrets. Loi fired again. Then again. The three plasma blasts left one of the turrets out of commission, and another damaged but still functional.

Jopp continued his screaming course right at the ship. Loi switched to the rapid bolters and unloaded the remaining half-barrel. The shots all connected but had little effect against the tough hull of the warship.

"Here we go!"

Jopp pulled them into a sharp upward trajectory, changing course just in time to avoid a pair of red beams from the now-powered up defense towers.

"Hopefully we did enough to get them to chase us."

"Let me see if I can help with that," Loi added, pressing the last available weapon icon.

The payload of trailer mines fell down behind them, peppering the Sanctuary with tiny explosions like a storm of fiery hail. The Sanctuary responded by lifting itself up out of the water.

"Wish granted!" said Loi.

"Great... shit... okay... Hey, Mola!" Jopp said into the ship's comm, "I think it's about time for you to bail."

"All over it, Joppopo!"

The cube ship continued soaring upward, right along the edge of the thick, dark clouds.

"Much luck, Gonchos!" echoed through the commline.

The next thing they saw was a silver figure riding a silver board with a large silver sail gliding over the clouds as if they were waves of water.

"I hope he doesn't die," said Loi.

"Yeah, I like him too."

"You, uh, might want to step on the thrust a bit."

Jopp looked down and saw the Sanctuary rising up after them at an increasing rate.

"Oh, yup!"

Higher the cube soared along the wall of swirling gray clouds, twinkling with bursts of green light.

"Okay," said Jopp, "I'm gonna need you to do a little triangulation once we get above the storm. Pull up the Gjenlu surface map, locate our position, and give me your best guess for when we're directly over the center of that rock-circle-possible-portal-thing."

"What are you planning?"

The ship lurched as Jopp jerked them to the side, barely avoiding a beam of red energy.

"You'll find out in like twenty seconds."

The ship cleared the top of the clouds. Jopp curled them into a horizontal trajectory along the Gjenlu's lower atmosphere, heading for the storm's center. After a few seconds, the Sanctuary appeared behind them.

"We getting close, Loi? Loi? Loi!"

"Shut up... okaaaaay stop!"

In one fluid motion, Jopp decelerated the cube and spun them around to face the oncoming warship.

The Sanctuary fired.

Jopp dodged the shot.

The Sanctuary got closer.

"Jopp?"

"Yeah, Loi?"

"What are we doing?"

"Waiting... don't worry. I've done this before... kind of. Hopefully the winds in the storm are somewhat similar to the currents of Nautaun."

"*What?!*"

The Sanctuary got even closer. It was just a few hundred meters away.

Jopp smiled. "You know that button I said not to press?"

"Yeah?"

"Press it."

As Loi reached for the big red button, Jopp whispered to himself, "*Thanks, Prof.*"

Loi pushed the button.

A protective, spherical barrier formed around the control room. The cube ship burst apart into eight sections that rocketed outward. In unison, the eight sections detonated with electromagnetic pulses. Brilliant blue arcs of energy surged through the Sanctuary. The behemoth of a vessel groaned. All the lights flickered and then went dark. And then, the Sanctuary fell from the sky.

For a moment longer, the core of the cube ship hovered in place.

"Holy shit," said Jopp, "It work-"

And then the gravitational stabilizers gave out. The spherical core plummeted straight down in a tight spiraling corkscrew. Jopp and Loi screamed as they fell through the dark storm clouds, burst through the underside, and continued to hurtle toward the curiously viscous, purple membrane within the rock ring below.

The core bounced off the inner edge of the rock ring, and then careened downward through the portal.

WORD SECTION 0052

"Alright!" shouted Bhanakhana, "Alright! Everyone cease screaming!"

Chuck and Rohi stopped. The being let its own scream trail off into a series of deep panting breaths.

"I suppose you're here to kill me," the being groaned.

"Absolutely not. We-" Bhanakhana paused and looked at Chuck and Rohi. "Did you understand that as well?"

"Yeah," said Rohi.

"Yep," said Chuck.

"Fascinating," Bhanakhana turned back to the being. "Are you able to understand what I am saying?"

"I'm gathering the gist of it, though you're about as eloquent as a small child who only just learned to speak last week."

"That's not nice," said Rohi.

"Yeah, man," Chuck added, "Don't be rude."

The being pointed at Rohi. "The Jergette sounds like a small child who learned to speak last week, who also has a mouth full of gublum..." then pointed at Chuck, "And is this animal your pet? What an awful sound it makes."

"What did he call you?" Chuck asked Rohi.

"I'm more concerned about what he called you," she replied.

"Are you sure you aren't here to kill me?"

"We are not going to kill you," said Bhanakhana.

The being sighed, "Oh, bother... well, what do you want?"

"Sir, are you... are you one of the Ak'alei?"

"I see... You're an idiot."

"Hey, screw you, dude," Chuck said.

"Your pet is growling at me. I'm not surprised. Animals don't like me."

"Bhanakhana, what is going on?" Rohi said.

"Okay... okay... okay..." Bhanakhana folded his arms. Then unfolded them and stroked his chin. Then refolded them again.

"I have a hypothesis: This person is an Ak'alei."

"Wow," said Chuck.

"Oh shit," said Rohi.

"Yes, Ak'alei," the being drolled, "I see your physical stature isn't the only thing about you that's thick."

"Why's he such a dick?"

"I don't like your pet. It's noises are unpleasant."

"More importantly," said Rohi, "Why can we understand it... or why can it understand us."

"*Understand* is generous. Your enunciation sounds like words being pushed through a fruit pulper."

"Our TellAlls," said Bhanakhana, "In the Sentient Coalition, there are four known races whose home world's held evidence of Ak'alei presence: Venovans, Puzuru, Bogteks, and my fellow Dronla. It stands to reason that the Ak'alei has influence over the manner in which our cultures and languages developed."

"So our TellAlls are connecting the dots and making educated guesses on what he's saying?"

"In a manner of speaking," Bhanakhana chuckled.

"But that doesn't explain why he can understand us," Chuck saw the look he was getting from the Ak'alei, "or I mean understand you two and not me at all."

"If you're not going to kill me, but rather going to make me sit here and listen to this gibberish, could you at least have the decency to get me a cup of tea."

"Some of the words I am saying must have originated from the Ak'alei language."

"What about me?" Said Rohi. "It understands me a little too."

"Perhaps the J'Kari origin planet was also visited by them."

"So that's a *no* on the tea, then?"

"It would explain why it can't understand Chuck at all."

"He still doesn't have to be a dick about it."

The Ak'alei gingerly climbed out of the bed-pod. Its legs wobbled under the weight.

"Oof... everything aches."

It walked past them toward the door.

"Uh, sir or madam, where are you going?"

The Ak'alei ignored Bhanakhana and stepped out onto the landing connecting the stairs to the bedroom. It saw the layers of dust, the general decrepitude of the tower, and turned back. It walked back into the bedroom and looked out the windows to the dark and lifeless town below.

"How long have I been asleep?"

"Well," said Bhanakhana, "we do not know... however, it has been almost two thousand standard annuals since your kind has moved amongst ours."

"It sounded like you said some kind of time frame. *Two thousand* something? How many periods is that?"

"We do not know."

"Your breed matures physically at twenty-nine periods. What's that in whatever you measure time in?"

"Generally speaking, we Dronla achieve physical maturity at nineteen annuals..."

The Ak'alei exhaled deeply. "Then I've been asleep for over two thousand six hundred periods."

"Two thousand annuals," amended Bhanakhana.

"Wow," said Rohi.

"Holy shit, how is he still alive?" asked Chuck.

Bhanakhana saw the Ak'alei eyeing Chuck.

"He asked how it is you are still alive. And despite his appearance, he is quite sentient. I can translate what he says for you."

"I can't imagine it'd be anything worth hearing," griped the Ak'alei, "And why wouldn't I be alive? I've just been sleeping..."

"Most sentient species age at a continual rate until their bodies give out and they perish.

"That's dumb."

"It's true," Rohi offered.

"I didn't say it wasn't true. I said it was dumb."

"Your kind does not die of old age?"

"No. I wish. What an easy release that'd be…"

"What happened to the other Ak'alei?"

"How should I know? I started my usual shift here in Overlook Tower. Took my sanctioned nap. Next thing I know, it's a few millennia in the future and I'm stuck with you lot."

"You slept through the extinction of your own race," noted a dejected Bhanakhana.

"Of course, this would happen to me. Nothing good ever happens to me."

"Do you have a name?" Rohi asked.

The Ak'alei sighed, "It's Ahfel."

"Oh, I am certain it is a perfectly fine name. We will not judge you. I am Bha-na-kha-na."

"And I am Ro-hi."

"Chuck!"

"So," said Bhanakhana, "Would you like to share your name?"

"I told you. My name is Ahfel."

"No need to be so morose-Oh! I see! Your name *is* Awful."

"Who's on first?!" said a grinning Chuck.

"We don't have time for this," hissed Rohi.

"Right!" said Bhanakhana, "Excuse me, Mr. Awful. But there are some other people who have come to your world with foul intentions. We intend to stop them; however we don't know how to locate them."

"Sounds unfortunate for you."

"Er, yes, well, mayhaps you could assist us?"

"Why bother?"

"Because they're dangerous to the rest of our worlds," replied Rohi.

Ahfel shrugged, which was quite an interesting thing to witness given its lack of neck and head.

"Hey," said Chuck to Bhanakhana, "This dude's mentioned dying like three times. Tell him he'll probably die if he chooses to help us."

"That is quite morbid, Chuck. You wish me to attempt to persuade him to assist us by telling him that assisting us will likely result in his death?"

"Okay, I'll help you."

Ahfel trudged back out of the room. After a moment of stunned hesitation, they followed after it.

"Excuse me, Awful?" Rohi said as they descended the stairs.

"You're not really saying my name right... I guess it doesn't matter... what?"

"Er, why are you so eager to die?"

"I don't *want* to die. I *want* to be left alone. But if I die, at least then I'll get some peace and quiet."

"You haven't enjoyed your life?"

"Why would I?"

"We tend to enjoy life... at least that is the ultimate goal, for the most part," countered Bhanakhana.

"That's your problem then, isn't it?"

They stepped through the tower doorway and paused on the hilltop. Chuck, Rohi, and Bhanakhana had been so focused on the tower itself they hadn't really registered their surroundings. This hill was situated in the center of a wide, shallow valley. Three dozen of the portal-tree-mountains, including the one they'd arrived through, could been seen scattered throughout the valley. They saw more 'towns' of domed buildings, and it looked as if the single massive dome they'd seen from atop the portal tree-mountain marked the center of the valley. The valley looked dead and dormant. The Gjenlu portal was the only one active. None of the buildings gave off any light.

"Something terrible has happened," lamented Ahfel.

"How can you tell?"

"Something terrible always happens." Ahfel pointed at the large single dome structure. "Structure One controls the power generation and pretty much everything else."

"*Structure One*... that's what you call it? Not *The Cortex* or *Prime Station Alpha* or-"

Rohi elbowed Chuck in the ribs to shut him up and said, "Looks to be about fifteen, maybe twenty-minute walk."

They heard a series of *thunks* and *thuds* and looked up in time to see about four or five sizeable chunks of metal fall through the Gjenlu portal. They clattered off the landing platform and toppled down to the ground below.

"That can't be goo-" Chuck started right as a metallic sphere, about the size of an Estal Cube core, burst through the portal. It hit the landing platform with an ear-splitting crack, and bounced off. The tree-mountain branch supporting the platform groaned, creaked, and then broke. The metal sphere hurtled through the air before smashing into the large dome, disappearing within the massive structure.

"Was that the control core of my ship?" asked Bhanakhana.

"This seems more trouble than it's worth," said Ahfel, "I think I'll go back to bed."

"Oh no you are not," Bhanakhana scooped up the alien and slung him over his shoulder. He turned to Rohi. "Fifteen-to-twenty-minute walk, you say?"

She shrugged, "Or a ten-minute run?"

"And now you're abducting me... savages."

Chuck looked up at the Ak'alei, put his finger to his grinning lips and went, "Shhhhh."

WORD SECTION 0053

Pale light crept in through the rough, circular hole in the dome. The air was filled with clouds of ancient dust. Directly below the hole, a metal sphere was partially embedded in the stone floor. A rectangular seam appeared in the side of the sphere. The section of metal within the seam vibrated for a second and then popped right off, landing on the floor with a clatter. A stout yellow being and a blue-skinned humanoid emerged from the rectangular opening and fell clumsily to the floor.

"Holy shit," said Loi, "We are never doing that again."

"Oh, you mean engaging in battle with a religious zealot-controlled warship... disabling said warship by self-destructing our *own* ship... only to then plummet through a mysterious portal leading to the undiscovered origin planet of an ancient, powerful, extinct civilization? How *ever* will you avoid such a common daily occurrence?"

Loi slugged him in the arm.

"Ah, seriously. People need to stop hitting me."

"Then stop saying asinine crap."

"Never."

Jopp stood up to dust himself off. Loi followed suit and started looking around. The minimal light leaking in from the hole they'd made revealed an empty, cavernous room. It was eerily silent, until Jopp had something else to say.

"Fuck... Bhanakhana isn't going to be happy about that hole up there. Chuck and me damaging historic relics is kind of his pet peeve."

They climbed back into the ship core to retrieve some e-torches and Jopp remembered his old pulse pistol was still crammed in one of the navigation console drawers. As he fastened it back on his belt he noted, "You know, it wasn't that long ago when the scariest thing I might have needed this for was a bunch of angry pineapples."

"What the phoob is a pineapple?"

"Apparently this indigenous tribe we were studying looked like some plant Chuck had back on Earth. He kept saying it, and it's a funny sounding word, so it stuck with me."

Loi's fingers traced over Serru's blade, still in her belt. "Well, I hope you're ready to use it. This isn't a rescue mission anymore."

They climbed back out of the core. A quick scan with their e-torches confirmed that, save for a few support columns, this room was empty. The only door they could find was on the far wall, leading deeper into the Ak'alei building. They looked from the door to each other, shrugged, and headed toward it.

• • • •

Bhanakhana, Chuck, and Rohi panted as they tried to catch their breath. The large Ak'alei dome rose up ahead of them, about a half a kilometer away. They had stopped because Ahfel had claimed an urgent need to urinate.

"You try sleeping for a few millennia and then tell me you don't need to do a little personal waste removal," it had argued.

While it relieved itself near a boulder, Chuck reached into his satchel and produced three nutrient bars and some hydration pouches. The three of them tore into the sustenance like a pack of wild animals.

When Ahfel returned, Chuck offered it a nutrient bar. The Ak'alei sniffed at it and scrunched its face up in revulsion.

"Tell your pet, no thank you."

"He can understand you," said Rohi, "And I would appreciate it if you stopped calling him that."

"I've offended you. I do that a lot. I'm not good at inter-being interactions. I never did much traveling to the other worlds. I never saw the appeal honestly."

"How does it work?" Bhanakhana asked, "The portals."

"I don't know all the mundane details. I'm just an operational observer. But I was alive when it started."

"Could you please tell us more about that?" Bhanakhana asked.

"It's not very interesting."

"Please."

Ahfel sighed as it pointed at the sky, more specifically at the black dot in the middle of all the swirling color.

"We used to have a real star. It was bright, yellow, and warm. The sky was blue. The ground had plants. Then the star turned into that and everything changed. All the other lights in the sky began to bleed. Our planet got cold and desolate. We went under the ground, found caverns full of plant life and water, some so enormous you could almost forget you were stuck underground. We dug deeper, discovered the pa'tika."

"The what?" Rohi said.

Ahfel turned to the nearest tree-mountain and pointed at the cluster of orange crystalline material clinging to its side.

"What is it?" Bhanakhana asked.

"We never fully knew. It sometimes acts like a metal, or a stone, or even a fungus... if left unchecked, it will self-replicate. That's what's going on with all that excess clinging to the Marams."

"Marams would be those tall tree-like structures."

"They're not plants. That would be dumb."

"He said tree-*like*! Don't be rude!" Chuck said.

"Chuck, it is okay," assured Bhanakhana.

Ahfel sighed and said, "Anyway, it takes heaps of volatile energy to supercharge the pa'tika to the point of spatial bridging. So they tried to keep the spatial bridges accessible while still being somewhat removed."

"Spatial bridges... the portals?"

"Obviously."

"We need to keep moving," Rohi said pointedly.

Ahfel raised its arms to Bhanakhana like a toddler reaching for their parents to pick them up. Bhanakhana looked down at it with an inquisitive raised eyebrow.

"Escaping seems like too much effort, and running, in general, is terrible."

He slung Ahfel back over his shoulder with a sigh.

WORD SECTION 0054

Jopp and Loi soon realized they'd caught a lucky break in that the door leading out from the room they'd landed in had been left partially open. They found many other doors along the darkened corridor, but none of them would so much as budge a millimeter.

"Must be some kind of electronic locking system," Loi noted.

"Great. So either we find the 'on' switch or this place becomes our tomb," grumbled Jopp.

"Ever the font of relentless optimism."

"Relentless pragmatism."

The corridor ended in a t-intersection. Their e-torches couldn't reach far enough to illuminate the end of either hall. Jopp noticed a diagram of lines, rectangles, and circles with small bubbles of Ak'alei text.

"Hey," he said, "Can you read this?"

Loi shone her light on the diagram. "It's a map. I think we're right here."

"How can you tell?"

"Because this dot says *You are here*."

"Fair enough."

"Okay, let's see... looks like there's maybe a bathroom and what I think could be a kitchen down the left hall..."

"Ooo, I'm starving. Let's go to the kitchen."

"Jopp, this place has been abandoned for like a thousand years."

"According to Big Red, it's more like double that... ah man, I wish he was here. He'd have gotten all giddy at me remembering some relevant factoid."

"You're only proving my point."

"Oh, c'mon! These guys figured out intergalactic portals for phoob's sake. You telling me they couldn't have also mastered food preservatives?"

* six minutes later *

"Oh my holy fucking shit!" Jopp sputtered in between coughing fits as they rushed back to the map diagram.

Loi forced back her gag reflex and said, "The smell of that kitchen will haunt my nostrils forever."

"I'm pretty sure that one pile of blue mold winked at me."

Loi shuttered and shined her e-torch back on the map.

"Okay, um, I don't know all of these words... but 'power' and 'control' are tagged to this room over here. It's a bit of hike... fuck, if I'm reading the scale of this map right, this place is *big*."

Loi captured a picture of the map with her data bracelet. They moved down the hall at a brisk but careful pace. The door at the far end, their desired destination, was sealed firmly shut. However, the door behind them on the left was open.

Loi checked the map, traced a potential alternate route. They found themselves moving through a series of small storage rooms filled with unmarked barrels.

At the end of the third room, they came to a door that was just barely ajar. The opening was roughly a quarter-meter wide.

"You should go first," Loi said.

"Um, excuse me?"

"You're... um, more... three dimensional then me?"

"Did you seriously just say that?"

"What's the point of me going through, if you end up not fitting?"

"Wow, fuck you."

"Oh, just go already."

Jopp turned to the side and started trying to shimmy through the door, all while giving Loi the stink eye. When he was about halfway through, his momentum stopped. He tried to move again but felt a tug around his midsection.

"Are you stuck?"

"No!"

"You're stuck."

"I'm not stuck."

"Then keep going."

Jopp wiggled and grunted.

"Fucking fine. I'm stuck."

· · ·

Chuck, Rohi, Bhanakhana, and Ahfel came around the bend in Structure One to see a decorative archway, some twenty meters tall carved into the dome. Ahfel lead them through the archway, and into a cavernous, dimly lit vestibule. Numerous statues were scattered around the room. They saw a Dronla, a Venovan, a Bogtek... and plenty of unfamiliar creatures.

"They liked to catalogue our collection of sentient species with these ridiculous displays," explained Ahfel.

"Your collection?" asked Bhanakhana.

"It was a like a game to the Travelers. They'd find planets with sentient species and try to get them to believe our kind was some sort of divine entity."

"That seems callous and potentially detrimental," said Rohi.

"I know," said Ahfel, "Bunch of sludgers, the lot of them. The universe has probably been much better off without us mucking about in it."

Ahfel lead them deeper into the dome. More than once, they entered a room with multiple doors, all but one being sealed shut. Ahfel never hesitated, always heading for the open door.

"May I ask where we are going?" asked Bhanakhana.

"Everything is off, which means something's wrong in the power terminal. The doors between there and the Structure One entrance can't close. All the other doors, if closed when the power goes out, stay closed."

"You're being quite helpful now," noted a skeptical Rohi.

"And we are quite appreciative!" added Bhanakhana.

"It occurred to me that the sooner you get your nonsense resolved the sooner I can be left alone in peace. My helpfulness is motivated by pure selfishness."

"He's a grumpy fucker, huh?" said Chuck.

Ahfel eyed Chuck who gave him a big smile and a thumbs up.

They entered an expansive room that was utterly filled with tubes, cisterns, gears, and workstation. The wall opposite their door was one big window. The room it looked out on was a large circular chamber covered in glossy blue metal. Far below the window, the entire floor of the room was one gigantic turbine. The turbine blades were made from a familiar orange crystalline material. Directly across from their window, they saw another window. The room behind it appeared to be coated in gold plating.

"This would be the power terminal, then?" said Bhanakhana

"You're the smart one? Okay then. Yes. You come with me. Tell the other two not to break anything."

"What're we gonna break? His whole planet's already broken," Chuck grumbled to Rohi.

She fought back a snicker.

Ahfel and Bhanakhana started inspecting the equipment, which mostly consisted of Bhanakhana prying off whatever protective plating was coating the machine and Ahfel rooting around inside it.

Meanwhile Rohi busied herself trying to catch some kind of signal on her data bracelet. Chuck used every ounce of self-control to stay in one place and not touch anything. And that got him a full two minutes before he started moseying around.

"No!" echoed Ahfel's voice, "Don't turn *that* knob. Turn the other knob."

"You said this one, I am certain of it," Bhanakhana's voice echoed back.

"No, I didn't."

Chuck gazed at a lattice of narrow tubes that ran up the length of the wall to the high ceiling.

"Try connecting the white wire to the purscane wire," said Ahfel.

"I don't know what purscane means," countered Bhanakhana.

"Your eyes can't see the color purscane?"

"I see a white wire and two blue wires."

"One of those 'blue' wires is actually purscane..."

Chuck walked around a tall cistern with a half dozen pipes connecting it to the wall.

"There seems to be some corrosion on this relay switch."

"You got any claws you can chip it off with?"

"I do not."

Chuck started strolling toward a large contraption that reminded him of an oil derrick. He froze mid-stride, his eyes focusing on the ground between the 'oil derrick' and the wall. He walked over and looked down at a cord. The cord, which was as thick as his arm, ended in a bulbous head with six prongs sticking out of it. Chuck looked at the patch of wall nearest to the cord and saw six holes grouped close together.

He looked back at the cord with the six prongs.

Then back at the cluster of six holes in the wall.

Then back at the cord.

Back at the holes.

Chuck shrugged.

He picked up the cord and inserted the six prongs into the six holes.

Then everything... literally *everything*... turned on.

WORD SECTION 0055

"Here. I'll push you," said Loi.

"No. Don't-"

Loi put one hand on Jopp's shoulder, the other on his hip, and pushed.

"Ow! Stop! Ow!"

"Almost there..."

"Loi! Cut it-"

Jopp burst through the other side with a pop and fell to the floor, his e-torch clattering a few feet away. Loi quickly slid through the door opening and held out a helping hand. As Jopp begrudgingly reached up, his eyes fell on the patch of space illuminated by his dropped e-torch. He saw a wide-framed humanoid standing against the wall.

"Look out!" Jopp shouted as he yanked his pistol free, raised it, and fired. Loi dropped to the floor. The pulse beam bounced of the figure's chest, before ricocheting around the room a few times, finally dispersing as it hit the floor uncomfortably close to Jopp's head.

"What the fuck?!" shouted Loi.

Jopp pointed. Loi rolled over to look up at the figure, which had not moved so much as a millimeter. She shone her own light at it. It was missing the orb of light above the shoulders, but it definitely resembled the statue of the Ak'alei.

"I don't think that's a person... I think it's... a suit? Or something."

The reptilian scales of the suit were a dark, almost black, purple. And the seams between the scales were dull orange. Loi stood and walked over for a closer look. The suit had no head, and she noticed a strip of smooth, glass-like material running across the chest. There was a scorch mark where Jopp's shot had connected. She let her light slide down along the wall, revealing a row of these suits.

Meanwhile, Jopp crawled over to his own e-torch and stood back up. He shined it against the wall opposite the suits.

"Maybe save your ammo for an actual living threat next time," said Loi. "More likely to both keep us alive and not further piss off Bhanakhana by damaging more relics."

"Oh, I think he'll have relics to spare..." said Jopp.

Loi turned around and looked at the opposite wall, where Jopp's light had revealed an eclectic array of equipment... tools... weapons? There were rods, orbs, items with handles that could have either been guns or vacuums or anything really.

Loi walked over next to Jopp, and they approached the wall of supposed gadgets.

"I don't see any kind of labeling..." Loi muttered.

"Yeah," said Jopp as he reached a hand out. Right as his fingers brushed against the wall... a single ceiling light turned on.

Jopp and Loi jumped back in surprise.

"What'd you do?!" said Loi.

"Nothing!"

They heard a series of low toned clicks reverberate through the building. More ceiling lights turned on. Narrow spotlights shined down on each of the strange suits. Then the entire wall of gadgetry lit up with orange and blue glow. Blurbs of Ak'alei text appeared next to each item.

Before they could read anything a loud scraping noise pulled their eyes to the far end of the room, where a wide pair of double doors was sliding open. They approached the door as the slabs of stone separated, and found themselves looking into a circular room full a short, wide, cylindrical pedestal in the center, five other double doors evenly spaced around the room, and multicolor tube lights running up the walls. One by one each of the other doors opened. The last door to open was the one directly across. Behind it stretched another hallway, and there was nothing particularly interesting about the hallway... except for the four Venovan men wearing Adherent attire standing in it.

"Oh..." started Jopp.

"...shit," finished Loi.

"Heretics!" One of the men shouted, "Herald Dac'eth! The heretics are here!"

Jopp reached for the wall and snatched a metal orb with a single switch. He flicked the switch causing the orb to light up with an ominous glow and hurled it across the circular room into the opposite hall. It bounced off the floor. The Adherent men tried to dive out of the way. The orb exploded in a cloud of thick, watery mist. When the mist dissipated, tiny green beads coated the floor, walls, ceiling, and the Adherent warriors. They sat up and looked around in confusion.

"What was that?" Jopp asked.

Loi peered at the label next to where the orb had been.

"A Ger- let me try to pronounce this right: Ger-min-ade. A Germinade... I think you just threw a wad of plant seeds at them."

One of the Adherent picked off a green bead and saw a small white flower sprouting from it.

"Quick!" said Jopp, "Find a weapon that's actually a weapon!"

Loi tried to read the nearby labels as fast as she could.

"Uh... livestock feed... hydro-supplements... this is all farming equipment!"

The Adherent had gotten over their surprise and were getting back on their feet. Jopp glanced back at them just in time to see Serru and three more Adherent come around the far corner of the hall.

"Loi! We need to run!"

Serru swept past the seed-covered Adherent, her glowing eyes focused on Jopp and Loi with calm determination.

Jopp raised his pistol and fired.

Serru tilted her head, letting the shot zip by with ease.

Jopp fired again.

Serru sidestepped.

Jopp cursed, "Phoobing worthless piece of junk!" and he hurled the gun itself.

Serru stopped at the doorway into the circular room and watched the pistol clatter of the wall next to her with an almost amused expression. When she looked back toward Jopp, she saw him standing in the opposite doorway, cradling four or five glowing metal orbs.

"No clue what any of these do," he said, "I hope at least one of them hurts."

He underhand-tossed the bundle of orbs into the circular room, before lunging for the sole lever next to his door. He yanked it down, praying it did what he thought it did. Sure enough, the doors slammed closed. He heard shouting and a muffled explosion from the other side.

Jopp whirled around to bark, "Loi, what the hell were you-"

She held up an oblong rucksack with a cross body strap.

"I found this and threw in a couple things that looked semi-useful. Let's go!"

They sprinted back through the rooms filled with barrels. Each time, closing the door behind them and taking a few moments to push over as many barrels as possible to block the path.

· · ·

Serru stood up cautiously from her cover behind the cylindrical pedestal. Two thirds of the circular room were now covered in green seeds, some kind of rainbow foam, and a foul-smelling black sludge. She peered at the closed doors where Jopp had stood, saw the outline of two humanoid heat signatures getting farther away.

Serru then turned around to her remaining cadre, four of whom now had tiny flowers blossoming over their bodies.

"Go after them. I want our Venovan sister kept alive. If necessary, the Yoblon can be sacrificed. With the power restored, I should be able to reach to the Origin Room. We have waited long enough for the Holy Gates to be opened."

WORD SECTION 0056

Chuck, Rohi, Bhanakhana, and Ahfel all stared down at the thick cord, now married to the wall.

"Are you sure that's what it said?" asked Ahfel.

"Yes," answered Rohi, "*HE* said that cord was lying on the floor next to the wall, and he just plugged it in."

"He doesn't believe me?" Chuck asked.

Ahfel stepped in front of Chuck.

"You. Put. Plug. In. Wall?" He was accenting his words with exaggerated hand gestures, miming the act of inserting the cord into the wall.

Chuck simply nodded.

Ahfel put his hands over his mouth, and let out a long, low groan. "Ohhhhh dear... ohhhhh dear... ohhhhh dear..."

He trudged over to the nearest workstation and collapsed into a chair, still groaning.

"What are we missing here, Awful?" Bhanakhana asked.

He looked up at them with a forlorn expression.

"For a while, the only way we knew how to make the spatial bridges was by building the marams, each one a total self-contained power source. You'd think the ability to pass seamlessly between worlds, even if each new world required building an enormous contraption like the maram, would be satisfactory. But not for our people, noooooooooo. They wanted to make it even more convenient. The first step was the branches off the marams, small local bridges between up there and key locations down here. But that still required one end of the bridge being connected to a maram, which wasn't good enough for the parliament. Bunch of spoiled yankers if you ask me. They wanted to have door-sized spatial bridges anywhere and everywhere. So, the engineers went to work. Took them a century or so, but they figured it out."

Ahfel let out a heavy sigh, "Of course, they wanted a party. Any excuse for celebrating themselves, those trogboggers. They set up a few dozen of the portable bridges."

"Heh," said Chuck, "portable portals... *portabatals*?"

Rohi gave him the ol' elbow-in-the-ribs.

"They thought it'd be soooo fun to have a party on a bunch of different worlds simultaneously. They started with a ceremonial toast. Then everyone was supposed to go through one spatial bridge, spend a little time on one world then come back and go to the next. The first stop was this new one they'd just discovered. The spatial bridge opened out onto a barren rock surrounded by water that stretched to the horizon in every direction. Everyone thought it'd be a great place for a party."

"When you say *everyone*, you cannot be referring to your entire civilization, can you?" asked Bhanakhana, "Why that must have been..."

"Three hundred and eighteen," interjected Ahfel.

"There were only three hundred and eighteen of your kind?" said Rohi.

Ahfel shrugged, "Have the star go black on your world. See what happens to your people."

Bhanakhana gave him a pointed stare. "But not *everyone* went through, did they?"

"I hate parties. I hate alcohol. It makes annoying people more annoying."

"Blasphemy," grumbled Chuck as he dodged Rohi's elbow.

"But those yankers made me join the ceremonial toast. All I wanted to do after that was go take a nap. I remember walking back to the tower. I like the tower. People left me alone in the tower. I remember leaving the Great Hall... quickest way from there to the exit is cutting through this room... that dumb drink made me all fuzzy-like... I tripped over something..."

Its eyes stared at the cord in the wall.

Rohi and Chuck stared back forth from the cord to Ahfel, their mouths hanging open in shock. Bhanakhana's entire body tensed, and he pinched the bridge of his nose.

"Are you conveying to me... that your entire civilization... a civilization that has fascinated and captivated the scientific community of our society for decades upon decades... was wiped out of existence because you accidently knocked out the power, trapping everyone else on a desolate rock in the middle of an alien ocean... and then you took a two thousand year nap?"

"I'm just the worst, aren't I? You can kill me if it'd make you feel better."

"Oh, I am considering it."

"Bhanakhana!" Rohi and Chuck exclaimed in unison.

The mound of red muscle sighed and said, "No, I will not harm you."

"So close," sighed Ahfel. "What if I called your breed-mum a trogblogging yanker?'

"I do not know what that means."

"It's really insulting. Trust me. You should be quite mad."

"Hold on," said Rohi, "if the power that fuels these portals has been out all this time, how come the one that brought us here worked?"

"This station has the ability to control the original marams. But they have internal power sources and can still function independently with an Onu-Key... I assume you lot found one?"

"Well," said Bhanakhana, "We had a key, however it is currently in the possession of our ill-intentioned adversaries."

"That's bad for you."

"Are there more keys?" asked Rohi.

"In the Origin Room. It's that ugly gold room you can see through the window, opposite side of the turbine. If you go through that door over there and keep going straight, you'll be in the Great Hall. The Origin Room overlooks the Hall. There's a stair."

At that moment they heard muffled shouting, the shrill ping of pulse pistol fire, and then an explosion. Chuck, Rohi, and Bhanakhana looked at each other and started sprinting for the door Ahfel had gestured toward. The Ak'alei slumped back in its seat, calling after them. "You lot go on ahead. I need to ponder things a bit."

WORD SECTION 0057

"Okay" <pant> "Okay" <cough> "Okay, I need to stop."

Jopp slowed to a walk and put his hands on his hips, breathing heavily. Loi, a few meters ahead of him, skidded to a stop to turn around.

"We are in the middle of a doorless hallway. If they come around that corner back there, there'll be no where for us to go."

"I literally lost count on how many rooms and halls we've run through. My lungs are on fucking fire. We had to have bought ourselves a minute."

"C'mon. Let's at least find a place with a little cover or something."

"Ugh, fine!"

Jopp followed after her at barely a jogging pace. The hallway curved to the right, ending in a door. Loi opened it and they stepped into a cavernous warehouse-like room. She looked to the right and saw a large pane of glass set into the wall fifteen meters above the floor. Up until this point, Loi would've described the decor of this building as *pragmatically dull*, but the room behind the large pane of glass was anything but. Every surface that wasn't a neon light, was covered in gold plating. She could make out the bottom halves of four tall golden statues spaced near the four corners.

Jopp looked to the left and saw a large metal dais. It was covered in complex-looking machinery and gear works, with two twenty-meter metal pylons rising upward. Hanging down from the ceiling was a massive mechanical arm that ended in a two-pronged claw.

The rest of this assumed-warehouse was filled with hundreds of the same, peculiar item: a ring made from copper-colored metal and an orange crystalline substance. Each ring was about two meters in diameter. Most of the rings were stacked against the walls, leaving a vast open floor space in the middle. At the center of this space, eighteen of these rings had been arranged in two concentric circles. The inner circle had a five-meter diameter, with six rings spaced around it. The outer circle had a twenty-meter diameter, with twelve rings evenly spaced. Unlike all the others, these rings hummed with life, and the space inside each ring was not empty. The outside of the rings, the side facing away from the center, was a solid wall of dull orange. The inside 'face' of the rings, however, appeared to have a translucent membrane. Beyond that, Jopp and Loi saw very strange sights. They saw a night sky, a solid wall of rock, a beach, a tangle of thorny red vines, a room that looked suspiciously like the closed storage sector of the Golatac Barge... Water trickled in from one portal, snow from another. Some of them were pure blackness.

Jopp and Loi walked over to inspect them closer.

"That's trippy," said Loi.

"Are those fucking portals to, like, other planets?" Jopp wondered aloud.

"They're actually *portabatals*: portable portals," echoed a voice from behind them.

They spun around to see Chuck, Rohi, and Bhanakhana stepping through a different door across the way. The five of them rushed to meet each other. Rohi yanked Loi in for a rough hug, "I'm glad you came back."

"Yeah, yeah, don't you go gettin' all squishy on me, Law Cog."

Before Chuck or Jopp could decide on what kind of greeting they'd have, Bhanakhana scooped them both up in an embrace.

"I am glad to see you, Jopp."

"Okay, okay," said Jopp, "You can put me down now, Big Red."

Bhanakhana set them both back down, and Jopp started brushing himself off.

"What caused you to change your mind?" asked Bhanakhana.

"I figured it'd look real bad on my resume, you know? Quitting in the middle of a contracted job."

"And because you love us," Chuck added.

"Excuse you?"

"It's okay, buddy. I love you too."

"Stop it."

"Ah," cooed Bhanakhana, "I hold warm, brotherly affection for you as well."

"Seriously. I will turn around and leave again."

"Boys," said Rohi, "We need to figure out a plan, immediately."

"Yeah, about that," said Loi, "Serru and her lackeys are in the building. We already had a nice little reunion, and they're chasing after us. How are you guys fixed for weapons?"

"Chuck still has his machete, and I have the Hand Cannon. That's it."

Loi unslung the rucksack and dropped it on the ground.

"Weapons?" asked a hopeful Rohi.

Loi shrugged, "Kinda."

She opened the bag.

"We found some equipment, mostly farming related... I don't know exactly what any of it does, but I tried to memorize the names."

She revealed a pair of large mechanical-looking gauntlets.

"I have seen something like that before," said Bhanakhana, "In a museum on my home world... though it was severely rusted, and missing most components..."

"Well, good, 'cause I grabbed them with you in mind... they're called, uh, Rock Chewers or something vaguely similar to that."

"I'll bet those Ak'alei dicks made your ancestors use them for hard labor," Chuck noted.

"How you know they were dicks?" asked Jopp.

"Oh, we met one," said Chuck, "He sucks. I'll tell you about it later."

"Wait... *what?*" said Loi, "There is a real live Ak'alei being *here?*"

"We don't have time-" Rohi started before she saw the Adherent warriors spill through the same door that Jopp and Loi had come from. There were seven of them, and they quickly fanned out to form a line, their halberds held in ready position. Rohi held up the Bloodfist Hand Cannon and shouted, "First one of you to take a step forward gets his head popped off!"

The Venovans hesitated.

Chuck noticed some of them had little flowers blooming all over their clothes. He glanced at Jopp and whispered, "*You do that?*"

Jopp nodded with a mischievous grin and the two of them fought back giggles.

The Adherent stood still, looking back and forth amongst themselves. Without a word spoken, they all appeared to reach a consensus.

"Don't do it," Rohi warned.

The one in the middle snarled, "Prepare for divine retribution, heretic!"

WORD SECTION 0058

The Adherent warriors charged.

Rohi fired. The shot tore through the leader's chest. He dropped. The others began zigzagging around the portals as they approached. Rohi fired again. Missed. She fired again, barely grazing the arm of her target, the force of the shot still making the man drop to the floor.

Bhanakhana examined his hands. The metal gauntlets each had a small circle of milky white crystal on the inside wrist, just below the palm. The right-side one was a convex sphere, the left-side one was concave. Bhanakhana shrugged and pressed his wrists together. Lights on the backhand of the gauntlets lit up and they began to whir with electronic life. He looked up just in time to see an Adherent lunging at him, halberd falling in a downward strike. Bhanakhana thrust his arm forward, catching the halberd by the shaft, just below the axe-head. He felt the gauntlet humming and tried to squeeze.

The metal shaft of the halberd shattered in his grip.

The Adherent warrior stared up in shock.

Bhanakhana wasted no time in delivering a left hook to the Venovan man's temple.

Rohi fired again. Nothing happened. She saw the red blinking light on the pistol grip.

"No ammo? Because why-fucking-not!"

She jumped out of the way, narrowly avoiding an Adherent's halberd thrust. With one hand, she grabbed the weapon and pulled him closer. With the other she flipped the pistol, catching it around the barrel, and then struck the Adherent across the face with the butt. She then immediately dropped the gun, shaking her hand. "Ow! Fucking hot!"

Chuck grabbed the first thing that looked useful from the rucksack, an item resembling a short sledgehammer, and rushed into the fray.

"You don't even know what it does!" called Loi.

"He'll figure it out," said Jopp, "What else you got in there?"

Loi held up a silver orb.

"More seeds?"

"The label said *animal snare*."

Jopp saw two Adherent closing in on Bhanakhana. He snatched the orb, flipped the switch, and hurled it. The orb hit the ground behind the two Venovan men, and ten tendrils of blue energy burst out in every direction. Both Adherent warriors had one of their ankles grazed by a tendril, which quickly wrapped itself around their leg. Then, in unison, all the tendrils receded back to the orb, pulling the two Adherent down and dragging them across the floor.

"That won't hold them forever."

"Nope," said Loi, "Take this."

She handed Jopp a half-meter baton with two prongs on the end.

"What's this?"

"Povee Tamer."

"What?"

"You don't know povees? We have herds of them all over Venova. Their milk makes killer cheese. Don't know why they'd need to be tamed. Povees are docile as fuck. Go stick 'em with the prongs. Probably gives them a nasty shock or something."

"*Probably?*"

Loi held her hands up, "Look around, man. *Probably* is the best we can hope for."

Jopp rolled his eyes and charged at the two Adherent still stuck in the snare.

Loi reached into the sack and pulled out the last item. It was a short baton with a switch and three buttons. She flipped the switch and a length of orange energy poured out from one end, coiling on the ground like a rope.

"*Herding Whip*," she murmured to herself, "Saved the coolest one for me."

She gave it a test crack.

"Ow!" screamed Jopp, "What the fuck?!"

"Sorry!"

"Go fight over by someone else!"

Loi saw Rohi grappling with an Adherent, each trying to rest the halberd away from the other. She ran to within a few meters of them, raised the whip and let it fly. The rope of orange energy lashed out... and wrapped itself tightly around the Adherent's wrist. Loi looked down at the handle, and pressed a button labeled with a tiny lightning bolt image. The light of the whip brightened. The Adherent's body glowed, every muscle spasmed, and he then toppled over. He lay twitching on the floor. Rohi wasted no time in hopping on his back and putting him in a choke hold.

Some movement in her peripheral pulled Loi's eyes upward, to the far end of the warehouse, to the large pane of glass and the golden room beyond. Standing at the window, she saw a blue-skinned woman with glowing orange eyes. Serru regarded the scene below her impassively. She then turned around and walked toward the center of the room. Before Loi knew what she was doing, her legs started sprinting for the stairs leading up to that room.

Chuck had an Adherent bearing down on him. He flipped the switch on his hammer, causing the handle to extend to double its length. The hammer's head lit up with red lights. He shrugged. The Adherent raised his halberd to strike. Chuck stepped inside of the axe head's reach and swung his hammer. The Adherent managed to step back to avoid the blow. But then something happened... the air around the hammer head rippled and whooshed forward, pushing the Adherent warrior off his feet and backwards a few meters. He landed on his back, his halberd clattering across the floor.

Chuck stared at the hammer, "Oh... that's rad. That is so rad."

He saw Rohi nearby, putting her lone pair of maglock cuffs on an unconscious Adherent.

"Thanks for the assist, Loi," she said as she looked up, seeing only Chuck.

"Where's Loi?" she asked.

Chuck scanned around and saw her climbing the stairs at the far end. He pointed. Rohi looked from Loi up to the window and saw Serru working at a terminal.

"Shit," she cursed.

"Go," said Chuck.

"You sure?"

Chuck patted his new toy. "We got this."

"Don't die," said Rohi as she snatched up the unconscious Adherent's halberd, and took off after Loi.

"Love you too, sweetie," Chuck called after.

WORD SECTION 0059

"Die!" screamed another Adherent as he came up behind Chuck, weapon held high. Chuck stared up at his impending death. A blur of yellow appeared, and Jopp thrust a metal baton up under the Adherent's exposed armpit. The Venovan man groaned, dropped his weapon, and dropped to his hands and knees.

"Room... spinning..." was all he managed to say before vomiting.

"That's gross," said Chuck.

"You're fucking welcome," said Jopp.

Chuck smiled, "You're a good friend and I love you."

"Stop that. It concerns me how much you're enjoying this."

"That's funny."

"Why?"

"Because it concerns me how much you *aren't*." Chuck gave Jopp a wink and sprinted toward Bhanakhana, who was inside the inner portal circle battling with the two previously snared Adherent. Jopp sighed and followed after.

Bhanakhana had been able to deflect most of their strikes, but he was also sporting a few new cuts on his upper arms and shoulders. As Chuck rushed up behind the two warriors, his eyes locked with Bhanakhana and he shouted, "Duck!"

Chuck swung his hammer.

Bhanakhana ducked.

The blast of air sent the two unsuspecting Adherent flying. One actually fell through a portal that led to an open plain of red grass.

Bhanakhana stood and looked right and left and then at Chuck, "That was interesting."

"Hell yeah!" said Chuck. "Gives me an idea... portal fight!"

"Wha-" Bhanakhana started to say, but Chuck was already running toward the grass portal.

Jopp caught up, reaching the inner portal circle. In unison, he and Bhanakhana pointed behind each other and said, "Look out."

They each spun around, now back-to-back, as four Adherent warriors entered the circle. One of them had a bloody swollen bruise covering the entire right side of his face. His good left eye glared at Bhanakhana with murderous intent. They steeled themselves for the attack.

"HEADS UP!" hollered Chuck as he burst back through the grassy plains portal. He skidded to a halt, spun on his heel and hit the portal ring with his hammer. The ring shuddered and a few small bits fell off it, but it remained active.

The four Adherent stared at him with confusion.

"Chuck, what are you-"

"WE NEED TO CLOSE THIS THING NOW!"

The Adherent warrior who'd originally fallen through the portal re-emerged. His eyes were wide with shock and fear. He took one step forward before a blue-gray tentacle appeared, wrapped around his waist, and yanked him back into the portal. After a few seconds of eerie silence, three more tentacles burst through the portal. Bhanakhana, Jopp, Chuck, the other Adherent scattered. One of them wasn't so lucky. A tentacle got a good grip and dragged him back, screaming all the way.

Bhanakhana looked from his gauntlets to the ring. He sprinted around, coming up behind the portal, and gripped one of the more vulnerable looking sections of metal. His felt the gauntlets hum with power as he squeezed. The portal's metal whined, but then gave way. Bhanakhana tore the ring apart. The portal winked out of existence. The two tentacles still on this side were severed clean off. They flopped on the floor for a few seconds before going limp.

"So..." Chuck started, sitting on the floor.

"...gross," Jopp finished, standing over him with an outstretched hand.

Before Chuck could take the hand, an Adherent appeared out of nowhere and tackled Jopp. They tumbled through the portal that was leaking water.

Chuck sighed, "Man... not again." And he quickly hopped up to follow.

Bhanakhana found himself alone against three warriors. Before they could coordinate an attack, he looked for something to throw. All he could see were portals. He lunged for the nearest and gripped it at the wide ends. This maneuver shocked the three Adherent and they paused for a brief moment before coming to their senses and rushing him. Bhanakhana pulled the portal free with surprising ease, raised it over his head and hurled it at them. Two managed to dive out of the way, but the portal got the third guy dead center. The ring bounced and clattered, coming to rest portal side up. The Adherent it'd hit was nowhere to be seen. Bhanakhana didn't have time to bask in the success of his move. He charged the nearest warrior, scooped him up, and tossed him through the closest portal. Bhanakhana then tried to break the portal ring, but as he was reaching for it, the remaining warrior swiped at him with a halberd. Bhanakhana tried to twist out of the way, but the axe-blade still managed to open a diagonal gash across his back. He grunted in pain and dropped to a knee, bracing both palms against the floor to stop himself from collapsing completely. The Adherent wasted no time in going for the kill. Bhanakhana felt the metal floor beneath his humming gauntlets warp and begin to give way. He looked up at the advancing warrior with a vicious grin as he dug his fingers into the floor, puncturing right through the thick metal plating as if it were paper. He got himself a solid grip and waited until the attacker was virtually on top of him.

The Adherent raised his weapon to strike. Bhanakhana let out a fierce roar as he pulled the floor apart. The metal plating tore open right underneath the Adherent's foot, and he stumbled and fell. Bhanakhana lunged, grabbed him around the neck with his left hand, lifted him into the air and brought his right hand around with a devastating haymaker punch. He let go with his left the same second his right fist made contact. The Adherent warrior slammed against the floor in an unconscious heap.

Chuck sloshed through the knee-deep water. Tall palm trees, whose leaves looked more like gigantic bird feathers than actual leaves, stood sparsely scattered around the shallows. Patches of blue seaweed sprouted from the seabed, waving back and forth with the current. In front of Chuck, the ocean stretched to the horizon. Behind him, the portal rested against a sheer, cliff face, a thin stretch of rock branching off a small, jungle-covered island.

The Adherent and Jopp grappled with each other. The Venovan managed to get on top of Jopp and push his head under the water. But he heard Chuck sloshing his way closer and was forced to release Jopp to turn and face the oncoming Earth man. Chuck didn't even give him a chance to stand upright before swinging the hammer.

The air blast created a wave that swept the Adherent off his feet. Jopp came up from under the water sputtering. Chuck crouched down. "You okay, bud?"

Jopp choked up more water and said, "Look ou-"

The Adherent dove into Chuck, sending them both under. Chuck felt hands reaching for his throat. *Been here before*, he thought, *luckily I once again have a blunt object to hit this fucker in the head with*. But because of the water, he couldn't get any real momentum on his swing. The hammer gently bounced of the Adherent's shoulder. No air burst came out either.

Oh shit.

Chuck's vision, thanks in part to being underwater and in part to being strangled, was fuzzy and distorted. But he was able to make out two round blobs of yellow with a blue strap appear behind his assailant.

Chuck felt the Adherent's hands let go and he sat up out of the water retching. His eyes focused and he saw the Adherent clawing at his own throat. Jopp was using a length of seaweed like a garrote.

"Don't <cough> don't kill him!" Chuck said.

"Seriously? He was literally trying to straight up murder you ten seconds ago."

"We're better than them."

Jopp grumbled to himself and let go. The Adherent dropped to his knees, coughing.

"Let's tie him up with more of that seaweed."

They quickly secured the Adherent's hands behind his back. While Jopp while propping him up against a rock, Chuck took a moment to scan their surroundings.

"Hey... does this island look familiar to you at all?"

"I don't know man, it's-"

"Holy shit, Jopp, look!"

Jopp looked where Chuck was pointing. Back on the soft, sandy shores of the island's beach, they saw dozens of purple pineapples with arms and legs walking out from the jungle.

"No. Freaking. Way."

"I got an idea," said Chuck. He started waving at them and shouting, "Hi! Hi! Remember us?"

One of the Pyenapor threw a spear that had no hope of actually reaching them. It sank into the shallow water and was quickly followed by a chorus of angry sounding words.

"I think they remember us."

Chuck waved his hands defensively.

"Wait wait wait!" He pointed at the Adherent. "Eeleeo! Eeleeo!"

The Pyenapor stopped shouting and the Chieftain pushed her way to the front of the crowd.

"Eeleeo?!" they heard her shout back.

Chuck gave her two big thumbs up and pointed at the Adherent warrior again.

"Eeleeo! Yes!"

They all erupted in a cheer. Four Pyenapor suddenly emerged from the trees carrying a long canoe-like boat.

"Damn," said Jopp, "Big Red could probably come back and finish his thing here..."

They turned to each other and shouted in unison, "Bhanakhana!"

• • •

Bhanakhana saw blue fingers emerge to grip the frame of the portal he'd thrown. He rushed over and looked down to see the Adherent clinging to the side of a mountain. Apparently very high up the mountain, given the clouds the swirled far below.

The Adherent froze when he saw Bhanakhana standing at the portal edge.

"Please believe me when I say I truly do not wish to kill you. If you give me your word... swear to your god that you will not attack me, I will help you up."

The Adherent glared at him for a few moments before responding, "I swear it."

Bhanakhana reached down and took the Venovan man's hand. He pulled him up through the portal with minimal effort. The second the man's feet touched solid ground, he pulled a knife from his belt and attacked. Bhanakhana's gauntlet took most of the brunt, but his upper forearm still felt the bite of a blade parting the skin.

Bhanakhana growled in pain and shoved him to the side, which happened to be the same side as the portal. The Adherent cried out as he fell back down the mountainside, through the clouds. Bhanakhana raised his foot and stomped hard on the portal frame, cracking it. The portal blinked away.

"You alright, B?" called Jopp's voice.

Bhanakhana turned around to see a soaking wet Chuck and Jopp stepping through one of the portals.

"I have been better. What happened to you two?"

"We'll tell you more about it later, but I think we patched things up with the pineapple people," Chuck answered.

"I must be delirious from blood loss. What did you just say?"

"I think there was wound-sealant in one of our satchels. Let me see if I can find it." Chuck started searching the room.

"So, they all down for the count?" said Jopp.

Bhanakhana nodded. "I threw one through a portal full of gear works and machinery. I do not know his fate."

Jopp scanned the room for the portal in question.

Chuck returned with a spray can. "Found the sealant!"

He started spraying lines of yellow foam along Bhanakhana's wounds. The muscular Dronla wincing at the sting from the antiseptic. Then they heard Jopp yelp, "What the shit is that?!"

Bhanakhana and Chuck turned in time to see a robotic arm poke through the portal. A bulbous metal sphere with a red mechanical eye was fixed to the arm's end.

"I vote we don't wait to see what that thing's attached to," said Jopp.

"Indeed."

Bhanakhana rushed over, gripped the ring with his gauntlets and broke it. The portal disappeared, cutting off the robotic arm. As it dropped to the floor, the round head with the red eye broke away from the length of arm. It sprouted eight tiny metal legs and started scurrying away. It rushed away from the open center of the room and disappeared behind a stack of portal rings.

"Nothing good is going to come of that," noted Chuck.

"Hey, uh, what happened to Rohi and Loi?" Jopp asked.

Chuck pointed a thumb toward the control room.

"Boss Fight."

WORD SECTION 0060

Loi allowed herself the briefest of moments to linger in the doorway, admiring the gorgeous Origin Room. Serru stood hunched over a large semi-circle panel that was covered in dial, switches, and neon displays. The four statues she'd seen earlier turned out to be life-size depictions of those armored Ak'alei suits. An orb of orange light hovered over each one, and they all held orange crystalline sabers. To her right, was the window overlooking the warehouse. To her left, was the window overlooking the power turbine. Six active portal rings stood lined up across the length of the long window. Each one appeared to lead to the elevated landing pad of a maram. Directly behind Serru was a waist-high pedestal, about five meters in diameter. It was covered with hundreds of tiny neon lights as well as sculpted diorama pieces.

"Be with you in a moment, Sis."

Serru didn't bother to look up from her work as Loi stepped through the door.

"It's over, Serru."

This time Serru looked up at her with a bemused smirk.

"*What's* over, Loi? Do you even know what I'm trying to do here?"

"Probably kill a bunch of people."

"Only if necessary. And in the process, I'll save thousands... millions even."

"Oh, yeah? How's that?"

"The technological possibilities here are endless. I mean, just look at me. Look at what the tiniest fraction of Ak'alei tech can do. Inside me are hundreds of thousands of microscopic machines, all made from the pa'tika."

"The what?"

"The orange stuff, Loi, the orange stuff. I can lift a six-wheel land-crawler. I can hear your heartbeat. I can see your muscles start to twitch before you even move. I can smell what you had for breakfast. Look around you, Loi! We're standing in an actual *portal factory*! Don't you get it?! Don't you realize what we can do here?! Resource scarcity is about to be a thing of the past. Destitute refugees stranded on Venova Prime? Open a portal. No more inefficient shuttle flights. No clean water? There are planets that have nothing *but* clean water. Open a portal. The Sentient Coalition, local planetary governments, corporations, the *fucking* Church of Rhonac..." she spit the curse out like it tasted bitter, "When I'm finished, no one will have to endure the childhood you and I did."

"You really think it's that simple?"

Serru smiled. "Yes. Yes, I really do."

"They won't just let you-"

"Yes, they will. All I have to do is show them what happens when they don't fall in line."

Serru cranked up a large dial and flipped the switch next to it. The lights all flashed for a second. Beyond the glass, the giant power turbine began to hum and slowly spin.

"What did you just do?"

"Setting an example. Hopefully the governing bodies of the Coalition will get the message and this will be the only necessary sacrifice."

"*Sacrifice?* Serru, what did you do?!"

"I'm charging up a new portal."

"Between where and where!"

"Between an active volcano on Erimalai... and Kovil-Rho."

"Are you fucking insane?! Kovil-Rho is the capital of your own damn religion!"

"Exactly. I'm sacrificing my own. And besides, they're mostly bastards. Trust me... the higher up the ranks you go, the more bastardly they get. The universe is better off without them."

"Serru... it's not just the Heralds... Kovil-Rho is virtually a city within a city. Thousands of people will die."

"... so I can save millions. And thus, we bring this conversation full circle."

Loi activated the energy whip.

"I can't let you do this."

Serru gave her a patronizing look, "*Let* me? C'mon, Loi. We both know you can't stop me by yourself."

"Good thing she's not by herself." Rohi strode through the door to Loi's side.

Serru's eyes began to glow.

Rohi and Loi spread apart, moving so as to come at Serru from opposite sides. Rohi gave the halberd a casual spin, testing its heft.

Serru held her hands up invitingly.

"Ready whenever you are."

Loi lashed out with the whip.

Rohi charged.

Serru caught the whip's end and before Loi could react, yanked hard. Loi was pulled off her feet. She let go of the handle and tumbled across the floor, slamming into the base of the diorama table.

Rohi raised the halberd high, pressed her thumb against the one button, and slammed the axe head into the ground. Serru leapt into the air, back flipping over the control panel just as an arc of orange electricity shot past, lightly singing the gold plating of the panel.

She tsk-tsk'd at Rohi. "Careful. Careful. You scorch the controls, and you guarantee that portal opens under Kovil-Rho..."

Rohi burst forward, bounding up onto the control panel and then up into the air. She swung the axe-head downward.

Serru didn't budge. In a blur, she clapped her hands together, catching the axe-blade between her palms, just a few centimeters in front of her face. The sudden momentum stoppage made Rohi's grip slip off the halberd, and she awkwardly fell to the floor. Serru tossed the halberd aside, picked Rohi up singlehandedly by the collar and tossed her across the room. Her body hit one of the statues, causing it to topple over. Its shoulder hit the back window, forming a spider web of cracks.

Loi screamed with rage as she lunged with the orange-bladed knife. Serru bobbed and weaved, dodging each stab and slash with minimal effort. She then snatched Loi's wrist and bent it back just enough to hurt without causing any real damage. Loi fought back the pained yelp, instead letting out a determined growl.

Serru's bright orange eyes stared into Loi's fierce yellow ones.

"Stop this nonsense, Loi. This is the last time I tell you."

Serru drove her open palm into Loi's chest, with enough force to take the wind out of her lungs and bruise her ribs without breaking them. Loi gasped in pain and collapsed.

Serru strode over to where Rohi lay face down.

"I can see by your elevated pulse that you're still conscious, I'm going to put you to sleep now."

As Serru leaned down, Rohi whipped around, swiping up with the statue's saber she'd had concealed under her body. Serru quickly pulled back, however the tip of the saber just barely managed to scrape across her right cheek. She took a step back, as Rohi scrambled away. Serru delicately touching her cheek, where pink blood trickled from a thin, three-centimeter cut. She looked at the beads of blood on her fingertips and started laughing.

"Valiant effort, agent. I respect your tenacity."

Rohi popped to her feet, brandishing the saber.

"I'll give you something to respect."

"What would you say is your purpose, agent? Why do you do what you do?"

Serru took a step forward. Rohi took two steps backward, she could the hear the hum of the portals on her right.

"You want to protect the good people from the bad, yes?"

Rohi tightened her grip on the blade. "Yes."

"I do too. We're fighting for the same thing."

"No. You're a murderer."

"And you're *not*? How many people *have* you killed, agent?"

"It's not the same."

"Isn't it?"

"Every life I've taken has been in self-defense. And yes, I remember them."

"You kill to defend your *own* life, as if it's worth more than others. I kill to defend hundreds, thousands, millions of truly innocent lives. In reality, you're *worse* than me."

"Oh, shut up, you fucking psychopath."

Serru picked up the toppled golden statue and hurled it forward. Rohi ducked, letting it sail over her head, as it knocked over a portal ring. The top end of the statue punctured a hole through the window, and the damaged glass creaked under the weight of the golden figure leaning against it. Serru's eyes no longer had pupils or irises, just solid orange light. She walked toward Rohi.

"What gives *you* the authority?! The U.L.E.? Who gave *them* the authority?! It's all made up. Some random fool made up an arbitrary set of rules and then chose other random fools to enforce it and the cycle has continued for centuries... with no one bothering to question it!"

She slammed her fist into the closest portal ring. It snapped off its ground-stand and hit the window, causing the entire pane of glass to finally shatter. The statue landed flat on the floor, its top end hanging out over the turbine below. The portal Serru had hit fell over the edge and slid down the bowl-like walls, coming to a stop against the slightly raised rim that encircled the spinning turbine blades.

Rohi backed up until she felt the wall. A rush of wind blew through the broken window to her right. The pulsing hum of the turbine filled the air.

Serru beckoned her forward, "You don't want to die cowering in a corner, do you?"

Rohi gritted her teeth and rushed at Serru, swinging the saber at her head. Serru ducked, which Rohi had been expecting and she curved the swing trajectory down and around, cutting a 'C' through the air. Serru had to dive roll to the side, almost going over the lip of the window pane. She looked up to see the point of the saber coming right for her face. Serru burst into the air, flipping clear over Rohi's head. Before Rohi could even begin to turn, Serru spun around with a sweep kick, taking Rohi's feet clear out from under her. Rohi fell hard on her back, hitting her head. Her vision exploded with stars and blurry shapes.

Serru stood over Rohi and raised her fist to deliver a killing blow.

"Hey!"

Serru paused, fist held aloft, and glanced to her left to see Chuck, Bhanakhana, and Jopp enter the room. Serru opened her mouth, but before she could say anything she felt something wrap around her raised wrist. She turned to see a length of orange energy coiled around her arm. She looked over her shoulder to see the other end of the orange rope attached to the baton in Loi's hand.

"Sis-" was all she got out before Loi pressed the lightning bolt button. Electricity surged through Serru. She felt every muscle spasm. Loi pressed the button again. And again. And again.

Serru dropped. She writhed in pain. Blood trickled from her left nostril. She started retching and then vomited a glob of pale, yellow bile. She got to her hands and knees and looked up at Loi. Her eyes had no glow. They just looked like normal Venovan eyes.

Serru grabbed the portal ring next to her and looked as if she was trying to wrench it free of its base. It didn't budge.

Loi readied the whip to strike again. "Oh no, did I fry all those fancy little machines inside you, sis?"

WORD SECTION 0061

Serru coughed a few more times and then, to their surprise, began cackling with laughter.

"Oh my," she said as she composed herself. "Thank you, Loi. Truly. It's been so long since I felt challenged in any way."

She lunged forward, sprinting straight ahead. Loi struck at her with the whip. Serru held her arm up, intentionally letting the whip warp around her forearm. But before Loi could do anything, Serru pulled hard, yanking the baton from Loi's hand. Loi scrambled for it, but Serru was already on her, delivering a knee to the midsection. As Loi dropped to her knees and looked up in time to see Serru's fist connect with her face. She crumpled.

"I don't need enhancements."

Serru snatched back her dagger from the floor next to Loi and brought it up just in time to deflect the grasping, gauntleted hands of Bhanakhana. She jumped backwards, avoiding another metal-handed punch. Serru moved herself next to one of the statues. She slipped the dagger into her belt and pulled free the statue's saber. She regarded the charging mass of red muscle with a smug grin.

"I've done nothing but train for fifteen years."

She slashed at Bhanakhana. His gauntlet took the brunt, however the saber managed to split the metal, just by a hair. Bhanakhana felt the blade's bite on the back of his wrist. He growled and threw a jab at Serru's side with his other hand. She tried to sidestep but wasn't quite fast enough. Pain exploded through her abdomen and ribcage. She refused to let it slow her, diving out of the way as Bhanakhana attempted to end the fight with a haymaker. Serru rolled and hopped up to find Jopp, Chuck, and Rohi bearing down on her.

She parried a slash from Rohi's saber, and then dodged Jopp's thrust with the animal tamer, before cutting it half. Before she could dispatch the weaponless Jopp, Chuck swung his hammer. Serru felt herself lifted up and pushed backwards by the concentrated burst of wind. A less skilled combatant would have found themselves tumbling awkwardly through the air. Serru managed to reorient herself midair and saw Rohi coming in hot. She planted her feet on the floor just in time to deflect Rohi's slash, and immediately leapt into a spinning roundhouse kick. Serru's heel caught Rohi in the side of the head and sent her stumbling back toward the shattered windowpane. She misplaced a step, tripped, and fell, barely catching herself on the arm of the golden statue hanging out over the turbine.

Serru saw Chuck rearing back for another swing with that pesky air hammer. She burst forward and with a crisp clean stroke, severed Chuck's left arm just above the elbow. He let out a gasp and staggered backwards before collapsing against the wall, sitting precariously close to the broken window edge.

Jopp was on him in seconds, unleashing an excessive amount of the wound sealant foam all over the remains of Chuck's left arm.

Bhanakhana came up behind Serru and when she spun around to strike, he caught the blade with both hands, squeezed, and shattered it. Serru didn't even flinch, but immediately lashed out with the hilt and the jagged orange shard still attached.

Chuck's skin was pale and clammy. His mouth hung open and his eyes blinked rapidly. Jopp snapped his fingers in front of Chuck's face.

"Hey! Hey! Buddy, it's going to be okay! Okay, Buddy? Okay?! Chuck! It's going to be okay!"

Serru feinted a thrust with the saber shard and when Bhanakhana moved to block that attack, she instead punched him across the jaw with the saber hand guard. Bhanakhana dropped to a knee, spitting out gobs of blood and a molar. Then Serru drove her heel into the bridge of Bhanakhana's forehead, putting him on his back.

Jopp opened Chuck's shirt and slapped a pain reliever patch on his left chest.

Rohi was trying to pull herself up when a figured appeared over her. Serru looked down at her with a pitying expression.

"In a few seconds, that wondrous machine below you will have generated enough power to open the gates. It's done, agent. If you're ready to accept that, I will pull you up. You can huddle in the corner with your scrappy menagerie and witness as I usher in the new era."

Rohi glared up at Serru. She looked to the side, saw Chuck against the wall with Jopp tending to his wound. She looked down at the spinning turbine below. Saw the detached, still active, portal ring resting against the lip directly below. As she looked down, something caught her eye: the two incendiary shinebombs she'd taken off her fallen comrade.

Rohi looked back at Chuck, who was now looking right back at her. Tears welled in his eyes as he nodded. Rohi mouthed the words *love you*.

"What's it going to be, agent?"

Rohi let go of the statue with one hand and placed it on the explosives. She grinned up at Serru.

"Fuck you."

Rohi pulled the shinebombs from her belt and let go of the statue. She activated the bombs as she fell and tried to toss them into the center of the turbine.

Chuck watched Rohi fall straight through the portal, tumbling onto the landing of a maram.

One of the shinebombs lodged itself neatly between two turbine blades.

"Oh shit!" said Jopp as he pulled Chuck away from the edge.

The other shinebomb hit the edge of the portal ring and fell through. The last thing Chuck saw was Rohi diving for the large interplanetary portal on the maram.

Outside the dome, one of the old portal marams exploded and crumbled to the ground below.

Inside the dome, the central power turbine erupted in bright white flame. Shards of turbine blades exploded in every direction. Everyone dove for cover as the tongues of white fire licked at the ceiling. After a few seconds, the fire pulled back into the turbine room. Serru felt pain in her right arm and saw it had gotten a streak of nasty burns. She laid back to take a deep breath and center herself, but then saw the length of turbine blade stuck in the ceiling overhead. The metal creaked and groaned and then fell. Serru frantically rolled out of the way, right over the edge, barely catching herself on the windowpane.

Her burned arm screamed in agony and she had to let go with her right hand. She stared down at the roiling pool of raw energy and liquid metal that had once been the key to fulfilling her destiny. She wracked her brain... *maybe the generator could be fixed... maybe there's another facility like this on the planet... maybe it's... maybe it's all over.* The realization washed over her. She felt fury.

She felt pain.

She felt peace.

Serru had done all she could. She'd tried to fix the universe and failed. *Maybe it's time I had a rest.* She let go of the ledge. But before she could fall, a pair of hands darted out and snatched her wrist. Serru looked up at Loi with sad eyes, letting her whole body go limp. Loi strained at the weight.

"What are you doing?! C'mon, help!"

"Let me go, Loi."

"What? No!"

"Loi..." with her burned arm, Serru pulled the dagger free from her belt, "I'm going to stab your hands."

"No!"

Serru slashed.

Loi couldn't help but let go.

Serru closed her eyes as she fell, enjoying a brief moment of serenity before the fiery molten stew consumed her.

WORD SECTION 0062

Bhanakhana, Jopp, and Chuck with the help of the first two, joined Loi at the window's edge. Jopp's eyes were misty, and tears flowed freely down the cheeks of both Bhanakhana and Loi. Chuck's expression was ice cold.

"Perhaps you lot *were* better off under our subjugation. Just look at this mess…"

They turned around to see Ahfel standing in the doorway.

"What the fuck is that?" asked Jopp.

"An Ak'alei," answered Bhanakhana.

"Oh," said Jopp as he gave Ahfel the finger and said, "Fuck you and your entire civilization."

"That's fair," Ahfel replied.

"Rohi," said Chuck through gritted teeth. "She went through one of those portals at the tops of the towers… the marams. We need to find out where she went."

"You need considerable medical assistance, Chuck," Bhanakhana started.

"Rohi saved all our asses!" Chuck growled. "We find her first!"

Bhanakhana addressed Ahfel, while pointing at the empty portal stand. "That spatial bridge led to a maram. Where did the maram's interplanetary bridge go?"

Ahfel had walked over to the control terminal and was messing with switches. Behind him, the wide pedestal table began to change. Some of sculpted pieces disappeared below the surface. The neon lights morphed and moved and changed colors. When the movement ceased, the table display held four different pieces, each one looking vaguely similar to the temples on Gjenlu. One of them glowed with an inner light. The rest of the table was scattered with hundreds of tiny lights.

"Your friend went there," Ahfel pointed at the glowing temple figurine. "These lights represent the lights in the night sky as seen from each Structure. They're all on the same world."

Chuck looked at Bhanakhana with bloodshot eyes, "Please tell you can do some kind of cross-referencing with the stars to find out where that is..."

"Um, well... it would be difficult... and take quite a bit of time..."

"No need," said Loi as she leaned over the table. "I recognize this constellation. It's Heaven's Maw... you see how it kind of forms a big mouth with sharp teeth and those two red stars are the eyes..." She put her hand over her mouth, trying to collect herself.

"Where is it?" Chuck hissed.

Loi avoided Chuck's eyes and instead looked at Bhanakhana. "This is in the Hua Tau system."

"Oh no," said Bhanakhana.

"Oh fuck," said Jopp.

"What don't I know?" said Chuck.

Jopp turned to him, "Buddy, Hua Tau is in The Verge. It's, um..."

Bhanakhana cut in, "It is a collection of star systems where the Sentient Coalition has zero jurisdiction. The Verge is complete anarchy, filled with militant factions battling endless wars."

Loi added, "And it's virtually impossible to get in or out. The Coalition has blockaded all anomalies leading to Verge systems."

"But you've been there," Chuck said.

"I was part of a crew of seventeen trying to hop in and out on a smuggling run. We were only in the system for twelve hours. Just two of us survived the trip."

"And Rohi's there alone," Chuck asserted, "So we need to get to her right now."

"Chuck," Jopp started, "Remember Pa Tahae? Secret pirate city? Seemed like a rough place, right? Pa Tahae is criminal daycare compared to The Verge."

"So we just leave her?!"

"No," Bhanakhana placed his hand on Chuck's shoulder, "No. We will not leave her. We will get back to civilization. We will get you the medical attention you require. We will inform the U.L.E. of everything that has happened, and request they send in a force to recover Rohi. And if they won't help, I will personally spend every Tahlian in my possession to hire us our own personal army. We will get her back. I swear to you."

A low rumble vibrated through the room. They heard a shrill, metallic whine reverberate through the walls.

"Oh dear," Ahfel said while looking at the control panel, "You lot should leave. The structural integrity of this facility has seen better times... understatement of the millennia."

One of the other portals had a chunk of turbine blade sticking through its frame. Another kept blinking on and off every few seconds. That left three viable options.

"Where do those spatial bridges lead?" Bhanakhana asked.

"Well, I wouldn't take that one as we were in the process of decommissioning the maram. The world it led too imploded. And that other one might not be the best... can you lot breathe sulfur? No? That last one there actually goes to her kind's world." Ahfel was pointing at Loi.

Loi sighed, "Fucking Venova..."

"We don't have a choice," said Jopp.

"Agreed," said Bhanakhana.

As they headed for the portal in question, Ahfel asked, "I doubt there's a decent answer to this, but why did you break so many portals down on the factory floor?"

"We had to prevent people and... *things* from coming through them."

"There's an activate/deactivate switch right there on the side."

"Oh, shit," said Jopp, "Look at that..."

"Kind of obvious now that he's pointed it out," added Loi.

Loi went through the portal first. Then Jopp. And Bhanakhana followed right after. They looked back expectantly as Chuck stepped up to the portal. He gave them a kind smile as he reached over with his remaining hand and turned the portal off.

Chuck spun on his heel and sprinted to the diorama table. He pointed at the shocked Ahfel, then pointed at himself, then at the glowing diorama piece. He repeated the action of pointing at himself and then at the table.

"You want to go there?"

Chuck nodded.

"*Chzzz... Chuck! Hey! hzzzz....*"

Chuck turned to the source of the noise and saw his data bracelet on the wrist of his severed arm. He ran over and pulled it free.

"Jopp?"

"*What the actual fuck do you think you're doing?!*"

"I can't leave her there alone."

"*Don't be an idiot, man! We had a plan!*"

"And it's a fine plan, Jopp. You three should stick to it. We'll be waiting for you when you come for us."

"*Chuck, this isn't a game!*"

"As the one of us who just had an arm cut off, I'd say I'm especially aware of that."

"*Even more reason not to do this!*"

"You guys made it clear how jacked up this place is, so there's no way I can ask you to come with... but I also can't, I just *can't* leave Rohi there alone. This is the only way."

"*Listen to you! The 'only way'?! You really are a dumb stupid ape, aren't you?! Yeah, go ahead! Go get yourself killed you scrog-slobbing yok knocker! See if I care!*"

"It's okay, bud. I'm scared too. I'm terrified. I meant it when I said you were a good friend."

After a moment of silence, Jopp's voice came through much tamer and weaker, "*Chuck, please... you're my friend. You're my best fucking friend.*"

"I love you too, bud."

"*Chuck?*" It was Bhanakhana's voice.

"Please don't try to talk me out of this, Bhanakhana. If you care about me, then help me."

After a sigh, "*...what can I do?*"

"Tell Mr. Awful what I want." Chuck held out the data bracelet toward Ahfel.

"He wants you to open a portal to the same place that our friend went."

"I gathered that. How does he expect me to power it up?"

"The generator is fried, yes. But what about where the power is stored? Serru said something about having enough to open her portal."

Bhanakhana relayed this to Ahfel. The Ak'alei turned a few dials and checked the display read out.

"Yes..."

A cacophony of rending metal and shattering stone echoed through the walls.

"The rim-side quadrant just collapsed. Oh well. Anyway, yes, there is enough energy to generate one small spatial bridge."

Chuck waved his hand in a furious circular motion, "Let's go. Let's go."

Ahfel started flipping switches. Through the window in front of them, at the far end of the warehouse, the mechanical dais came to life. Arcs of white, orange, blue electricity sparked between the tall pylons. Overhead, the robotic arm reached down to pluck the nearest portal ring off a stack. It placed the ring between the pylons.

Meanwhile, Chuck picked up his satchel and slung it over his shoulder. He then grabbed the air hammer and tried to collapse the extended handle. Ahfel saw the difficulty he was having and came over to help. The Ak'alei tied the condensed hammer to Chuck's satchel with a loose strap.

Chuck gave him a thank you nod, and then picked up one of the sabers.

Ahfel pointed out toward the factory floor. The dancing electricity had ceased, and the portal ring was now active. From far away, all Chuck could see through it was a dark sky.

A chorus of metallic creaks pierced the air. Cracks started running up the walls. Down in the factory, Chuck saw the floor starting to split. An eery orange light shown up from below.

"You had best flee," said Ahfel.

Chuck leaned close to the data bracelet on the table.

"Thank you, guys. I love you both. Loi, I don't know you all that well, but you seem pretty chill. Take care."

Loi's voice responded, *"You got one serious pair of yub nubs on you, Earth Man. Good luck you crazy fucker."*

Then came Bhanakhana's, *"Chuck, as your friend I abhor your current plan of action. However, I have to respect your determination. Please look after yourself."*

Finally, Jopp, *"Don't get yourself killed you dumb ape. This universe would be a lot less fun without you."*

Tears flowed freely down Chuck's cheeks, "Thanks Buddy."

He took a step toward the door.

"Hey Chuck?"

"Yeah, Jopp?"

"We'll find a way to get you out of there. I fucking swear it."

"I know you will, bud."

Chuck took off, loping down the stairs, nearly slipping multiple times. The cracks in the warehouse floor were widening and he had to leap across gaps filled with scorching orange energy. Dust and bits of stone began to fall from the ceiling. Then a ceiling chunk the size of a fridge slammed into the floor just a few meters behind him.

Chuck hopped another crack and bound up the dais. The muffled sounds of building collapse were getting much louder and much less muffled. Chuck stopped in front of the portal and looked back at the Origin Room. Ahfel stood at the window, looking down at him with an expression that could've almost been but wasn't quite a smile.

Chuck gave him a final nod and dove through the portal just as the warehouse roof gave way.

•　　•　　•

Outside, standing high up on a maram landing pad, Bhanakhana, Jopp, and Loi watched the massive dome of Structure One cave in on itself.

"You think he made it?" Loi asked.

"Yes," answered Bhanakhana, "Yes, I do."

"Of course he did," added Jopp with a smug grin, "It's Chuck. That plucky little shit always makes it out okay."

The ground around the rubble of Structure One split into fissures that fanned out in every direction The fissures, while quite jagged, each seemed to be heading for a maram. They watched the ground beneath their own tower begin to split apart.

"Time to depart," noted Bhanakhana.

They turned to look up at the interplanetary gateway.

"Let's do it," said Jopp, "So how's Venova this time of year?"

"Gorgeous. Hope you packed your beachwear."

"Really?"

"Fuck no."

Bhanakhana rolled his eyes, scooped Jopp and Loi up in each arm and barreled through the shimmering portal, just as the maram spire began to crumble and fall.

WORD SECTION: EPILOGUE

Rohi sat on the rocky ledge and looked down at the unfamiliar city at the center of the unfamiliar valley. High above the buildings, bright lights filled the night sky. Or more accurately, explosions filled the night sky as two unfamiliar star cruisers waged war on each other with pulse beams and concussive rockets, all while two opposing squadrons of scout fighters swarmed around the space between creating a morbidly beautiful laser light show. She watched a fighter jet get shot down and crash into one of the city's towers.

She heard the crackle of electricity behind her and turned around to see the air itself tear open. The opening hovered about a meter above the ground, and was tilted forward at an odd angle. Orange sparks popped around the edges of the opening as it molded itself into a circle.

And then Chuck fell through, landing on the ground with a thud.

"Oof!" He grunted.

The opening sputtered and winked out of existence. Chuck rolled himself to a sitting position and looked up at the stunned Rohi staring back at him.

"Hey, Beautiful."

"Holy fucking Bjordax, Chuck... your arm!"

"Yeah... yeah... it's not an ideal situation. But don't worry, I'm alright." He forced a chuckle and held up his lone right arm, "Get it? I'm *All Right*."

"I feel like you're way too calm about this."

Chuck tapped his chest. "No-Pain-Patch. I got about another two hours or so before it wears off and I start screaming like a teething baby."

Rohi helped him up. Chuck held out the saber.

"Got you a present."

She smiled. "Much better than flowers."

Rohi led him to the ledge where they sat side by side.

"Wow," said Chuck as he took in the embattled scenery.

"Yeah... my money's on the white cruiser with red trim. The gunners over on the green one don't know what they're doing."

As if illustrating her point, a pulse beam from the white cruiser tore through a primary thrust engine of the green.

"I know where we are, by the way," Chuck said, his eyes fixed on the unfolding battle.

"Somewhere in The Verge?" Rohi replied, also keeping her eyes forward.

"Uh, yeah."

"I figured... surviving this isn't going to be easy, Chuck. Especially with your current health status."

"I know. There was this saying on Earth... something along the lines of nothing worth having ever comes easy."

"You think whoever said that had considered wading through a chaotic war zone on a far flung alien planet?"

Chuck laughed, "No. Probably not."

Rohi took his remaining hand in hers and turned to look at him. "I'm glad you're here with me."

Chuck turned his head to look back at her. "I'm glad too."

They leaned in for a kiss while, off in the distance, the green cruiser erupted in a burst of dazzling blue fame.

The End
...For Now, At Least

Thank you for reading. I really hope you enjoyed it. Seriously, from the bottom of my heart, thank you.

Your pal,

Pat

ACKNOWLEDGMENTS

Again, thank you so much to Katie, Gabbie, Grace, Graham, Mom, Dad, Erin, Al, Kristie, Tony, Shannon, Margie, and Pat G. I am so very lucky to have you all as my family.

In the time since my first novel was published, I've had some new friends come into my life. And I cannot thank them enough for the incredible outpouring of support they've shown over the past few years. These people have been truly amazing allies in my career:

Ash, Sam, Bret - Over the past few years, you three have honestly become some of my absolute closest, dearest, and most treasured friends. I am so thankful that our paths crossed.

Rick Heinz - Who knew back when we met in person at my first ever book signing that we would eventually form a working partnership and embark on some truly batshit crazy writing projects together.

Justin Barcelo - Your work inspires me on a regular basis. I can't wait to witness what I am certain will be a long and marvelous career for you.

CertainPOV - To Case, Storm, Matty, and everyone else on the delightful CertainPOV network of shows. Y'all are a most pleasant and truly talented gang of podcast nerds.

Geekly, Inc. - To Tim, Michael, Jane, Jennifer, Josh, and the many many *many* truly wonderful people that make up this one-of-a-kind community. You have no idea what the constant love and support has meant to me over the years. I am eternally grateful.

And don't think I've forgotten about You. Yes, you, the person reading this. Thank you so much for sharing some of your time with this story. I hope it made you smile.

ABOUT THE AUTHOR

Patrick was born and raised in the greater Chicago area, with a brief stint in Los Angeles along the way. A former collegiate football player, Patrick is a die-hard fitness fanatic.

Being two big kids who refuse to grow up, Patrick and his wife, Katie, got married in Disney World during EPCOT's Food & Wine Festival. They then settled down in Cincinnati to raise their three children.

In addition to his novels, Patrick is co-host of the Let's Rewatch podcast and TTRPG enthusiast, having written for multiple published games and books.

NOTE FROM THE AUTHOR

Word-of-mouth is crucial for any author to succeed. If you enjoyed *Space Tripping 2*, please leave a review online—anywhere you are able. Even if it's just a sentence or two. It would make all the difference and would be very much appreciated.

Thanks!
Patrick M. Edwards

We hope you enjoyed reading this title from:

www.blackrosewriting.com

Subscribe to our mailing list – *The Rosevine* – and receive **FREE** books, daily deals, and stay current with news about upcoming releases and our hottest authors.
Scan the QR code below to sign up.

Already a subscriber? Please accept a sincere thank you for being a fan of Black Rose Writing authors.

View other Black Rose Writing titles at www.blackrosewriting.com/books and use promo code **PRINT** to receive a **20% discount** when purchasing..

www.ingramcontent.com/pod-product-compliance
Lightning Source LLC
Chambersburg PA
CBHW010726100726
47899CB00009B/2945